HARPER BLISS

Pink Bean Series

BOOKS 7-9

lady lit_

Copyright © 2018 by Harper Bliss
Published by Ladylit Publishing – a division of Q.P.S. Projects Limited - Hong Kong
ISBN-13 978-988-74415-9-5

LOVE WITHOUT LIMITS

PINK BEAN SERIES - BOOK 7

To my beta reader Carrie for her unwavering enthusiasm and loyal support.

Chapter One

I THOUGHT it would have taken me much longer to get used to this domesticity, but when I get the chance to crawl under the covers with Jo, it's like I'm glowing on the inside, all warm and lit up and ready for a prolonged snuggle.

Jo doesn't look so pleased to be sharing this intimate moment with me.

I scoot closer and curl an arm around her waist. "Look on the bright side," I say. "You get to go to bed early with Caitlin James."

This makes a smile appear on her face. "Aren't I the lucky one," she says.

"No, that would be me." I kiss her shoulder. "I get to have an early night with Josephine Greenwood."

"I should really sleep in the other room," Jo says. "My coughing will only keep you awake."

"I refuse." I curl my arm around her tighter. "Stay."

"Your choice, but I don't want any complaints about this in the middle of the night." Her face scrunches together before it erupts into a sneeze. I instinctively recoil a little.

After she has blown her nose, she asks, "Are you sure?"

I nod, although I hope I don't catch this cold. I shuffle a little closer to her again.

She sighs. "I don't even mind about the money so much. It's letting the audience down that I care about. This is the twenty-first century. How can no-one have found a cure for the common cold yet?"

"Fair question. Maybe you should go over to the science department tomorrow and ask one of the brainiacs there."

"I don't know what I'm doing in bed yet. I'm not tired."

"You need to sleep, Jo. You don't get nearly enough sleep."

"I don't need that much." Her voice is scratchy from coughing.

"A good night's sleep will boost your immune system. With a bit of luck, you'll feel much better in the morning."

Jo looks at me from under her lashes. "You just sounded a lot like Amber. All these yoga lessons you take with her must be rubbing off on you."

"Amber only ever has good advice to dispense."

Jo's lips draw into a pout, but she doesn't say anything.

"What?" I ask.

She shakes her head. "Nothing."

"If you're not ready to go to sleep, we might as well talk."

She adjusts her position so she can look at me better. "You know how the brain can make these crazy associations, jump from one random thing to the next?"

I nod.

"Thinking of Amber made me think of how you slept with her once and that made me think of something else... Something I've been meaning to ask you for some time."

"Shoot."

"We've been together a while now." Jo reaches for a handkerchief and wipes the underside of her nose. "I guess

I've been wondering when you're going to bring up the inevitable question."

"The inevitable question?" I know what she's getting at. Of course I do. But before I can bring up this subject, we'll have to work on our communication skills a bit more.

"You know." Her facial expression tightens. "Sleeping with other people."

"Darling, I'm not sure tonight is the right night to start that conversation. You're a little grumpy about having to cancel your gig, which I understand completely. And you're sick." I stroke my thumb over her hand. "Tonight, you just need to be pampered."

"I just would like to know. I feel like this has been hanging over my head since we got together. That at any time you can sit me down and tell me it's time we started sleeping with strangers."

"I would never even dream of broaching the subject when you're so defensive. Although I'm beginning to think we should have talked about it already, as it's clearly weighing on you. You make it sound like something I'm going to force on you, while that's absolutely not the case."

Jo's features relax and she sinks a little deeper into the pillows. "Frankly, I don't even know where we would find the time."

"To have a conversation?" I envelop her hand in mine.

"To find other people to sleep with. I barely have time to spend with you." She locks her gaze on mine.

Even though Jo has moved in with me, she's very adamant about her financial independence, so I have to tread carefully. "How many colds have you had this winter? It seems you've barely healed from one when another's already waiting in the wings. Maybe your body is trying to tell you something."

"I'm not even thirty. I can take it."

"It wouldn't hurt to listen to the cues your body is trying to give you a little more. It's not normal to suffer from so many colds. This is not the first gig you've had to cancel. Maybe it's time for something else to give?"

Jo pushes herself up a little. "How did this turn into a conversation about my health? I thought we were talking about something else entirely?"

"Being under thirty doesn't make you superhuman. You need to take care of yourself. You were already stretched too thinly when we met, between working at the Pink Bean, working on your PhD and being Sheryl's Teaching Assistant."

"Which is why I'm no longer Sheryl's T.A."

"I can tell you're not in the mood to talk about this, but—"

"You just need to tell me one more time." Jo's lips draw into a soft smile. "Maybe it's time to stop working at the Pink Bean."

"You can't keep on doing all the things you've been doing."

"So I can have more time to sleep with other people." She tilts her head.

I shake mine in response. "You're being deliberately contrary."

She clasps a hand to her chest. "Who? Me?"

"Yes, you." I sneak my hand along her belly. "If you weren't sick, I'd punish you."

"Oh really? How would you do that?" She puts her hand over mine.

"I have my ways, but if you want to find out, you need to get better first."

"Yes, Ma'am." Jo leans forward and kisses me on the forehead. "I just hate not being able to sing." She lets herself drop against the pillows again.

"Don't I know it." I give her a smile.

"If only you could hold a tune, I could send you as my replacement." She chuckles.

"What are you insinuating?"

"Same as always." She puts her head on my shoulder. "You're a woman of many talents, but singing's not one of them."

"My voice is just more of an acquired taste, that's all."

"No, honey." Her chin bumps against my shoulder as she shakes her head. "It's really not."

"Go to sleep now," I say. "We'll continue this conversation later."

As we settle under the sheets, I know it will be a while before I'm able to nod off. My mind is too preoccupied with things left unsaid.

Chapter Two

"Come on, Sheryl," I urge. "How many times are you going to make me beg?"

"It's not me making you beg, it's you who can't stop begging."

"This is exactly why I want you on the show. So you can say things like that on camera."

"I have no desire to be on TV, Caitlin. Besides, there are many people more interesting to interview than me."

"Completely false. To me, there's no one more interesting than you."

"Really?" Sheryl cocks up an eyebrow. "You'd not rather interview yourself?" She bursts out in a chuckle.

"I don't know where I got this self-centered reputation. Am I really that bad? As my friend, tell me the truth."

"I wouldn't dare." Sheryl shoots me a wide grin. She looks over at the counter where Jo is busy with a customer. "You should have Jo on."

"That would be a conflict of interest."

Sheryl rolls her eyes. "Excuses, excuses."

"Maybe I would, if she weren't so exhausted all the time."

"She has already quit working for me. Something I hold you personally responsible for, by the way."

I know Sheryl doesn't mean it. Not that she wasn't sad to lose Jo as her T.A.

"You should have paid her better than your wife does. In what universe does working in a coffee shop pay more than working at the university?"

"Being a Teaching Assistant is more of a prestige than a money job."

"A sad state of affairs," I say. "No offence to Kristin or the Pink Bean, but I so wish she would stop working here. It's too much."

"But it's not your decision to make."

"I know. It needs to come from her. I just don't understand why she's so stubborn about it. She makes good money singing. She has royalties from the book."

"It was already a big decision for her to stop being my T.A. For the first time, she's making ends meet. She might be scared that her luck will run out."

"I was like her when I was her age, so I do understand. But I have the benefit of hindsight. If I could be her age all over again, I would take more time to enjoy life instead of working all the time."

"Singing is not a job for Jo. And I dare say she gets more than money out of working here. Next year, she'll finish her PhD. Everything will change then."

"I have the most uncanny buzzing in my ears." Jo suddenly stands next to our table. "As though you were talking about me behind my back."

Instinctively, I bring my hand to her back. "You're my girlfriend and Sheryl is my friend. It's only natural I should talk to her about you."

"Only good things I hope." Jo looks at Sheryl.

"How could we ever say anything bad about the great Josephine Greenwood?" Sheryl says.

"Oh, Christ. It must have been really terrible then." Two new customers walk in. "Excuse me." Jo walks away, leaving my hand to tumble down.

Sheryl hunches over the table. "We all have to make our own way in life, no matter how experienced the woman we share our life with."

"But isn't that one of the big advantages of being in a relationship with a woman who's twenty years older? To learn from the wisdom she has acquired?"

"I don't think it's your age that made Jo fall in love with you." Sheryl sits there smirking. "Nor your life experience."

"Just my general loveliness then." I lean back and smirk at Sheryl.

"What else could it be?" She sips from her coffee.

I roll my eyes at her and glance at Jo, who is chatting to a customer. I think of all the conversations we've yet to have and how, if she hadn't pushed me to think about it yesterday, I wouldn't have brought up opening up our relationship for a good long while.

"So," I straighten my posture again. "Is that another official no from you? Jessica's not going to be pleased."

"Who is this Jessica you keep mentioning, anyway? And why does she want you to interview me so badly?"

"She's my new boss at the network and an executive I actually get along with. She does, however, very much enjoy suggesting guests for my show."

"But why me?"

"Maybe she'd like to get to know you better." I quirk up my eyebrows.

Sheryl shakes her head. "You tell Jessica that not every person on the planet wants to be on TV."

"Fine, but remember when I made you look good by guest lecturing at the university?"

"As if you would ever let me forget. Besides, you enjoy lecturing. It was no hardship for you. And it allowed you to woo Jo. You can hardly say I'm the only one who benefitted from that."

"Nor would I be the only one to benefit from you coming on my show. You have important things to say and we need more women like you on television."

Sheryl paints on a knowing smirk. "The answer is still no."

"I bet the dean would love it."

Sheryl holds up her hand. "Stop, please." She looks at her watch. "I need to get to the university, where I will tell the dean all about this missed opportunity, of course."

"I'd better go too. Off to disappoint my boss again."

We both rise and kiss each other goodbye. I stop by the counter to blow Jo an air kiss.

"See you tonight, darling," I say.

"I'll be home late," she replies. "Jimmy and I are rehearsing a few new songs."

Chapter Three

WHILE I WAIT for this week's brainstorming meeting to begin, the one where we come up with a bunch of questions that will be pared down to the most inquisitive ones, I look over the research on this week's guest. As a way of placating Jessica, I have agreed to interview Kathy Kramer, the star of Australia's longest running and most popular reality TV show.

A far cry from interviewing the likes of Sheryl, I think, although I have to admit that in the few months since I took over *The Zoya Das Show*—and turned it into *The Caitlin James Show*—some of the guests of whom I expected the least have surprised me most. And Jessica was very persuasive when she made her case for Kathy Kramer. That's the problem with Jessica—she has very convincing ways. And I haven't quite figured out yet how to say no to the new boss.

While Zoya is off in Paris, living a life of romance with her French girlfriend, and befriending the French president Dominique Laroche, I'm stuck with Kathy Kramer.

In the document my team have prepared, there are

endless links to tabloid articles, which I refuse to follow, until my mouse trigger finger accidentally opens one. The link takes me to a *Daily Post* article about how Kathy has supposedly split from her boyfriend. I roll my eyes, but before I can close the tab, my eye is drawn to a headline lower down the sidebar. "Media mogul Edward Porter's daughter nabs top exec job at ANBC".

I can't help but click on it. However small, the picture of Jessica next to it is too compelling to ignore.

The article speaks of Jessica's appointment in her father's company as though it were a scandal—as though Jessica has no skills that would merit her a job at ANBC. The article also speaks of Jessica's sexual orientation, as though it has something to do with her professional life.

I'm quickly reminded why I don't read rags like the *Daily Post* and click away before I get sucked into the gutter of humanity that is the comment section.

When I first started presenting the show, I asked my team to collect all press clippings about it, except from the *Daily Post*. Life's too short for their disrespectful tone and double standard for women.

I try to refocus on the research about Kathy Kramer, but even though I've only read a few pages, I already feel I know all there is to know about her. I should really learn to hold a firmer stance against Jessica. I refuse to think of her in terms of only getting the job because her father owns the company, but I do wonder if she has picked my show to meddle with because it's just as new as she is. Because it makes her feel more comfortable.

Someone knocks on the door and it opens without me having the chance to say "Come in".

"How's it going?" Jessica asks. "Am I still welcome in your office after pushing Kathy Kramer on you?" She walks in and leans against my desk.

It's not the first time she has dropped by unannounced. As a new exec, doesn't she have anything more pressing to do?

"We'll make it work." I look into her eyes.

"It'll be a ratings hit, which…" She leans over my desk. "Is exactly what we need."

Jessica's predecessor, who hired me and was very enthusiastic about me filling the empty spot Zoya's departure had left in the network's schedule, barely even mentioned ratings. He knew what the show was about and realized that, just like *The Zoya Das Show*, it would never be a big commercial hit, but a welcome addition to balance out the more popular programming. Jessica Porter does not seem to agree with this.

I scan her face. Her lips are tilted into a small smile. There's a glint in her eyes that I can't decipher—not in this context anyway.

"I thought ANBC had plenty of hit shows already. *The Kramers* being one of them."

"Can I sit for a minute?" Jessica points at a chair.

"Sure."

Before she sits, she pushes the door shut. She then leans back in her chair and crosses one leg over the other.

"Your show is great, Caitlin. I'm a huge fan. You do a great job. I'm just not sure anyone here is aware of its true potential—of *your* true potential. I'm talking about a possible prime time spot."

I scoff and shake my head. "You know my show is not designed to be prime time material. It's much too serious for that. Not enough sensation."

Apparently, it's Jessica's turn to shake her head. "Zoya Das made it serious but it doesn't necessarily need to continue in that vein now that you've taken over. We could lighten it up. Get more commercial guests on."

I furrow my brow. "Then I don't understand why you've

been nagging me to invite Sheryl. She's a professor. An interview with her would hardly be light entertainment."

"I agree, which is why we'd need her on the show before we change its format."

What's with the *we*, I want to ask. And the change of format? Jessica is starting to get on my nerves with her presumptuousness and, for a split second, I feel myself agreeing with the *Daily Post*. Who is Jessica, a person who only got this job because her father owns the parent company, to interfere with my show? Then I regret my thought—and reading the article—and take a deep breath.

"Miss Porter," I say, trying to sound respectful. "I have no desire to change the format of the show. If I did, it wouldn't be my show anymore. I don't mind humoring you and trying to find an extra dimension to the likes of Kathy Kramer because it would please you, but I don't intend to stoop so low every week." Oops. That didn't come out very respectful.

"Please, call me Jessica." She doesn't lose her smile. "I do understand where that remark is coming from, Caitlin." She puts emphasis on my name. "How about…" Her tongue flicks over her lower lip. "I take you out to lunch to talk this through a little more." She leans in my direction a fraction. "Or better yet. Dinner?"

I do my best to not expel a sigh. So that's what this is about.

"I can do lunch." I make a point of looking at my calendar on my computer screen. "How about tomorrow?"

"Tomorrow it is." Jessica paints a wide smile on her face and, all of a sudden, I can't make heads nor tails of her again. She remains seated while neither of us speaks for a few moments, then she scoots up. "I think you and I will have lots to talk about."

After she's left my office, I lean back and think about our

exchange. Is Jessica really interested in changing my show, or is she after something else?

Probably a bit of both.

Chapter Four

Jo ARRIVES HOME AFTER ELEVEN, just as I've given up waiting for her and am getting ready for bed.

"Good rehearsal?" I ask as I gather her in my arms. Even though she told me this morning she would be late, I'm a little pissed off—but I'm happy to see her regardless.

"Sorry I'm so late. We had trouble getting a song right. Jimmy wrote a new arrangement for it and the changed melody made it very weird for me to sing. I just couldn't get the hang of it."

"Which song?" Maybe if I'm lucky, I can get her to sing it for me. The cold she suffered from a few days ago seems to have gone away.

"'So Cruel'."

"U2?" I can't keep a hint of disappointment out of my voice.

"I know you dislike them, babe, but Jimmy hero worships the Edge."

"By rewriting his melodies?" I nod. "It can only make the song better."

Jo kisses me on the cheek. "How was your day?"

I contemplate for a second whether I should tell her about Jessica. It's late and it could spark a long conversation. But I have to tell her, if only in the spirit of the complete openness I want to create between us.

"My new boss wants me to lighten up my show and thinks the best way to get me to do so is by openly flirting with me."

"Jessica Porter?" Jo asks and takes a step back.

I'm glad she has remembered Jessica's name. Sometimes Jo seems so preoccupied with all her activities, I fear she barely listens to me at all.

I nod.

"What did she say?" Jo's interest seems piqued.

"She asked me to lunch, then swiftly changed her mind and asked me to dinner."

Jo brings her hands to her sides. "What was your reply?"

"I agreed to lunch. I thought dinner was a bit much."

Jo shuffles backwards and sits on the armrest of the sofa.

"It's just a business lunch," I'm quick to say.

"But she did flirt with you?"

"I think so, yes."

"So she's after more than just lunch?"

I feel awkward just standing in the middle of the room like this. "My gut says she is, which is why I didn't agree to dinner."

Jo scrunches her lips together. "Is this when we have the talk?" She sits down in the sofa properly.

"It could be, but just to be very clear, I have no desire to sleep with my boss." I walk to the drinks cart. "Splash of something?" I ask.

Jo nods then lets her head fall back.

After I've poured us both a generous measure of whisky —which reminds me of the very first time she came to my apartment and she nearly gagged when she sipped from it—I sit next to her.

"I have no intention of responding to Jessica's flirtation in kind, babe." I take a sip from my drink. I've had this conversation a few times in the past but this time around, it seems so much harder. The words don't sound right as they roll from my lips. "Not just because she's my boss, but also because I'm not sure you and I are there yet. I know you brought it up the other day, and I do think we should talk about it. I'm just not... sure how you actually feel about it."

"That's because I don't know."

"You saying it was like something hanging over your head shocked me. Like it's a very unwelcome destiny you can't escape."

"I fell in love with you. I knew all about this and it didn't stop me from falling deeper and deeper in love. I know this is who you are. This is what you want," Jo says in a nervous voice.

"The problem is that when you put it like that you make it sound like something I need to convince you of. That it's my job to open you up to the possibility of desiring other people. That's a difficult spot to be in."

"Then let me make it easy for you." She grins at me. "Don't. Let's just not. We're good the way we are. Why make things so endlessly complicated?"

I drink to gather my thoughts. "Because if we were to do that, I truly believe we would be doing ourselves, each other, and our relationship a great disservice." I find her gaze. "We should at least be able to have the conversation."

"Then why does even the prospect of the conversation already wear me out so much?"

"Because you're tired. You don't get nearly enough sleep, let alone plain old rest. When was the last time you spent more than a few hours doing nothing at all?"

"There we go again." Jo puts her whisky tumbler on the coffee table. "If you want to play with other people while I'm busy building my career, just go ahead. Just do it. I'm not in a stage of my life where I have the time or the inclination to explore this. I'm perfectly happy coming home to you after a long day. And before you say anything, I know you have loftier goals than to just sleep with other people. I get that you want our relationship to be different, to be less traditional. And I should respect that more, but you know what? To me, you are enough. I just wish I could be enough for you."

I swallow hard then take her hand in mine. I think about what to say next, because I don't want it to be as hurtful as what she just said to me. I don't want things to escalate. It's too late in the day for that. I also don't want to sound like a lecturer on open relationships, because it's very clear my words will never convince Jo that what I chose as way of life a long time ago can actually be a rewarding and wonderful process.

I'm going to have to rely on something else than just my words.

"May I make a suggestion?" I rub my thumb along her palm.

"Of course." Her voice has softened.

"You have fans. Adoring fans. I see how some girls look at you when you're on stage."

Jo is already shaking her head.

"Just hear me out, okay?"

"Okay." She holds on to my thumb.

"When someone you like comes up to you after a gig and they give you a compliment, when they are a little flirtatious… flirt back a little. Just to see how it makes you feel. Just say something cheeky. That's it. No ulterior motives. Just some flirty banter."

Jo has the kind of skin that can flush in an instant. Her cheeks are instantly rosy red. "Just because someone compliments my singing doesn't mean they're flirting."

"You'd be surprised." I scoot a little closer and put a hand on her knee. "But you need to be open to it to notice. Most people are not. Just try to be open to it at your next gig. That's all I ask. Then we'll talk about how it made you feel."

"I'm not like you, babe. I'm not... hot like you."

I tilt my head. "Trust me, you're very hot. Especially when you're on stage."

"I'm more of an acquired taste. When someone sees you, like that Jessica for instance, I can so easily imagine her thinking, 'Oh yes, I would like some of that'. Whereas for the life of me, I can't imagine anyone thinking such a thing when they look at me."

"That's only because of how you see yourself." I squeeze her knee. "Most of the time. Except when you're singing. Then you forget to think. Then you exude confidence and charisma and sensuality. Take it from me." I take her hand in mine again. "People are attracted to that."

"But when I talk to them I'm not on stage anymore. I'm not singing anymore."

"I've seen you after gigs, darling. There's this window of time after you walk off the stage that you're a different person."

"That's just it, though. I'm not me. I'm a different person."

"I think those moments are more *you* than any other time. Since you've started performing on stage, you're coming into your own more and more. You're not the same shy girl I met a year and a half ago. Remember when I first asked you out? First you followed your gut and said yes—you responded to my flirtation. But then the overthinking took over and you said no. You overthink much less these days. A direct consequence of the confidence you gain by singing for an audience."

"Have I really changed that much?"

I give her a slow nod. "You have." I take her hand in mine again and kiss her palm this time. "Think about what we do in bed these days as opposed to when we first got together." The thought sends a frisson of excitement up my spine. It was never my intention to end this conversation, even this day, like this, but now I can't stop myself. I kiss the inside of Jo's wrist, hoping she will catch my drift.

Her voice is soft when she asks, "How about you? How have you changed?"

I look her in the eyes and say, "I only want you more each day." A cop out if ever there was one, but I'm done talking. I want to make love to my girlfriend.

———

We're naked in bed and Jo lies on her back with a dildo strapped to her pelvis. Once I started kissing her on the sofa, it seems like we ended up naked in a matter of minutes. When I opened the drawer where we keep this particular sex toy, Jo knew, without me having to say a word, what kind of foreplay I had in mind.

My hand drifts down to the toy while I kiss her. I'm going to make it nice and wet before she fucks me with it. When we break from the kiss she looks up at me and says, with nothing but authority in her voice, "Suck my cock."

The mere fact that she can say such a thing to me now is such a testament to how much she has changed. I may sometimes have to point out her transformation, but I like to believe that, deep down, behind all those insecurities that sometimes make her life much harder than it has to be, Jo knows this as well. As I look at her face right now, I know she does.

I kiss her on the lips once more, then make my way down. I trace a moist path along her neck and halt at her beautiful, luscious breasts. I take my time sucking her nipples into my mouth, but she starts pushing me down. When I first took Jo to bed, I'd never imagined her to be this bossy between the sheets. It took her a long time to get here, but here we are nonetheless. I love her all the more for it.

I kiss the edge of her pubic hair, all blond and soft and fragrant. Then I pivot and straddle her so that my pussy is mere inches away from her face.

The silicone cock stands high and mighty in front of me. I kiss the tip, lick my way around it to make it slippery enough for when I let my lips slide over.

I feel Jo's hands on my butt cheeks, her nails digging into my flesh. Then she pulls me toward her and kisses my pussy lips. Her tongue skates along them the next second and when I feel it lapping at my clit, I know it's time to open my mouth wide. I let my lips slip down half the length of the dildo, an action that never fails to leave my clit extra hard, extra ready for her tongue.

As has become our habit, we have discussed this particular sexual act at length, but I've never been able to accurately describe why it turns me on so much. Not every partner I've had has wanted to do this with me—lesbians and their phallic aversion—and if I hadn't had so many lovers, I would never have known I enjoy this so much.

I lick the dildo's shaft as I bob my head up and down. Jo's tongue is insistent on my clit. She sucks it into her mouth and I'm pulled between the sensations on my lips and my pussy. Jo's hands on my behind and the cock in my mouth. Slowly, I slide into a state of total surrender—there's no other way to do this. Either I'm fully in, or I'm out. There's no in between.

The silicone is soft against my lips, its girth spreads my lips wide. On the other side of me, Jo slides a couple of fingers inside, spreading me equally wide. Getting me ready. I'm almost there. Almost at that point where I want to turn around and look this woman I love in the eyes while she fucks me.

I take the dildo in my mouth as far as it will go, give the tip one last lick as I let it slip from my lips. I give Jo the time to slide her fingers out of me, then swivel around—not gracefully, limbs overtaken with blind, clumsy lust—and position the dildo at the entrance of my pussy. It's slick with my saliva and I'm wet enough for it to slip inside easily, as though this is the only possible apotheosis of my day.

It feels so damn good inside of me, the length of the toy filling me so intensely. I look at Jo. She has that smirk on her face that drives me wild. When we do this, we don't only do it for me, even though I'm the one getting the most physical pleasure from this particular position. But as we both know, physicality is only half of this equation. The other half is made up of how I feel when I look at her and what she gets back when she sees the look in my eye. My lust for her, for this, for us. I hope she sees in my glance that she is enough for me, that how I choose to conduct my relationships doesn't have the slightest thing to do with any of that.

I push myself up and down on the dildo and Jo brings a hand between my legs. Her thumb finds my clit and every time I bounce down, she gives it a soft flick. She bucks up her hips and her face changes. I see surrender in her eyes now, echoing mine. She flicks faster, I bounce harder and, together, we orchestrate my climax. It's one that takes me all the way out of myself because of the overload of sensation, the dildo, her finger, her hips slamming into me, my hands pushing into her as I hold on to her shoulders. It's wild and full of abandon and love.

I collapse onto her chest, the dildo still half inside of me, to catch my breath.

I kiss the side of her breast. She wraps her arms around me. When I can properly breathe again, I glance up at her.

She smiles a smile that says, no matter what she said earlier, she bloody well knows how scorching hot she is.

Chapter Five

"THANKS FOR JOINING ME." Jessica holds up her glass of Sauvignon Blanc.

"When you said lunch, I thought you meant a quick bite in the cafeteria." I hold up my glass of water. We're sitting in a booth at a small French restaurant around the corner from the ANBC building. This lunch might be all about signals and how the other interprets them, so I thought it better not to order wine when Jessica did.

"I thought I'd go for a more intimate setting." Jessica doesn't beat about the bush. Only a few minutes into this lunch, and my suspicions have been confirmed.

"May I ask why?" Two can play this game. I dare to bet I'm much more experienced at it than her. I'm all for openness but she's just being blatantly obvious now—and severely unprofessional.

She paints on a smile. "I enjoy your show and I would like to get to know you better. The ANBC cafeteria is not the right spot for that."

"Right." I drink some water.

A waiter arrives to take our order. After he's gone, I

decide to steer the conversation. I might as well get something out of this. I've only been doing the show for a few months and I would very much like for the format to remain the same. It suits me. An interview with a person deemed interesting enough to question for that long. This gives me an idea.

"Would *you* be interested in coming on my show, Jessica?" I ask with my sweetest voice.

"Me?" She plays coy too well. Maybe Jessica's not that interested in me personally. Maybe this is what she's been playing at all along. "Oh, no. That's not my thing at all."

"It would give you a chance to rebuff the rumors that you only replaced Jason Hewitt because your family name is Porter."

She waves her hand. "I don't give a rat's ass about what the *Daily Post* writes about me. Besides, who believes anything printed on that waste of paper? I know why I got the job. I won't sit here straight-faced and claim my father owning ANBC had nothing to do with it, because of course it played a part." She shrugs. "Let's not be overly naive about that."

Her reply surprises me. "Is that a no?" I shoot her a sympathetic smile.

"I know I've been meddling with your show, Caitlin. I can't shake the feeling it annoys you, while annoying you is the very last thing I want to do."

"I get that it's a TV exec's primal instinct to increase ratings, but some shows will just never be a hit. Not unless you change them drastically. My show is one of them." I tilt my head. "Truth be told, having to interview Kathy Kramer is already a bridge too far for me."

"But you agreed. To please me." She reaches for her wine glass again.

"You're the new boss. I felt like I didn't have much choice."

"My sincere apologies for compromising your integrity. I really wanted to get stuck in and be hands-on with this new job. I might have gotten carried away and you may be the victim of that."

"Why the focus on my show? There are so many on ANBC."

"Pertinent question." She grins. "I guess that's why you're so good at your job."

I grin back at her because of the compliment. "Am I allowed to press you further on this matter? Or should I back off because you're the boss?"

A laugh comes from the back of her throat. "Please, don't ever hold back because of the title on my business card." She leans over the table a little. "You're the only out lesbian on ANBC. I'm the only out lesbian in management. I guess it instinctively drew me to you."

"Good answer." I narrow my eyes. "Although I can't shake the feeling it's a bit of a cop-out."

She gives a slow nod. "Did you want me to say outright that you're the most attractive host we have and, well, I know your reputation."

"Ah." I almost want to slap my hand against the table triumphantly because I got her to admit this out loud—and it wasn't all that hard. "There we have it."

Our dishes are brought to the table and the conversation pauses. It gives me time to consider whether I should be frank or cautious. But I don't really do cautious, not after she has been so frank with me.

"A reputation can be a funny thing," I say as I spear a roasted potato on my fork. "It can most certainly give people the wrong impression."

"I read the book, Caitlin. Your entire life philosophy printed black on white."

"I wrote that book more than fifteen years ago."

"Has something changed?"

I chuckle. I'm beginning to see why she was put in the job of a ruthless executive.

"That's not really the point." I wish I had a glass of wine in front of me. "If my so-called reputation is the reason why we're having lunch, we shouldn't be sitting here at all. You're my boss. If I were a different kind of person, I could perceive this as another thing entirely."

"But that's where your reputation comes in. I know you're not the kind of person who will misinterpret this invitation."

"That is the biggest line of bullshit I've heard in a while." My voice shoots up. "If you were a man—"

"But I'm not, and I believe that changes everything." Jessica doesn't let me finish my sentence.

"Not everything," I hiss.

She takes a deep breath. "Caitlin, I'm truly sorry. I was just flirting. Just trying to get a feel of the possibilities. I don't even consider myself your boss. I see you as a colleague. An equal. And I got carried away by what I read about you, by what it might promise." She sighs. "I certainly never meant to offend you or assume, um, certain things."

"If you don't consider yourself my boss, then could you please stop suggesting guests for my show. My team and I have a long list of people we'd like to ask. We can only welcome your input to a certain extent. You must understand that in your position it's easy to put pressure on people. That's just how it is."

She holds up her hands in supplication. "I'll back off, I promise. On both accounts." She looks at her plate, which she has barely touched. "Have I completely blown things with you?"

"We can start over." I suddenly feel like I owe her some lesbian solidarity, however false that sentiment might be.

"Just lay off a little." I try a smile. "And stop flirting. It's not going to go anywhere. I don't think I should complicate my life by sleeping with my boss or any co-worker."

She drinks more wine. I don't know her well enough to gauge whether my words have wounded her. If she wants to start over, and become friendly with me, it will depend on how she responds to them.

"I guess I'd better start harassing the people from *Worlds Apart* then. That show's ratings have truly been flailing lately." She sends me a cheeky grin, showing me that, even if she hasn't recovered from what I've said, she's at least willing to pretend for the sake of further conversation.

"How about this." I look her straight in the eye. "We consider this lunch and what's been said annulled, and we start by a friendly chat over coffee?" I relax and lean back in my chair. "You don't happen to live near Darlinghurst, do you? Because I know just the place.

"I live in Pott's Point," she says. "So, close enough."

Chapter Six

WHEN JO SINGS, I forget about everything. I'm more than ready to forget about my first truly disastrous interview since I started the show.

Interviewing Kathy Kramer felt like pulling blood from a stone. She was overly defensive from the start, and no matter how hard I tried, I was unable to put her at ease. In fact, the more I tried, the more she clammed up. Every other question I asked was met with a yes or no reply and my follow-up questions didn't fare much better. The show's producer, Jack, and I spent the better part of the day with our colleague Annika in the editing suite trying to salvage this train wreck —to no avail.

It's Friday night and the show started airing five minutes ago. I've switched off my phone so as not to get any notif- ication about overzealous Twitter trolls. And, of course, also not to be disturbed when Jo sings. This is by far the highlight of my week. Jo doesn't sing at the Pink Bean that often anymore—the place has become too small.

She finishes the song and the crowd that did manage to

squeeze itself into the Pink Bean bursts into raucous applause.

"This next song is for Caitlin," she says as she finds my gaze. "U2 are her favorite band, so…" She winks at me from the stage and despite her teasing me, I melt a little inside.

I bring a hand to my chest and bow my head. I might hate the original, but I'm sure I'll love her and Jimmy's rendition of it.

Jo keeps her gaze on me throughout the entire song, as though she's singing it to me. I try to ignore the lyrics of the chorus, but find it nonetheless disconcerting when she sings, "Sweetheart, you're so cruel". Is she trying to send me a message?

I shake off the thought and meet her gaze, while enjoying her voice, which, in my love-warped opinion is a million times more enjoyable than Bono's. Does she know how much she turns me on when she croons, "Ooh, love" like that? I'm pretty sure she does. Maybe that's why she's doing it. And because of that chat we had earlier this week. I wonder what she'll do when the gig is over. This branch of the Pink Bean has a liquor license now and these open mic nights tend to go on full throttle until Kristin kicks everyone out at midnight.

After the gig has finished, I stay in my chair for a minute to watch Jo. I keep my eyes on her, the way I've done countless times, but then realize this will not encourage her to be more receptive to flirting.

I find Sheryl who is chatting to Micky and Amber. They always show up to support Jo when she sings.

I keep an eye on the side of the stage while I try to find out what they're talking about.

"Hey Caitlin, why don't you harass any of these fine ladies to be on your show?" Sheryl asks. "Amber here would make the most wonderful interviewee, with all the enlightened wisdom she has to offer."

Amber shakes her head. She's a funny one. Even though she has explicitly told me she has forgiven me for sleeping with her under what she called false pretenses a few years ago, she can still be so skittish around me. After the train wreck interview we recorded this week, I'm not taking any more chances.

I put a hand on Sheryl's shoulder. "You're off the hook, Sheryl. I managed to get Jessica off my back."

"Oh." Sheryl juts her bottom lip. "It was that easy to make her lose interest in me?"

"I've invited her for coffee at the Pink Bean this weekend, so she might go gaga for you again if you were to be around."

Sheryl rolls her eyes. "What's with this woman blowing hot and cold like that?"

"I've yet to figure that out." I look away from our group and try to find Jo. She's no longer near the stage but by the bar, holding a glass of wine. Did Kristin give it to her or did someone else buy her a drink? I sip my own wine to get myself in check. If I can't stop eyeing my girlfriend after asking her to have an open mind, there wasn't much point asking in the first place.

She's chatting to someone, however. A woman of her age who's standing rather close to her, although that could simply be because there's a crowd at the bar.

"Caitlin?" Sheryl asks.

"Um, yes, sorry. Miles away." I glance at Sheryl.

"Micky asked you a question, I believe."

"Are you coming to my pity party next Saturday?" Micky asks.

"I'm sorry, your what?" I didn't follow the conversation at all.

"Micky's a grown woman who was single for quite some time, but now that she's found lesbian bliss with Robin, she finds it hard to be home alone for a weekend," Amber says in that tone she always uses when she's mocking Micky.

Micky juts her friend in the elbow. "I just want to cook for my friends. What's wrong with that?"

"You never invite us when Robin's not on a business trip."

"What are you talking about? Of course I do."

While they bicker, I glance over at Jo again. She's smiling, then her smile bursts into a full-blown laugh.

"So, are you and Jo coming, Caitlin? I hardly ever see Jo anymore."

I focus my attention back on Micky. "I'll need to check with her. I don't know for sure if she has a gig next Saturday, but chances are she has. So you may have to make do with just me."

"I can probably live with that." Micky grins. "Where's Jo anyway?" She rolls her eyes. "Has she now gotten so popular she no longer has time for a quick chat with her former Pink Bean colleague?"

"I guess you'll have to make do with me right now as well," I joke. "It's not easy to get a slice of Jo these days."

For a split second, I think I must be mad to have asked Jo to flirt with other women tonight. She's so busy, we've barely figured out our own schedule. The last time we had a quiet night at home was when she was sick with a cold.

I glance over at Jo again. She's still talking to the same woman, who now puts a hand on her arm. Jo looks like she's having fun, like she's basking in post-show confidence. She looks like the very picture of what I wanted for her. But then why does it suddenly feel like it's the opposite of what I want?

Jealousy is an emotion so foreign to me, I barely recognize it as it sneaks up on me. But that's what this is. It's the only thing it can be.

I'm jealous.

Chapter Seven

When we get home after the Pink Bean gig, Jo is still in high spirits. It usually takes her a while to wind down after she has been on stage. Weather permitting, it has become a habit to sit on the deck with a glass of whisky so she can let the last of the evening's excitement drift from her body.

"What a night," she says. "And to come home with you afterwards to this place." She glances at me. "I sometimes wonder when all my dreams started coming true."

These days, Jo is such a far cry from the girl who barely dared to address me because she was too much of a fan girl. It warms my heart when she says something like this: that I'm one of her dreams that came true.

"I suppose it started the day you met me," I say. I hope she can hear the joke in my words.

"It's true." She leans back and puts her bare feet in my lap. "That day you signed my copies of your books. I didn't know it then, but that's when things started changing."

I rub her ankles. "I loved your version of 'So Cruel'. Wonderful arrangement." I fix my glance on hers and send her a smile.

She wiggles her toes. "You have to say that because I dedicated the song to you."

"That didn't stop the woman from chatting you up afterward." Is it jealousy making me say this? Or am I just curious? It bothers me that I can't tell the difference.

Jo nods thoughtfully. "You were right. She was flirting. I flirted back a little. It was… kind of fun." She looks at me from under her lashes.

"What did she say?"

Jo chuckles. "That she's a big U2 fan."

I roll my eyes ostentatiously. "And you managed to chat with her for that long?"

Jo doesn't reply. She seems lost in thought. "I'm glad you, um, advised me to be more open to flirtatious signals. Having that conversation made me feel…" Silence again as I wait with bated breath. "I'm not sure how to put it." She sinks her front teeth in her lips. "Extremely alive is the best I can come up with." She rolls her head from side to side. "Like life is, in fact, full of endless possibilities." She snickers. "Although I must admit that I drank a bit too much of the wine she kept offering me, so I might just be babbling." She sips from the whisky. "And this isn't helping."

That explains her ease to talk about this. Two voices do battle in my mind. One wants to push and ask more. The other—the jealous one—wants to shut this whole thing down.

"Would you like to engage in some flirting like that again some time?"

"It was pleasant." She nods, her head bopping up and down a bit too wildly. "Is that what you had in mind when you suggested this? I mean, it did make me feel sexy. As though I would want to get it on with you as soon as we got home." She smirks. "Although now I feel a little too tired and tipsy."

I have to laugh at how adorable she is as she sits there saying this.

"While you were flirting, did you feel like taking things a step further? Like getting it on with her?"

Jo scrunches her lips together, as though pondering my question heavily, though she looks in no fit state to do so. "I don't think so. It was just fun. It made me feel good about myself."

How can I possibly be jealous when she says that? When she says the almost exact words I wanted her to say. When my mission has been accomplished so perfectly.

"Was that your goal all along?"

My turn to nod. "Yes, along with what you said about endless possibilities."

"What did I say about that again?"

I lean over and take the almost empty glass from her hand. "Come on. Bed time for you."

"For you as well, I hope." She manages one last lazy grin.

"Oh yes." I haven't switched my phone back on. Whatever messages there are—and nasty *Daily Post* reports about Kathy Kramer being treated unfairly by Caitlin James—can wait until tomorrow.

When we're in bed, Jo turns to me. "I have to work on my thesis tomorrow. I have no choice."

"But that's tomorrow." I scoop her hand in mine. "You'll get a good night's sleep first."

Before I've even finished my sentence, I hear a gentle snore starting up next to me. I lay with her hand in mine for a while longer, pondering that I had, perhaps, not expected her to be so keen on the flirting.

Chapter Eight

"AM I FIRED?" I ask as soon as Jessica arrives at the Pink Bean.

"I should be fired," she replies. "It was my mistake."

"Maybe we shouldn't have aired it." I sigh. "What can I get you?"

"I should have let you do a quick back-up interview with me." She chuckles and looks up at the blackboard above the counter. "I'll have a large Americano, please."

"Coming right up." I'm so used to Jo being behind the counter that it's strange to place my order with someone else. But it's Saturday and Jo is trying to finish a chapter of her thesis—not that she looked as though she felt like getting up at all when her alarm went off this morning. But I held my tongue and didn't bring up that she could have weekday mornings off to work on all the thesis chapters she wanted, if only she quit working at the Pink Bean. I just hoped she would reach that conclusion by herself before she gets too burned out.

Jessica is glued to her phone screen. While I wait for our coffees, I glance around the Pink Bean. In the furthest corner, I see a face I vaguely recognize, but can't immediately place. Then an image from last night pops up in my mind. Jo smiling, laughing at something that woman said. It's her. She has come back—maybe hoping to run into Jo.

I stare at her, hoping she will look up at me, so I can send her a territorial smile. She shoots me a quick glance but looks away quickly—like a kitten that knows it's been naughty.

"Here you go," Mandy says and hands me the coffees.

I head back to our table and sit with my back to the door so I can keep an eye on the woman.

"I've been here before," Jessica says. "But I didn't know this was your regular coffee shop. I like it."

"My partner works here during the week."

"Josephine Greenwood?" Jessica surprises me. We haven't had many personal conversations and I haven't had a chance to mention Jo.

"The one and only."

"It probably won't surprise you that I googled you," Jessica says.

I shake my head. "Not in the least."

"Did you, um, tell Josephine about my failed flirtation attempt?" Jessica's tone couldn't be more self-deprecating.

"I did."

"And?" Jessica blows on her coffee. "Does she dislike me before she has even met me?"

I chuckle at Jessica's forwardness as well as her down-to-earth-ness. Part of me wants to confide in her about the current state of my relationship with Jo, but the prevailing part thinks it's none of her business. Jessica and I are having coffee today to gauge whether there is any friendly chemistry between us, I remind myself. Although I probably wouldn't have invited her if that initial spark hadn't been there.

"You might not be Jo's all-time favorite person right now,

but she doesn't dislike you." I glance at the woman in the corner. "I wouldn't worry about it."

"Who are you looking at?" Jessica asks.

"A woman who was here last night at Jo's gig."

"Jo sang here last night?" Her voice shoots up a little. "I would love to see her perform. Will you let me know next time?"

I get the impression Jessica is trying very hard to be my friend—to force the brittle process of a burgeoning friendship. She's new to ANBC, but as far as I know, she's hardly new to town.

"Sure." I lean over the table. "Can I ask you a personal question?"

"Isn't that why we're here?" She grins.

"I suppose." I grin back while thinking of the best way to put this. "Why did you take that job at ANBC? Didn't you have your own company?" After Jessica first turned up in my office, I did a little research on her myself, but information on the internet was scarce.

"I did. For many years. Until I ran it into the ground." She purses her lips together. "But that's a very long story."

"As you just said, isn't that why we're here?"

"Touché." She nods slowly. "It's just not that easy for me to talk about. I failed a lot of people, not just myself."

I nod my understanding. "So ANBC is like a new start for you? A clean slate?"

"Very much so," she says, then looks up.

"Hey, babe." Jo's voice behind me surprises me.

Before I get up, I sneak a quick glance at the woman in the corner, who is most definitely looking in our direction now. "Hello darling." I kiss Jo on the cheek to inform the other party that not much flirting should be expected today. "Did you chuck in the thesis writing?"

Jo huffs out an exasperated breath. "It's not really coming together today." She looks over at Jessica.

"This is Jessica, my boss," I say.

Jessica gets up and holds out her hand.

Jo takes it in hers. She's courteous enough to smile at her, but it's not her usual hearty smile. "I've heard all about you," she says, then turns to me. "I wouldn't go on the internet today if I were you. The Kramer Army is out to get you."

"I'll gladly take that advice." I pull a chair up for Jo.

I see her stiffen for a split second. She has probably noticed the woman. "I'm just going to have a quick chat with Mandy," she says. "I'll be right back."

I wish Jessica weren't here so I could ask Jo how she feels about our conversation last night now that it's just a regular Saturday morning with no alcohol or supreme post-show confidence flowing through her veins. Because, in the end, that's what will matter most. What will make or break that particular part of our relationship. If we don't find a way to successfully communicate about it in the broad daylight, there's no point.

"That was a little awkward," Jessica says. "Are you sure there are no hard feelings?"

"It's fine. Really." I glance at the woman again. She has gotten up and is making her way to the counter. I follow her with my gaze. If she has the nerve to strike up a conversation with Jo in front of me, I may have to step in. Or should I just let this play out? I seem to be losing my cool quickly.

Jessica looks over at the counter as well. She must wonder what is happening. If we were friends, I would explain it, but I don't want to talk about it with her. And I want to hear what this woman is going to say to Jo, but I'm sitting too far away from the counter to hear.

Jo looks surprised to see the woman, even though I'm sure she spotted her before. The woman immediately puts a hand on Jo's arm—like she did last night. And it's too much for me. It crosses a boundary that Jo and I haven't yet explicitly set.

"Please excuse me a second," I mumble to Jessica. "I'll be right back."

I walk over to Jo and, in an obnoxiously possessive way, curl an arm around her waist. "Who's your friend, darling?" I say.

Poor Jo. She looks like a deer caught in headlights. None of this is her fault. She has no tools to deal with this situation. And, I realize, this may set us back quite a bit in our quest for balance in what we want out of our relationship.

"This is Bryony. We met after the open mic last night."

"Nice to meet you Bryony." I don't hold out my hand. I wouldn't want Bryony to think I'd like to engage in some small talk with her.

"This is my partner Caitlin," Jo says, her voice trembling a little.

"Oh yes. Caitlin James. I knew I recognized your face from somewhere. I was just reading an article about you on my phone. What are the odds?" She cocks her head. "That Kathy Kramer, eh?" She throws in a chuckle, as if she has any idea what she's talking about. And wasn't just hitting on my girlfriend in front of my very eyes. This woman clearly has no shame—which is something I can usually admire in someone, but today that sentiment eludes me.

"Can you bring Jo's coffee to the table please, Mandy," I ask. "Come on, babe. Jessica is waiting for us." I hope Jo will catch my drift.

"It was good to see you again, Bryony," Jo says. "We should get back to our friend."

"I'll bring your cappuccino right over, Jo." Mandy winks at us. She's a good sport.

Just then, Sheryl walks in through the back door behind

the counter.

"Hello, hello," she says in her low voice. "I was hoping to find you here." She looks at me. I vaguely remember saying something last night about meeting Jessica here today. Sheryl looks keen—much keener than I would have expected after her adamant refusal to be a guest on my show.

Bryony scoots off and the three of us head to the table, where Jessica sits slack-jawed.

We've barely sat down when Mandy brings over Jo's coffee and Sheryl orders an espresso. I take advantage of the hustle and bustle to gather my thoughts. What the hell just happened?

————

Jessica seems instantly smitten with Sheryl and keeps asking her questions about her research and the subjects she teaches. Apparently she saw a few of her lectures online and has had a soft spot for Sheryl, which she isn't shy about, ever since.

This gives me a chance to put a hand on Jo's back and ask, my voice a whisper, "Are you all right, babe?"

She narrows her eyes as she speaks. "Are you?"

"I am if you are." What the hell am I saying? I'm supposed to be the expert at this. I'm supposed to guide the way. I'm not doing a very good job of that, what with uttering platitudes and such.

"You were rather rude to Bryony." Jo holds my gaze.

"I know. I'm sorry."

"We can't talk about this now," she whispers. She looks over at Sheryl as though hoping she would engage her in the conversation, so that Jo doesn't have to speak to me anymore.

I lean back in my seat. I know I screwed up. Now I just need to figure out why.

Chapter Nine

"I'm sorry, darling," I say on the way home. "I don't know what came over me."

"It looked very much like plain old jealousy to me." Jo stops in her tracks. "Which is fine with me. It was just a little unexpected."

"If we're going to do this, we're going to need clear rules."

"Did I say anything at all about you having coffee with Jessica this morning? Even though you told me yourself she's after you."

"No, you didn't." I hate how sheepish I sound.

"That situation just now was just absurd. I'm not sure what I would have said if Sheryl hadn't turned up."

"Which is why we need—"

"Rules," Jo says on a sigh, "yes, you made that clear."

Only complete honesty can break the tension between us. I sling an arm around Jo's shoulder. "I was jealous. I hate to admit it, but I was. I was jealous last night when I saw you with her and I was extra jealous just now when she came up to you. I don't really know why. I'm usually not the jealous type. I trust you. I was the one who suggested you put your-self out there. It has surprised me as well."

"I'm flattered that you were jealous." Jo leans into my arm. "Even though there's plenty of me to go around, you don't want to share."

We arrive at our building and spend the elevator ride up in silence.

"Did Jessica hit on you again?" she asks with a smirk on her lips when we're inside the apartment.

"No, babe. We had a chat. She apologized for being too forward. It's all about being friends now."

"She seemed quite keen on Sheryl."

I sit down and think about what Jessica has told me about herself, which isn't a whole lot. "I get the impression she's lonely. Or that, at the very least, she's looking for something new. A new circle of friends, perhaps. Something happened with her former company, but she wasn't ready to give me the details."

"There's something wounded about her." Jo sits next to me. "I recognize it in people, what with being a terribly wounded soul myself." She follows up with a snicker.

"She would like to hear you sing." I rest my gaze on Jo, stare into her gorgeous brown eyes for a moment. "That should do wonders for her wounded soul."

Jo sends me a smile. "So, tell me. What are the rules?"

I appreciate Jo's forwardness. "Good question."

"I'm relying on you for this. On your vast experience."

"Yet rules setting should be a collaboration." I draw my legs underneath me.

"But we have to start somewhere." The way she's pushing me a little makes me wonder how much she likes Bryony. To me, she didn't look like anything special, but that might be the jealousy speaking. Again.

"That we do." I somehow feel like I've been pushed into

a role reversal. That Jo wants this more than I do now. But it's a silly thought I need to shake off there and then. "Rule number one should be to remain respectful toward one another. It's paramount."

Jo nods. "No flirting in front of each other."

"I guess that was my mistake."

"Maybe you hadn't expected me to actually go through with it. Truth be told, if Bryony hadn't come up to me, I probably wouldn't have. But there she was. And then it seemed like an opportunity I had to grab. Not only to prove something to myself, but to you as well."

"I get it." I think for a second. "Are you comfortable with Jessica and me being friends?"

She taps her fingertips on a sofa cushion. "Jessica's fine. She's your boss. I can't imagine her ever being a threat to our relationship."

"I'm truly not interested in her that way."

Jo nods. "I know." She holds up two fingers. "So, rules number one and two, respect each other and don't flirt with anyone else in front of each other."

"Should we write these down?" I joke.

Jo doesn't take my words as a joke. "We should." She gets up to get pen and paper from a drawer. "What?" she asks after she has sat back down.

"You're right. We should write them down. It's important."

"Did you never write down the rules before?"

"Not for a long time."

"Not with Michelle either? You were together for a while. You must have had rules."

"We did, but my relationship with Michelle was very different. We lived in different cities, for starters. It's hard to flirt in front of each other when you only see each other every other weekend."

"Just a sec." Jo writes down the rules we've already set. "What's the next rule?" She looks up again.

"We need to discuss if we want to know about what the other gets up to or not."

She drops the pen. "I've been thinking about that. It's a tough one. I think not knowing would drive me crazy. It would make me imagine all sorts of things. But knowing would be equally hard. I'm not sure. Because how do you keep from trying to compare? Trying to gauge whether it could be a threat?"

"Experience has taught me it's better not to know. Because, in the end, it's all about trust." I never thought this would be such a loaded question. "Do you trust me?"

"I do," Jo is quick to say. "I'm just struggling with the practicalities of all this."

"Let me give you an example." I sit up a bit straighter. "Say you've finished a gig and you meet someone like Bryony. I wasn't in the audience so you have all the space to flirt with her. You like her and you think, um, yes, I can see this happening." I shoot Jo a smile. "Then you just text me to let me know you'll be home late."

Jo shakes her head. "But then you would know. That would be the equivalent of telling you."

"Not specifically. You're just letting me know you're safe."

"Besides, I would never… do that. Meeting someone for the first time and, you know."

"Have sex with them?"

"Well, yes."

"Maybe not now. But maybe later you might."

"I'm not sure I agree with this rule."

"It's not a rule yet. It's a debate."

"I just know that if you were to text me one night to say you're not coming home, it would drive me nuts. Because there would only be one reason for that."

"That's true, but I wouldn't be doing anything behind your back. You would know, because of our arrangement. And there will always be some acknowledgment of the fact, which would be okay, because we have agreed on all that beforehand. What I meant was that we shouldn't tell each other all the details of our encounters. I can only speak for myself, of course, but *I* don't want to know about any of that. For me, the point is knowing that being with me is not holding you back in any way, shape or form. That it allows you to explore and fulfill needs that I can't."

"I do see what you're trying to say, babe. I just have a hard time imagining it all play out. It's funny because being with you has made me think about this a lot. Sometimes I get really excited about the prospect of freedom, of the sort of happiness you propose outside the regular norm for relationships. And other times I just get really tired just thinking about it."

"That's completely normal. The mere thought of going against the grain, going against what everyone expects of you, can be exhausting." I quirk up my eyebrows. "But I know my why. I know very well why I've written the books that I have and why I speak so passionately about my chosen subjects. I'm not going to live my life in a certain way simply because the majority of people have always done it that way. And I'm not so vain to think that I, just one person, can be everything my partner needs."

"To me, you are everything I need."

I break out into a smile. "Because we're still in the honeymoon phase of our relationship. We're still madly in love." A gush of warmth pours through me. "We don't have to open up right this minute. We'll know when we're ready. But for me it's important to know that the option will be there. That it's something you want as well. And most importantly, that it's not something I'm forcing on you."

"Sometimes it's hard to know the difference." Jo taps the pen against the paper. "But at the very least you being who you are and being very vocal about it, has made me think. Or better, re-think what I have believed in all this time." Jo twirls the pen between her fingers now. "I don't have much of a relationship track record. All I know, really, I know from books and movies. And they're not the most reliable source."

"I know non-monogamy gets a bad rap. That it's all about sex and sluttiness and what not. But that's not what it's about at all."

"It's hard work though."

"It requires more communication, for sure, but that's not a bad thing. Look at it this way, only a few decades ago, it was very hard for most gay people to come out. Because there were hardly any examples. No positive role models. Gay men were the butt of the joke or their lives were portrayed as miserable. We were all seen as lonely creatures, freaks, unnatural. Well, I can tell you what I believe is the most unnatural thing of all: monogamy." I tilt my head and look at Jo. She looks lost in thought. Before she has a chance to say anything, my phone starts ringing.

I look for my purse in which it is still safely stashed. I quirk up my eyebrows at the name appearing on the screen.

"It's Michelle," I say to Jo. I haven't heard from her in a long while.

"Hello." My brain tries to calculate the time difference with New York. I used to be able to do it automatically, but I've been back in Australia too long to have retained the automatism.

"Caitlin, hi. I hope I'm not disturbing you."

"No, of course not. How are you?"

"I'm jet lagged in Singapore," she says.

"Singapore?" I'm still processing my conversation with Jo and now I have to talk to my ex. "What brings you to Asia?"

"Work," she says curtly. "Which will also bring me to Sydney next week. Which made me think of you."

"You're coming here?"

"Yes, and I would love to catch up. If you're up for it."

"Sure. Where will you be staying?"

"The Hilton. I'm arriving on Thursday morning and will be staying until Tuesday."

We exchange some more chit chat but by the time we hang up I'm still flabbergasted that she even called me. Our split wasn't the biggest disaster, but it wasn't extremely amicable either. But we were together for three and a half years, and it has been a few years since. Maybe it's time for that final closure conversation.

"Did I hear that right?" Jo asks. "Was that your ex on the phone?"

"She'll be in Sydney next weekend."

Jo's eyes grow wide. "I'd love to meet her. Pick her brain on how to deal with Caitlin James."

"She wasn't that much of an expert. We broke up for a reason." Thinking about next weekend makes me remember Micky's question from the night before. "By the way, I forgot to ask, but we've been invited to dinner at Micky's next Saturday. Are you free?"

Jo shakes her head. "We're playing the gig we had to postpone last weekend when I had a cold." She rises and stands close to me. "Sorry. But maybe you can take Michelle." She quirks up her eyebrows.

I chuckle. "Wait until you meet her first," I say.

"Oh, now you've got me all curious."

"I'm just teasing."

"I'm serious. Apart from Amber, I've never actually met someone you've been with."

"Amber and I had a one-night stand."

"It'll still be interesting." Jo cups my cheeks with her

palms. "Shall we continue our conversation later? I'm interviewing someone for my thesis in an hour and I need to look over my questions."

I kiss her on the lips to say okay.

———

When Jo is at her meeting I go into my study and sit at my desk. I get out my personal diary and stare at a blank page for a while. I usually write in my diary first thing in the morning, but I sometimes dig it out during the day when I feel like I have something extraordinary to process. Seeing Jo with that woman earlier, our subsequent conversation, and that phone call from Michelle are plenty of extraneous circumstances to make me want to write for a bit.

But first, I indulge myself and take last year's diary out of the drawer. I keep previous diaries on a shelf on the other side of my study, but I've kept this one close. Just to be able to go back and read my entry from the day after I met Jo. The fact that I mentioned her says so much. Even though, just like Jo, I had no idea it would be the beginning of something so beautiful, everything changed for me that day as well. It's wonderful to have a record of the occasion. To be able to track the progress of how we fell in love.

I put the old diary away and start filling the blank page. As I write, I don't think. Or at least, it doesn't feel like I'm thinking. I just let my hand go, let it guide me, until it feels as though my mind is no longer in control, but my hand is guided by whatever my subconscious wants me to process. It's an addictive activity, one I've come to rely on to sort out what's going on in the part of my brain I can't easily reach.

When I read back what I've written, fast and trance-like, my handwriting barely legible, I see this: *I wonder if, after a year and a half together, I'm still Jo's idol. Or has she become mine now?*

It's my private diary, where I can get away with these kinds of questions. The ones I would never dream of asking her, or anyone else, out loud.

As for the answer, I have none. All I know is that, between us, it just works.

Chapter Ten

I MEET Michelle in the bar of her hotel on Friday evening. She looks the same as she always did, but also, in a way, different. I can't really put my finger on the difference, so I focus on what I recognize instead. The bright white of her teeth when she sends me a wide smile. The strange familiarity of her hug—after all this time. Her kind, wide-eyed gaze.

I'm somehow happy I've fallen in love again since we broke up. It makes it easier to look the face of our failed relationship in the eye. Although, perhaps, for that I need only look into a mirror.

"Girl," she says, as though I'm not well above forty. "You look fine."

Immediately, I'm struck again by what drew me to her. What's on display the most: her gregariousness. How outgoing she is. Inviting, warm, a perpetual kindness about her that's hard to resist.

"You don't look too bad yourself." I sit down opposite her and wish I had suggested a different spot to meet. Somewhere a bit more cozy than a generic hotel bar.

"Too many time zones between me and looking my best." She waves off my comment even though, if she hasn't changed too much, I know she enjoys it.

"How was Singapore?"

"Strangest place I've ever been. Everything is just so… sanitized. And so damn humid all the time. I don't know. I can't give my final verdict on the place yet. I'm still processing."

"Welcome to Sydney. We have more grime on the streets here. More disarray."

"That should suit me just fine then."

A waitress comes around and first gives Michelle a confident smile. Only then does she look at me to get my order.

I glance at Michelle's drink and point at it. "I'll have what she's having."

"And another one for me please, Lola," Michelle adds and, right there in front of me, winks at the waitress with whom she's already on a first-name basis.

Lola nods and lets her gaze linger on Michelle before scooting off.

"I don't believe you," I say.

"What? I can't be friendly to the people who work here?"

"There's friendly and then there's *friendly*," I say, quirking up my eyebrows twice. This reminds me of the conversations I've been having with Jo, which are so much more challenging than the ones I had with Michelle when we started seeing each other. When we met, just like now, Michelle seemed down for anything.

"It's lonely on the road and, well, let's just say there isn't much eye candy to have a harmless flirt with in my field of employ."

"How is the world of Artificial Intelligence these days?"

"Making leaps and bounds and very, very exciting to be a part of." Her eyes light up.

"As long as you can assure me that feminist TV show hosts won't be replaced by robots in my lifetime, it's all good with me."

"I think you're safe, although…" She tilts her head. "I watched your last show earlier. The one with Kathy Kramer. No offense, girl, but that kind of looked as though it was being performed by two robots with failing algorithms." She chuckles.

"None taken." I chuckle with her. "That interview was a total disaster." I roll my eyes. "Does that mean you've done some research on me?" I give her an amused smile.

"Why, of course. I'm not going into a meeting with Caitlin James cold." She stirs her cocktail. "Don't tell me you didn't at least quickly google me before you came here."

"Guilty as charged."

The waitress arrives with our drinks—some kind of pimped-up gin and tonic—and makes a big display of putting them on our table in just the right way.

Michelle continues to openly flirt with her. Lola flirts right back. By the time she leaves our table, I'm surprised they haven't exchanged phone numbers yet.

"You haven't changed much." I hold up my cocktail.

"You *have*, from what I've found on the internet." Michelle holds up her own glass in response. "Whatever happened to defeating the patriarchy?"

"I believe a lot has happened in that regard already." I sip from the cocktail. It's a bit too sweet for my liking, but it'll do. "And I believe I've played my part in making it happen."

Michelle looks at me from under her lashes in silence for a few seconds. "Tell me about Josephine Greenwood then."

"Did you not google *her*?" Warmth glows underneath my skin as the topic shifts to Jo.

"Of course I did. I started with a video of her singing an Annie Lennox song, then I couldn't stop. The girl's got the gift, Caitlin." She looks me in the eye. "I would love to meet her."

"She has a gig tomorrow evening. We can go together if you like." I hope I haven't spoken too soon. I have no idea how Jo will feel about me taking my ex to see her perform. But maybe Michelle will say no.

"We can?" Michelle says.

"Of course. Why not?"

"New lover. Old lover. All of that." She runs a hand through her slicked-back hair.

"Jo's curious about meeting you. And I love taking people to her gigs."

"In that case, I would love to join you." She gives a curt nod.

I make a mental note to cancel my attendance at Micky's dinner party. I take a few sips from my drink.

"So," I say.

"So," Michelle repeats, the way she used to do when we were together.

"Are you seeing anyone?" I ask.

"Sort of." She looks into her drink. "It's complicated." She glances up. "Sometimes I think that at my age it really shouldn't be that complicated anymore, but maybe I'm just drawn to things being complicated. I'm trying to figure that out." She looks me in the eyes with that inquisitive stare of hers. "Can I ask you something?"

I nod, sensing what's coming.

"Are you and Jo… open?"

"Working on it."

"So monogamy still isn't your thing?"

"And I still believe it's not many people's thing, but I have stopped trying to convince the masses."

"Have you managed to convince Jo?"

"Convincing really isn't the right word for it. I've opened

the dialogue so we can discuss it." I rest my gaze on Michelle. "I don't want to convince her of anything. I've made that mistake before." I shoot Michelle a smile. She knows all about my mistakes.

"Your mistake wasn't so much trying to convince me. Cleo and I aren't exclusive either."

"You're not?" My eyes widen.

She shakes her head.

"Would you want to be exclusive?" I use the word reluctantly, because I've always found it so inappropriate—so incredibly inapplicable—for relationships.

"No." She sounds adamant. "Hence my flirting with the waitress."

"What changed your mind?" I lean over the table a little. "When we were together, it seemed to be such an obstacle."

She juts out her bottom lip. "I don't think that was the biggest obstacle between us."

"You don't?" I get the feeling I'm about to learn something I was previously too ignorant to see.

"You didn't want to move to New York for me."

"I would have, in the end. But I was getting really sick of the US. When it's not your home country, quite a few things get harder and harder to stomach."

"You didn't love me enough to stay," Michelle says matter-of-factly.

I scrunch my lips together. "I think that's putting it all wrong. I think I didn't give our relationship enough of a chance. We didn't have enough time together. It always felt like a bit of a struggle. But I loved you very much."

"Then why was it so hard?" She quirks up one corner of her mouth.

"I don't know. I truly don't. Maybe we just weren't right for each other?"

"Was I too old for you? Too secure and steady in my ways? Too black, perhaps?"

I wonder how many of these cocktails Michelle has had and whether jet lag is still messing with the part of her brain that decides what's appropriate to say to an ex after all this time.

"What are you talking about?" I ask.

She shakes her head. "It's just strange seeing you again. And I always believed the problem lay with you. That you simply weren't capable of an adult, long-term relationship, but now you're in one, and you seem happy enough. So maybe the only conclusion is that it was me who sucked at the relationship part."

"You didn't suck at it. I loved being with you."

Michelle waves her hand. "All water under the bridge, anyway."

"Does that mean there are no hard feelings?" I find Michelle's gaze and keep it.

"Of course not. It's not as if we didn't have any good times." She smiles. "Because we had many."

I smile back. "I think maybe it was the combination of the two of us together. In some ways, we were too alike, while in others we were too different."

"Incompatible." She says it slowly, drawing out the word. "Are you and Jo more compatible?"

"I believe so. She's much younger than me, yet she teaches me new things about life all the time. Because we are so different and she's not constantly in the same bubble as me. And when she's up on stage..." I pause to picture it again. "She impresses the hell out of me." My mind slips to what I wrote in my diary earlier this week, when I wondered whether I'm still Jo's idol, or whether the tables have turned once and for all.

"I can't wait to meet her."

"I can't wait to introduce you." Another gush of warmth travels through me.

"How's that family of yours? Do they still think you're the devil's spawn?"

"I have no idea." I try to sound light, yet whenever I think of my family, and their lack of respect for me, my heart sinks. "No contact has been established. Even though I've been back in Australia a while. My face is on national TV once a week. I hear I make the tabloids on a regular basis. They must know I'm back, but they don't seem to care."

"Have you tried reaching out to them?"

I shake my head firmly. "I refuse."

"Still a hard-ass then." Michelle smirks. "Some things never change."

The waitress appears at our table. "Same again?" she asks.

"Why the hell not?" Michelle says.

I order a regular G&T this time and when she has left, I ask, "Is it really your intention to sleep with her? Or are you just playing?"

"I'm not sure yet." Michelle draws her lips into that irresistible smile. "We'll just have to wait and see."

Chapter Eleven

It's strange to get ready to go out with Michelle. What makes it even weirder is that we're going to see Jo perform. I've barely seen Jo all day and I'm not sure she's had the time to fully register that I'm bringing Michelle to her gig.

When I got back last night, she was fast asleep and when I woke up this morning, I heard her typing away in her office. I assumed she was having a good day and was making swift progress on her thesis. By the time she emerged from her writing cave, I was getting ready for a party my show's producer Jack was throwing to welcome his new-born daughter into the world. When I arrived home, there was barely time to kiss Jo goodbye as she was about to leave to meet Jimmy before their gig. A typical weekend at the James-Greenwood residence.

I'm meeting Michelle beforehand for a drink, even though I'm not entirely sure either of us is up to that after last night.

Jo and Jimmy are playing a proper concert venue, small, but no longer a bar where they're background entertainment —although, to me, when Jo sings, she could never fade into any background. Everyone there will have paid for a ticket to get in, as opposed to having bought a few drinks. Jo's been playing this kind of gig for a few months now and no longer playing in bars has meant a massive boost to her morale. It's a step up, another hurdle she has cleared in her growth to... I'm not sure how to call it. To me, she's already a superstar. But, if I weren't her partner, I would say it was another step in the direction of this no longer being a hobby. Jo's not the type to abandon her PhD at this stage, but judging by the way things are going now, she'll be going on the road rather than into academia after she gets her doctorate.

Another thing we should probably start talking about, but it's difficult to discuss that part of Jo's future with her, because she always claims she doesn't want to jinx anything by dreaming too big. She just sings for fun. But she doesn't see herself on stage. She's not in the crowd when she belts out note after glorious note. Her voice moves people in ways I'm not sure she fully grasps. But I can't be the one to push her to the next level. That has to come from her.

I apply lipstick and arrange my hair. I wonder if Bryony will be there. And what Jo will think of Michelle and vice versa. It's a weird thing to introduce a new lover to a former one. A strange blend of pride and hope and trepidation. The past meeting the present. Michelle was right about one thing: she and Jo couldn't be more different.

One last look at myself in the mirror and I'm out the door.

―――――

"I can see why you fell for her," Michelle shouts into my ear. The crowd around us goes wild.

"I fell for her before she ever took to the stage," I yell back.

The audience bursts out into a slow clap while shouting for more. Michelle follows suits and hollers "Woohoo" enthusiastically.

"Do you want to wait for her backstage?" I ask.

"Hell no. I'm staying for the encore."

Jo and Jimmy walk back on stage and it's during moments like these that old and new Jo are so brilliantly on display. I can see how astonished she is by the admiration of the crowd, by their cheering, as though she will never be able to believe those cheers are for her. But at the same time, I see the pride in her eyes. The confidence she has gathered from moments like this one. The meeting of the two makes her all the more irresistible.

Next to me, Michelle is jumping up and down enthusiastically.

"Thank you so much." Jo addresses the crowd. At that she has also gotten better. I try to find her gaze, but it's impossible. This isn't the Pink Bean where everyone politely stays in their seat. Besides, Jo's too busy being adored to look for me in the crowd. Something I can't hold against her at all. "Please give it up for Jimmy." She sends Jimmy a kiss.

"Now tell me," she says, a wide smile appearing on her face. "Are there any lesbians in the audience?"

Nearly everyone roars wildly—Michelle included—though there are quite a few men in the crowd as well. I smile at the spectacle.

"Have you heard of a band called Heart?" She brings her hand to her chest.

The crowd roars again.

"Good, then you'll know this last song we've got for you tonight."

Jimmy plays the first notes of "No Other Love" and they get to me immediately. Once again, I can't shake the feeling that Jo is singing for me and the privilege of being with her nearly brings a tear to my eye.

Michelle is singing along loudly. I let go and burst into song as well, not caring that I can't hold a tune to save my life—something Jo has mocked me for greatly throughout our affair.

As I look up at her, at how self-possessed and incredibly sexy she is up there, I see quite a few women look up at her with nothing but adoration in their eyes. I conclude that, yes, the tables have indeed turned. Jo is my idol now. But perhaps that doesn't have to mean I'm no longer hers.

I also understand why she gets so cranky when she has to cancel a gig. To have to forego this. The energy these people are giving her. The applause for something she does well.

When the song is about to end I nudge Michelle in the ribs. "Come on. I want to be there when she gets off stage." I take Michelle by the hand and drag her outside, then inside again to a door I only find because Jo sent me instructions beforehand.

It has happened more than once that the security guard doesn't recognize me and makes a big display of checking my name on a list—often just a piece of hand-written paper that Jo gave him earlier. Tonight, the person knows who I am and Michelle and I are waved through effortlessly.

The backstage area is tiny and we nearly bump into Jo and Jimmy as they exit the stage.

"That was one of the best gigs we've ever played," Jimmy says excitedly.

I don't believe I've ever seen him this animated.

Jo throws her arms around me and kisses me brazenly on the lips. "I'm so glad you're here."

"Hi Caitlin," Jimmy says, his voice back in its normal register. "I'm going to put on a clean t-shirt. See you in a bit."

"You must be Michelle." Jo extends her hand.

"And your newest biggest fan." Michelle bows to Jo, then takes her hand and kisses a knuckle. "That was truly amazing. And what a way to get the lesbians eating out of the palm of your hand." She only then seems to realize she's still holding Jo's hand and drops it. I reach for it and take it in mine.

"Let's not stand around here," Jo says. "I'd invite you to my dressing room, but Jimmy and I share it and we barely fit in. I'll see you in the bar in five."

———

It takes much longer than five minutes for Jo to join us. On her way over to us she is accosted by a few people who want to chat with her. I scan the room for Bryony and am relieved when I don't spot her anywhere near us.

I keep my eye on Jo and her progress toward us. I've ordered her a white wine, which will be too tepid for her to enjoy if she doesn't come over quickly.

"How does it make you feel, Caitlin?" Michelle asks. "To see your partner so adored."

I take my eye off Jo and glance at Michelle, who sports a wicked grin. She still knows me too well after all these years. I always think it's only the essence of a person that stays with you when you don't see them for a while, like Michelle's gregariousness has stayed with me, despite the bad memories of our split and the years since we last spoke. Is my vanity really what has stuck with her all this time?

"I'm happy for her." I send Michelle a wide smile, in case she thinks I'm not serious. That I haven't changed for the better, at least a little bit. "The way she is now is almost unrecognizable from when we met. She was so insecure." I shake my head. "You have no idea."

"You're right," Michelle says. "I don't." She holds my gaze. "So, when you're walking around in the city and someone comes up to you two and asks for a selfie with Jo instead of you, that doesn't irk you?"

"Why are you needling me like this?" I cock my head. "Are you frustrated because after all the work you put in last night with that waitress, you went to bed alone?"

"Ouch, girl." Michelle feigns a sudden pain in her chest. "You're shooting sharp tonight."

"No sharper than you." I smile. It's a pleasant surprise that we can tease each other like this. I had expected things to be more tense between us—maybe because I had forgotten how easy Michelle is to be around.

"Sorry it took so long." Jo finally arrives. "Ah, is that for me?" She sits in the chair between us. "Thanks, babe." She blows me a quick kiss.

"Josephine Greenwood," Michelle starts. "You are a superstar in the making." She looks at Jo intently. "It's an honor to be sitting at this table with you, and that's not an exaggeration whatsoever." She holds up her arms and leans forward with her entire body as though worshipping. "Your voice is so… soulful."

"Thank you," Jo says sheepishly. I can tell she's enjoying the compliments. I don't know if the blush on her cheeks is post-show excitement or a direct result of Michelle's words. "It was an exceptional gig. The crowd was so into it."

"I loved your version of 'So Cruel'," Michelle says, no irony in her voice.

"Did you really or did Caitlin ask you to say that to goad me?" Jo asks.

"Goad you?" Michelle quirks up an eyebrow.

"She thinks Bono is so full of himself he would stick his head up his own ass if he could." Jo smirks at me.

"Oh yes, Caitlin's disproportionate dislike of U2. I had

forgotten about that." Michelle leans back in her chair. "It didn't show when you played the song. I really couldn't tell her taste in music is so prejudiced. What does it even matter that Bono wants to suck his own dick? He has a hell of a voice." Michelle holds up her hand for Jo to high five.

Knowing Jo, I don't think she will. But then she does. Her hand meets Michelle's in a soft slap in the air in front of me.

"You should hear the two of you." I shake my head in despair. "As though having a great singing voice gives you license to be an asshole."

"You thought she asked me to goad *you*." Michelle grins broadly at Jo. For a split second, I expect her to hold up her hand for an impromptu high five again.

"It's great to finally meet you," Jo says. "How long are you staying? I have a lot of your brain to pick."

"Until Tuesday." Michelle holds up her glass of red wine. "Until then, you can ask me anything you want."

"Do say if you need some privacy," I joke, slightly taken aback by the two of them hitting it off like that.

"We can put up with you for now." Michelle puts her hand on my arm. "Who's up for another round?" She looks around fruitlessly for a waiter.

"Bar service only in Australia," I say.

She rolls her eyes. "Where's Lola when you need her?"

"Who's Lola?" Jo inquires.

"The waitress at the bar last night, whom Michelle was hitting on as if there was no tomorrow." I examine Michelle's face for any signs of regret.

"Yet a new morning broke regardless." Michelle shoots me a smile. "Nothing came of it, by the way. After you left, I went up to my room and Skyped Cleo." Michelle gets up. "I guess I'll head to the bar then."

"Who's Cleo?" Jo asks after Michelle has left.

"Her partner. I think." I take the opportunity to hold Jo's gaze for longer than a second. "Hey, you were wonderful. Again." I lean in to kiss her. "What do you think about Michelle?"

"She's, um, very…" She weighs her words. "American. But I like her straightforwardness. And, well, she's hot."

"Really?"

"She's your ex. Surely you had noticed." Jo slants her head. Michelle teasing me seems to have rubbed off on her.

"That's usually not how you speak of people. In terms of *hot*."

"I spoke of you like that when we met."

"Only when we met?" I lean in to kiss her again.

"You're still hot." Jo kisses me on the lips. "And so is she. More so in real life than in the pictures you showed me. She's very likable also."

"Enough compliments for my ex already." I put a hand on her upper thigh.

"Sorry for disturbing you lovebirds." Michelle has already made it back to the table. "But I come carrying booze." She sits. "Hot damn, you two look so disgustingly happy together."

Jo straightens her posture. I have no choice but to follow her example.

Someone clears their throat behind me before saying, "Excuse me, Josephine."

Jo bursts out into a practiced but genuine smile and turns to the person.

"Can we take a selfie together?" a girl, barely eighteen by the looks of it, asks.

"Of course." Jo shoots up.

"How about I take it for you," Michelle offers.

The girl looks at her phone then decides to take Michelle up on her offer.

While they go through the process of taking the picture, I conclude that this girl has no idea of who I am. To her, I'm Josephine Greenwood's girlfriend. It's not a thought that irks me, as Michelle would put it. But if I'm truly being honest with myself, there's another emotion there, other than only pride. I don't much care for getting to the bottom of it.

The girl leaves thanking Jo and Michelle profusely. Then Michelle digs into her purse and unearths her own phone. "While we're at it," she says. "Let's take one of the three of us together."

"Really?" I roll my eyes at her.

"What? Just because you're not down with the kids anymore. This is going straight onto my Instagram."

I reluctantly pose for the picture and look on as Michelle and Jo proceed to take a couple of the pair of them.

"Now if you would sign this napkin for me," Michelle says. "For when you blow up in the States. I can sell it on eBay if I ever need money."

"Autographs are not really a thing anymore." Jo finds my gaze. "Although for Caitlin and me, they do have a great significance."

"Do tell," Michelle insists.

"I asked Caitlin to sign a few of her books," Jo says. "Which she did. I never, ever thought it would lead to anything more. To all of this. But it did."

"Wow." Michelle drinks from her wine. "So you'd already read her books before you met her."

"Read them? Devoured them more like," Jo says.

This is getting a little awkward. I'm all for a bit of praise, but from her tone I can tell Michelle is still trying to goad me.

"And you agreed with everything she'd written?" Michelle asks.

"I could easily understand it," Jo says. "If you read it in a well put together book like that, it's an irrefutable logic that's easy to follow."

Michelle nods. She suddenly looks as tipsy as last night when she was heavily flirting with the waitress. Then, under the table, I feel her leg against mine.

I shoot her a look but she doesn't respond. Her leg remains in place. Maybe it's just a coincidence. We are huddled closely around this table. But I can't help but wonder what her other leg is up to—whether it's sliding up to Jo's shin on the other side.

I drink and relax. If Michelle wants to play, I'd like to see where she's going to take things next.

Next to me, Jo doesn't give any outward signs of feeling an untoward leg against hers.

"It sounds like all your dreams came true," Michelle says.

Jo grins. "It's funny. I said the exact same thing to Caitlin the other day. She has made many of my dreams come true."

"What about your dreams, Michelle?" I ask.

Her leg presses into mine. This is definitely not a matter of not enough room for all our legs under the table. I'm sure of that now.

"I have a few I'm working on," she says.

I inch my leg away from hers. It only takes a few seconds until I feel it against mine again. Under the table, Jo takes my hand. I try to read her face, but it hasn't really changed.

"I can tell." I push back against her leg a little, wiggle it about a bit.

Michelle looks from me to Jo, then back to me. "How about showing me that fancy penthouse of yours?"

I can't suppress a giggle. "Not tonight."

"Are you sure?" Her leg rubs against mine.

"Yes." I look at Jo. Is that a hint of panic I see in her eyes.

Or something else? "How about we call it a night? You must be exhausted."

Jo nods. "Maybe Michelle can come round tomorrow," she says. "After we've all had a good night's sleep."

"I would love to." Michelle's leg retracts. "Text me the address." She gets up brusquely. "I'll be there." She walks around the table and slings an arm around us before kissing each of us on the cheek. "It'll be fun."

With that, she makes her way out of the bar.

"Is she going to be all right?" Jo asks.

"She's a grown woman. She can take care of herself." I remember the taxi stand around the corner. "Are *you* all right?"

Jo pokes her tongue in her cheek as she looks at me. "Was she…"

"Hitting on us?" I burst into a giggle.

"Was her leg touching yours as well?" Jo whispers.

I nod. "How do you feel about that?"

Jo scoffs. "I'm not sure."

"We don't have to talk about it now."

"I don't mind." Jo twirls her wineglass between her fingers. "She's very shameless."

"Oh yes." I don't say it's one of the things I've always admired about Michelle.

"Is that what drew you to her?"

"Amongst other things." I take Jo's hand in mine.

"Did she hit on you last night?" Jo's voice has gone down to a whisper again.

"God no, she was far too busy flirting with the waitress for that."

"What about Cleo?" She shrugs. "I mean, I do under-stand. They have an arrangement. I've just never been so blatantly confronted with that kind of thing."

"Are you shocked?"

Jo considers my question. "Not shocked. But I am surprised."

"Are you by any chance also… flattered?"

Jo draws circles on my palm with her thumb. "Maybe." She scrunches her lips together. "Tell me honestly, babe. Has this happened before? That someone has hit on us. Together. And I just didn't see it? Because tonight there was no way for me not to notice."

I shake my head. "Not that I'm aware of."

Her thumb halts its circling and she clasps my hand tightly in hers. "Do you, um, want to consider it?"

I grip her hand safely in mine. I can only answer this question with another one. "Do *you*?" I tilt my head. "You were quick to invite her to ours tomorrow."

She sinks her teeth into her bottom lip. "I would need to sleep on it."

"But you're not saying no?" I feel something opening up between us. A crack in Jo's armor that hasn't been there before.

"Maybe… I don't know. It would make for a good opportunity to… test the waters."

"Do you feel attracted to her?"

Jo tries to look me in the eye. "She's quite something."

"Is that a yes?"

She nods slowly. "But how about you? She's your ex? Isn't there a rule against that?"

"We only have two rules so far." I smile.

"Maybe we need some more before we do this."

"I agree." I finish the last of my wine. "How about we get a good night's sleep first."

"Yes, please. I'm knackered."

"Talk of threesomes will do that to you," I whisper in her ear.

Chapter Twelve

ON SUNDAY MORNING I wake early from a fitful sleep. Jo's still sleeping and I look at her. It's not as if her personality changes completely in the morning after a gig, but I can't help but wonder whether her willingness to discuss taking things further with Michelle had as much to do with her post-performance high than anything else. I wonder how she'll feel about it this morning. And there's the question she asked me last night just before we left the bar. Michelle is my ex. Jo and I can't possibly approach her from a level playing field because Michelle and I share a history. That's what has kept me up through the night. Because "no exes" should be a rule. No doubt. Unless, perhaps, for threesomes.

My gut tells me it might be a bad idea. On the other hand, this feels like an opportunity. Provided Michelle still feels up to it and it wasn't just the booze talking last night. That mixed with the nostalgic atmosphere of us seeing each other again. Her meeting Jo. Jo liking her. That certain something in the air. It might all have vanished with the morning light.

I close my eyes and try to get back to sleep, but I know

instantly it's not going to happen. I gingerly slip out of bed because I don't want to wake Jo. She doesn't get to sleep in often and soon her alarm will go off so she can call her sister Bea first thing—an hour later than before we got together. It's hard trying to convince Jo of things when they concern her sister and might present a change to Bea, who has Down syndrome.

She went about it slowly and introduced it to Bea as a game. Every day she would call exactly one minute later, until a full hour had passed. The process seemed to be harder on Jo than it was on Bea. But really, what did I know? I only wanted for Jo to be a bit more rested. Whatever success is waiting for her in the future, I want her to be ready for it and not burnt out and unable to enjoy it.

I go into the kitchen and make myself an espresso, then take it onto the deck so I can overlook the city. I try to imagine what would have happened if we'd taken Michelle up on her offer last night. Would she have stayed? And would everything be extremely awkward right about now?

Then I ask myself if I truly want this. If I'm not going along with it because I want to prove a point to Jo. But the two are so inextricably linked, I can't come to a clear conclusion.

The thought of sleeping with Michelle again would probably never have occurred to me. I'm not the type to give in to that kind of nostalgia. But one of the reasons I'm such a fan of not restricting who my partners sleep with is the freedom it allows me as well. If, one day, I ran into an old flame and would be overcome with desire to sleep with her, nothing would stop me from making a move. Especially not a misplaced sense of loyalty to my partner. And it could feed my soul in a way that sex with my partner wouldn't. Which is the very thing most people who rage against non-monogamy are so afraid of. Fear is at the root of their dismissal. It's exactly that type of fear I want to eliminate between Jo and me.

I go back inside and I hear Jo talking to Bea on the phone. I head to the bedroom and mouth she should give her sister my love, which she does. I haven't spent a whole lot of time with Jo's family, but they embraced me right from the start. Her parents always send her a text when they've watched my show. Something like *Caitlin did great*. Every single week. If only my own parents would extend me the same courtesy.

Jo's phone calls to Bea don't last long and when she puts the phone down she pleads with me to come back to bed, which I gladly do.

She wraps her entire body around me and kisses my neck and cheeks profusely.

"Thank all the goddesses in heaven it's Sunday," she whispers in my ear.

"Did you sleep well?" I ask when she's done kissing me good morning.

"Like a log. Always, after a gig." She sends me a sweet smile. "You?"

"I had some things on my mind."

"I figured you would." She kisses me on the lips. "You taste like coffee." She draws her lips into a pout. "Whatever happened to the unspoken rule that you bring me coffee in bed on Sunday."

"Forget I was even here just now." I kiss her forehead. "I'll be right back."

I prepare her a cappuccino and bring it to her. She looks so relaxed in bed, so unafraid of showing her body, so at ease.

"Better, Ma'am?" I ask.

We both sit with our backs against the headrest.

"Don't tell Kristin, but your cappuccino is so much better than the ones we make at the Pink Bean."

"It's just different. You've gotten too used to Pink Bean cappuccinos. As we both know…"

"Variety is the spice of life," we both say in unison.

We burst out into a chuckle. I wait for her to say something first, but she gazes in front of her as she enjoys her coffee.

"Speaking of variety," I begin.

She turns to me. "That possible threesome was the first thing that popped into my mind as soon as I woke up as well," she says. "Have you heard from Michelle?"

"No. She's probably waiting to hear from us. Or not. I don't know."

"Should we find out?" Jo asks.

"I think we should talk first." I inhale the scent of coffee. "Figure out what *we* want before involving her."

Jo nods. A silence falls. On any other Sunday it would be a peaceful kind of silence, but this particular Sunday it's charged with possibility—not only the possibility of what could happen, but of saying the wrong thing, pushing too hard, of that dizzying sensation that comes with feeling around in the dark.

"I'm up for it." Jo puts her cup on the bedside table and looks at me. "If you are."

A grin breaks on my face. "Yes."

"No ambiguity," Jo says. Her voice doesn't carry the necessary force to pull off saying that word without actual ambiguity.

"I sense a but coming." I cross my legs underneath me and swivel around so I can look her in the eye properly.

"It scares me." She looks over my shoulder. "I mean, this body." She sighs. "It's not always my best friend."

"No woman's body is." I rub the inside of her wrist gently.

"You know what I mean." There is far less desperation in her tone than there used to be when she spoke of her body. "When I look in the mirror I don't see a woman who could even contemplate having an open relationship."

"Yet it's all in your mind."

Jo shakes her head. "Last I checked, sex very much involves the body."

"It does, but it's a much smaller part of it than we think." I scoot a little closer. We've had this conversation so many times —some patterns are hard, if not impossible to break. "Michelle is a feminist like us. She doesn't believe in the so-called ideal body shapes impressed upon us by TV, advertising, and social media. Besides, she came on to both of us. And she loved your performance. There was chemistry between you. At my expense, I might add." I find her gaze. "In that respect, it doesn't have that much to do with any of our bodies at all."

"What if..." She's struggling to find the words. "During, um, the thing... I don't feel secure enough and I can't... come."

"First of all, if at any time you feel insecure or you want to stop, then it stops. Simple as that."

"You make it sound as if it's simple, but I don't think it is."

"Oh yes. No ambiguity there. None, babe. Do you understand? Intimacy is not a finish-what-you-start activity."

She nods. "Should we agree on a word? Or a sign?"

"There is a word for that already." I narrow my eyes. "Stop." I lean in closer. "It's understood by everyone who will be in this bed."

"That's another thing. Can we do it in this bed? The place where we sleep? Our nightly sanctuary?" She chuckles.

"We can invite her into the guest room. We can rename it."

"To the threesome room," she jokes. Jo inhales deeply. "I want to do this with you. The prospect excites me."

"Me too." I slant forward and kiss her on the cheek. "As for either one of us reaching orgasm, I think that shouldn't be the focus. If it happens, that's great. But it will be equally rewarding if it doesn't happen."

"Just go with the flow," Jo says.

"That sounds about right. Enjoy the moment. Discover things about yourself you didn't know before."

"Should we have specific rules, though? As in what can and can't happen?"

"If you feel that's necessary."

"I have no idea." She chuckles. "I think we should call her now."

"And go with the flow?"

Jo tilts toward me and kisses me on the lips.

Chapter Thirteen

I SERVE all three of us a cup of tea while Jo pours us a whisky. It's early afternoon and the light outside is not right yet. It feels off for what is about to transpire. I'm hoping the whisky might help.

"I'm glad you called," Michelle says, a satisfied smile on her lips, which she has painted a deep red for the occasion.

I'm beginning to think this could only be possible with Michelle. Not because she's my ex, although that has its importance, but because of how she is. She's not coy about this. She's the perfect candidate to christen our guest room with a threesome.

"We're glad to have you here." My voice sounds a bit harder than I would like because of the nerves. If it were just me, I wouldn't be this nervous, but it's as though I don't have enough bravado to cover up both my and Jo's nervous energy.

"Here you go." Jo's hand shakes when she offers Michelle the tumbler.

"Thank you, gorgeous." Michelle fixes her gaze on Jo. "I

don't suppose I can ask you to sing us a song this afternoon?" She smiles broadly, her bright white teeth on full display.

"I save my voice on Sundays." Jo sits next to Michelle. There's not much space between them. Seeing the two of them sit together like that, and all the possibilities in the small space between them, turns me on. There's not a hint of jealousy inside me, because this situation is completely different than Bryony chatting Jo up in front of me.

This is a setting we've created, with respect and communication. It makes all the difference.

I sip from my whisky and sink back in my chair. I could sit here leisurely the next couple of minutes and just watch things unfold. I know Michelle. She'll ramp up the flirting soon enough. My nerves ease, then flare again as I try to predict Jo's response. Will she clam up? At the last minute deem this whole thing a terrible idea? Or will she, as we agreed upon, go with the flow? Right about now, she very much looks as though she wants to give the latter a go.

"Ah, Sunday," Michelle says on a sigh. "That day of great possibility." She looks away from Jo and finds my glance, as though asking for permission.

I blink and give her a small nod. As long as Jo is okay with it, she can put the moves on my partner.

Michelle turns her attention back to Jo. "Last night, when you were playing the encore."

"'No Other Love'." Jo's voice is brittle.

Michelle nods. "There was this woman standing a few feet away from me. She wasn't shouting or singing along like the rest of us crazy people. She was looking up at you, listening so intently, it was as though she was in a trance." Michelle puts her whisky down without taking her eyes off Jo. "To have that kind of effect on people must be... magical." She reaches out her hand, palm upward.

Jo looks at Michelle's outstretched hand. She slowly

moves her own hand, stretching out a finger. She lets the tip skate lightly over Michelle's palm.

"On stage I don't really notice any of that." Jo looks at what her finger is doing, as though she can't quite believe it belongs to her. "I just sing."

"And how better off we all are because of it." Michelle looks down at their hands. Slowly, she brings her hand up, and Jo's finger along with it. When their hands are near her mouth, she traps the length of Jo's finger in her palm, and kisses Jo's fingertip.

I witness the intense eye contact between them that follows. Michelle gently tugs Jo closer by the hand she's still holding.

"You're so sexy," she whispers.

Jo's face lights up and then I feel that light flicker inside of me as well. This afternoon is all about her—for her. It doesn't bother me that Michelle doesn't have much eye for me—I guess it figures. We slept together so many times when we were a couple. It doesn't appear to be in her nature to go after what she has already had. And I wasn't the one up on stage singing my heart out last night—and touching other hearts in the process.

Then it's Jo who makes the next move, by leaning forward and planting her lips on Michelle's. It's a tentative kiss, soft and exploring. Until Michelle drops Jo's hand and cups her cheeks in her palms. Their lips part and tongues dart into each others' mouths and for a short moment I don't know what to do with myself. Do I just keep sitting here? Do I insinuate myself into the situation at the risk of interrupting what they've got going on between them? I can't disturb that fragile moment of the first kiss.

I drink again and just watch. I can no longer ignore the pulse that has started beating between my legs.

I watch their kisses grow more ravenous, more intent.

There is only one possible direction where things are headed: the bedroom.

As if they somehow had the opportunity to agree upon it, they break from the kiss and they both look at me. Jo stretches out her hand. I put my glass down and walk over to them and, in turn, hold my hands out to both of them. They follow me into the bedroom silently and, already, we are intertwined by the touch of our hands—like we were last night when this started, by the touch of our legs under the table.

I lead them into the guest room and once inside, Jo pulls me toward her and kisses me hard on the lips. What must be going through her head? There's no point me pondering that question now. We will talk about all of this later. Right now, it's all about the joy this can bring.

There is no fear in her kiss. I feel excitement and the willingness to let go. To let this happen and enjoy it.

When Jo and I break from our kiss, Michelle has already unbuttoned her blouse. Jo surprises me again by being the one to push the garment off Michelle's shoulders. Their lips find each other again while Michelle claws at the hem of my top.

I can't help but wonder how Jo will deal with all this undressing in front of each other. She has no qualms about it with me anymore, but she and Michelle only met last night. Then again, Jo initiated that kiss, pushed Michelle's blouse off. It says something. It tells me she's ready for this. I'd like to think that alongside finding her groove on stage, the extreme joy and confidence that singing brings her, I might have something to do with that. I know I do, because I watched her change in front of my very eyes. This woman who used to want the lights off so she could undress in darkness.

This room, today, has plenty of light.

Jo's hands roam across Michelle's abdomen. I help Michelle hoist my top over my head. She starts on the button of her jeans next. I unzip the back of Jo's dress. This stops her kissing Michelle and Michelle seizes the opportunity to plant her lips on mine.

It's strange to kiss her. I hadn't expected it to come with so much emotion, but there it is. A slew of memories of when we first kissed in New York. Of picking her up at the train station in Boston. Of saying hello and goodbye over and over again. Of the promise a kiss can hold, and how, given time, it can turn into something else entirely.

She presses her fingers into my flesh as she pulls me close and I lose myself in another kiss. When our lips part, Jo is standing next to us in just her underwear, her dress an easily discarded puddle of fabric on the floor.

Both Michelle and I turn to her. Michelle kisses her neck and I take that as my cue to kiss Jo on the lips—and to check in with her.

"Okay?" I whisper.

She gives a quick nod. "You?"

"Yes, my love." I kiss her again and when I put my hand on her back, it meets one of Michelle's.

We kiss each other while undressing until all three of us are only clad in underwear. I can see why Michelle was so keen to get her clothes off. She seems to have dressed for the occasion. Her lace-edged bra and panties match the color of her lipstick. How did she feel when she put those on before coming here? It's probably not a question I'll get to ask.

We shuffle to the bed and Michelle sits down. She keeps a hand on Jo's back while she pulls me close and plants moist kisses above the waistband of my panties. My clit has become like a second frantically-beating heart. I will happily take my pleasure first—unlike Jo, I don't expect any trouble reaching the heights of orgasm. I've had a lot more practice in doing so under extraordinary circumstances.

Jo's hand travels to my upper back, where she unhooks my bra with one confident flick of the fingers.

Michelle's mouth has trailed south and I can feel her breath on my clit through the fabric of my panties. Instinctively, I spread my legs further. It's Jo who starts tugging down my underwear and I step out of them. I'm the only one fully naked and the sensation fills my veins with another burst of heat. Watching them kiss earlier in the sofa has turned me on. Having both their hands on me is taking me to greater heights. This is no longer a matter of choice. I want to come soon. This could very well turn into a multiple orgasm occasion and I want to take the edge off—so I can give Jo all the focus she needs.

Michelle hooks a hand under my knee and lifts my leg onto the bed. Jo stands behind me and kisses the back of my neck while her hands roam to my breasts. She takes my nipples between her fingertips and tweaks them softly. When Michelle flicks her tongue along my clit, I let myself fall against Jo. She's there to catch me. She's here with me all the way.

I feel the hardness of Jo's nipples through her bra. But most of all, I feel Michelle's tongue on my clit, more insistent now. I close my eyes. Michelle's fingers dig into the flesh of my behind. Jo's fingers are all over my breasts. She alternates cupping them with kneading and torturing my nipples. All the while, I'm safely enclosed in her arms, while my legs are spread wide for Michelle.

I imagine Michelle's red lipstick smeared all over my pussy and Jo licking it off later. The thought of it sends such a burst of desire through me, the next flick of Michelle's tongue sends me into a different orbit.

"Good God," I moan, as I clasp one hand behind me to

hold onto Jo and I let the other roam through Michelle's hair. "I'm c—" I try to announce but the words die in my throat as I surrender to orgasm and I collapse into Jo's arms.

This orgasm might feel a little different emotionally than when I come at Jo's tongue and fingers alone, but that doesn't make it any less intoxicating. As much as any other climax, this one was born in my mind, in that place where I allow myself to be the person I am. The woman my parents despise. The non-monogamous feminist most of society doesn't know how to deal with. But here, in this room, with these two people, I am the most me I can ever possibly be.

I take my foot down from the bed and lean forward, my hands resting on Michelle's shoulders. After I've caught my breath I glance backward at Jo, who still has a hand on my back.

She smiles at me. It's not a polite smile. Her eyes are brimming with desire. Seeing Michelle lick me has turned her on. This is a moment I have to seize. I turn around and beckon her over to the bed. I sit next to Michelle and pull Jo onto my lap so she can straddle me. Michelle gets up and takes the position Jo was in earlier, standing behind her. She takes off Jo's bra while I kiss her with a fire burning so fiercely in me, it takes me aback. Perhaps because I'm currently being very much reminded why monogamy is not my thing, even though I'm holding the woman I love tightly grasped in my arms.

"Lie on your back," I whisper in Jo's ear. I remember very well what I said about her coming not being a priority this afternoon, but now I want her to experience it. I want her to know what it's like with someone else in the room—someone who will do anything to make it happen.

Jo shuffles around until she's on her back. She looks me in the eye and I smile at her. This is not shy, self-conscious Jo in bed with us this afternoon. This is the version of herself she has grown into over the past year. A woman aware of her effect on others. A woman who has come to love her body and, in the process, found out it wasn't so hard after all.

Michelle hooks her fingers under the hem of Jo's panties and tugs them off. Then there she lies. My Jo. Naked between us. Ready for whatever we have to offer her. I glance at Michelle to see if we're on the same wavelength. She winks and I know. We're in this together and she wants the same for Jo. Of course she does.

We flank Jo. I bring a hand to her chin and turn her face toward me so I can kiss her. My tongue protrudes deep into her mouth and Jo receives my kisses eagerly. When we part, Michelle touches Jo's chin with her finger and turns her attention toward her. I watch as they lose themselves in a passionate kiss, and my clit starts throbbing again. This afternoon is far from over, of that much I'm sure.

After they stop kissing, I push myself up and find Michelle's lips. We kiss in front of Jo while our hands roam across her body. When I lean down to kiss Jo again, Michelle follows me and our tongues twirl together in their own mini-version of a threesome.

When we part from the kiss, which has made Jo spread her legs wider, Michelle bites her lip, then bends over and kisses Jo's breast. I do the same to her other breast and underneath me I can feel Jo expel a deep sigh of contentment.

Michelle's hand ventures down first and I let go of Jo's nipple for an instant to watch how she skates a fingertip along Jo's pussy lips. I'm not sure it's anatomically possible, but I feel just as turned on as Jo looks. She lets her knees fall a little deeper into the mattress and bucks up her hips. I feel my own juices trickle along my upper thigh.

Michelle leans down and starts kissing Jo the way she kissed me earlier. Starting high but her attention drifting lower swiftly. And I'm torn between looking at Jo's face and what I see unfolding in front of me. I can't tear my gaze away from Michelle getting ready to fuck Jo. It lights me up inside in a way I haven't experienced in years, maybe ever. I want to see her fingers disappear into Jo's pussy.

Breathless, I scoot a little closer. I'm not even participating anymore, that's how transfixed I am. I don't think either one of them minds. They're lost in their own world. Michelle in her sphere of giving, Jo in that intimate space where it's possible to receive the highest pleasure.

Michelle lifts her head and brings two fingers to the entrance of Jo's pussy. For a minute, I want to say that Jo likes it gentle and slow at first, but I don't need to instruct anyone today. Besides, from the way Jo's hips are bucking upward I don't think she wants things to go slow at all.

Michelle licks her lips before sliding her fingers inside Jo's wet pussy. The slow, rhythmic motion of her fingers fucking Jo hypnotizes me. Until Jo starts moaning behind me and I feel her fingers dig into the flesh of my hip.

I turn around to look at what this is doing to her. Her mouth has fallen open, her eyes are narrowed to slits. Her hand is clawing for something. For mine. I intertwine my fingers with hers and clasp her hand tightly in mine. I bring my other hand to her breast and tweak her nipple the way she did with mine earlier, twisting it between my fingertips until the moans in her throat become deeper, darker, sound more as if there's no return.

Her open mouth is irresistible to me and while my one hand remains firmly clasped in hers, I move my free hand from her breast to her mouth and, just like Michelle inserted two fingers into Jo's pussy minutes ago, I slip two fingers into her mouth.

Her lips clasp shut around my fingers instantly. Her eyes widen a bit and she fixes her gaze on me while she sucks my fingers into her mouth, twirls her tongue around them, while I feel her writhe against me more intensely.

This time, I can't look away anymore to see what Michelle is doing to her. But I can read it off Jo's face. My woman who this morning believed she might not be able to come, might not even be able to turn on another woman with her body, is about to reach an obliterating climax.

I see her expression change, but most of all, I feel how it starts thundering through her. Her lips slacken around my fingers for an instant, only to suck them back into her mouth with full force a second later. She's gasping for air but unwilling to let go. Having my fingers inside her mouth makes me feel as though I'm part of this, because I'm inside her too. I'm inside and I get to see what this does to her. It's a privileged position to be in. All the while, the fire in my clit rages on.

Jo's grip on my fingers loosens entirely and they slide out of her mouth, languishing wet against her chin.

My lips spread into a smile because of the pure joy I see on her face. I give her a few seconds, but then I can't resist kissing her any longer. Our hands are still clutched together when my mouth finds her and I lose myself in the kiss.

When I finally push myself away to see how Michelle's faring, she is sitting on the other side of Jo, a wicked glint in her eyes.

"I see what you did there." Michelle's voice is husky, as though she's up to no good.

She reaches out her hand, the one she fucked Jo with, over Jo's body, toward me, and holds her fingers in front of my mouth. They're glistening with Jo's juices and I don't need to think twice. I slide my lips over Michelle's fingers and suck Jo's wetness off them. I close my eyes and consider how quickly we've reached the next level of being totally intertwined.

Chapter Fourteen

"IN BED WITH TWO COUGARS," Jo says. "Talk about dreams coming true."

Jo and I are draped along Michelle, who is still recovering from her last orgasm. The pale color of our skin contrasts deliciously with her much darker one.

"I didn't know that was a dream of yours." I find her gaze.

"Just as I'm sure I don't know all about your dreams." Jo appears to have found a new level of confidence. She has come too hard at Michelle's fingertips to have any qualms left, it seems.

"Next time either one of you has a dream," Michelle says, "call me."

We all burst out laughing.

"Or better yet, plan a trip to New York." She turns to Jo. "Have you been?"

Jo shakes her head. "I've never been out of Australia."

Michelle looks at me. "What are you waiting for? Take your girl to the Big Apple already."

"I just might." I push any thought of Jo not having time

for that and her stubborn unwillingness to accept me paying for her ticket out of my mind. It's not the time or place for any of that. "What about Cleo?" I ask, wanting to needle Michelle a little.

"Cleo can join us for the hottest foursome on the planet," Michelle says unabashedly.

"Can I ask you something… about Cleo?" Jo asks.

"Shoot." Michelle looks so at ease in our bed, like she has no intention of getting out of it any time soon.

"Are you going to tell her about this?" Jo asks.

Michelle inhales deeply. "Yes."

"Because that's the arrangement you have?" Jo wants to know everything.

"We like to relive all the frisky details together." Michelle paints on a wide smile.

"What's the deal with you and Cleo, though?" I want to know. "Why are you on and off as you called it the other night."

Michelle scrunches her lips together, then says, "What's with the third degree after my third orgasm of the day? Wear me out first to get to the truth?"

"God no," Jo is quick to say. "We don't mean to pry. But I for one am just really curious."

"Cleo and I love each other," Michelle says on a sigh. "And we're both down with the open relationship thing, but Cleo, well, she would like to take things in a slightly different direction. Open up to an actual relationship with another person, not just occasional unattached fun. And I guess I haven't evolved that far yet. I don't know. It's an issue for me at this moment in my life. Given time, I can probably be down with it as well. Just like back in the day when Caitlin and I were together I wasn't completely ready for an open relationship, and I am now. I just need more time to think, to analyze, to foresee all possible outcomes first. For a while."

She chuckles. "I have a hard time shutting off my analytical brain sometimes."

It's as though I can see the wheels of Jo's mind churning. I have a question of my own.

"Do you really tell each other all the details when you've been with someone else?"

Michelle nods vigorously. "Always. No question. Not only because then we get to relive it and be turned on all over again, but also because we don't believe in secrets. If you're going to have an open relationship, then throw everything wide open." She grins at me. "You can be sure Cleo will hear all about you sucking my fingers into your mouth. Damn, that was hella hot." She pushes her hip against me. "Makes me want to do it all over again." She bursts out into a chuckle. "But my coochie needs a little rest." She wriggles herself from underneath us as best she can. "And I need a shower."

I make room so she can hop out of the bed. Before she leaves the room, she blows us both a kiss.

"Bloody hell," Jo says when we're alone. "Who and what is that woman?" She shuffles closer to me and hooks her legs in mine. "I can totally see the two of you together. Well, I just did. And it was indeed *hella hot*."

"Tell me." I pull her as close to me as I can. "I already know you enjoyed yourself, but how do you feel after the fact?"

She thinks for a minute then pushes herself up so she can look me in the eye. "Like I finally understand what all the fuss is about."

———

After Michelle has left, Jo and I lie in bed together, freshly washed and mentally and physically exhausted.

"I think I'll skip yoga tomorrow morning," I say.

"My legs might not feel up to a run either."

"Do you feel up to a chat right now?"

She glances at the alarm clock, then nods.

"Were you jealous at any point this afternoon?"

"No," she says. "That's the funny bit. I was just so turned on the entire time."

"Me too."

"I was thinking that maybe I felt that way because you know her. She's not a total stranger you can develop feelings for and who could come between us." She turns on her side and lets her head sink into the pillow. "Has that really never happened to you before when you were in an open relationship? That you slept with someone and afterward wanted to sleep with her again? More than with the partner you were in a relationship with?"

"I would be lying if I said it hadn't. These things happen. Sometimes a relationship gets tested. Open and closed relationships get tested all the time. But because an open relationship requires much more communication, it's much easier to talk about these things. Honesty and respect are the pillars of any good relationship, no matter how you define the boundaries."

"That's what scares me about this the most. I enjoyed sleeping with Michelle. I was able to let go of all my inhibitions much more easily than I had expected. I think because you were there. But I still do have a lot of hang-ups and I worry that, when you're out and about doing your thing, you may meet someone far more suited to you than me."

"Ah." I can't suppress a grin. "Talk about hitting the nail right on the head." I caress her cheek with my fingers. "I'm glad you were able to say that to me, to voice your deepest fear. Because now we can talk about it and address it."

"I think, as Michelle put it, I might be down more for full disclosure as well." Jo kisses my knuckle.

"Tell me this, darling. And tell me honestly." I scoot a little closer to her. "Do you want to do that again some time?"

"I would definitely be up for a threesome again." Jo scrunches her lips together. "I'm just not sure someone like Michelle is going to come along again any time soon."

"It might happen sooner than you think if you're attuned to the signals." I smile. "Take Bryony, for instance."

"Bryony?" Her voice shoots up.

"If you see her again, you could always… allude to it."

Jo narrows her eyes. "You would be up for that?"

"I'd be open to it." I think of Bryony and wonder whether I might have found her attractive if I hadn't been so jealous of her. What would make her most attractive to me, I conclude, is Jo's attraction to her.

"I don't know."

"You think she wants you all to herself?"

"I truly don't know. When I met her, I really wasn't considering that… option."

"You might never see her again, but something tells me you might. We both might. Let's just see what happens when we do. Just something to keep in the back of our minds. But I think you will see things differently from now on."

"I'm already seeing them differently." She smiles. "What about Jessica?"

I scoff. "She's my boss." Only after my quick reply do I think to ponder Jo's question deeper. "Do you find Jessica… appealing?"

She quirks her lips into a lop-sided smile. "I wouldn't say no."

My eyes widen. "Seriously?"

"Are you jealous again?" She chuckles.

I'm not sure. "I can't tell if you're pulling my leg right now or being serious."

Jo reorders her features into a solemn expression. "I know she's your boss, but I do find her attractive. When I first met her at the Pink Bean I was a bit miffed because you told me she hit on you. But once I got over that, I had to admit that she's pretty gorgeous."

"She's a bit highly strung and... I don't know. There's something about her."

"Something wounded. That might also be what I see in her." Jo sighs dramatically. "I've suddenly started seeing so much more into everything. It's exhausting. Maybe my life was better when I was ignorant." She cackles loudly. "You've ruined me forever because now there's no way back."

I scoot closer to her. "You know what I'm thinking about right now?" I whisper in her ear.

She sinks her teeth into her bottom lip and shakes her head.

I lean in so close my lips touch her ear when I speak. "You fucking Jessica with that strap-on of yours."

She looks me in the eye. "You can't say things like that anymore and not expect them to have consequences."

"I'm not expecting that at all, my love." I kiss her on the lips. "This conversation is far from over."

"I think it will never end," Jo says, mock-sighing, before pulling me close to her again and slipping her tongue in my mouth.

Chapter Fifteen

THE FIRST PERSON I see the next day is Jessica. We're in the elevator together. Our gazes meet in the reflection of the doors.

"Good weekend?" she asks.

Inwardly, I chuckle. If only she knew. Then I wonder how she would react if she did. Meanwhile, I'm reminded of what Jo said about her before we went to sleep.

"Jo had a gig. One of her and Jimmy's best."

"At the Old Oz Club," Jessica says, surprising me. "I saw on her Facebook page she was playing there. I considered going but I wasn't sure if you'd be there and I didn't much feel like going alone."

There's a sadness to Jessica I can't figure out. I decide there and then to get to the bottom of it. Not in this elevator, of course, which will soon be dropping us on our desired floors, but this week. I find her intriguing and a little depressing at the same time.

"You should have called," I say, even though I know full well my weekend would have been entirely different if Jessica had tagged along. Perhaps she and Michelle would have hit it off. Perhaps a night with someone like Michelle is exactly what Jessica needs.

The elevator dings and we both get out on the same floor even though Jessica's office is a few floors higher than mine.

"I didn't want to intrude," she says.

"How about this." I shoot her a wide smile. "Next time I'm going to see Jo, I'll call you. We'll set it up in advance." This should make Jo happy. I'm almost sorry we're visiting her family in Northwood the coming weekend and I can't make it happen then.

"That would be great." Jessica straightens her spine, as though she needed to take her time to go into corporate mode, but is now fully powered on. "By the way, I'm this close to reeling in Sheryl for the show." She holds up her hands. "I know, I know. I promised not to interfere any more, but I have to make an exception for her."

"You've been talking to Sheryl?" My interest is piqued. I make a mental note to call Sheryl as soon as possible.

"I went by the Pink Bean this weekend and she was there. We got chatting." She gives me a thumbs-up. "Oh, and last Friday's show was really good. You were at your best, Caitlin."

"Interviewing our country's only out lesbian member of parliament is more up my alley than trying to squeeze some intelligible words out of Kathy Kramer."

"I know. That's why... hands off." She makes the actual gesture of pulling her hands away.

"Let's have lunch sometime this week," I say.

"I would love to. I'll call you later." She looks at her watch. "I'm late for something." She pushes the elevator button. "But I look forward to it already."

As I walk to my office I conjure up the image I mentioned to Jo last night.

———

When I arrive at my desk, I see I have a missed Skype call from Zoya. I do a quick time zone calculation in my head. It's around midnight in Paris. I probably shouldn't call back, but are the French not notorious night owls—dinner at ten PM and all that. Perhaps Zoya has taken on the habit of going to bed late as a matter of integration. She tried to call me about half an hour ago. I waste no time and hit the call button straight away. She picks up after the second ring.

"What are you doing up so late on a Sunday evening?" I ask, trying to make my voice sound steady. Zoya leaving Sydney for Paris has affected me much more than I ever had the nerve to tell her.

"Trying to catch you, of course. I wanted to call earlier after seeing the Kathy Kramer interview, but something always came up."

I roll my eyes. I'm not sure the connection is good enough for her to catch that.

"Why on earth did you invite her on the show?" Zoya asks. So much for offering me her commiserations.

"Things have changed since you left. The new boss felt inclined to push things in a new direction. She felt the show could get better ratings if we, how to put this, lowered the accessibility threshold of our guests."

"They try to do that once in a while. Especially new execs who feel like they have something to prove. Why didn't you tell her to stick her advice you know where?"

"Because she's Edward Porter's daughter." I look into Zoya's face. Her bringing up Kathy Kramer has almost made me forget how happy I am to see her.

"Ah. That makes sense."

"Don't worry, I've got her under control now." I smile into the camera. "Was it really that bad?"

107

"I have nothing but sympathy for you. I know what it's like when an interview doesn't go the way you want it to."

"Tell me about you. How's the Missus?"

"All's well here, although my French should be better by now. It's bloody hard picking up a new language at our age. How's Jo?"

I know it's meant to be a straightforward question, but because of the activity Jo and I engaged in over the weekend, it sounds so loaded to me.

"Is something going on?" Zoya asks when I don't immediately reply.

"We're fine. I mean, she works too hard and I don't get to see enough of her, but when I do see her, well…" When I lived in the US, I was part of a community where I could easily talk about the evolution of my relationships. I haven't found the same kind of community in Sydney yet—I only have to mention the words *open* and *relationship* in a sentence together and Sheryl gives me the evil eye. "Things are really good."

"That's great to hear." Is that a hint of sadness in Zoya's tone? Either way, it's probably not a good idea to discuss the ins and outs of my relationship with Jo, and the next level we reached this weekend.

"Are you sure you're okay?" I ask.

"I miss you guys, that's all."

"We miss you too, Zoya." I know how hard it can be to find a community to belong to after moving to a new place, and I imagine the language barrier must make it even harder for Zoya.

Zoya looks up and glances behind her. "That's Camille coming home. She was over at Flo's babysitting Emma."

"Ah, that's why you called me," I joke. "Your missus was out and you were lonely."

"That's exactly it." Zoya has a mock sneer on her face.

I hear Camille walking into the room. She bends down to look into the camera. "G'day Caitlin," she says, trying to mimic an Australian accent, which clashes horribly with her French one.

"*Bonsoir* Camille." My French accent is much worse than her Australian. "How's the little one?"

We chat a little about this and that, but it's much more superficial than the deeper conversation I was after when I called Zoya. Maybe that's why it was so good to see Michelle after all this time. We might not have been on the exact same page when we were dating, but we are now. I never thought I'd get tired of having to explain myself, but maybe my age is getting the better of me and I long to be simply understood and, even more so, accepted for who I am.

I tell Zoya and Camille all about how everyone they know is doing and about the second Pink Bean branch in Newtown.

When we end the call, I have a browse through my diary and, after consulting Jo's Facebook page, decide to invite Jessica to dinner instead of lunch.

Chapter Sixteen

"YOU'RE HAVING Jessica over for dinner without me?" Jo asks, her hands on her hips.

"It's just dinner, darling." I narrow my eyes, trying to gauge whether I've really made a faux-pas or Jo is simply exhausted—even though it's only Monday evening—and she's taking it out on me.

"Not after what we talked about last night. How can it *only* be dinner then?" She looks at her watch. "I don't have time for this."

I don't say anything. Does Jo really expect me to wait until she has freed up some of her precious time to get to know my boss and possible friend better? I could wait weeks until she has a suitable opening in her agenda.

"Have you eaten?" I ask. "I bought bread."

"I had a salad." She shifts her weight from one foot to the other. "I would have appreciated a heads-up. That's all."

"Do you know what I did before I picked the evening to invite Jessica over? I had to go on your Facebook page. You're performing four times this week, Jo. That didn't exactly leave me with much choice."

"That's not the point. And you know this week's exceptionally busy because we're going away next weekend."

"What do you expect from me? That I wait for you at home alone every night until your gig is finished?"

"What? No. That's completely beside the point." She fiddles with the wristband of her watch. "Jimmy is waiting for me. I really have to go."

"I'm not keeping you." I give her a hard stare. "I wouldn't know how if I tried," I mutter under my breath.

"I didn't catch that," she says.

"Just go. I don't even know what we're fighting about. All I know is that you don't have time to talk about it. So just go already."

"Fine," she says but keeps on standing there for a few seconds longer, until she finally turns around and heads into the hallway.

We might have had an amazing Sunday, but no matter how many great days we have together once every two or three weeks, they won't magically erase the tension about this between us. At its core, this issue is one of being at completely different stages of our lives. I see a lot of myself in Jo, the me when I was her age, approaching thirty and building my career, not much caring for a home life, let alone a relationship. But here I am now, feeling petty and misunderstood because my partner is doing the exact same things I used to do.

The problem with Jo is that she wants to be so independent she sometimes makes me feel as though our relationship is inferior to that. She insists on paying rent. A monthly sum I reluctantly take and put into a separate account from which I hope to pay a full year of her sister's school tuition soon—if only I can convince Jo to let me. I thought it would get better the longer we were together, but Jo has had to fend for herself for such a long time, it's not a habit she can quickly shake.

I stare at the hallway door for a few minutes, hoping her gig will have miraculously been cancelled at the last minute and she'll be spending the evening with me. A selfish wish, for sure, and an idle one at that, yet I'm not willing to un-wish it.

———

When I have Jessica over for dinner on Wednesday evening, Jo and I have barely talked. She's been getting up at the crack of dawn to go for her morning run before starting work at the Pink Bean. I've been too stubborn to go by the Pink Bean before work because I'm beginning to feel like a dog pathetically begging for its owner's attention.

When she slips into bed after midnight I always wonder how two people can live together yet lead such separate lives. Something's going to have to give soon, or else I'm not sure how this will end—but end it will.

"Just the two of us?" Jessica says when I take her coat. She starts walking around my apartment, clearly no longer expecting a reply. "Good grief." She turns to me. "This place."

"I'm glad you like it." I'm happy to see Jessica—happy to have another person in my home. I offer her a glass of champagne.

"Like it?" She chuckles. "That's the understatement of the year."

"Let's sit outside," I say, anticipating her reaction to the view from my deck.

"I don't mean to be indiscreet." She leans against the railing of the balcony. "But how much did they pay you to have your face on TV in the US?"

"First of all, it wasn't my face they were paying for. It was my opinions." The setting sun brightens her eyes. "And you work in television. You know it's the most overpaid business of them all."

"I guess I still have a lot to learn." She holds up her glass. "Thanks for inviting me."

"My pleasure." I fix my gaze on her for a millisecond, then look away into the distance. Was I really so wrong to invite her?

"I wasn't always in television," Jessica says.

I lead the way to a couple of chairs and we sit down.

"But your family has been."

"Which is why I deemed it necessary to do something different." She utters a self-deprecating scoff. "And look at me now. The prodigal daughter has returned. You should have seen my father's face on my first day at ANBC. I wouldn't quite call it smugness. He's not really the sort for that. More like terribly misplaced pride."

"Are you enjoying working at ANBC?"

"I am. I don't even know why I resisted it for so long. Family will do that to you."

I huff out a sigh. "Ah yes, families. They're never simple, are they?" I've become accustomed to not thinking about my own family very often. Years of estrangement will do that to you.

"So much goes unsaid, yet so much is expected." She sips from her champagne. "In mine, anyway."

I think of the upcoming visit to Jo's family we have planned. "Jo and I are visiting her family next weekend. We're going all the way to Northwood."

"Did she have a gig tonight?" Jessica puts down her glass.

I shake my head. "She's out with her best friend. They do a girls' night every few weeks, no significant others allowed." I'm not sure I fully succeed in keeping the bitterness out of my voice. In a week with four gigs, Jo could have kept an extra evening free to spend with me.

Jessica just nods. She probably doesn't know me well enough to notice the inflections in my voice.

I take a long swig of my drink and feel the bubbles fizz out on my tongue. "Can I be indiscreet in return?" I ask, emboldened by the fresh hit of alcohol.

"Be my guest." Her eyes shine as she gives me a quick nod.

"As any interviewer worth their salt would, I googled you. I found startlingly little."

A small smile forms on her lips. "Who knew that these days you need to pay good money to keep your name off the internet? My family's not short, so that's what they did." She reaches for her glass and stares into what remains of the liquid.

"You don't have to tell me. I'm just curious." I give her a warm smile back. "My curiosity is not something that needs to be indulged at all times."

She waves off my comment. "It's not easy to talk about." She takes a quick sip. "I made a big mess of things and failed quite a few people in the process."

"Don't we all sometimes?"

"I doubt *you* do." She tilts her head. "Then again, that's only my impression of you."

"I screw up all the time," I say.

She arches up her eyebrows, as though doubting my statement—or, perhaps she's waiting for me to give her a few examples. But I prefer to keep my mistakes to myself.

"I owned a successful advertising agency for about a decade, until I ran it into the ground." She taps a finger to her temple. "Mental health issues, which indirectly led me to losing us one big client, which seemed to have a domino effect on our other clients. I failed to keep it together. The company folded. Seventeen people lost their jobs. All because I couldn't keep it together."

I glance at her in silence before speaking. "I'm sure you're being too hard on yourself right now."

"It's just a quick summary of what happened. That's always going to sound harsh." She finishes the last of her champagne. I take it as a cue to refill our glasses.

"My therapist would not agree with how I just put that, by the way." A grin appears on her face. "She would have me analyzing how I phrased that and why quick as days. Bless her."

"Then how would you explain it less harshly?" I feel like I'm stepping into the role of Jessica's therapist.

"I would say that I"—she looks at her hands— "suffered from depression triggered by burn-out, which is an illness. A chemical imbalance in the brain. It's biology and chemistry, therefore I should stop blaming myself for what happened, which is hard when you have the unemployment of seventeen people to account for. Seventeen good people who didn't have a rich daddy to bail them out and give them a second chance." She puts down her champagne flute with a hard knock on the table. "Daddy Porter provided the cash for handsome severance packages, of course. That's what men with deep pockets do when their good-for-nothing daughters get in trouble."

I'm getting much more than I bargained for. And I'm not a therapist. But I can see that what Jessica needs most is someone who listens—someone friendly who isn't paid to.

"You built a successful company. That must stand for something."

"Not really." Her voice is small. "Not when you lose it." A finger flicks to the corner of her eye. "I'm sorry. I don't really talk about this a lot outside Mrs. Buchman's office." She inhales deeply. "Christ." She looks at me sheepishly, then glances away. "Now you must think I'm a mental case as well."

"I think no such thing, Jessica." I lean forward and rest my elbows on my knees. "You are human, just like the rest of us. No better, no worse. How about that?" I keep myself from putting a supportive hand on her knee. "How about some dinner?"

"That's why I'm here." There's that smile again. It's the same one she beamed at me after we got out of the elevator last Monday. It feels practiced, yet there's authenticity about it as well.

———

"My prediction," I say, only vaguely aware of my preachy tone—the one Jo, if she were here, would try to coax me out of by gently patting my shoulder—"is that fifty to a hundred years from now, the majority of newborns will be mixed-race, most people will eat a plant-based diet, and non-monogamy—well, it will never be the norm, but it will be regarded and perhaps even respected as a valid alternative for ever-failing monogamous relationships."

What I am aware of is that my earlier spat with Jo bothers me far more than I let on, and I've been greedily drinking away my growing frustration. Jessica has been a willing drinking partner.

"Australians will never go off beef. Or lamb," Jessica says. "Or a creamy rock oyster."

"I know I just served you veal." I bow my head in acknowledgment. "I haven't been able to work up enough of a guilty conscience to forgo meat. Because I do believe that will be the turning point. When our collective conscience finally tips over the edge and we start feeling truly ashamed for eating animals."

"I think your vegetarian prediction is a bit off. We'll need at least another two to three generations to weed out the fastidious meat lovers." Jessica shrugs. "But what does it matter anyway? We won't be here anymore."

"Oh yes, I forgot to say. That's if we don't destroy our planet first, of course. Although I do believe we're intelligent enough to find a solution. Maybe just in time. But I don't think the human race is about to become extinct just yet."

"To a beautiful mixed-race future then." She reaches for her glass of wine. "I really can't say anything about monogamy, but I don't mind indulging your view of the future."

"What's your relationship history?"

"Sketchy to say the least." Jessica seems to find her assessment of her love life hilarious. "I'm sorry. I've just had… really shitty luck with women. There was someone I loved but when things got hard, she was the first to bail, so…" She makes a throwaway gesture with her hand. "Good riddance."

"That must have hurt."

"It showed me her true character, which in turn made me wiser." She grins. "I've also been learning to see the brighter side of things."

"How's that going for you?"

"Wonderfully well this evening." Jessica rests her gaze on me. She makes for a fantastic drinking buddy. "I'm so glad I got to meet you." Her eyes are still on mine.

I hold her gaze. I want to see what she's made of. She has shared some of her secrets and, most importantly, I like her. I want to test the waters for whenever Jo and I ever have time for a threesome again.

"So am I, despite you shamelessly hitting on me." I throw in a smile.

"I'd like to think we're past that now."

I sink my teeth into my lip and nod. "Jo and I had a further chat about it."

Her glance flits away for a moment. "You did?"

"Yes." I slant my head. "Jo finds you very attractive."

Jessica's eyes widen. She doesn't say anything.

"So do I." I narrow my eyes, hoping she will put two and two together and fill the silence. I'm going out on a seriously tipsy limb here.

"I, um…" The light in the room is low, yet I can see Jessica's cheeks flush. "I'm not sure I understand what you're trying to say."

"If one day the occasion and the mood were to strike, we would like to invite you into our bed." I sound ridiculously solemn, as though I'm extending an invitation to an official and very pompous soirée.

"You mean for a… threesome?" The disbelief in her voice is so strong it can't possibly be fake.

I nod, and scan her face.

Her lips tighten. There's no more room for that practiced smile. I've thrown her massively off guard. Perhaps the booze has made me misjudge the sense I had of us being on the same page.

"Look, Caitlin, I, um, am attracted to you." She gives a nervous giggle. "I did flirt with you for that reason, but a threesome…" She shakes her head.

"Fair enough." I give her a warm smile. "Threesomes aren't for everyone."

Jessica drinks again. "I mean, I guess I could get to know Jo better. I would love to, actually." She puts her glass down. Her lips have loosened into a hint of smile again.

It's very much my move. If only Jo were here. I suddenly feel as though I need to make this happen for her. "I think it's safe to say Jo feels the same way." At the same time, I don't want to rob Jo of the delicious journey that could lead to having Jessica in our bed—it really is half the fun. I glance at my watch. If she's out with Eva, there's no predicting when Jo will come home.

Jessica empties her wine and stares at the glass.

When I reach for the bottle to give her a refill, she holds up her hand. "I think I've had quite enough for one night." She pushes her chair back. "God knows what I'll say next if I have another glass." Her cheeks are flushed.

"Should I call you a taxi?"

She shakes her head. "I'll walk it off." She rises and stands with her hands clutching the back of the chair.

I get up as well and walk over to her. All of this is extremely unprofessional of us. I put a hand on her shoulder. "I'll see you tomorrow then."

"Give Jo my love," she says and heads to the hallway.

At the front door, we kiss each other quickly on the cheeks and before I even have time to consider if our budding friendship has already progressed into different territory, the elevator has taken Jessica away.

———

By the time I've stacked the dirty plates in the dishwasher, I hear a key in the lock.

As soon as she's closed the door behind her, Jo walks over to me and throws her arms around me. "I'm so glad you're still up," she whispers in my ear. "I was being an ass earlier. I was jealous and unreasonable. I take it all back."

I arch up my eyebrows then kiss Jo softly on the cheek.

"What?" she asks. "Why are you looking at me like that?"

"If only you'd been here…" I wrap my arms around her waist. "I'm pretty sure Jessica would still be here."

"Don't tease me like that. Tell me what happened." Jo wriggles herself free from my embrace.

"How about I tell you all about it over a nightcap?"

Jo nods and we sit in the sofa, our feet propped up on the coffee table.

"She wants to get to know you better." I send her a sly smile.

"Please, babe. It's late. I've had too much too drink. And I have some news to share. Just spit out what you want to say."

"Oh Christ, you're no fun to tease tonight." I lean into her with my shoulder a bit more, wanting to be closer to her. "The other day you said you might be up for some fun with Jessica. I made, um, an *overture*."

"An overture?" Jo turns to me so she can look me in the eye. "You mean you propositioned her?"

"I might have." I bite my bottom lip.

Jo's eyes grow wide. "I, er, don't really know how to react to that." She purses her lips together for a split second. "What did she say?" Are her eyes lighting up?

"What I just said. That she wants to get to know you better."

"Why?" Jo drinks from her brandy.

"Because I very much think she's interested in my offer." I smile at Jo and tilt my head. "You don't mind that I brought it up while you weren't here?"

Jo shakes her head.

She seems lost in thought. When she doesn't speak for a few moments, I ask, "How was your night? How's Eva?"

"She's only going to get married," Jo says matter-of-factly.

I sit up a little straighter. "No way. Already?" I shake my head.

"She turned thirty last month, babe. She's not exactly a child bride." Jo shoots me a grin. "Please be at least a little bit happy for her."

"If she's happy and you're happy, I'm happy."

Jo rolls her eyes. "Promise me you won't give her the 'marriage is just an invention of the patriarchy speech' when you see her next."

"Only if you promise me you will never, ever propose to me. I *will* say no."

"Don't I know it." Jo holds on to my hand a little tighter. "Caitlin James is nobody's wife." Her eyes narrow as she smiles. "You can just be my unwedded old lady forever."

"That I can do."

"I will be Eva's maid of honor, so you'll have to deal with that."

"When's the wedding?"

"They haven't set a date yet."

"Plenty of time to prepare myself then." I pull her close to me. I only hope seeing her best friend prepare for marriage won't put any unrealistic ideas into her head. Same-sex marriage might be legal now, but that doesn't mean I will avail of my right to wed another person—to swear ludicrous oaths like faithfulness and to never desire another. In the grand scheme of things, same-sex marriage is definitely progress, more equality always will be, but isn't it about time someone rewrote the standard marriage vows? With divorce rates going up every year, when will people figure out that what they label infidelity is just nature taking its course?

"Come on." Jo rises. "You look as though you'll fall asleep any second."

I let her pull me up and lead me into the hallway.

"Next week, please keep a few more nights free for your old lady," I ask as we shuffle to the bedroom.

"Deal." She tugs at my hand. "Time to take my old lady to bed." We topple onto the bed and I fall into her soft embrace.

Chapter Seventeen

I'VE BARELY HAD time to sit down at my desk when I get a phone call from Jessica. It's as though she asked someone to tell her when I arrived at work. Her name flickers on the screen while I debate with myself whether to answer or not. I want to talk to her but I'm afraid that if I do so first thing I won't be able to get certain images out of my head for the rest of the day.

Reminded of Jo's smile last night, I pick up. "Good morning, Jessica," I say.

"Morning, Caitlin.." Her voice is unsteady. "Can I stop by your office real quick? I would like to ask you something in person."

"Sure." I'm intrigued. Will her question be professional or purely private?

"I'll be there in one minute."

I don't know how she managed to get to my office so quickly, but it seems like less than a minute since she hung up the phone. She must have sprinted down the stairs. Or maybe she gets to use a special executive elevator reserved for family members of the owner of the company.

"Thanks for seeing me." She closes the door behind her. "Can I sit?"

"Sure." I observe her as she sits. Her ginger hair is pulled back into a pony tail. She hasn't managed to conceal the dark circles under her eyes. I, too, have a hint of headache pulsing at the base of my skull, despite the ibuprofen Jo lovingly laid out for me this morning.

"I had a really good time last night," she says. "Sorry to have rushed off like that."

"Perhaps the conversation was getting a little too... heated." I try to hold her gaze. At first, she looks away, but after a few seconds she looks me square in the eye.

"The way I see it." She slants her head a little, making her long neck appear even longer. "I opened up to you and you, in return, opened up to me."

"That's one way of putting it." I grin.

"In the spirit of that, I would like to invite you and Jo to dinner at my place on Saturday next week."

I nod. "That would be lovely." I glance at Jessica from under my lashes. "I need to check Jo's schedule, of course."

"Of course." She doesn't look as though she wants to get up from that chair any time soon. I conclude we have crossed into the next level of friendship—a level unreachable by most. Today, however, we're sitting in my office at the network her father owns. The dynamics are a little different.

"I'll let you know." I lean back in my chair. I'm not going to ask my boss to leave my office.

"I'll leave you to it then," she says, but still doesn't get up. She fixes her gaze on me and I see so much in it. I see how much being able to sit here with me and have this brief but loaded conversation means to her. How much she hankers for something different in her life—to put the past well and truly behind her. We may have different motives, but as seconds tick by, I'm getting more and more convinced Jessica, Jo and I all want the same thing.

Jessica finally gets up and pulls the same disappearing act as last night. With a few swift moves, she's out of my office and I'm left staring, a little perplexed, at the door she just vanished through.

Chapter Eighteen

"No THANK YOU," Jo says to the flight attendant who just offered her a bottle of water.

"It's free, you know." I grin at her.

She shakes her head as though she greatly despairs of me. "Nothing's free. And I don't want to get used to a certain standard of living." She turns to me. "It's a one and a half hour flight, Caitlin. You're such a princess."

"It's just a bottle of water." I told her when we booked the flights that if I was going to see my partner's parents, I wouldn't skimp on travel comfort and promptly paid for both our flights in business class. Although Jo has a point that it's not really worth the extra money. On a small plane like this, the seats aren't any bigger and there's no extra legroom. But at least Qantas has a makeshift business class. The budget airline she wanted to fly didn't. "What if you get thirsty?"

She points to her backpack underneath the seat in front of her. "That's why they invented refill bottles. Did you know you can bring your own water onto the plane? That they have water fountains past security where you can refill your own bottle?" She talks to me like a school teacher would to small children.

"How about you just enjoy the flight—and the service. Maybe what you need is a G&T." I lean over the empty seat between us. "Or are you nervous about me spending time with your family? Is that what this is about?"

"You know I hate being watched. I feel so on display here. Like I don't belong."

"They'll close that curtain behind us as soon as we take off."

"That's not what I mean."

"Darling, come on." I put a hand on her knee. "Would it help if I admitted to having some princess-y ways? I'm perfectly willing to own up to that." I throw in a smile. "I'm older than you. My creaky bones need more comfort."

There's a hint of smile on her lips. "My old lady is a princess."

"For what it's worth, I'm really looking forward to better getting to know the people who are responsible for bringing you into this world and hence making my life so much more complete."

"I *am* a little nervous."

"No kidding." I give her knee a squeeze. "How about that gin and tonic?"

"It's too early and I don't want to smell of booze when I hug them. I haven't seen my parents in so long."

"You know I'll be on my best behavior, right?"

"So will they. Just… you know you won't be lodging in grand luxury."

"Darling, I know I'm a princess when it comes to certain things, but I'm not a snob."

She quirks up her eyebrows.

"I'm not."

"Most of the time you're not."

I roll my eyes. "The point is that we're flying to North-wood to spend time with your family. For us to get to know each other better, in person. There's no need for you to worry about anything else."

"I know I shouldn't worry," Jo says and folds her hand over mine, which is still resting on her knee. "I can't seem to help it."

"Think about Bea. She's going to be over the moon."

Jo nods. "She will be." Her voice cracks a little. "Expect to see the very image of joy personified." She relaxes. "I should go home more often," she says on a sigh. It doesn't sound like a reprimand to herself, more like a simple observation.

I refrain from saying that she could. I want Jo to enjoy the journey to her family, not get into another argument about money and independence and what she can and can't do.

"I feel very lucky I get to go with you," I say.

"Is it hard for you?" She searches for my gaze.

"Not at all. It's wonderful." I attempt a smile.

"But you don't get to take me home to your family."

"Which leaves all the more time to spend with yours. The plane fare I save from not being welcome at my parents' house, we can spend on flights to yours. It works out well that way." It's not even hard to keep a brave face, nor is it hard to be on the way to visit Jo's family. Besides, I've met them all. I've felt their warmth and the respect they have for each other—and how they've embraced me as one of their own.

"I will never understand how someone can shun their own flesh and blood for no good reason at all. Is there ever really a reason to sever all ties like that with your own child?" Jo muses.

"Speaking of children." I don't want to talk about my parents and their failings any longer. "Will Eva and Declan be wanting some? Is that why they're following the prescribed route of marriage?"

"Eva is very broody. I think they're trying already. You don't have to wait to be married anymore these days, you know," she says with a snicker.

A silence falls. Jo glances out of the window. When she looks back at me, she says, "Do you regret never having any?"

"Goodness me. If I had known flying business would turn you into an inquisitor of my deepest emotions I would have thought twice."

"Such a perfect example of a very typical defensive Caitlin James reply." There's kindness in her eyes.

"Have you and Eva been talking about children?" I might be defensive, but I can also put two and two together.

Jo nods. "She and Dec want four. I mean, she says that now, but let's wait until she's had the first."

"And?" I shuffle around to get a better look at her.

"It *has* made me think. I'll be thirty soon. It's the time for me to consider these things. What did you think when you were thirty?"

"That I was far too busy and, perhaps more importantly, too single to even consider it."

"But those are rational arguments. What did you feel in your heart?"

"Honestly, Jo, when you come from the kind of family I come from, having children simply doesn't seem like the best idea."

"From what I've heard about your parents, you're nothing like them."

"I'm sure when they had me they never believed they would one day start pretending I don't exist. But it just goes to show how life can go. And that having a child isn't always a fairytale."

"They hurt you. The very people who were always supposed to protect you."

"Let's not get too dramatic about it." I find such support in Jo's glance. "So what have you been thinking?"

"I'm not sure this is the right place to have this conversation," Jo says. "In fact, I'm certain it's not. Even in business class."

"Should I brace myself for when we get back?" I manage a smile. I was well aware of the age difference between us when we fell in love, but up until now Jo has been too busy to have this conversation which, truth be told, suited me just fine.

"Not really." Jo turns to me. "We barely get to spend two evenings in a row together." It's as if she's reading my thoughts. "If I do have a ticking biological clock, it's been somewhat drowned out by my other activities." She gazes at me longingly. "Of which not nearly enough include the simple pleasure of watching you." She smiles. "So I might just do that for the rest of the flight."

I bat my lashes. "I might just do the same with you."

Our moment is rudely interrupted by a flight attendant stopping at my seat with a cart. "Can I offer you a drink, Miss James?" she asks.

I accept her offer with a smile.

Chapter Nineteen

AT THE AIRPORT we're met by Jo's father, Ron, and her sister, Bea.

Ron speaks very fast and I have a little trouble following him. But when I look into his eyes, I see Jo's kindness reflected at me.

"Jojo." Bea is bouncing up and down on the balls of her feet. She can't seem to let go of Jo.

"Jo's her hero," Ron says as we watch them hug.

"Jo talks about Bea lot. She adores her."

Ron nods and, in silence, we watch them interact until Jo turns Bea toward me.

I hold out my hand to her and she looks at it for an instant first before taking it in hers.

"You're Jojo's girlfriend," she says. "Because girls can be with girls and boys can be with boys."

"That's right," Ron says.

"Do you want to give Caitlin a hug, Bea?" Jo asks.

She tilts her chin down but keeps her gaze on us. "Okay." She opens her arms wide and I step into her tight embrace.

In the car, I sit in the front with Ron while Jo and Bea snicker unstoppably in the back.

"It's always like that when they see each other. I know Jo calls her every day, but it's not the same over the phone, is it?" He glances in the rearview mirror and a smile appears on his face. "I don't get to see them together often enough."

"It's wonderful to witness." I turn around and smile at them. I can hear Jo's love for her sister in every word she says to her—and I understand better why she works so hard to give her sister the best life possible.

It's a forty-minute drive from the airport to the Greenwood home and Ron and I fall into a companionable silence while we listen to Jo and Bea sing songs in the back. I haven't been out of the city in too long and it's wonderful to not see any high-rises and bumper-to-bumper traffic.

As we approach Northwood, Ron raises a hand to every single person we see. When we arrive at the house, Jo's mother is waiting for us outside. I can see how she quickly wipes a tear from the corner of her eye as she wraps her arms around Jo.

She gives me an apologetic smile before she folds her arms around me as though I too am one of her children who hasn't been home in too long.

"How wonderful to see you again, Caitlin." She rubs a hand over my shoulder. "We watched your show last night. Wonderful as always."

"Thank you." The warmth bestowed upon me by this family shouldn't come as a surprise. I live with their daughter and she's just like them, but it takes me aback a little nonetheless, just as it did the first time I met them. Because I'm not used to such displays of affection between family members, to Bea's exuberance, to the love in Ron's eyes when he looks at his daughters. We've spoken on Skype numerous times, but seeing them in the flesh, all their love on display like this, is an entirely different experience.

"Jojo, will you sleep in my room?" Bea asks when we go inside. She doesn't let go of Jo's hand.

"We talked about this, honey. Remember?" Ron says. "Jojo and Caitlin will be sleeping in Jo's room. They are partners. That's what partners do. Like mommy and daddy."

"You mean they are girlfriends, like girlfriend and boyfriend but two girls," Bea says.

Jo slings an arm around her sister's shoulder. "I'll be in your room until you fall asleep, Bea. I promise. And in the morning I don't have to call you, because I'll be right here."

"You must want to freshen up after your journey," Kathleen, Jo's mother, says. "There are fresh towels on the bed." She holds out a hand to Bea. "Come on, honey. Let's say hello to the goats while Jojo and Caitlin change."

Bea looks at her mother's hand pensively, then a smile breaks on her face and she nods eagerly.

———

"Can I help?" I ask. Jo, Ron and Kathleen are busy laying the table and putting the finishing touches to lunch.

"Oh no," Kathleen says. "Jo has given us strict orders. You are not to help us at all. I believe the P-word was mentioned." She and Jo both burst into a chuckle.

"Don't mind them." Ron comes to my aid. "They get a bit giddy when they're around each other. Usually they take it out on me." He winks at me. "So I, for one, am very happy to have you here."

"Meanwhile my reputation has been tarnished." I play along. "What other lies has Jo told you about me?"

Jo turns away from the drawer she's rummaging through. "Me? Telling lies? How dare you insinuate such a thing in front of my parents. Next you'll try to make them believe you're not a princess at all."

"It's true that we don't get many princesses around here," Ron says. "Except when Princess Beatrice comes home, of course." He grins at his youngest daughter.

Jo clears her throat.

"Oh yes, and Princess Josephine, of course. But I do believe you've just undone the point you were trying to make about Caitlin, love."

We all sit around the table, our elbows touching.

"I hope this is to your liking." Ron pours a splash of red wine into a glass and offers it to me. "Do you want to, um, try it?"

"Dad." Jo rolls her eyes at him.

"I'm sure it will be perfectly fine." I fix my gaze on Ron briefly.

"Fill up our glasses already," Kathleen says. "I want to drink to all my girls being home." She sits there beaming. "That includes you, Caitlin."

I'm at a loss for a quick reply. I can only smile in gratitude.

We all hold up our glass, four filled with wine, one filled with sparkling water.

"I have champagne," Bea says as she looks into her glass. "It bubbles."

Jo gives her sister's glass an extra clink. She radiates such joy when she's around Bea.

"I hope you'll all visit us in Sydney soon," I say. "There's plenty of room at our place."

"I want to go to Sydney," Bea cries. "When can we go?" She looks at her mother with great expectation in her eyes.

"We'll see, honey," Kathleen says.

"Lovely as that would be," Ron says. "It's difficult for us to get away."

Underneath the table I feel Jo's hand on my knee, as though she's trying to tell me something. Have I been too exuberant with my invitation?

"As Kathleen says, we'll see." I try to erase whatever faux-pas I committed with a warm smile. It's probably about money. Any tension between Jo and me is either about money or time—and surely this isn't about time. Or maybe it's difficult to travel with Bea, who must be used to her routine.

"I finally finished the book you and Jo wrote together," Ron says. "Sorry it took so long, love. Too much brainiac language for your old dad."

Instinctively, I want to say that we've paid attention to the language, to not make it sound too high-brow but make it accessible for everyone, but I feel Jo's hand on my knee again.

"What did you think of it?" I ask, instead.

"Oh, wonderful," is all he says.

"Sounds like a job well done. I'm not much of a reader anymore. My eyes have gotten too bad," Kathleen says.

"You should get an e-reader," I say. "Then you can adjust the size of the letters."

Kathleen waves off my comment. "I'm not one for electronics either."

I nod my understanding. It's not just Kathleen's aversion to electronics I get, but I'm beginning to understand Jo's inclination to put herself down. Self-deprecation seems to be a family trait.

"I love reading," Bea shouts. "I want to read Jojo's book."

"I'll read to you from it tonight," Jo says.

Bea sits there grinning.

"Time for food." Kathleen puts her glass down and scoots out of her chair. "It's nothing fancy." She looks at me and there's that apologetic smile again. "But the girls love it.

Bea practically demands that I make this pasta bake every time she comes home."

"I'm sure it'll be lovely," I say.

———

"All right, give it to me," I say to Jo when she finally comes to bed. "How many times did I say something I wasn't supposed to say today?" I'm exhausted from traveling and all the conversations of the day.

"You can say anything you want, babe." Jo quickly undresses and slips under the covers with me. The bed we're supposed to sleep in is about half the size of the one we have at home. "My parents will forgive you anything for taking me off the shelf."

I shake my head.

"That was a joke." Jo runs her cold hands along my back then brings them to my front.

"Stop that." I put my warm hand on her ice-cold one.

"Stop what?" She tries to worm her hand from under mine.

"I don't just mean stop touching me with your freezing fingers." I clasp my hand around them. "What's with all the self-deprecation? I didn't know Northwood was the capital of putting yourself down?"

"It's just modesty. Not something you're very used to so I can imagine it seems vey foreign to you." Jo paints a grin on her face.

"It's more than that, Jo."

"You're reading too much into things. Maybe you're still in work mode. Let me switch that off for you." She abruptly plants a kiss on my lips. "How's that?"

"Lovely." I let my hand roam across her back. "Didn't you pack a pair of pajamas?"

"I'll put them on when I need to." As cold as her hands were, that's how hot her skin glows against mine already.

"This bed is tiny. How are we meant to sleep in here?"

"I can sleep in the living room if you need more space."

"No." I pull her closer to me. "Stay here with me."

"Your choice." She kisses me again but on the cheek this time. "My parents adore you. And Bea is just as smitten with you as I am." She pecks me on the cheek again. "Then again, what's not to love?"

"I love how relaxed you are here. How at ease."

"They're my family and I grew up here. And it's so good to be out of the city and out of the usual maelstrom of work and gigs and intellectual conversations. Here, I can just be. Not do, but just be."

"I've always dreamed of a place in the countryside. Somewhere to get away from everything, to just relax." I glue my body a bit closer to hers. "Be with my woman without distractions." I kiss the tip of Jo's nose.

"That does sound lovely."

"Do you have any old friends left here? Someone who can enlighten me on what teenage Jo was like?" My only other visit to Northwood was so brief, there was no time to consider spending any moment away from Jo's family.

"Not as far as I know. Young people don't stay in a place like this if they don't have to. There's no work here. The nearest decent-sized city is a plane-ride away. Even Bea's school is an hour's drive from here."

"So I'll just have to quiz Ron and Kathleen more."

"They only have good things to say about me."

I smile at Jo. "They're clearly very proud of you."

"As they should be." The skin around her eyes crinkles as she grins.

"That's what I like to hear." I let my head fall into the pillow. "Should I not have invited them to Sydney?"

Jo scrunches her lips together before she speaks. "I know your intention was good, but the air fare to Sydney is a lot of money for them."

"I would pay for—"

"Not everyone wants you to pay for everything all the time, Caitlin." Jo silences me with her words.

"Oh, I think I know that."

"I'm a chip off the old block. I can't help it." She caresses my arm. "I know you mean well, but it's important for me, and for my family, to pay our own way. It's a matter of pride that we've always managed somehow, even though there was never much to go around."

"You could easily pay for their flights. You make more and more money from singing. You have royalties from our book. You have your job at the Pink Bean and your PhD stipend."

"I guess, but this situation is new to me. And I know that a rainy day will come. It's inevitable. I want to have some money in the bank for when it does." She sighs. "Besides, my parents would never take money from me. It took forever to get them to accept that I would pay for Bea's school. But if I didn't, Bea would not be getting the best care possible, so they did accept it in the end." She shakes her head. "Because of that reason, they would never accept anything more from me—or you."

"I understand. But aren't there limits to everything? And aren't we running around in circles here? Your parents didn't want to accept your money, even though you had it. And you don't want to accept mine, even though I have it. They changed their minds in the end. Why can't you?"

"Because the circumstances are totally different. The only reason they ever allowed me to pay for Bea's school is because it was in Bea's best interest and if we wanted to put her in that particular school, it was the only option. I don't need to accept any of your money because I'm doing just fine on my own."

"Are you really?" I ease my lips into a smile. "I'm not talking about money. I'm talking about time. It seems a difficult conversation to have with you while we're clearly both suffering from your lack of it."

"But we're here now, squeezed together in my teenage bed. Can't we just enjoy the weekend?"

I can't suppress a sigh. "Why is it so hard for you to admit? That's really all I ask at this point. That you admit that you've been neglecting our relationship because you don't have the time to dedicate to it."

"I know I'm busy—probably much busier than you would want me to be. But this is only temporary and I can't have someone else tell me, not even you, how hard I should work."

Here we go again. We've only just started and already we've been sucked into the same old loop. She's basically forbidding me to say anything else about the matter because she's dead set on construing it as me telling her what to do. I don't really have much choice but to play the emotional card.

"What about me? It's never really been my style to sit around and wait for my partner to come home."

"I know it drives you a little mad. I'm not going to lie, I find it kind of flattering." Her warmed-up hand skates along my back. "Caitlin James waiting for me in her penthouse apartment."

"As romantic as the notion sounds to you, it's pretty unbearable for me."

"Unbearable?" She grins. "Because the princess doesn't get the attention she thinks she deserves?"

I shake my head. "Don't make this about me, Jo. This is not about me. It's about us. And it's about you not being willing to sacrifice anything to spend more time with me. Yes, we have this weekend, where I do have to share you with your family, but I've barely seen you all week."

She sinks her teeth into her bottom lip and her glance skitters away. "I just… never pictured you as someone wanting to spend all this time at home."

"I never really was before," I admit. "I guess I've changed. And I guess I want a little more than what you've been giving. I respect your desire for independence and I can clearly see where it comes from, but I have desires too. Why can't we meet somewhere in the middle?"

"Where's the middle according to you?" Her gaze lands back on me.

"It would be nice to have breakfast together in the morning."

"In other words, the middle for you is me giving up my job in the Pink Bean."

"Yes." No need to mince my words any longer.

Jo sighs. "I just can't imagine not working there."

I grin at her. "Could you ever have imagined me lying in this bed with you?"

She chuckles in return. "Not in a million years. I read and reread your books in this bed. But no, I could never have imagined this."

"Well, here we are. Change is scary and so much has changed for you already. I'm very fond of the Pink Bean as well. But it's just around the corner. We can go by every day. You don't have to work there."

She lets herself fall onto her back. "I'm just scared that if I let go of my Pink Bean job I'll be removing a piece of the puzzle that got me where I am now. I've worked there since the beginning. Kristin and Sheryl are like family. It's where I met you. It's just very hard to let go of."

"But darling, you have a safety net." I crawl a little closer to her, even though in this bed it means having to climb half on top of her. "You have me."

She huffs out some air. "That's just the thing. I'm not used to having a safety net." She turns her face toward me. "What if you get tired of me? Then I won't have my job at the Pink Bean anymore, nor my so-called safety net."

"We've been together a year and a half. I'm not going anywhere." I stroke her cheek. "I hope you know that."

"I do, but then again, you never know what might happen. The way our relationship is going now…"

"We've talked about this."

"Have we?" There's sudden harshness in her tone which she seems to regret immediately. She pushes her cheek into my palm like a cat would.

"I thought we had," I say.

"I enjoyed that afternoon with Michelle a lot. Much more than I had expected. But I'm still unsure about the rest."

"We can go as slow or as fast as you want." Most of our conversations seem to end up here—off topic and dealing with Jo's fear of losing me. One emotion can't be separated from the other. Her clinging to her job at the Pink Bean has another reason than losing the money it represents.

"Right about now I would like to go very slow." A small smile tugs at her lips. "I'm exhausted."

"Will you be able to sleep? I can't give you much more space than this."

"We can sleep like this." She slings a leg over mine. "Nice and cozy."

"If only," I mumble, and close my eyes anyway.

———

We say goodbye to Jo's parents late Sunday afternoon. On the way to the airport we've taken a detour to drop Bea off at her school, where a big production was made out of showing me her room.

At the airport, Kathleen wipes another tear from her eye after she finally lets Jo go from her embrace.

"Take care of my girl," she whispers in my ear as she curls her arms around my neck.

Suddenly I wonder whether Kathleen has ever leafed through any of my books on the shelves of Jo's bedroom when she still lived at home—whether she's aware of my views on marriage and relationships in general. Maybe that's why she claimed to not be much of a reader—to avoid the subject of my books. To keep the peace. To not have to imagine things about my relationship with her daughter.

"I will." I give her arms an extra squeeze to emphasize my intention.

Jo tears up a little when we walk to security, where there is a surprisingly long line.

"Where are all these people flying to on a Sunday afternoon?"

Jo's barely listening. She's still waving at Kathleen and Ron. I can't begin to imagine what it's like to feel so sad to say goodbye to your family.

I put a hand on her shoulder. "We'll come back for Christmas."

She just nods, then says, "And Bea's birthday."

"Anytime you want, babe."

The line moves swiftly and we wave goodbye to Kathleen and Ron one last time.

Chapter Twenty

ON MONDAY MORNING Jo is up and away early as usual. I stretch out in our bed luxuriously. A smile spreads on my lips when I think of Kathleen and Ron's warmth. And Bea's sheer exuberance at being with her sister. The smile remains on my lips a little longer because I'm lying in a bed where I can actually stretch out. I suppose it would be too much of a princess-like thing to order a larger bed for Jo's old room. I shake my head at the thought and my mind wanders to my own family.

I haven't been to the house in Evanston in over fifteen years. I'm not sure my parents even still live there. I don't know if they're doing well. I don't know anything at all. Ordinarily, I would push the thought of them away immediately—after all, they don't seem to be spending any time thinking of me—but I'm incapable of doing so this morning.

Seeing Jo's family makes it harder. I've made myself forget the harsh words my mother spoke to me after she read my first book, but I did write them down in my diary. It's easy enough to find them again—to remind myself why it's futile to even think of my mother because what I do remember is the day she said them to me. February 17, 2001. I've only to take my diary from that year off the bookshelf in my study and thumb to that particular date. I haven't done so in a long time although moving back to Australia has made me think of my family more often. The shortening of the distance between us has brought them closer nonetheless.

Sometimes I wonder if, subconsciously, it wasn't one of the reasons I decided to move back. It's easy enough to explain my return by the political developments in the US and the end of my relationship with Michelle, but maybe there was more to it than that. A woman I briefly dated told me once that children will always keep seeking the approval of their parents, whether they know it or not.

I throw the covers off and slip into a robe. I walk straight to my study and stand in front of the shelf with my diaries.

When Jo first moved in I told her I had no intention of hiding them from her and that she was free to pick any of them and read. The look on her face was priceless. But the past is the past. It has happened and it can no longer be changed. As far as I know Jo has yet to avail herself of the diary reading privileges I've bestowed on her.

I let my finger glide over the spines until I reach the year 2001. I page through it until I find the entry of February 17. My book had come out on Valentine's Day, which was some sort of cruel coincidence that I hadn't dared to challenge the publisher on—it was my first book, after all. In the end I managed to see it as sweet irony that it came out on a day like that, because the book made it clear its author despised the tying of romantic love to ever-growing consumerism.

Snatches of what my mother said to me that day are written in blue ink on the paper in front of me.

"Of course I haven't finished it."
   "How can you stoop so low? I don't recognize you."

"You're a slut. That's all you are. You are no daughter of mine because my daughter would never write such utter nonsense."

"Did you really have to go public with this? Was it really so hard to keep this to yourself? Did you think about your father and me for one second when you wrote this? About our reaction? No parent wants their daughter to behave the way you do, let alone write about it."

"You'd do best to not contact us again. You've disappointed and hurt us too much."

I snap the diary shut. I try to do that thing that Amber teaches in yoga. To feel where the emotions reside in my body. But I don't feel anything. Granted, my first book was rather scandalous. It was a memoir mixed with research and the odd salacious detail. It was, in part, written to shock.

But I had to write what I did as I didn't have any other means to get my point across. Not then. It was uncompromising and unflinching. Of course I thought about my parents reading it at some point, but I couldn't let that interfere with writing it. I couldn't let their possible negative reaction influence it.

I did take myself more seriously back then than I do now. While I still stand by my words, I don't necessarily still agree with the style I wrote them in. Incendiary and bold and completely unapologetic. I'm still unapologetic, but I'm no longer as young and naively arrogant.

I put the diary back and walk to the window. Am I still seeking their approval? Or maybe just their respect? But even if I am, is it not too late for all that? Or is it never too late when it comes to family? And if it's not, shouldn't I take the first step toward reconciliation? After all, I'm the one who wrote the book. I'm the one who hurt them by doing so. I know whom I need to talk to about this. My oldest friend, Sheryl.

———

The next evening, when Jo is at rehearsal with Jimmy and Kristin is volunteering at the charity kitchen, I have Sheryl over for dinner. I'm glad I have her all to myself. I'm fond of Kristin, but I've known Sheryl for such a long time and it's good to hang out, just the two of us. It's a bit like going back in time. Besides, Sheryl knows a thing or two about strained relationships with a parent.

"At last I'm invited back here. It's been ages," Sheryl quips when I open the door to her.

Out of respect for her sobriety, I don't drink any alcohol, and we sit on the balcony holding glasses of sparkling water.

"Has Jessica been in touch?" I ask.

Sheryl shakes her head. "She seems to have come to her senses."

"Last I heard, she was very close to snagging you."

"And last I heard it wasn't Jessica's job to book people for *The Caitlin James Show*." This is why I love Sheryl—why I've been friends with her for decades.

"It would be weird to interview you in front of a camera. I like to think I have some professionalism, but I think I know too much about you." I offer a smile.

"Let's not forget all the things I know about you." Sheryl winks at me. She turns in her seat and leans toward me as if wanting to say something confidential. "Kristin and I were talking about you and Jo this weekend. We were wondering what stage your relationship was in now."

I chuckle. "Somehow I can't imagine you and Kristin not having something better to do on a Sunday afternoon than talking about Jo and me."

"When two friends get together, it's going to be a topic of conversation. That's just the way it is."

I shroud myself in silence for a few seconds. Then I find Sheryl's gaze. "We've progressed."

"What does that mean?"

"It means we're no longer in a strictly monogamous relationship."

"Really?" Sheryl juts out her lip.

"Why the sudden interest?" Sheryl and I might be best friends but she has never agreed with my view on relationships.

"Simple curiosity." She draws her lips into a smirk. "Kristin and I were wondering if, perhaps, being with Jo would have changed your ways."

"Why would being with Jo change me?"

"Because relationships always change people."

"I might have changed in some ways, but that part of me will always remain the same."

"But you're doing well despite it?"

I give a slow nod. "Very well, thanks for asking." I can't help but sound a little smug. "We visited her family over the weekend. All very nice and wholesome. They're so wonderful. I didn't even know parents like that existed. You know, with the unconditional love and such."

"I hear you." Sheryl gazes out in front of her. "And I've seen it with Kristin's parents. They're always so disgustingly proud of her. I mean, that they would be proud when she brought me home, sure, I get that." She chuckles. "But let's have some boundaries, please."

"You and I didn't grow up with proud parents."

"Yet here we are." She smiles at me. "Do you need me to tell you that I'm proud of you? Because I am." She gives me a sarcastic thumbs-up.

"I'm proud of you too." I drink from my water and wish it were something stronger. "And I don't mean that sarcastically."

Sheryl fixes her gaze on me. "You seem to be in a funny mood."

I expel a sigh. "Spending time with Jo's family has made me think of my own."

"Aha." Sheryl doesn't say anything else.

"All these years I've blamed them. I pleaded innocence because I was convinced I had a right to my opinions *and* their love. That one should not exclude the other. Although clearly it did."

Sheryl nods. She's never too shy to voice her opinions but she can also be a patient listener.

"I suppose I've come to an age where I'm willing to take my portion of the blame. They grew up in a different era, after all. They've lived in Evanston all their lives, not exactly a hotbed of anarchy and forward thinking."

"All true," Sheryl says. "But still."

"My mother said some things that are hard to forgive, but in hindsight, I can understand why she said them. At the time, I was furious. And sad, but mainly angry. But now that I've been back here for a while and Jo and I are having all these conversations about relationships and I'm no longer safely ensconced in my bubble with like-minded people, I can see things differently."

"You want to forgive them," Sheryl says.

"It's probably the first step if I want to ever talk to them again."

"The question is: can you forgive them?"

"I don't know. I guess it depends on whether their opinion about me has changed or whether they still think I'm the most hardcore slut Australia has ever produced."

"There's only one way to find out."

I nod. "The hard way."

"Something like this is never going to be easy. Even if

there's a happy end in it, the road to it will be… all sorts of difficult things. Embarrassing. Awkward. Tense."

"You forgave your father in the end."

"Yes and I'm all the happier for it now. Holding a grudge takes so much more energy than forgiveness."

"That sounds very zen."

"Too much yoga with Amber." She smiles. "In the end, you reach an age where you need to stop blaming your parents for your own mistakes. Because it's your life and if you keep blaming certain things on other people, you're just shirking responsibility."

"They're just so… judgmental. The character trait I hate most in anyone."

"Age might have done a number on them as well. Growing older will do certain things to you, mainly make you see things in perspective. I can't imagine they never regret the way they treated you. You're their daughter. Their flesh and blood. They raised you and cared for you. Becoming a parent doesn't just suddenly absolve a person from making mistakes—on the contrary."

"But that they never sought contact after all these years. My face is on television every single week."

"Maybe they're afraid. Or ashamed. Or too much time has passed and they've become lethargic about it." Sheryl quirks up her eyebrows. "We can sit here and speculate about it until the cows come home, but we'll never know until you get in touch with them."

"All these years, it has just been so much easier to not think of them. To just push it all away."

"Understandably so." Sheryl offers me a grin. "Why do you think I had a love affair with many, many bottles of wine for so long?"

"I admire you quitting the booze so much."

She tosses her hand. "Admiration is the last thing I need."

"What do you need then?"

"Just for all my friends to get their heads out of their asses and do the right thing." She grins at me.

"Tell it like it is, why don't you?" A smile breaks on my face.

"Am I wrong? I don't think so." She shakes her head. "Micky, Amber, Jo, Martha... you."

"So you think I should make contact."

"I do now, after this chat. If this is how you feel, you should do something. Don't let these feelings fester inside of you."

"You're the expert."

She raises a finger. "Don't you forget it."

I nod and Sheryl allows me a few moments to arrange my thoughts. These days, everyone is easy to find on the Internet. Or maybe my parents still have the same phone number. Or perhaps a phone call is too intrusive off the bat. A written message might be better.

"Can I ask you something that has nothing to do with this?" Sheryl asks, pulling me from my reverie.

"Sure." I look at her with one eyebrow cocked up.

"Who did you sleep with?" There's a sparkle in her eyes.

"Do you really want to talk about that?"

"Is that so surprising?" She slings one leg over the other.

"You never used to."

"I consider Jo a colleague and a friend. She's intelligent and, these days, brimming with confidence and self-respect. If you've somehow managed to convince her that sleeping with other people is a good idea, it's making me very curious about the details."

"Professor Johnson, I never knew you to be such a gossip queen."

"It's not gossip. It's information."

"First of all, I didn't *manage to convince* Jo. That makes it sound as though I needed to talk her into it."

She tilts her head. "Really? You're telling me that the Josephine Greenwood I know didn't need convincing to give non-monogamy a try?"

"Let's not get caught up in an argument about semantics. It's not important. What matters is that Jo and I are more or less on the same page about it. Obviously I'm older than her and I've had these convictions for much longer, but our first experience was, well, let's say rather successful."

"Now you're going to have to tell me more."

I try to suppress a triumphant smile—but I can't help it from forming on my face when I think of our afternoon with Michelle. "We had a threesome with my ex, Michelle, when she was in town last weekend."

Sheryl's eyes grow wide. She shuffles in her seat. "You know, in all honesty, I've never really known how threesomes work exactly. Isn't it all extremely awkward?"

"No, it's not. Or at least it doesn't have to be." I give her a smirk. "Trust me."

"I just can't imagine it. We've been friends for so long and sometimes I think that our conversations about this go a certain way because we've been having them for so long. You defending, me questioning. Maybe I could do with a little more open-mindedness about it."

"Well I never." I sit up a little straighter.

"Don't get any ideas into your head. Kristin and I are not opening up our relationship." She holds up her hands. "I'm just willing to be more amenable to your point of view."

"Oh my, lucky me." I clutch a hand to my chest.

"You know what I mean." Sheryl's lips ease into a smile. "Maybe I'm getting too old to give you a hard time about this."

"My turn to ask you a probing question," I say.

She opens her palms to me. "Be my guest."

"You and Kristin have been together for such a long time. Can you honestly tell me that during all that time your relationship couldn't have benefited from some... outside activity. That there haven't been times when you couldn't fulfill each others' needs and wished you had an arrangement?"

"Christ." Sheryl reaches for her glass of water. "I'm not sure I can answer that question without giving it a long hard think."

"You don't have to answer me now."

"We've had rough times, that's for sure, but whether sleeping with other people would have been the solution... I highly doubt it."

I'm impressed with how Sheryl is willing to consider this in such a levelheaded manner. I'm not trying to get her to come to a conclusion. I'm just teasing her mind into a different direction than it's used to heading into.

"Not a solution, but just another way of approaching everything. Life. Relationships."

She looks me in the eye. "We should have you and Jo over for dinner. I'm curious whether she can be as frank about this as you."

"Me too," I say, meaning it. "Now, shall we eat?"

Chapter Twenty-One

I RING Jessica's bell and a tingle starts up in my belly.

As if she was waiting for us in the hallway, the door swings open a fraction of a second later. I barely recognize my boss. She's dressed in a tightly fitted black velvet dress that splits at the knee.

"Welcome." Jessica throws her arms around us and kisses us on the cheeks. She very much comes across as if she's putting on a show.

She guides us into the living room and to my surprise, someone is waiting for us there.

The woman is dressed in a deep-red fancy jumpsuit. As she rises, she's all long legs, delicious curves and plunging neckline.

She walks toward us with a confident stride, hand outstretched. "Hi, I'm Katherine," she says in a sultry voice. As I shake her hand, she takes another step toward me and kisses me on the cheek as if she's known me forever. She repeats the process with Jo.

As we sit, I try to find Jo's gaze, but she can't seem to keep her eyes off Katherine—or Jessica. I, too, feel as though we've stepped into a scene we were unprepared for. I was expecting dinner—and some heavy flirting—with my boss, a chance for all three of us to get to know each other better. But having Katherine here changes the anticipated atmosphere into one I can't quite put my finger on.

"Katherine is a…" Jessica hesitates.

"Very good friend," Katherine says, her voice still sultry and low. Is that really how she speaks all the time? Or is she putting on a show the way Jessica is doing? There's something forced about the vibe between them. I'm not entirely sure they're friends at all but I will give them the benefit of the doubt.

"Champagne?" Jessica asks holding up a bottle.

Both Jo and I nod eagerly.

While Jessica pours I take the opportunity to study Katherine in a little more detail. She sits poised, her head lightly tilted, one knee over the other, her body slanted toward us.

"What do you do for a living, Katherine?" I ask.

"She's in finance," Jessica says.

What's with the answering each other's questions?

"I manage a hedge fund," Katherine says, making the words hedge and fund sound like I've never heard them before. Like it's actually a sexy profession. "No need to tell me what you two do. I know all about it." She winks at us.

Jessica sits next to Katherine and holds up her glass. We all follow suit.

"Thank you for coming." We clink rims and drink.

I, for one, am very happy to have some alcohol slide down my throat. There's a tension in this room I can't define —and I certainly hadn't expected. I glance at Katherine, then at Jessica. Is it sexual tension between them? Jessica certainly did not tell me about meeting someone, not that she automatically would, but it doesn't gel with what she *has* told me.

"I hope you don't mind that I asked Katherine to join us." Jessica pins her gaze on me. "I thought it could be... interesting." Her lips form into a smile that's not quite as confident as I'm used to from her. I think I'm beginning to understand her relationship with Katherine, who, if I'm not mistaken, makes the money she manages by spending time with other women. Everything about her is just a touch too perfect, too put on.

But I can't help it. My body tingles with the thrill of this new insight. And with the fact that I can still read a room. It took me all of ten minutes to figure out what's going on here. I glance at Jo. Does she know too? There's no way for me to read that off her face. What I can do, however, is steer the conversation in a certain direction.

"How long have you known each other?" I hope my voice sounds innocent.

"Oh, ages." Jessica slaps her hand on Katherine's thigh exaggeratedly. Katherine is probably not even Katherine's real name. It could very well be that before tonight she had no idea who Jo and I were.

"We go way back." Compared to Jessica, Katherine is calm personified. She doesn't bat an eyelash. She's got this routine down to a T. "I've seen Jess through some hard times." She does that tilt of the head again. "How about you ladies?"

"We've been together about a year and a half," Jo says, her tone earnest. I don't think she has an inkling of what's going on here at all.

That Jessica puts me in this position is fine with me. I can deal with it. I might even enjoy it. Jo also deserves to know what's happening right under her nose before this goes any further.

"Jessica, could you *escort* me to the washroom, please?" I ask.

"It's just down the hall. The door next to the stairs," she says.

"I'm so hopeless at finding things." I rise. "Could you show me anyway?"

Jessica looks at me then gets up. "Sure."

We walk into the hallway. I close the door behind us and pull her away from it as far as possible.

"What is this?" I narrow my eyes.

"What do you mean?" Jessica widens her eyes but I'm not falling for her bad acting.

"Are you going to stand here and tell me that woman is not someone you have paid to be here tonight?" I whisper.

"W—what?" she stammers. "Katherine and I are friends."

"I'm sure you are. But usually when you have a friend over for dinner you don't have to pay them at the end of the night."

Her shoulders sag. "How did you know?" she asks.

"By not being born yesterday," I say. "It's written all over her. What were you thinking?"

She looks at me with despair in her eyes. "Maybe I wasn't thinking at all. Or I thought it could be fun." She shrinks in front of my eyes. "I guess I didn't much feel like meeting you and Jo alone. I haven't... exactly been brimming with confidence lately."

"But an escort? Really?"

"That's all Katherine is," Jessica says. "An escort. A companion. She's not a sex worker or anything."

"That's not the point." I sigh and weigh my options.

"It *is* the point. There's no need for you to be this offended, Caitlin. Katherine and I *are* also friends."

"But you do pay her."

158

"I've known her for years."

"You can do with your money what you want. I just would have appreciated a heads-up, that's all."

"Katherine's very discreet if that's what you're worried about."

"And if she isn't, Daddy Porter will just have it all erased from the news, won't he?" I sneer.

"You're free to leave if you don't approve of my choice of companion." Jessica does that thing I've seen her do a few times. She goes from almost-crumbling to the very picture of a ruthless television executive. "I thought you were a fun-loving person. In fact, you made it very clear that you are."

I meet her gaze and hold it. I can't believe how presumptuous she's being, but at the same time I can't help but admire her audacity and her willingness—and ability—to think outside of the box.

"Katherine seems perfectly lovely," I say. "It would be rude to leave now."

A smile breaks on Jessica's face. "She's much more than lovely." She arches up one eyebrow, as if waiting for me to say something else.

"I have to tell Jo."

"Why?" Jessica leans against the wall.

"It's the right thing to do."

"I know you have no reason to trust me, but… why don't you let me take care of Jo?"

I shake my head. "I'm not sure what you're implying, but I don't think so."

"Look, Caitlin, either you stay or you go." She speaks to me as though she's my boss in this house as well. "But if you stay, I need you to have an open mind." She tilts her head. "You know, that open mind you pride yourself on so much." A smile forms on her lips. "I'm not one to organize a regular old boring dinner party. Not if I'm out to impress." She narrows her eyes. "Don't tell me you're not curious." She pushes herself away from the wall and takes a step towards me. "In fact, no need to tell me. I know you are." She's so close I can smell her perfume.

For the life of me, I can't figure out Jessica. One minute she's a vulnerable little thing suffering from the burdens of her rich white privilege, the next she's this vixen going in for the kill.

"We should get back to Jo and Katherine," I say. "They'll be wondering where we are."

Jessica doesn't smile, she just looks at me with a look of gratitude and promise in her eyes—a look I like very much.

———

"Even Nigella is skinny now," Katherine says. "What has the world come to?" She looks at me as though I have somehow had a hand in this, then takes a piece of bread from the basket. "Can you imagine Nigella forgoing scrumptious food like this and only eating"—she shrugs—"I don't know. Lettuce, I guess."

"Not on her show," Jo says. "You can't sensually lick lettuce from a spoon."

"You can hardly criticize a woman for losing weight," Jessica says.

"You can if it's Nigella." Katherine stands by her point. "Watching her show now is not the same experience anymore. It feels like a betrayal of all of us more voluptuous women." She slaps a hand against her hip as if to accentuate her point—and to which camp she belongs.

"I can't believe we're talking about this," Jo says. "In the end, skinny or not, does a person's size really matter?"

"I've read your book." Katherine looks from me to Jo. "I know that's the whole crux of it, but it's all about representation. I mean, we did send Rebel Wilson to Hollywood. That's a feather in our Australian cap. But if even Nigella is skinny now, who's going to teach girls that it's okay to not conform?"

"Representation is important," I say. "And I agree with you wholeheartedly that many more larger women should be in the spotlight, but you can't hold it against someone when they suddenly look different. Then you're applying fat fascism in reverse."

Katherine waggles her finger. "Oh no, no, no. Don't give me your politically correct bullshit. There is no such thing as skinny shaming." She pauses and gives me a once over. "No offense, but what would you know, anyway?"

"I believe I know a thing or two about body fascism." I look her straight in the eye. I can't help a grin from breaking on my face when I do.

"You might know about it, and teach it, but, and do correct me if I'm wrong, you've never experienced it."

"I haven't, but I've experienced plenty of other scorn, judgement and wrath because of my views."

"Ah, but there's a big difference between your views and how you look. A point of view is much more easily defendable than a larger body."

"I won't argue with you on that, Katherine." How can I? When I met Jo, she was so defined by her body and how she believed others saw it, that she barely had any confidence. "You've made your point."

"Before you think I'm someone who always needs to be proven right, I'm working on it." She winks at me. "And that's not all I am."

"I think I know that." I hold her gaze again and allow myself to drown in her glinting dark eyes for an instant.

After Katherine looks away, she focuses her attention on Jo. "I won't put you on the spot and ask you to sing us a tune after dinner, but do let me know when your next gig is. I would love to see you on stage." She cocks her head again. "I'd love to see you represent for us larger ladies."

"I believe Jessica is most up to speed about Jo's concert calendar." I can't help myself.

"I might be." Jessica smiles. "That's what happens when you're trying to get to know someone better."

"Stalking?" Katherine asks.

"Jo's a public figure so checking her concert calendar can hardly be called stalking," Jessica defends herself.

"Christ," Jo says, "I certainly don't see myself as a public figure."

"Yet you are," I say.

"Caitlin might be on TV but she's lucky to have you," Katherine chimes in.

"I am," I concur. I lean toward Jo and touch my head to her shoulder. "You have no idea."

"Then why don't you try giving me one?" Katherine looks straight into my eyes again, her glance bold and brazen. She's challenging me again, but she's also flirting with me.

"Gladly." I tear my gaze away from her and glance briefly at Jo, trying to gauge whether this is embarrassing her. But the turn the evening and conversation have taken has made her relax. She just sits there grinning.

"I'm waiting," she says.

"I was going to say that you're one of the most modest people I know, but maybe I should rephrase that." I blow her a kiss. "Jo is kind and has a heart the size of this country," I say.

"And an ass," Jo butts in and follows up with a loud cackle.

Katherine holds up her hand and Jo high fives it.

"I was being serious and heartfelt here," I say.

"Who needs that when you have laughs?" Katherine says.

Jo leans in and kisses me on the cheek. "You don't need to tell me out loud. I know how you feel about me."

"Now that we've gotten that out of the way," Jessica says. "How about we retire to the other room?"

My ears perk up. Which other room is she referring to? I've known her to blurt out a thing or two, but surely she can't be referring to the bedroom—yet.

———

The *other room* turns out to be a library, small in size, but infinitely cozy with its walls lined with built-in book cases, all filled to the brim. In the middle of the room there are four leather club chairs. A cabinet on the side holds an impressive collection of liquor.

Jessica goes to a shelf on the right of the door and picks out a book. It's the one Jo and I wrote together. She holds it up. "Don't worry, I won't ask you to sign it."

"Just take a selfie with it," Katherine says. "Selfies are the new autographs." She comes to stand between me and Jo. "As a matter of fact, Jess. Can you take a picture of me with these two beauties." She moves behind us and slings an arm around each of us, pressing her bosom into our backs—well, at least into mine. I can't see Jo's.

"I don't have my phone on me," Jessica says.

"Here." Jo fishes her phone out of the back pocket of her jeans. "Use mine. I'll send you the picture later."

I still remember how utterly shocked she was the first time someone asked her to take a selfie with her. As though a dubious privilege like that could never be bestowed upon the likes of Josephine Greenwood.

As Jo steps forward to hand Jessica the phone and take the book from her to pose with, Katherine's body remains firmly glued to mine. We might not be in the bedroom, but I'm getting a fair idea of where Katherine would like this evening to progress. I know Jessica was spinning me a tale when she said Katherine was not *that kind* of escort—simply because I don't believe they exist. I certainly don't believe Jessica is as naive as to think they do—nor did she expect me to believe her lie.

Jo joins me again in Katherine's embrace and pushes her hip against mine. I take her free hand and she holds up our book in the other. Katherine, who's even taller than Jo, lowers herself and plants her head on my shoulder, the arm that's wrapped around me squeezing me a little tighter.

Jessica snaps the picture and no matter the course this evening might take later, we'll always have the memory of this moment. When everything vibrated with possibility, the innuendo grew louder, and delicious tension crackled in the air. Sometimes I think it's moments like these I'm most addicted to. That they represent so perfectly what freedom means to me, the freedom I crave so much. That this kind of tension will always be part of my life, of our lives. When we feel the thrill of being alive rumble through us. Whether we take the opportunity or not, the fact that it was there is half the joy.

After the picture taking has ended—a few more have followed in various configurations of people—we sit down while Jessica pours us our tipple of choice.

"The night is young," she says after she has sat as well. "The sun has set." Her eyes glitter in the light of the lamp next to her. "Let's see what happens next."

It's my guess that even though what will happen next is unpredictable by definition, she knows very much where she wants it to go. That makes two of them. I check my own desire. I certainly didn't come here with this in mind, but I wouldn't mind staying a good long while still. But this is easy for me—second nature by now. My senses are honed to scope out opportunities like these. I really need to check with Jo. She will make the final decision.

I glance at Jo, who's sitting in the chair closest to me. She looks into my eyes. She puts her hand on my knee, squeezes, and lets it drift upward a little, for me to feel and for Jessica and Katherine to witness.

"Yes. Let's see," Jo says as her hand scoots up a little higher still. Her gaze lingers on mine and she narrows her eyes. I guess that means yes. I give her a smile. Her glance turns away from me and I find myself waiting with bated breath for what she will do next.

A silence falls as we sip from our drinks. Katherine is the first to put her drink down. I follow her every motion with my eyes. Jo rids herself of her glass next. To my surprise, she's the one who gets up first. Katherine quickly follows. She holds out her hand to me which spurs Jo on to reach out a hand to Jessica.

A frisson of excitement runs through me as I take Katherine's hand. Her grip is strong and promising. She pulls me out of my chair. There's something fluid about her movements, as though she has shifted into a higher gear. Into that effortless space where she's used to operating. Where she knows exactly what to do to make others feel at ease.

Katherine leads us out of the room and up the stairs.

Chapter Twenty-Two

WITHOUT LETTING GO of my hand, Katherine flicks a switch and a bank of dim lights blinks on behind the bed. She must have surely been here before. I look at Jessica's fingers which are intertwined with Jo's.

Katherine gives my hand a quick yank and pulls me close to her. She brings her mouth to my ear, and whispers, "I'm going to make you come so hard." She plants a delicate kiss just below my ear and I believe every word she says.

When I look into her eyes there's no doubt in my mind that she will because it's her very reason for being here tonight. What I'm not sure of is what they have discussed beforehand. Whether it's a consequence of how the night has gone that Katherine is the one holding my hand and Jessica's is now snaking up Jo's arm.

I put my free hand on the back of Katherine's head, my fingers twirling through her hair. She needs to lean down a little for me to be able to kiss her on the lips without stretching my neck. As her lips touch mine, I feel a hand in the small of my back. Jo was standing next to me so I assume it's hers—she's telling me, once again, that she wants this too.

Katherine's tongue probes into my mouth and I lose myself in the kiss. Before I close my eyes I catch a glimpse of both Jessica and Jo watching me—us. It makes me welcome Katherine's tongue into my mouth with even more fervor. When I open my eyes next, Jo's lips are glued to Jessica's. I watch them kiss and desire starts to flare inside my belly. The image I had in my head about Jo fucking Jessica leaps to the front of my brain. I'm not sure what will happen tonight, but the thought of it is enough to propel me in their direction.

When they break from their kiss I lean in to find Jo's mouth. She feels and tastes the same as always, yet there's a subtle hint of difference. It's that hint I'm after. It's what fuels me. What makes me come alive inside. Katherine's earlier promise reverberates inside of me, grows stronger, connects with my clit. After tonight, I may very well never see Katherine again, but before that, we will make some memories neither one of us will ever forget.

When my lips leave Jo's I stare into her eyes for a second. She gives me that smile again and I don't think I've ever felt so connected to her. I sometimes feel this way when she looks at me from the stage and deliberately searches for my gaze in the crowd while she belts out an emotional melody, but this is different. Because I'm not in the audience now. I'm here, with her. And it means everything to me.

Katherine tugs at my hand and before I can even turn my head, Jo has leaned in to kiss Jessica again.

Katherine pulls me toward her, tilts her head and says in that gravelly voice of hers—which is having more effect now than at the beginning of the evening when we were just introduced—"I've been wanting to take this off you for a while now." She takes one of my blouse buttons between her fingers and undoes it. Her eyes follow the movement of her fingers and it's as though I can feel her glance on my skin. She slowly unfastens a few more buttons until I stand there with my blouse gaping open, only the flimsy fabric of my bra protecting my bare skin from her gaze.

When I glance to my side, I see it's Jo who has taken the initiative. She's zipping Jessica out of her black dress. A tingle runs through me as I see Jessica's milky white skin contrasting with the black lingerie that's being uncovered.

What on earth will we say to each other when we run into each other at the office on Monday?

She looks at me from under her lashes and pulls her lips into a sly grin, as if to say, *look where I got you.* Or maybe that's just how I'm interpreting it in this split second because the next moment she flashes me a wide smile and there's not a hint of smugness to be seen on her face.

Katherine has brushed down the shoulder straps of her top. I reach for them and pull the top down her torso. Her bra is red like her entire outfit—even her lipstick perfectly blends into the color scheme she has chosen for tonight's game of seduction. Although I can't really remember who seduced whom. Did it happen when I spoke to Jessica in the hallway? When Jo and I exchanged glances earlier? When Katherine argued so deliciously with me over dinner? Or is it all these moments that have brought us together here, four kindred souls, ready to take this journey to a higher level of pleasure.

Katherine steps out of her jump suit and stands in front of me in her underwear. Her skin looks so smooth my hand is drawn to it automatically. It looks made to be caressed. She pushes my blouse from my shoulders and I hear rustling beside me. Jo's jeans are next to join the pile of clothes on the floor. Then I'm the only one wearing more than lingerie and it's Jo who comes for the button of my jeans and flicks it open—as though she's opening the lock of the last door standing between us and what's next.

I kick off my shoes and wriggle out of my pants. Here we

are then. We press together in a bundle of flesh and it's as if I can smell the arousal in the air.

I take another deep breath and the next thing I know a pair of lips is planted on mine. I think they're Katherine's but I don't look. I close my eyes because I just want to feel. A hand snaps open the catch of my bra. A finger skates along the waistband of my panties. A pair of lips is skimming my neck as well.

When I maneuver my bra off, it's Jessica's hands which cup my breasts first. I turn my head to Jo and let my tongue slip inside her mouth. I find Katherine's bra fastening and unhook it. Soon we're standing in our sexy circle with just our panties on. Jessica steps away from us and guides us closer to the bed. I glimpse at it. It's king-sized, but will it have enough room for all four of us to maneuver around on comfortably? I'm sure we'll find a way. Logistics are of minor importance at this stage. And there's Jo's mouth again, hungry on mine. When I look into her eyes, I don't see reason or sanity. I only encounter lust. They brim with it, with this desire I feel course inside of me as well. Everything I feel I see reflected in her glance.

Jessica crawls onto the bed and takes Jo with her, as if their hands have become welded together. Jo lies next to her and, instinctively, I drape myself next to her. Katherine glues herself to me on the other side.

First, I watch how Jo kisses Jessica deeply again, her hand cupping Jessica's jaw. I feel Katherine's finger on my jaw and she slowly turns my face toward her. There's unexpected kindness in her glance, as if she understands my need to check in on Jo. Ever so slowly, she lowers her lips to mine and kisses me much more tenderly than before. Her hand wanders down to my breast and she lightly circles my nipple with the tip of her finger. It sparks a fire underneath the entire expanse of my skin. The fire brightens when she repeats the process with my other nipple. All the while, her lips are on mine, her breath mixes with mine, her body is glued to mine. The other side of my body is sunk against Jo's. I can feel her heat radiate into me. She rubs against me as though Jessica is already doing something very thrilling to her, but I can't see, because I'm kissing Katherine, whose hand is all over me. The circling of her fingertips is turning into pinching and I moan a little into her mouth every time she squeezes my nipples between her fingers.

As soon as Katherine's lips leave mine to kiss their way down my neck, I turn my head to catch a glimpse of Jo. Her head is turned away from me and I only see the slant of her neck as she kisses Jessica.

My attention is pulled back to my own body when Katherine wraps her lips around my stiff nipple. My nipple has been licked a thousand times before, yet because of the situation I find myself in, this particular lick translates into a fierce arrow of lust shooting through my entire body.

"Ooh," I groan. I find her gaze. "I want you," I say on a sigh. Good god, I want her so much. I want those long fingers of hers inside of me. I want her tongue to linger on my nipples forever. I want Jo and Jessica to watch me as I come. I want so many things and perhaps not all of them will come true but a certain number will and that thought catapults me onto an even higher plain of arousal.

What we are doing is not *making love*. We are indulging ourselves, giving in to our purest instincts—the ones most people pretend they don't have.

Katherine takes one of my nipples between her teeth and pulls at it while she looks at me from under her lashes. She plays this game well. I wonder how much her hourly rates are. Then she clamps down and I don't wonder anything anymore.

I flick my head back into the pillow and undergo her deli-

171

cious ministrations with my eyes squeezed shut. When I open them again she smiles at me and crawls toward me.

"What do you like?" she asks. "Tell me what to do and I'll do it." Her voice has grown sultrier still.

With anyone else I would give instructions, but not with this woman. I intend to take full advantage of her experience. "Surprise me," I say.

"Okay." Her lips ease into a smile. "But let me know when you want me to stop." She adds in a quick wink and I do wonder for an instant if I haven't overplayed my hand. I just gave a professional at this carte blanche. I'm much more aroused than worried, though, and I give her a wide smile back while I nod my agreement.

She kisses me again and I can feel more intent behind this kiss, like it's the start of the next stage.

"I'll be right back," she says and flashes me a wicked grin. She hops off the bed and disappears into a door to the left.

I take the opportunity to get a good look at what Jo's doing. She's lying half on top of Jessica—my girl has clearly taken the lead. It's at the same time expected and a surprise. Jo has definitely become the one to lead where things are going when it's just us in the bedroom. Perhaps I hadn't expected her to do so this quickly when others are involved. Her true nature can't hide.

I hear some noises in the room next door. My anticipation grows as I watch how Jo's hand maneuvers between Jessica's legs. She traces her fingers along the panel of her panties very lightly and it's clearly driving Jessica mad.

I glue my body to her back for an instant and she pushes her behind into me. I kiss her neck, inhale her scent, let my hand wander to her breast. I'm so ready for it all and halfway toward insinuating myself into Jo and Jessica's foreplay that I don't even hear Katherine come out of the other room.

In her hand, she holds a flogger. On her hips, she has fastened a harness that holds a dildo a shade darker than the color of her skin. She stares at me, one eyebrow cocked up, with a hint of question in her eyes.

I swallow hard. I'm not sure it's only arousal that I feel. I have been on the receiving end of a spanking quite a few times, though not recently. But, as if my body is overruling any objection my mind could have, I gently nod my head, not breaking eye contact with Katherine.

Jo and Jessica look up as well. Jo looks at me with her bottom lip sucked between her teeth. I can so easily tell what she's thinking.

She doesn't need me to give her permission. She knows what I want as well. She does need Jessica's permission, of course. And her own toy to play with.

Katherine stands there grinning, enjoying her big entrance into the room. Jo shifts beside me and she whispers something in Jessica's ear.

Jessica's eyes sparkle. "Katherine has brought a box of toys," she says. "Check the bathroom."

Jo scampers off the bed and disappears into the bathroom. I hope she finds what she's looking for.

I glance back at Katherine.

"Caitlin," she says, not a hint of sultriness left in her voice. "Come here."

It's not the sort of tone that would support insubordination—and that flogger isn't helping either. My panties cling wetly between my legs as I make my way off the bed and stand in front of Katherine. I can't take my eyes off the dildo. It's a good size larger than the one Jo and I use at home. But everything about tonight is larger and more intense.

"Face the bed," Katherine commands. "Spread your legs and bend over."

Before I do, I see Jo slip back into the room. She's in her element as she strides to the bed, fully strapped on, the dildo standing tall between her thighs. The sight of her makes me break into a thrilling sweat.

I know Jo. I know what she's going to make Jessica do. And I'll have a first row seat to the spectacle. And a flogger torturing my behind while I do it. The mere prospect is almost too much.

Katherine doesn't seem to move a muscle behind me. Maybe she's waiting as well. Maybe she's an expert at reading a room like this one.

Jo settles onto the bed with her back against the head rest. She takes the dildo in her hand, the tip sticking out.

"I need some lubrication," she says, then she looks me in the eye. This time, I have no idea what I see in her gaze. She has crossed over into a different realm of reality as well. We're in this together, fully, no holds barred.

Jessica snaps to and, on hands and knees, crawls to the dildo.

Jo caresses the back of her head. "Suck it," she says in a very low voice.

Jessica licks her lips and just as she lowers her mouth onto the dildo, a crash of pain thunders through me. My breath stalls in my lungs. My muscles tighten.

"Fuck," I cry out.

I barely have time to brace myself before the next blow from the flogger hits me. The pain shudders through me in a different way now. Less acute, more pleasant.

Jessica is swirling her tongue around the dildo. I remember my first time in her current position vividly and conclude there's no way this is her first time doing this. I'm also beginning to think this might, after all, be the beginning of a beautiful friendship.

I look into Jo's eyes as I brace myself again. Katherine is taking her time. I try to read in Jo's eyes what Katherine might be up to next, but she doesn't give anything away. She has her hand on the back of Jessica's head. I feel a hand on my behind, caressing my tender buttocks the way Jo's hand is caressing Jessica's scalp.

Then Katherine pulls down my panties. Not all the way, just enough to expose my ass cheeks. My skins stings as it meets the air. Katherine cups my cheeks in her hands for a few seconds, then her hands retreat.

Jessica is taking the dildo deep into her mouth and the sight connects directly to my clit. I'm so excited by what I see I fail to brace myself again and the next hit, the first one on my bare skin, causes a loud yelp to leap from my throat.

I drop my head to catch my breath. Is Katherine testing me? Or is she just warming up? I have no idea. Which is the biggest turn on of all. No. What turns me on the most is having Jo watch me go through this. We're here together. We're making a memory that will feed us for long years to come. It's bonding of a different kind, but bonding nonetheless.

The flogger touches down again, this time on only one cheek. It rains blows in quick succession. They're not as hard and unmerciful as the previous ones, but they're plenty and they leave me gasping for air, my arms bending at the elbows, my entire body looking for support.

Katherine focuses the flogger action on my other buttock and all thoughts flee my head. I'm just pain and arousal blending into a cocktail of utter delight in my flesh. I'm just a body at the mercy of another body. I can't even look at Jessica sucking Jo's dildo into her mouth anymore. All my energy is being spent on withstanding the blows of the flogger because, for the life of me, I don't want to give in.

The flogging action ends and I hear a thud. The flogger is on the floor next to the bed. I feel the air shift behind me and Katherine pulls my panties all the way down. She pushes my legs apart and I feel her dildo between my legs. She rubs it back and forth against my pussy lips, occasionally brushing against my clit.

She leans her torso over my back and finds my ear with her mouth. "I think you're ready," she says.

She replaces the dildo with a few fingers and I feel them skate delicately along my wet lips.

"Look at Jo and Jess," she whispers in my ear next. "Look at them while I fuck you."

I snap my head up. Jessica has let Jo's dildo drop from her mouth and it glistens with her saliva.

Katherine's fingers slip inside me.

"You're so wet," she croons into my ear. "I'm going to fuck you so hard."

Again, I believe her. Her words make my head spin as, on the bed, Jo maneuvers Jessica onto her back and relieves her of her panties. Jo bows down between Jessica's legs. Meanwhile, Katherine keeps fingering me and my legs go a bit wobbly with increased lust. How much more of this can I possibly stand? But these are only Katherine's fingers inside of me. I want so much more.

In front of me, Jessica is panting heavily. I can't see much because her thigh is in the way, but I can very easily conclude that Jo is licking her clit.

Jo pushes herself up and I get a good glance at Jessica's glistening pussy. Jo looks behind her and finds my gaze. We look at each other for an instant. Then she taps Jessica on the hip, indicating she should move a little.

Jo wants me to have a better view. She wants me to see

how her dildo slides inside of Jessica's pussy. I gasp for air. Katherine's fingers slip out of me. The next moment, I feel the head of the dildo press against the entrance of my pussy. It's wide and hard and I can't wait for it to slide inside me.

On the bed, Jo has positioned herself so her toy is grazing the rim of Jessica's pussy. I can't see everything, there are too many body parts in the way, but the glimpse I get is enough.

I see on Jessica's face that Jo has already entered her. It distorts into an expression of disbelief, her mouth opening into an astounded O, her eyes growing wide.

At the same time, Katherine pushes into me and I imagine my own face mimicking Jessica's expression.

"Oh god," I exclaim.

Katherine eases in gently first, but once she's in she thrusts deep and I need all the power I have left in my arms to brace myself. Then it all starts blending together. The dildo, so big and so much of it, so unabashedly burrowing inside of me, thrusting me into yet another realm of blissful sensations. The one where I lose myself completely because of this feast being bestowed upon my senses. The image in front of me. Jo thrusting the way Katherine is thrusting into me. The utter delight on Jessica's face. My own arousal growing by the second. I close my eyes and think this is my life, it's the life I want to lead, and now I've found someone who wants to lead it with me.

When Katherine slings an arm around my hip and touches a finger to my clit I'm already so far gone, so transported onto this cloud of pleasure and close to orgasm, that it takes only a few flicks before I come the way she said I would. *Hard.*

She slips out of me and I crash onto my knees, my upper body collapsing onto the bed. I hear Jessica moan close to my ear, but I'm too spent to look. I bask in my own private bliss for a minute and when I look up again, Katherine sits on the edge of the bed, next to my head, the wet dildo still standing proud between her legs.

She looks behind her and I see her exchange a glance with Jo. They're up to something but my brain is too muddled from the orgasm to think much of it.

Jessica lies loosely limbed on the bed, a big smile on her lips.

Jo crawls over to me and kisses me on the lips. I embrace her body as if I've been separated from her for days.

She kisses my cheek, my forehead, the top of my head, my earlobe, then she says, "Suck my dildo dry." I look at her in disbelief while something chases up my spine. A thrill. A marvel at how she speaks to me in front of others in the confines of this bedroom.

Katherine twists her torso so she can look at Jessica. She makes a come-hither movement with two fingers. "Come here, Jess," she says.

Jessica rolls off the bed and crawls to the end on all fours. Katherine points the dildo in her direction. "Lick," is all she says.

I'm envious of the energy Jessica attacks the dildo with, but seeing her do it makes me want to follow her example.

I spread my mouth wide and lower my lips over the dildo, licking off Jessica's juices. Jo winds her fingers through my hair and, when I close my eyes, this could so very easily be a scene from our own bedroom, but it's not, because I'm licking a dildo she has just put into another woman's pussy and, right next to me, Jessica is doing the same.

Once I feel I've followed Jo's orders sufficiently, I let the dildo drop from my mouth and start tugging at the straps. I want it off her, because I want her.

"Take it off," I say, my breath snagging in my throat.

Jo gets up and loosens the straps so she can lower the

entire contraption off her. I'm no longer focused on whatever Jessica and Katherine are doing. I only have eyes for Jo. She sits back down and puts her feet on my shoulders. I kiss her inner thighs and think about how far we've come. Is this the same woman who couldn't reach climax in front of me—the woman she had fallen in love with—because of too much noise in her head? She's about to come in front of an audience of three.

I let my lips touch down on her clit and she shudders in response. This night is far from over, that much I know, but even if it ended here, with my tongue flicking over Jo's clit, I would be truly content.

Chapter Twenty-Three

I WAKE up in a bed that's not my own. Jo breathes heavily beside me. She's sprawled on her back, her arms spread wide, the sheets thrown off her. I blink and look around. Light is coming through the curtains. I soon realize we're in Jessica's guest room. The flesh of my behind stings.

I lie on my side as I watch Jo. Before I get up and face Jessica—and Katherine if she's still here—I want to talk to Jo, but she doesn't look like she'll be waking up any time soon. She gets little enough sleep as it is so I slip out of bed gently and try to remember where the bathroom is.

As I wash my hands I hear a faint knock on the door.

"Hey." I recognize Katherine's voice.

I open the door to a slit. I'm not dressed, which, after last night shouldn't faze me, yet it does.

"Morning," she says, a coy smile on her face. It's always a little weird the morning after to come face-to-face with a woman who has fucked you so thoroughly the night before. "I heard noise so I thought I'd knock. I'm taking off."

"Oh." I shake the last remnants of sleep off me.

"I had a wonderful time." She tilts her head the way she

did last night before leaning in to kiss me. "Give my love to Jo."

I nod. "Can I ask you something?"

"After what we did last night, you can ask me anything." She smiles.

"Are you and Jessica really friends?" What I would really like to know is whether they slept in the same bed. And how much it costs to have someone like Katherine over for dinner and all-night play time.

The smile remains on her face while she regards me intently. "We are," she says. "Although I'm not exactly a hedge fund manager."

"Then why did you say you were?"

She leans against the wall with her shoulder. "Am I on *The Caitlin James Show* all of a sudden? Being interviewed by a naked Miss James no less?" She pushes the door open a little wider. "I've learned the hard way to not announce my real profession to people I've just met. It has a tendency to put people off." She gives me a once-over, a smile reappearing on her face briefly. "Not you, though."

"I don't want to give you a cross-examination this early on a Sunday morning. I'm just curious."

She steps a little closer. She smells of flowery soap. "If you need any more information, give me a call. Jess has my number. I always answer."

"I bet you do."

She leans in and whispers in my ear. "I enjoyed fucking you very," she pauses, "very much." She kisses me on the cheek and puts some distance between us. She winks at me one last time, turns around and disappears down the hallway.

When I get back to the room, Jo's awake.

"Were you talking to someone?" she asks.

"Katherine. She came to say goodbye."

"Christ." She sits up and holds out her hand. I take it and let her pull me back into bed. "Who was that woman? She was so… forward. Or no, *you* are forward, she's… beyond forward."

"You haven't figured it out yet?" I press myself against her warm skin.

"Figured out what?"

"She's a professional escort. Jessica hired her for the night. They both claim to be friends as well, which I do think is true."

Jo's muscles stiffen. "What the hell," she says. "No way. I can't believe that." She sits up higher brusquely. "You knew? Why didn't you tell me?"

"I wanted to, but I didn't really get a chance. Besides, I thought you'd figured it out as well." I caress her arm. "Babe, does it really make a difference? Would you have called the whole thing off if you'd known?"

"It makes a hell of a lot of difference." Her voice shoots up.

"Why? We had fun. In fact, we had an amazing night. Don't you think?"

"I need to process this information." She pushes her palms against her temples. "I'm not sure I'm okay with this at all." She drops her hands. "And you should have told me. If you knew, I had a right to know as well. I feel so… duped."

"Clearly Katherine is someone who has chosen what she does very deliberately. She's smart, articulate, and probably very rich if she has the likes of Jessica Porter hiring her."

"It's the principle that counts."

"You didn't pay her. To you she was a woman you had a good time with."

"Indeed, she *was*. I don't know what to think now." She huffs out some air. "That's prostitution, Caitlin. No matter

183

how much money she makes or whether she does it out of nothing but free will. Money still gets exchanged for sex. That's something I don't want to be associated with."

"Really?" I do my best not to go into teacher mode. "You can try to pretend things like that don't exist as much as you want, but that won't make them nonexistent. You'll have your PhD in Gender Studies next year. You know better than to victimize women like Katherine."

"I'm not victimizing her."

"Are you victimizing yourself then?"

She rolls her eyes at me. "Everyone else in that bed last night had information I didn't have. How would it make you feel if it was you in that position?" Her eyes are narrow slits. "And what on earth was Jessica thinking? Is that woman completely crazy?" She shakes her head, then lets it fall into her hands. "And what about those dildos she brought?" She looks up again. "Does she buy brand new ones before every job?"

I can't help but chuckle.

"It's not a laughing matter." Jo throws a pillow at me.

I put my hands on the pillow. "You're right, it's not." I take a breath. "I understand you're upset. I should have told you as soon as I found out."

"Your punishment is that you need to ask Jessica what the sex toy protocol is for sex workers."

"According to Jessica, Katherine isn't a sex worker."

"According to me, Jessica suffers from a delusion or two," Jo says.

"That may be, but it didn't stop you from having a whole lot of fun with her last night."

A smile forms on Jo's lips. "Christ, what a night."

"One for the books, darling." I caress her back. "Your old lady is a little sore in some places. What do you say we go home and watch Netflix for the rest of the day?"

"I can't. I have to at least start the next chapter of my thesis. I'll never get it done if I keep stalling."

I take her hand in mine. "You will finish your thesis on time. You always finish everything on time."

"It's easy for you to say. You only have one job."

I bring her hand to my lips and plant a kiss on her palm. "Let's take a shower and go home." My lips touch down again but I keep eye contact with her. "We'll talk through your next chapter together, and then we'll talk about last night a little more, and in between, we'll rest. Okay?" I don't get up, but sit there with her a little longer, holding her close, until she nods her head.

———

At home, I draw Jo a bath and don't leave her side while she soaks her weary body in it. Afterwards, she falls asleep with her head in my lap. She has been mostly silent since we left Jessica's. I know she'll start talking when she's ready. She hasn't mentioned her thesis again and I hope she gives herself the day off—she usually does on Sunday.

Images of last night keep flashing back into my mind, even though I'm trying to watch a movie. My initial reaction to finding out about Katherine was shock as well. Jo is allowed her indignation. But there's one thing she can't deny despite it: we all enjoyed the experience.

When she wakes up she looks at me with those big, kind eyes of hers. She blinks a couple of times.

"God, I needed that," she says.

My behind has been stinging excruciatingly for the past fifteen minutes, but I decide to bear it a little while longer.

She rolls her head from side to side. "How long have I been out?"

"Not too long." I run a finger across her cheek. "There's still plenty of time left in the day."

"I really, really don't feel like getting up," she says on a sigh.

"Then don't. It's Sunday." I bow and plant a kiss on her forehead. "We all need to rest. Even the young ones like you."

"A night like that makes me feel very different than the day after a gig."

"How do you feel?" I smile down at her.

"Tired but strangely elated."

"A couple of orgasms will do that to you."

She chuckles. "I know I had a bit of a fit about it this morning, but working on my thesis is the last thing I feel like doing. I feel quite zen actually." She fixes her gaze on me. "Whereas the day after a gig I can feel so extremely depleted. Because of all the eyes I've had on me all night and how deep I have to dig to meet those eyes. It requires a different kind of energy."

"You had three pairs of eyes on you last night."

She grins. "But those eyes belonged to people who were busy elsewhere most of the time."

"You know what I mean."

"I think I'm beginning to understand why you're so big on non-monogamy." A hint of smile on her face. "I also think it has less to do with the principle behind it than with how it makes you feel."

"One will always be linked to the other," I say.

"Maybe. Or maybe you were curious about the theory behind it, but practicing is what really pulled you over the edge."

"Is that what's happening to you?"

Jo takes a moment before replying. "To answer your earlier question: I can't be sure, but I do think I would not have run off, even if I had known who Katherine was. You *should* really have told me, but now that I've had some time to let it all sink in, I can look at the night with a bit more perspective. And I have to say that I wouldn't mind doing that again some time." She squints up at me. "If you promise to share all the information you have, no matter how obvious it seems to you. As we saw last night, I'm not as perceptive to certain things."

"I promise," I say. "And a repeat performance can be arranged."

"Can it?" She lifts her hand and starts playing with a strand of hair that has fallen to my shoulder. "How? I can't shake the impression that last night we just got lucky. We had no idea this was going to happen. Jessica is your boss. What will you say to her tomorrow at the office?" She chuckles.

"Jessica is… I don't know. She keeps surprising me."

"She's a strange one. I don't want to judge, but I don't know many people who are 'friends' with a high-end sex worker."

"I think she gets out of it what she needs."

"Isn't that weird? How can you even pay for friendship?"

"She's an enigma and I have no idea what I will say to her tomorrow." I narrow my eyes. "My question to you, however, is did you enjoy fucking her?"

Jo draws her lips into a smirk as she nods. "And I enjoyed you watching me do it." Her hand travels down my shoulder to my wrist, which she circles with her fingers. "In fact, for now, as I explore this side of me, I would very much like it if we could explore more together."

"As opposed to exploring on our own, you mean?"

She nods.

"Deal." I fold my arm and bring her hand close to my lips. "Let me know when you have the next Saturday evening off."

She shakes her head. "The next Saturday I have off, I'm spending with you and you alone."

"Music to my ears." I kiss her hand.

"As long as you don't start singing." She pushes herself up. "I love you very much, but that won't be music to my ears at all." Her attempt to get up fails and she falls back into my lap. "My body is exhausted."

"The way you were fucking Jessica, that does not surprise me one bit." I wink at her. I want to bring up another subject, but I don't really know how. Maybe because it doesn't come up very often.

Jo lies there with a grin on her face. Maybe she's reliving last night's memories the way I was doing before. We don't speak for a while, both of us lost in thought.

"What's on your mind?" she asks. "I know that look."

"Since we visited your family, I've been thinking about my parents more and more." I purse my lips. "I've been thinking about contacting them."

Jo nods but remains silent.

"I've never spent a lot of time with the parents of a partner before, but spending time with yours has really made me think. What if all they're waiting for is some sort of sign from me? What if things can be repaired between us? What if this estrangement is completely unnecessary?"

"These are good questions, babe," Jo says. "And I believe in the power of forgiveness, but…" She does push herself up this time. She swivels around and sits facing me with her legs drawn underneath her. "You shouldn't get your hopes up too high in case nothing has changed."

"It's been so long and, well, I came from them. They made me. How can it possibly be that they don't have a progressive bone in their body? Or at least some tolerance…"

"You're absolutely right. You can't know any of that unless you get in touch with them."

"I've drafted an email. Will you read it?"

"Of course." She holds out her hand for my phone.

"Not now, though. Tomorrow. Or the day after." Seeing as it's up for grabs, I take her hand in mine.

"My parents have asked about yours. I didn't tell you because I didn't want to upset you for no reason, but they're curious. They're not exactly well-trained in meeting my previous girlfriends' parents, but I guess it's a logical question to ask."

"What did you say?"

"That your relationship with them is complicated and you don't see them."

"That pretty much sums it up." I smile at her sheepishly.

"All of that being said…" Jo finds my gaze while she pauses. "I think *you* would make a fantastic parent."

I scoff. "Yeah right."

"I'm serious." Her gaze remains on mine. "You have so many things figured out that most people struggle with their entire life. Look at me. I've been with you for less than two years and I've changed so much—all for the better."

"But you're not my child. You're my partner. And I'd like to think I've changed a little myself because of being with you."

"Oh, you have. I think. You still like to hog the limelight, but that's okay." She grins at me. "I never thought you needed much changing, by the way. But I get the impression that our relationship is very different than your last one. It's much more intense. We live together. I'm experiencing so many firsts. You're giving me all the time I need to process them. Sometimes, you're even patient with me when I have too much on and I don't have enough time for you."

Warmth blooms in my chest. "Sometimes."

"For the record, I know I'm stretching myself too thin. Will you trust me when I tell you that I'm considering making a change, I just need some more time to figure it out."

I nod. "I do trust you." I scoot a little nearer to her. "It may sound strange after last night, but I don't think I've ever felt so close to anyone. Or let anyone come as close as you have. You've changed that about me." I lean in to kiss her. When I shut my eyes her words from earlier pop back into my head. "What did you actually want to say when you claimed I would make a good mother?" I try to hide the sudden panic in my voice.

She cups my cheeks in her palms. "It was just an observation."

I tilt my head. "Not a suggestion?" I put a hand on her chest. "There's no clock ticking away urgently in there?"

"Even if there was, I'm a bit too busy to notice."

"My scarce experience with wannabe-mothers is that they hear that particular tick-tock very clearly above everything else that's going on in their lives."

"There you have it then." She kisses me on the lips. "Mine isn't ticking nearly loudly enough."

Chapter Twenty-Four

WHEN I WAIT for the elevator at ANBC the next day, I can't help looking around to see if Jessica is arriving at the same time as me. As it turns out, I have the elevator all to myself and I make it to my office without a sign of her.

In hindsight, it wasn't the best idea to spend the night with my boss, even if there were two other parties involved. The memory of a night like that should not have any effect in the workplace, which is exactly why the advice is *always* not to mix business with pleasure. But it happened and here I am—just as it has happened to millions of other people before me and will happen to many in years to come. Good advice has never stopped anyone from doing the exact opposite.

But my mind is preoccupied during the team meeting and I fail to answer promptly a few questions—I find myself gazing into the distance trying to figure out what to say to Jessica when I do inevitably bump into her. Maybe I should just get it over with and give her a call. Clear the air. Get that first awkward office encounter out of the way so we can move on.

In the afternoon I call her mobile, but don't get a reply. I try her office.

"Jessica Porter's office," a female voice which doesn't belong to Jessica, says.

"Caitlin James for Miss Porter," I say.

"Miss Porter is not available," the woman says. "She has taken a leave of absence. I've yet to send the memo."

"A leave of absence?" I ask. "For how long?" She has only just started this job, I want to say. And what's with the leave of absence starting the Monday after Jo and I spent Saturday night with her?

"That's undetermined."

"I tried her mobile, but she's not picking up. Is she okay?"

"I don't have any further information, Miss James," the woman says. "I suggest you try her mobile again later."

We ring off and I stare at my phone for a while. What on earth is going on? I need to speak to Jo but on Monday afternoons she teaches so I won't be able to reach her either. For a split second, I wish I had Katherine's number—which, she assured me, I could get from Jessica if I wanted to—but I'm fairly certain she doesn't know much more than I do.

I try Jessica's mobile again but get no reply so I send her a few texts instead, hoping that, no matter what's going on with her, she will respond to those.

After work, when I still haven't received word from Jessica, I sit in my car for a while, pondering whether I should drive straight home or make a stop in Pott's Point. I decide to give her another day to reply and if she hasn't been in touch by tomorrow evening, I'll stop by her house then.

———

When I arrive at work the next morning, there's an email addressed to all employees in the department Jessica heads. It's very short and uninformative.

Jessica Porter has taken a leave of absence for an undetermined period of time. During her absence Nicolas Morton will make sure everything runs smoothly. Please direct all inquiries to Mr. Morton.

That's it. It's as if Jessica has vanished into thin air. I've never had any dealings with Porter Senior but I'm of half a mind to call his office and ask for an explanation. I also catch myself worrying over this far more than I would over any other executive who would take a sudden leave of absence. But it's the unexpectedness of it—and the timing. Something's off. I need to find out the truth.

Then again, if Jessica considered me a friend, an intention she has made clear many times, why hasn't she kept me in the loop? This makes me worry for her even more. I try her mobile again and send a few more texts. After work, I drive by her house, but no lights are on and nobody answers the door.

It's only the day after, when I'm in the Pink Bean for my morning coffee, that I finally get a text from Jessica.

Sorry for being out of touch. I'm fine. Don't worry about me.

I go up to Jo behind the counter. "Do you have a minute?"

She must be able to tell from my tone of voice that it's

important because she gives me a quick nod, serves the customer she was dealing with and sends Mandy an apologetic smile.

"What is it?"

I show her the text. I've told Jo all about Jessica being missing in action.

"That doesn't make much sense," Jo says.

"Should I call her?" I ask.

Jo nods. "You can try. Follow me."

We go into the storage room where we have privacy. My heart pounds in my throat as I dial Jessica's number. It rings four times, five, then someone picks up but doesn't say hello.

"Jessica?"

A tortured sigh on the other end of the line. "Caitlin." It's Jessica's voice even though I have to strain to hear it.

"Are you all right?" I ask.

"I'll be fine. I, um, I had surgery yesterday. That's why I didn't respond."

"Surgery?" I make eyes at Jo. "What happened?"

"It's nothing to worry about, Caitlin." It's hard for her to make this particular point when her voice sounds so weak.

"Yet I am worried. Are you still in hospital? Can I come see you?"

"No, no. There's no need."

"Please, Jessica," I plead.

"You have to take my word for it, Caitlin. I'm going to be fine. But I don't want any visitors. This is private, okay?" Her voice is slow and labored. "I'll be in touch when I'm ready."

I don't dare argue with her anymore for fear she'll lose the last ounce of energy that comes through in her voice. "Okay, but promise me you'll be in touch."

"When I'm ready," she says. A barely audible sigh comes through, then she hangs up.

I quickly recount the conversation to Jo who scratches her head in response.

"You have to respect her wishes," Jo says after a while. "There's no other choice."

"Or we can go on the internet and try to find Katherine. Maybe she knows what's going on."

Jo steps closer and puts her hands on my shoulder. "You have to let it go, babe. No matter how hard that is. She said she'd be in touch when she's ready. It would be disrespectful to try and find out what's going on behind her back. She clearly doesn't want anyone to know."

"But it's strange." I sound like a petulant child.

"It is, but life is strange sometimes."

"It must be something serious. She only just started at ANBC a few months ago. It can't have been a procedure planned long in advance."

"I'm sorry, babe, but I have to get back to work. Take a few deep breaths." She stands there watching me as if she wants to witness as I inhale deeply.

Instead of breathing deeply I walk out of the storage room. Even though I've just spoken to Jessica, I'm none the wiser. But Jo is right. I need to respect her wish for privacy, no matter how worried I am and how much I want to find out what's going on.

Chapter Twenty-Five

KRISTIN HAS PERFORMED her usual magic in the kitchen and I sag back into my chair with a contented smile on my face. "That was once again delicious, Kristin," I say.

"Why do people always assume it's Kristin preparing the food around here?" Sheryl says with a contradictory grin on her face.

"Because it is," Kristin says and blows Sheryl a kiss.

"I've always taken on a more cerebral role in our relationship," Sheryl says. "I won't deny it." She glances at me, then at Jo, and gives us a smirk. "When you moved back home, I would honestly never have thought we'd be having dinner parties with the two of you as a couple, but," she raises her glass of sparkling water, "it's not because it was unexpected that it doesn't delight me every time I see you two together."

"I certainly never expected it." Jo holds up her glass as well. She turns to me and looks at me with so much love in her eyes I feel myself go warm inside. "But here we are."

"You tamed Caitlin James," Kristin says. "I didn't think it was possible."

"I've hardly tamed her," Jo says. "It is like living with a wild animal sometimes." She chuckles. "A wild animal with excellent manners and conversation skills."

"She's a former Gender Studies student. You can fault us many things," Sheryl says, "but lack of communication is not one of them."

"The exaggerated need for communication is more what I would call it," Kristin says.

Sheryl rolls her eyes. "You're outnumbered tonight, babe," she says. "Best mind what you say."

"I'm simply communicating." Kristin grins at Sheryl. She holds up her glass. "To communication," she says, her tone serious but her eyes smiling.

We clink our glasses together and a short silence falls.

"I would like to, um, bring something up," Jo says. She has another quick sip of wine then fixes her gaze on Kristin. "You have been so good for me. Working at the Pink Bean has changed my life." She points her thumb at me. "What with meeting the love of my life there and all that."

"You would surely have met Caitlin at the university if you hadn't met her at the Pink Bean first," Sheryl says.

"Probably," Jo says and turns her attention to Kristin again. "Either way, I think my time as a Pink Bean barista is about to come to an end. As much as I have always enjoyed working for you, Kristin, it's all starting to be a bit much. Jimmy and I play more and more gigs. I'm so close to finishing my thesis. I—"

Kristin holds up her hand. "You don't have to explain, Jo," Kristin says. "I never expected you to work at the Pink Bean for this long. It's only normal for your life and circumstances to change."

"And I imagine Caitlin is quite high maintenance," Sheryl says.

I sit there stunned. Jo didn't tell me she was going to resign tonight.

"Well, there's that," Jo says. When she looks at me she has a wide smile on her face.

I smile back because by resigning she's fulfilling my very wish. She's making one hell of a compromise for our relationship. No more gruelingly early mornings after all the late nights she has.

"I will give you official notice, of course," Jo says to Kristin. "But I wanted to bring it up tonight. After all, you are much more than my employer."

"I'll miss you," Kristin says. "You're the most dependable person I've ever worked with. You'll be hard to replace."

"I'm sure Sheryl has a pool of grad students to choose from," I say.

"Or maybe a new Micky will come along," Sheryl says.

"No matter who will take the morning shift next," Kristin says, "it will never be the same without Jo. She was the first person I hired at the Pink Bean." She smiles at Jo. "You've been through all the highs and lows."

"Goodness me, Jo," Sheryl says. "You've succeeded in making my missus sound emotional in front of other people."

"I'm honored," Jo says. "And I will miss you too, Kristin."

"We'll be at the Pink Bean all the time," I say.

"And you'll still do an open mic from time to time?" Kristin asks.

"We should have a goodbye party slash open mic," Sheryl says. "We can't possibly let you go without making some fanfare about it."

Jo nods. "That would be lovely."

Kristin tilts her head. "Remember when I first asked you

if you wanted to sing at the open mic? I've never had such a quick and categoric *no* in my life."

"Things change," Jo says. "People change." She puts a hand on my knee.

"So I've heard as well," Sheryl says. She shoots me a quick wink then looks at Jo with a glimmer of expectation in her eyes. You can always count on Sheryl to steer the conversation into awkward territory.

Jo looks at her. "If we're not transforming in life, what are we doing?" she asks. "Someone posed that very question in my first year at the university. I believe it was a professor in the Gender Studies department."

"I'm glad I've taught you well." Sheryl gives Jo a warm look. Out of all of us, she has known Jo the longest.

"I'm just glad I'm no longer bearing the brunt of Sheryl's tasteless jokes about non-monogamy." I narrow my eyes. "When I say tasteless I actually mean unworthy of a professor in the Gender Studies department."

"Up until now, I've just never had much reason to believe it could actually work. I've seen quite a few open relationships fail," Sheryl says. "Which has nothing to do with what I teach."

"But you could—" I start, but Jo squeezes my knee.

"It's not for everyone and I agree that there aren't many positive examples in today's society," Jo says. "Maybe Caitlin and I should write our next book together about non-monogamy." She chuckles. "Well, once I've had a bit more experience with it, of course."

"I like the sound of that." I put my hand on Jo's.

"I admit I've given you a lot of flack over the years," Sheryl says, "but you've never given me any less for being in a so-called old-fashioned norm-abiding relationship."

"I'll give you that, but there's a difference between criticizing what's the norm and what's considered abnormal, aberrant, immoral and all the other things people like to assume I am. There's a power dynamic supported by society that will always give you the righteous edge."

"How about I get dessert," Kristin says, "and we agree that all forms of relationships are fine as long as everyone in them is happy?"

"I'll give you a hand." Jo rises. Before she follows Kristin into the kitchen, she plants a quick kiss on the top of my head.

"I hardly recognize her sometimes," Sheryl says.

I break into a smile. "I'm so in love with her." I lean forward a little. "Even though we've talked about it, I had no idea she was going to resign tonight."

"Something had to give. Quitting as my teaching assistant was not enough for the life she leads now." She nods slowly. "And if anything, we'll get to hear her sing at the Pink Bean more often. There are worse consolation prizes." She tilts her head. "I've been meaning to ask. I haven't heard from Jessica in a while. Has she given up on me?"

I shake my head. "She has taken a leave of absence and I have no idea what's going on. I spoke to her briefly and she was very vague. She was in hospital and had just undergone surgery."

Sheryl's eyes grow wide. "Is she all right?"

I shrug. "She said she was, even though she didn't sound like it. I've been thinking about going around to her house again. In fact, I've driven past it a few times, but she told me she would get in touch when she was ready. Jo thinks I should respect her wishes."

"Christ." Sheryl pulls a hand through her hair. "That's a tough one."

"What would you do?"

Sheryl arches her eyebrows. "If she has explicitly told you

to leave her alone, then you have to leave her alone." She strokes her chin. "Was she adamant?"

"I guess." I lean over the table a bit more. "But you have to understand that the weekend before she—" I can't finish my sentence because Kristin and Jo walk into the dining room with dessert in their hands.

"Lemon posset anyone?" Kristin asks and deposits a small bowl in front of me.

"That looks scrumptious," I say, trying to push my worry for Jessica out of my conscious mind, but ever since I spoke to her on the phone, I haven't been able to stop thinking about her.

Chapter Twenty-Six

"HERE YOU GO." I get up from my chair and motion for Jo to sit. "Let me know what you think."

"Okay." She sits and peers at my laptop screen to read the email I've composed to my parents. I read along over her shoulder.

Mom, Dad,

I've been back in Australia for a while now. I'm doing well. My partner Josephine and I have been together for almost 2 years. I work for ANBC. I'm glad I came back.

I hope you're both doing well. I've thought about you a lot the past 10 years. It pains me that we parted on such bad terms.

If you would like us to, Jo and I would like to come and see you.
Best,

Caitlin

Jo looks up from the screen and swivels the chair around. "What do you think?" I ask.

"It's a bit dry," she says. "Very unemotional."

"Maybe. But what do you expect?" I lean against the window sill. "A declaration of love?"

"No, but perhaps a tad more than what you're giving."

"But I don't want to give anything more."

"Then maybe you're not ready to contact them."

I shake my head. "I don't know."

Jo rises and walks over to me. "Family relations can be so complicated." She curls her arm around my shoulders.

"Not in your family."

"In every family, mine included. There are always unspoken things bubbling beneath the surface. There's always something that's better left unsaid." She bumps her hip into mine. "What if we do one day write a book together about non-monogamy. How do you think my parents are going to take it?"

"Were you serious about that, by the way?"

"Why not? We make an excellent co-writing team, don't you think?"

I curve an arm around the small of her back. "I think we make an excellent team in just about anything."

"So do I." She leans into me a little more. "But back to the matter at hand. It all depends on what you're trying to accomplish, but what that email says to me is that you're willing to seek contact, obviously, but not much more. You're leaving the ball firmly in their court. Is that really what you want to convey?"

"Of course the ball is in their court. They're the parents."

"It is widely but often wrongly assumed that parents always know best. They don't. Not even my parents, whom you seem to adore so much. They're great, but not perfect."

"So what do you suggest I write?"

"I don't think it's my place to suggest, babe. If it doesn't come from your heart or if what you've written is the best, most heartfelt you can come up with, then perhaps you aren't ready. Either way, you don't have to do this."

I snuggle into her embrace a bit more. "I think I might be afraid of being rejected all over again. What if I send them this, or another more emotional message, and I hear nothing back? Or all I get back is more vitriol and accusations."

"That's the chance you take. It's up to you whether you want to take it or not. Whether you think it's worth it."

"I get what you're saying, but I don't think I want to change anything of what I've written. This is all I have in me because I may have hurt them, simply by being who I am, but they have hurt me so much more by breaking all contact. I never wanted that."

"I know, babe." She turns to me and kisses me softly on the cheek. "But what do you want now?"

"If only sending that email could be enough. If only the very act of clicking the send button wouldn't fill me with a bunch of expectations. And then, if they don't meet them, I'll feel what they felt all those years ago, when I failed in their expectations of me as a respectable daughter."

"There's some warped logic going on here, darling," Jo says in her soft, understanding voice. If I hadn't met her, and her parents, I'm absolutely certain I would never even have considered writing this email, let alone sending it—I wouldn't have spared my parents an extra thought.

"Then let me ask you this." I know Jo will give me an honest reply. "Since we've known each other, have you ever at any point thought I was bitter because of my relationship with my parents?"

Jo shakes her head adamantly. "The word bitter has never even occurred to me when it comes to you. You're anything but bitter. You're so full of life and ideas and opinions. You're a force of nature. That's what I thought the first time I saw you in the Pink Bean and it's still what I think now when you breeze in through the door. For me, nothing about you has to change." She smiles at me. "Not even your lack of modesty."

I bump my hip into hers. "I'm the very picture of modesty."

She loosens herself from my sideways embrace and stands in front of me. "Sure, and you're also a shy wallflower who'd much rather not have her face on TV every week."

"You know me too well." I put my arms on her shoulders.

"I know you intimately." She kisses the side of my neck.

"Now you're distracting me." I kiss her on the lips.

"Well then, how about you sleep on whether to send this email or not. There's no rush."

"Sleep, huh?" I nuzzle her neck. "Not much sleeping will be done."

"As long as Kristin hasn't found a replacement, I still have to set the alarm at five."

"I think I may volunteer to assist Kristin with that particular task. I can't wait to snuggle up to you on a Monday morning."

"Soon." Jo scoops the back of my head into her hand.

"Thank you," I say, "for making more time for me."

"Let me show you how welcome you are," she says, and slips her tongue into my mouth.

Chapter Twenty-Seven

"I've worked at the Pink Bean for so long," Jo says. "It has become my second home." She holds a hand out toward Sheryl and Kristin. "Sheryl and Kristin have become family." She blows them a kiss. "So it's with a heavy heart that I say goodbye to this place." She chuckles. "Well, at least to the barista apron and the cleaning of the coffee machine. I'll still be here all the time, having my cup of coffee *made for me*." She emphasizes the last few words and a collective giggle travels through the crowd. "So let me sing you a song or two to say goodbye to this special place."

Enthusiastic applause erupts all around me.

Jo looks at Jimmy and he plays the first chords. She closes her eyes and gets ready to lose herself in the song. I keep my gaze firmly on her, ready to lose myself in her performance.

When she starts to sing a few people clap, but most just seem to hold their breath. Because this is still such a special, precious thing. Sometimes, when I'm part of the crowd and I look at her up on the stage—even the make-shift stage in the Pink Bean—I think it's a miracle that she's up there. The girl who swore to never sing in front of an audience. And look at her now.

This is the perfect way for her to say goodbye to the Pink Bean, the place where so much clicked into place for her. A huge rush of warmth travels through me at the thought that I'm a part of that. Because Jo is special and I think I felt that from the get-go, from the very first time she approached me —all flushed cheeks and crippling shyness—to ask me to sign her books.

When the song finishes she stands there beaming. She's taking the time to enjoy herself, to feel every moment.

"This next song is for a very special woman I met here at the Pink Bean," Jo says. She briefly looks at me, winks, then her glance moves away from me. "Micky Ferro. It was an honor to train you in the art of barista-ship, especially the meticulous craftsmanship it requires to make a wet cap. And you meeting the love of your life in here was quite inspiring as well."

"Woohoo," Robin shouts beside me.

I applaud with the rest of the crowd. Jo seems to have a little speech prepared for everyone, even her best friend and former flat mate Eva gets a song dedicated to her. By the time she makes it to the ninth song, I'm beginning to wonder if she'll have anything to say about me at all.

"I'm going to go completely overboard with the last song of the evening," she says. "But women with bold personalities require dramatic songs to be sung to them. Believe me, after a year and a half with Caitlin I know that subtlety is not a requirement." She breaks out into a grin. "The lyrics may seem a bit contradictory, but to me they ring true. I wouldn't be the person I am today if it weren't for Caitlin and... the wind she is beneath my wings."

To my surprise, Jimmy puts his guitar to the side and leaves the stage. She's going to sing this one a cappella. I'm nervous for her, even though there's no doubt in my mind she can do it.

By the time Jo reaches the chorus you can hear a pin drop in the Pink Bean and I have tears streaming down my face. I can't stop them. Her voice and the song she has picked for me have that effect on me. I feel my love for her multiply with every beautiful, spot-on note she sings. Together, we have been on a huge journey already and I can't wait to see what the future has in store for us.

As she launches in the next chorus, I realize, for the first time, that Josephine Greenwood is my soulmate. She's the person I needed to meet so she could teach me a thing or two about myself. She's my sounding board. My partner in what my parents would describe as crime.

I didn't send the email to them after all. And now, as I stand here, brimming with pride and gratitude and love, I know I never will. Because finding Jo is enough for me. Spending a weekend with her family, and have them accept me for who I am, is enough. Being with Jo has brought more than enough love into my life.

I try to wipe my cheeks dry of tears by the time Jo finishes the song, but they keep on coming, so I give up. Then I feel an arm wrap around my shoulders. Sheryl gives me a tight squeeze and doesn't let go until the song has ended.

"Thank you very, very much," Jo says with obvious emotion in her voice, then rushes off the stage, into my arms.

———

When most people have left, and it's only the hardcore Pink Bean customers and friends who remain, Jo and I sit down.

I let my gaze roam across the near-empty Pink Bean when it lands, not for the first time tonight, on Bryony.

"Have you seen who's here?" I ask Jo.

She nods.

I turn in my seat and scan her face.

Jo sends me a smile. "Do you want to invite her for a nightcap at ours?"

"Maybe next time," I say. "But not tonight." I scoot closer to her and put my head on her shoulder.

"All right. Tonight's for you and me, my hero," Jo says.

I chuckle. "I'm a beautiful face without a name? Really?" I remind her of the words she sang in her last song.

"If I had known it would make you cry so hard, I would have thought twice about singing that." She pulls the corner of her mouth into a crooked grin. "But hey, at least for once you were content to let me shine." She lifts my head from her shoulder and plants a kiss on my lips.

"I want to see you shine forever," I say.

CRAZY FOR YOU

PINK BEAN SERIES - BOOK 8

To all the survivors.

Chapter One

JESSICA STOOD in front of the mirror with her eyes closed. She let her robe slip off and took a deep breath. She opened one eye to a slit through which she couldn't really see anything, then screwed it shut again. It was amazing how much of your own body you could avoid seeing if you applied yourself to it. But she had to look. It was time. Laurel would be there in fifteen minutes.

Jessica had seen the scars before, of course. She'd caught glimpses in the mirror. In an unguarded moment in the shower, she'd run a finger over their coarse texture—the red lines of remembrance. She'd never done that again.

Showering had never been a long dragged-out affair before, but now it had become an even more frenetic process. She disrobed with her back toward the mirror, hopped in, soaped up as quickly as she could, and only allowed herself to relax when hot water cascaded down her skin and she knew the ordeal of washing—of being confronted with her naked body—was over again.

Jessica sighed. She knew she couldn't avoid this forever. That was one of the main reasons she had made an appointment with Laurel. It would force her to confront what she was missing in a way she did not feel ready for at all. But she would never be ready if she didn't push herself out of her comfort zone. *Comfort zone.* Jessica hated the term. Her father had used it a few too many times when she was younger. But now she was using the exact term to get herself to do something she didn't want to do. It just went to show. In the end, she was a chip off the old block indeed.

"This. Is. Ridiculous," Jessica said to no one. Not even to her mirror image because her eyes were still closed.

She turned around, picked up her robe from the bathroom floor and pulled it safely around her shoulders. Only then did she open her eyes.

She couldn't do it. Yet. So what?

She took another deep breath. Should she cancel Laurel? It was probably too late. Canceling was always possible, of course, but she would have to pay the full amount if she canceled this late before the appointment. She knew the rules. In that case, Laurel might as well come over. If just to have a chat. She had no idea what had happened to Jessica. If she and Laurel only talked, Jessica could pretend nothing had changed.

Her body hidden away by the fabric of the robe, she looked into the mirror and examined her face. Strangely, little about her face had changed. Granted, her cheeks were a little hollower. Her eyes, at times, a little more sunken, but most of her features had remained the same. As if nothing had changed at all.

Jessica brushed her hair and forced a smile to her lips. She'd been lucky. One surgery and everything had been taken care of. It could all have been so much worse.

The smile remained without her having to strain to keep it. She'd have it ready for Laurel. How long had it been since she last saw her?

Jessica turned away from the mirror again and went into her bedroom. She'd taken clothes from her walk-in wardrobe earlier and laid them on the bed. The wardrobe had too many mirrors and she only went back in there once she was fully clothed.

She dressed and counted the weeks since Laurel had last come to her house. It had been so long that she lost count. Christ. It was time.

She headed down the stairs and waited. Outside, darkness had fallen. The clock read three minutes to nine. Laurel was never too late and never too early. Jessica knew the bell would ring at precisely nine o'clock.

She had opened a bottle of Cabernet earlier to let it breathe. Laurel liked red wine. Jessica didn't know why she wanted to please Laurel so much. She was the one paying her. Laurel was coming over with the sole purpose of pleasing Jessica. Yet she felt guilty for not having booked her for so long. For being out of touch. It was the craziest thing to feel bad about. No feelings had gotten hurt. Maybe that was what stung the most.

The bell rang as the big hand of the clock slid to nine.

Chapter Two

JESSICA INHALED DEEPLY and turned the doorknob. In a split second she would come face-to-face with Laurel's dark complexion, her surprisingly kind eyes—the warmth in them had always taken Jessica aback—and her easy demeanor. It was this particular quality of Laurel's that Jessica craved most right now. Since her surgery, it seemed that no one was willing to be easygoing around her anymore. As though acting normal would somehow break her even more than she'd already been broken.

Jessica opened the door wide.

"Good evening," the woman standing on her stoop said. A woman who was decidedly not Laurel.

"Who are you?" Jessica blurted out.

"Hi, Jessica." The woman held out her hand. "I'm Elizabeth, but do call me Liz."

"I was expecting someone else." Jessica ignored Liz's hand.

Liz nodded apologetically. "I know you were expecting Laurel. May I come in and explain?"

"No. I mean, not before I see, er, some sort of credentials. You could be anyone."

"I hate to say it, but I don't have my police badge on me." The woman produced a wide smile. She was nothing like Laurel with her soft curves and enchanting eyes. Liz was more angular. Taller. She looked somehow more unmanageable to Jessica. What the hell was going on here?

"Why didn't the agency tell me they were sending someone else?" Jessica asked.

"I'm desperate to explain," Liz said. "If you'll allow me." She tilted her head and painted on a dazzling smile.

"You can explain standing right there." Jessica crossed her arms in front of her chest, a gesture that still caused a strange sensation to run through her.

"Laurel has left the job," Liz said.

"What?" Jessica suddenly felt caught out. As though what she did with Laurel was all perfectly fine and legal as long as she did it only with Laurel.

"A few weeks ago," Liz said. "I've been taking over some of her clients." She took a step closer and leaned against the door frame.

Jessica instinctively stepped back. "That may very well be, but why was I not informed? You can't show up here and tell me this. I should have been notified in advance. I should have been—" Jessica swallowed the rest of her sentence. She didn't want to sound that crass. That's why transactions like this were not conducted verbally. It was all just too lewd to say out loud.

"I agree," Liz said. "Some wires got crossed at the agency. You weren't informed of the situation when you made the booking and they realized just a few minutes ago, when I texted to say I was on the way to you. I thought it better to explain in person."

"This is not the level of service I pay for," Jessica said. She really didn't want to have this conversation. She wanted Liz to leave. She certainly wasn't going to show her mutilated body to this stranger.

Liz nodded. "I completely understand." She narrowed her eyes. "But maybe we can talk about it? Work it out?"

"I wouldn't know what else to talk about with you." Jessica looked Liz in the eyes for the first time.

Her eyes were too light. Her brown irises had flecks of green in them. Her skin was too pale. Her smile too wide. She simply wasn't Laurel.

"I can think of a thing or two," Liz said. "Unless, of course, I'm completely not your cup of tea. There's no arguing over that." She crossed one ankle over the other and leaned against the doorframe, giving the impression she wasn't going anywhere soon. "But please allow me to say that I think you are one gorgeous woman, Jessica P."

"And you're obviously not very discreet." Jessica wanted to slam the door in Liz's face, but she couldn't do it. Her arms wouldn't move. Her body refused to go through the required motions.

"That's where you're very, very wrong." Liz's voice had dropped an octave. She looked around. "Let me ask you one last time. May I come in, please?"

Liz didn't have her profession written all over her, but Jessica didn't want her neighbors to start asking questions regardless.

"Fine." She dropped her arms and gestured for Liz to come in.

They walked into the living room and Jessica invited Liz to sit. Jessica picked a spot on the couch as far away from her as possible. She didn't want Liz to get any ideas into her head. As the thought ran through her mind, she realized it was one of the more ridiculous ones she'd had that night, which was quickly turning into an absurd farce. Things were definitely not going according to Jessica's plan.

It hadn't been easy for Jessica to send that message to the agency. But she had strongly believed that seeing Laurel would help her and had pressed *Send* after all. Only to end up in this situation. She would give whoever had been at the receiving end of her message a piece of her mind later after Liz had left. And call Katherine to tell her this was unacceptable. What did they think they were dealing in? The prices these women charged came with the expectation of absolute perfect management. But Jessica could hardly leave a bad review on Yelp.

She glanced at the bottle of wine. She could do with a drink right now and it would be too rude not to offer a glass to Liz, especially as two glasses stood waiting next to the bottle.

"Drink?" Jessica asked.

"I would love one," Liz said. Her teeth almost sparkled when she smiled, that was how white they were. "Thanks."

Jessica poured them both a glass then handed one to Liz.

"Cheers." Liz held up her glass. "To happy misunderstandings."

"What do you mean?" Jessica glared at her over the rim of her glass.

"Clearly a mistake was made and I understand you're shocked and unhappy about it. It's unprofessional and I'll make sure whoever is responsible for this cock-up never makes the same mistake again, but…" She paused to take a sip from her wine. "I, for one, am very happy to be here."

Because you get paid an exorbitant amount of money. Jessica didn't say that out loud. She couldn't say something like that out loud because she was completely complicit. And money mattered far less to her than the comfort Laurel brought her.

"What happened to Laurel?" she asked.

"She quit. It happens. This isn't a job you do until you reach the legal retirement age." Liz chuckled.

Jessica did admire her candor—and her sense of humor. Across from her sat a woman who displayed the same ease as Laurel had, perhaps even more.

"I suppose not," was all Jessica could say to that.

"This wine is divine," Liz said. "You have good taste."

"I don't need to be flattered or talked into anything—"

Liz held up her hands. "I know. Just to be clear, you won't be charged for tonight."

"That's not what I meant," Jessica said. She took a long swig of wine. However divine it might be, its exquisiteness was quite lost on Jessica tonight.

"It's all good." Liz picked up her glass again. "Any time you want me to leave, I'll go. Or, we could just chat for a bit. I have all the time in the world." She twirled the stem of the glass between her long fingers. "I'm a really good listener."

Strangely enough, Liz came across completely genuine. There wasn't anything fake or put-on in the way she sat there or the things she said. It was a gift, Jessica believed, to be able to talk to strangers as though you'd known them forever. Laurel had the same gift.

"Can I ask you a question?" Liz asked.

"Sure." Jessica took another big gulp.

"The first time you met Laurel… what was that like?"

Jessica scoffed. It was easy to see what Liz was trying to do. She could choose to rebuke her or she could play along. The latter would probably be most fun. Not having Laurel turn up had been a shock, but she was getting over that now. She was sitting on her couch drinking wine with an attractive woman who was, in fact, being very kind to her. Wasn't that what she was paying for in the first place? She could at the very least see where it would lead.

"Quite similar to meeting you." Jessica had a few very vivid memories of that first night with Laurel, but none were of the time not spent in the bedroom. "It's hard to pretend this isn't awkward."

"It doesn't have to be." That glittering smile again. "Anyway, I think it's time to move the topic of conversation away from Laurel. How was your day?"

Jessica broke out into a nervous chuckle. "Sorry, but that just seems too mundane a question."

"Would you like me to tell you about *my* day instead?" Liz pivoted in the couch and pulled one knee up, angling her body to Jessica. She wore a denim shirt of which the top three buttons were undone. Compared to how Laurel had always looked, Liz was quite casually dressed, even though on Liz a mere denim shirt somehow looked elegant. Her trousers were tight and black and glossy, not leather, but a soft-looking fabric nonetheless.

Truth be told, if Jessica had passed Liz in the street, she would have stopped to look twice.

"Sure. Do tell." Jessica drank again and allowed the alcohol to relax her.

"Let's see." Liz fixed her gaze on Jessica's, as though she was about to tell her the sexiest story instead of a recap of her day. Or perhaps her day had been sexy. "I woke up late. Went for a run in Centennial Park. Had lunch—smashed avocado on toast, for your information." She paused. "In the afternoon I went to a TRX class." She flexed her arm and pretended to feel her biceps. "Got to keep these babies toned." The grin she shot Jessica next was goofy rather than seductive. "Then I read the newspaper, wasted some time on the internet, took a long bath, had a disco nap followed by a light dinner, and now I'm here." She arched up her eyebrows. "Pretty mundane indeed."

"A run *and* a TRX class?" The mere thought of it

exhausted Jessica, even though she wasn't quite sure what TRX stood for. Physical conditioning was next on her 'to do list'—but first she wanted to work on her self-respect a little more. "You must be very tired."

Liz shook her head. "On the contrary."

Jessica imagined Liz running in the park. Her shoulders were broad, filling out her shirt in the most magnificent way. She pictured Liz in a tank top, a sheen of sweat glistening on her skin. The image ignited a light tingle in her lower belly. She was glad to discover that her most neglected organ still showed signs of being alive.

"It gives me energy and, well, my body is my biggest asset," Liz said matter-of-factly.

Jessica nearly sputtered out the sip of wine she'd just drunk. One thing was for sure, Liz had no qualms about being open about the job she did.

"Is it really, though?" Jessica asked. She hadn't meant to ask the question, hadn't thought about it, she'd just blurted it out. It was the closest she'd come to a real conversation with Liz since she had turned up.

"How do you mean?" Liz lightly ran a fingertip over her knee.

The motion distracted Jessica. She was pretty sure her meaning was clear to Liz, but Jessica didn't mind answering the question. So Liz wanted her to say certain things. Now that she had a bit of wine in her, and was getting used to the not unpleasant sight of Liz, that was fine. "Of course, I can see how your body is important, but I dare to guess other skills are equally, if not more, important."

"Which skills might they be?"

Jessica chuckled. "Do you really want me to have a go at trying to sum up your social skills?"

Liz shook her head. "Absolutely not." She grinned at Jessica. "Now would you like to tell me about *your* day?"

Jessica sighed. "There's really not much to tell. I mainly watched a lot of Netflix, but don't even ask me which shows. I was just passing time more than paying attention."

Liz narrowed her eyes. "Not what I expected. You don't strike me as the kind of woman who sits around and does nothing all day."

Jessica didn't reply immediately. Then she mumbled, "I'm still convalescing, I guess."

"Sorry? I didn't quite get that." Liz shuffled a little closer.

"I had surgery a while ago. I haven't gone back to work yet. Going back next week, though." Jessica forced her voice to be louder, making it sound unnatural.

"How do you feel about that?" Liz asked.

What was this? Rent-a-shrink? Jessica shrugged. She didn't have strong feelings about anything lately. As though something inside of her had gone numb when they'd taken a scalpel to her body and removed a body part she could live without.

"I'm sure it'll beat watching Netflix all day," she said laconically.

"Are you in pain?" Liz asked. "After your surgery?"

"Not anymore," Jessica lied, because sometimes she felt the most acute pain in the very part of her body that wasn't there anymore. A pain she could do nothing about because it was all in her head—where else could it possibly be?

Liz glanced at her and sent her a soft smile. She put her glass down, held up her hands, and wiggled her fingers. "I give a mean massage," she said. "As hard or soft as you like."

Jessica didn't know what to say to that so she just stared at Liz's hands—and her long, strong fingers. It was decision time again. "That's very nice of you to offer, but I'm good."

"Let me know if you change your mind." Liz drummed her fingertips on her thigh. "You look a bit tense around the shoulders."

Jessica huffed out some pent-up air.

"I'm sorry. I didn't quite catch that either," Liz said, a wide smile on her face again.

"I was trying to picture how I'm coming across. Obviously, you know who I am. You did your research. I'm sure the agency has a file on me. Part of me would like to know whether Laurel shared certain details about me, although the other part of me prefers not to think about that. I can only imagine this evening is not going according to your plan at all. And that you hadn't counted on meeting such an uptight rich girl, having to slog through this awkward conversation with me."

"That's not how I think of you at all, Jessica." Liz's voice had gone all soft and buttery. "And just to put your mind at ease, no details are shared between us at the agency. Discretion is the key to our success. There are no files, although I have, of course, looked you up online." She sank her teeth into her bottom lip for a split second. "Can't say I found much. Discretion seems to be very important to you as well."

"It should be to more people." Jessica didn't feel like divulging the real reason for the meagre results a Google search of her name yielded.

"That's so very true." Liz smiled again. "All of that being said, and since we were talking about my possible other skills earlier…" She looked Jessica in the eye again. "I can clearly sense you're feeling ill at ease. Not so much about me, although having me turn up when you were expecting Laurel has understandably thrown you. You don't seem to be very comfortable in your skin. Perhaps the surgery you talked about earlier has something to do with that?"

Jessica hadn't seen her therapist since before the surgery. She was beginning to think that was a mistake. Liz was playing shrink with her and it was having an unmistakable effect on her—the jury was still out on whether it was a positive or negative effect, but Jessica was just glad to be feeling something other than the dread she faced when looking into the mirror.

"You know what, Liz?" She smiled back. "I think I might be up for a bit of a shoulder massage."

Chapter Three

"IT WOULD BE MY PLEASURE." Liz rose and looked around the room. "Why don't you sit in that chair over there." She pointed at the low-backed armchair in which Jessica liked to curl up with a book—even though she hadn't read more than the odd page lately. "Put your feet up." Liz dragged the ottoman close. "I'll do the rest."

Jessica followed her instructions. By the time she sat, her shoulders were so tense, she couldn't wait for Liz's fingers to dig in.

"I'm just going to massage you over your blouse. Is that okay?" Liz asked, her voice a soft whisper.

"Yes." Jessica concluded that one of Liz's other skills was a sixth sense as to which items of clothing her clients were comfortable removing at any given time. Jessica was nowhere near ready to lower her blouse, let alone take it off in front of a stranger. Although, when she was clothed, if you didn't know about her surgery, and didn't look too closely, you probably couldn't tell.

Liz ran her fingers over the back of Jessica's head, then the base of her skull, as though she was trying to get a feel and read the level of tension residing in that area of Jessica's body.

Her fingertips caressed the exposed skin above the collar of her blouse. They dipped in a fraction, stroking her neck, before moving to her shoulders, over the fabric of Jessica's blouse.

Jessica was glad she was wearing a long-sleeved blouse because her skin broke out into goose bumps. She hadn't been touched like this in so long. With tenderness, as opposed to the directness of a nurse's skilled hands when she changed Jessica's bandages.

Over Jessica's blouse, Liz circled her thumbs next to Jessica's shoulder blades, the very spot where Jessica always suffered from various stress-related aches. When Liz's thumbs sunk in, Jessica couldn't suppress a gasp of pure pleasure.

Liz reacted by applying more pressure and gradually expanding the area she was working on. She dug her fingers into the hard-knotted muscles of Jessica's shoulders, pressed her knuckles against the most persistent knots, and worked magic with her thumbs until Jessica felt a wave of tension just flow out of her, as though Liz was absorbing it through her fingertips.

Jessica had lost track of time and had no idea how long Liz had been massaging her shoulders, but she hadn't strayed beyond the boundaries of her blouse. The motion of Liz's hands slowed and then Jessica felt Liz's breath near her ear.

"Would you like me to do your neck as well?" she whispered, making it sound like a very sexy proposition.

"Yes, please." Jessica barely recognized her own voice.

"Okay," Liz said. "Just relax." She started by pushing the collar of Jessica's blouse down a little. Jessica responded by undoing one button so she could expose a little more skin on her neck.

"I'll just be a second," Liz said.

Jessica watched Liz go over to the couch and pick up her bag, which she'd left next to it. When Liz returned to her position behind her, Jessica heard her rustling through the bag. She heard more rustling, followed by a squirting noise, and the sound of hands being rubbed together with some lotion or oil between them.

Liz's hands were slick and warm when they touched down on Jessica's neck.

Innocent though it seemed, Jessica hadn't been touched this intimately since she'd shared a bed with three other women, one of whom she'd paid for her services.

So many thoughts ran through her head. When would she be able to share intimacy with someone she loved again? She had a long way to go before that could happen. First, she'd have to be able to show herself—*to* herself. That was the first step. Perhaps this evening wasn't going as planned, but it was helping. The sensation of Liz's skilled fingers kneading her neck, running up and down the sensitive skin along the side of it, was taking down a little more of her guard with every tiny motion.

For a brief moment, Jessica considered asking for a full back massage, that was how divine Liz's hands felt on her flesh. But she didn't. The words didn't come out of her mouth and she knew that was because she wasn't ready to speak them—she wasn't ready for anything other than her blouse collar being pushed down a fraction.

"That was divine," Jessica said when the neck massage was over.

"I'm glad." Liz's hands hadn't ventured any lower than Jessica had felt comfortable with. She hadn't pushed Jessica's boundaries in any way. Maybe she sensed that Jessica wasn't ready. Maybe her sixth sense was her superpower. "Can I wash my hands somewhere?"

Jessica pointed Liz to the bathroom in the hallway and

took the moment alone to regroup. What would happen next? It was entirely up to her. She could ask Liz to leave. She would never have to see her again. Or she could pour her another glass of wine and they could continue their chat. Jessica might not be ready for a number of things just yet, but she was up to having a more candid conversation. Maybe if she just spoke the words to someone new, if they were out there in the atmosphere, it would be easier to open her eyes next time she stood in front of the mirror.

Liz's hair fell into her eyes and she brushed it aside with an exquisite hand gesture as she returned and headed toward the couch.

"Would you like another glass of wine?" Jessica asked.

"I would love one." Liz sat on the corner of the couch closest to Jessica's armchair.

Jessica started to rise, but Liz held up her hand. "Let me," she said. "You just relax a little more."

Jessica watched her hop out of the couch with elegant swiftness. She wondered how old Liz was. Come to think of it, she'd never known Laurel's age. She'd seen every nook and cranny of her body, and she had hazarded many a guess, but Laurel had never confirmed nor denied a number she offered.

Liz topped up their glasses and when she handed Jessica hers, she sent her a small smile. It was the kind of subtle smile that made Jessica imagine all sorts of things. Things she could have happen at the drop of a hat if she wanted them to. That was why Liz had come here in the first place.

"Thanks," Jessica said and held Liz's gaze. What had she had against the color of her eyes earlier? That they were lighter than Laurel's? How silly. Just like Laurel, Liz had beautiful eyes.

Once Liz had sat again, her body leaning against the armrest of the couch, Jessica said, "I had a mastectomy.

Breast cancer. I guess I was lucky that only my right breast had to be removed." Her shoulders hunched, as though she was trying to obscure her chest from view.

"I'm so sorry. That must have been hard." Liz didn't sound very surprised.

"It was hard, but I also got lucky. I got to keep one." Jessica had to stop herself from putting a protective hand on her left breast. "The biggest one." She managed a chuckle.

"You haven't had reconstructive surgery?" Liz asked, a warm smile forming on her lips.

"I was advised to wait at least half a year, in case I still needed radiation after the surgery. But I got lucky again. No radiation necessary. So far."

"That's good." Liz looked into her wine glass, then up again. "You are lucky, even though getting cancer might not make you feel so lucky."

Jessica drank before she spoke again. "It could have been a lot worse. I understand this very well." She sighed. "I've been made very aware of my… mortality, I guess. Along with some other issues."

Liz looked at her but didn't say anything. In her profession, being a good listener was probably as important as keeping a fit body.

"I suddenly found myself at the age of forty-five without many people I could call genuine friends, without a family that cared beyond getting me the fanciest room in a private clinic, without a significant other, and without my right breast." Jessica was aware of how pathetic she sounded. She squared her shoulders, making sure not to push her chest forward as she did, and looked Liz in the eye. An honest analysis of her life didn't automatically make her pathetic. It was just how things were—and she wasn't after Liz's pity.

"That mustn't be easy for someone who most people think has it all."

Jessica waved off Liz's comment. "I stopped caring about what others think of me a while back." She painted on a wide grin. "And at least I have money. No matter how badly I fuck up, I will always have money. As crass as it may sound, there's some comfort in that."

"I don't think there's anything crass about money." Liz mirrored her grin. "That would be quite hypocritical, doing what I do."

Jessica narrowed her eyes. "Is this your only job?"

Liz nodded. "And a well-paid one at that."

"Don't I know it." Jessica actually chuckled.

"But everything's free tonight." Liz leaned over the armrest a bit more. "Are you sure you don't want another massage? Take advantage of the situation?"

"I'm not after a freebie." Jessica shook her head. An idea popped into her head. "But since you're still here, I'd like to ask you for another favor, if you don't mind."

"Anything except plumbing," Liz joked. "I'm really no good at that."

"I haven't been out all day." Jessica scrunched her lips together. "In fact, I haven't been out since my last visit to the hospital three days ago. Will you come with me for a walk around the neighborhood?"

"It would be my pleasure." Liz jumped up energetically. "It's a lovely spring evening."

"Great." Jessica rose from her seat with considerably less energy.

Chapter Four

WHEN THEY'D STOOD outside Jessica's door, Liz had offered her arm for Jessica to hook hers through, and she had happily taken the opportunity. Walking around this Sydney neighborhood, to which she'd only moved a year ago, and under the current circumstances in which she often felt too fragile for the outside world, was so much easier on the arm of this gorgeous woman.

They walked in silence along MacLeay Street, meandering into smaller side streets. A few pubs had put out tables and chairs on the sidewalk already, but it was still a little too chilly to sit outside.

"Good thing I'm a sensible shoe girl," Liz said after a while.

"*There*'s a phrase that could be taken in more ways than one," Jessica replied. She steered them around. They'd walked for twenty minutes and still had to make it back to her house. She was getting tired.

Liz laughed heartily. She held on to Jessica's arm a little tighter. "I know you're going through a hard time right now and you're probably not yourself entirely, but I get the impression that sometimes glimpses of your old self come through. I like it."

"Ah, my old self." Jessica breathed in a fresh gulp of evening air. "If I focus really hard, I sometimes remember her."

"That sounded very dramatic." Liz lightly bumped into Jessica.

"Drama might very well be the Porter family specialty. Or better, how to be inundated by it while all you try to do is avoid it."

They both chuckled and it felt so good to have a little giggle with another woman by her side. Until Jessica remembered that she was paying for the experience—there was no way she would accept not paying after all the time Liz had spent with her. It wasn't her fault that Jessica had no idea she would show up. And now that they were walking along the dark streets of Pott's Point, she'd all but forgotten about Laurel.

"Is this what they call *The Girlfriend Experience?*" Jessica asked.

A deep laugh bubbled from Liz's throat. "Not quite."

"Is that something you get asked to do often?" Jessica had never dared ask Laurel questions like that. The vibe between them hadn't really invited them. Tonight, however, she was experiencing intimacy—paid for, but intimacy nonetheless—of a different kind.

"I'd rather not talk about that." Liz turned to face Jessica and painted on a wide smile—probably to make her rebuttal of Jessica's question go down a little easier.

"Fair enough," Jessica said.

"Ask me anything else instead," Liz said.

Their footfalls could barely be heard on the sidewalk.

Jessica had worn comfortable shoes as well. She was going for a walk, not attending an ANBC board meeting. Although she wished she'd worn heels so Liz didn't dwarf her so much.

"Anything?" Jessica asked. "Are you sure?"

"Anything," Liz confirmed.

"How long have you been in this job?" Jessica had a number of pressing questions battling for the upper hand in her brain, but this was the one she chose to ask.

"A few years," Liz said.

"That's pretty vague. Kind of makes me feel I wasted my question." They were approaching the dead-end street Jessica lived on.

"Ask me another one then. And make sure I can't give you a vague answer." There was obvious glee in Liz's voice.

Jessica tried to sort through her thoughts. In the end, she found herself only capable of asking one very specific question. "Will you come back some day and finish that massage?" The question surprised her as well. Of all the things she could have asked she asked a question she could have gotten the answer to just by making a request to the agency. But she wanted to hear the words come from Liz's mouth.

"I would love to." Liz held on to Jessica's arm a little tighter. They turned into Jessica's street and, although she was slightly out of breath and getting more tired with every second that passed, Jessica suddenly found herself regretting that their walk was about to end. "Any time," Liz said.

"Will you make sure they don't send someone else?" Jessica asked as they halted in front of her house.

"I give you my word." Liz let her hand slide from Jessica's arm to her hand and slipped her fingers through Jessica's.

Jessica couldn't think of a better example of what she thought of as *the girlfriend experience*, but instead of ruining the moment by describing it, she decided to enjoy the touch of this beautiful woman's fingers sliding against her own.

"Will you come in for a brief moment?" Jessica asked.

Liz nodded.

Jessica unlocked the door and they stood in the hallway. Because Jessica had expected Laurel, she had put the agreed-upon sum in an envelope and put it in a drawer in the hallway cabinet, that way she could pay Laurel as she let her out—and the exchange of money could be relegated to a brief afterthought.

Jessica opened the drawer and retrieved the envelope she had prepared. She gave it to Liz. "Please. No arguments."

Liz regarded the envelope. How many of these did she hold in her hands every week? Jessica had so many questions popping into her head again. Questions she was always so easily able to push to the back of her mind when she was with Laurel. Probably because the transaction with Laurel had always been very different—much more to the point.

"I want to protest," Liz said. "But I also don't want you to feel bad about not paying me. In the end, it's your call."

"Take the money," Jessica said. "The time you spent with me was worth far more than what's in that envelope."

"Thank you." Liz smiled, a glint of overhead light catching in her eyes. "I appreciate that." She leaned forward and kissed Jessica on the cheek. "I can stay longer if you want me to."

"I'm really tired. Too much excitement for one day." It wasn't even a quip. Who knew feeling alive for a few brief moments could take up so much energy?

"I understand." Liz touched her hand lightly against Jessica's shoulder. "I hope to see you again soon." She opened her arms wide and drew Jessica in for a hug.

"Me too," Jessica mumbled against Liz's shoulder.

After Liz had left, Jessica stood staring at the door for a while longer, leaning against the cabinet out of which she had taken the envelope of money. Jessica couldn't quite get her head around what had happened tonight. It hadn't come close to anything she had expected.

Chapter Five

"I LIKE YOUR HAIRCUT," Katherine said. "Shorter hair suits you."

"I thought it would be more age appropriate," Jessica said.

"Oh come on. Please don't tell me that was the main motivation for cutting your hair."

"Of course. Mid-forties means mid-length hair. Ask any woman in my family."

"If it's all the same to you, I'd rather not ask the women in your family anything at all—except you, of course."

They both chuckled.

"How are you feeling?" Katherine asked.

"Good," Jessica said. "Although there's something I've been meaning to ask you. Most likely something you're not too keen to talk about. But I can play the C-card, of course."

Katherine shook her head but had a grin on her face nonetheless. "You've played the C-card too often. It has lost its power."

"Damn." Jessica leaned back in her chair. "I thought I'd be able to use it for at least a year after my surgery."

"Maybe that works with other people, but not with me." Katherine put down her grapefruit mimosa. Jessica had invited her for brunch, although she wasn't partaking of the mimosas herself. Her doctor had advised her to not drink too much alcohol and, since her diagnosis, Jessica had drawn the line at daytime drinking. But it was good that Katherine already had two drinks down her. It would make her more amenable to the subject Jessica was eager to discuss.

Jessica looked her friend in the eye. There seemed to be no other way to ask this question, not for her. Eye contact was required. "What happened to Laurel?"

"Laurel?" Katherine said. "Why do you ask?"

Jessica rolled her eyes. "Why can't you simply answer a question with an actual reply instead of another question?"

"Come on, Jess. You know I can't give you any information about Laurel. We have a code of conduct."

"And is that code still valid once someone's no longer with the agency?"

Katherine sighed. "The truth is that I don't know what happened to Laurel after she quit. She's probably just living her life, like we all do, except she doesn't do certain things anymore." Katherine narrowed her eyes. "How do you know Laurel quit?"

"I, er, booked her for the other night. Someone else turned up."

Katherine's eyebrows shot up. "Are you serious?"

Jessica nodded slowly.

"God, Jess, I'm so sorry. That should never have happened."

"It worked out fine in the end."

"Did you make a complaint?"

"It's been dealt with."

Katherine tilted her head. "You're taking this surprisingly well."

"Believe me, I didn't at the time. But let's just say that the woman who turned up helped me change my mind over the course of the evening."

"Who was it?" Katherine asked.

"I'm not sure I'm allowed to say. Code of conduct and all that," Jessica said.

"The code doesn't apply to you," Katherine was quick to say.

"She called herself Liz. Probably not her real name. She didn't much look like a Liz."

Katherine nodded. "I know Liz."

"You do?" Jessica's heart skipped a beat.

"I like her. She's got a good sense of humor, which is a necessity in our line of work, although not everyone possesses the required amount. Liz does."

"Nothing happened," Jessica blurted out. "We just talked. Went for a walk."

Katherine looked at Jessica from under her lashes while she took another sip of her drink. "Would something have happened if Laurel had turned up?"

"Who's to say, really?" Jessica said wistfully. "I knew I wasn't ready but I wanted to force something. Now I'm not even sure I still want to use an escort agency to fulfill this need inside of me." She shook her head. "Sometimes I think having all this money has made me so fucked up in the head." Jessica was glad she could at least talk to Katherine about this. She wouldn't dream of broaching the subject with anyone else—not even someone as open-minded as Caitlin. It wasn't about the other person's open-mindedness anyway. It was about her own feelings of shame.

"Take it from someone who knows, Jess. For someone with too much money to know what to do with, you're a very decent person." Katherine grinned. "If you feel fucked up, it's because of the cancer. And the other stuff that happened before. The past few years have been rough on you."

"Is that an excuse to hire an escort, though?"

"You don't need an excuse. You don't need to justify yourself to *anyone.*"

"Myself," Jessica said. "I had a lovely evening with Liz, but it was just that. An evening. God knows what she's doing with another woman right this moment. It's all so fake, yet it feels like all I'm capable of."

"It's not fake in the moment," Katherine said.

"I'm not sure I get what you're saying." Jessica looked at her friend. "You don't fake it with clients?"

"*You* are not faking it in the moment. What you feel is real. That's all that matters. That's why you asked Laurel to come over. Because, however briefly, you knew she could make you feel something real."

Jessica huffed out a breath. "I don't think so."

"Think about it for a day or two, then let me know if my words of wisdom still don't have a whiff of truth to them." Katherine found Jessica's gaze. "And don't forget, we have feelings too. We are humans just like you."

Jessica mixed Katherine another mimosa. Before she had cancer she wouldn't have dared to continue this line of questioning but since meeting Liz, her curiosity had been piqued. "Can I ask you something else?"

"You might as well. That's why you keep topping up my glass, isn't it? Although I would like to state for the record that it's no fun drinking alone. Won't you have a tiny glass with me? It's not going to kill you any faster, is it?"

Jessica burst out laughing. Comments like this were the very reason she and Katherine had become friends.

"Oh, all right." She quickly drank the contents of her water glass, poured a splash of champagne and a good glug of grapefruit juice into it, and held it up. "To tipsy Sunday brunches."

"And good friends." Katherine watched Jessica take a sip. "Now, shoot," she said. "What's the pressing matter on your mind?"

"Have you, um, ever developed feelings for a client?"

"I don't want to say you're easy to read, Jess, but I saw that one coming from a mile away." Katherine chuckled.

"How could you possibly have known what I was going to ask?"

"I see and hear so many things. A lot depends on me being able to read people. And you're my friend. I know you well." She drew her lips into a soft smile before speaking again. "And I couldn't help but notice the sparkle in your eyes when you spoke of Liz."

"What?" Jessica's cheeks flushed. "No, no, no. That's not why I'm asking." She drank from her mimosa. "And, once again, you're not answering the question."

"Okay, Little Miss Defensive... although I dare say the lady doth protest too much." She winked. "The answer to your question is no. This isn't *Pretty Woman*."

"Agreed. Not one Richard Gere in sight and thank goodness for that." Jessica fiddled with her hands. She regretted having asked the question—had she given away too much? To herself included?—yet she couldn't quite let it go. "You've never met anyone of who you thought that, under different circumstances you might hit it off with?"

"Ah, but that's the key right there. Circumstance is everything. I'm not saying emotions are that easily controlled all the time, or that it's the same for everyone, but I'm just not one to develop romantic feelings for someone who pays me money to sleep with them. There's a psychological line I can't cross, no matter how charming or nice or dazzling the client. It just doesn't happen. It's like, as a lesbian, you have to learn early on to not fall for the straight girls because you know there's just no way, and you know you'll only end up getting hurt."

"That didn't stop me from falling in love with many a straight girl in my time." Jessica scoffed.

"Yes well, hormones and puberty and such will do that to you. But now you know. You learned your lesson and you evolved. It's part of you."

"That just sounds a little too easy. Sometimes you simply can't help falling for a straight girl. If I had a penny for every adult lesbian hopelessly in love with a straight woman at this very moment, I'd be very rich indeed."

"You're rich already, Jess."

Jessica waved off Katherine's comment. "I don't agree with your analogy."

"It's a matter of give and take. Of giving the right signs. Or, if you're receiving signs that someone is developing a little crush, of not throwing oil onto the fire. And of being mature about these things."

"Let me ask you this then," Jessica said. "Have any of your clients had a noticeable crush on you?"

Katherine leaned back, taking her mimosa with her. After a while, she nodded. "It happens. It's a thin line when you spend time in bed with someone."

"How did you handle it?" Jessica's ears perked all the way up.

"Never by milking it, if that's what you're wondering." Katherine narrowed her eyes to slits.

"Who's defensive now?" Jessica asked.

"I'm just a bit baffled by your sudden curiosity about my job."

"I've always been this curious, Kat. I think before I was just too embarrassed to ask."

"But is it a coincidence that you want to know about it all

mere days after you met Liz?" Katherine quirked up her eyebrows.

"Yes and no." Jessica grinned at Katherine.

"Please elaborate."

"It had been months since I last saw Laurel. I had bloody surgery—I had a breast removed. My mind hasn't really been pondering the ins and outs of the escort service. Then meeting Liz, and having too much time on my hands, brought up a lot of questions. Does that explain it?"

"You could have had all those questions when you were a regular client of Laurel's. We were friends then. You could have asked me then."

"But that was before I knew I had cancer. Back then, I wasn't the type of person to ask questions like this."

"Ah, so if I understand correctly, your diagnosis, surgery, and convalescence have all worked together to ignite your curiosity about being a luxury escort. Are you considering a career switch, Jess?" Katherine had a smug smile on her face.

Jessica nearly spat out the sip of mimosa she just took. "Christ, imagine my father's reaction." She chuckled. "Or no, my stepmother's. Hers would be priceless. A drama for the ages. Woe her." She shook her head. "I'm just curious. That's it. And you *still* haven't answered my question."

"I'll answer more than your question." Katherine pushed a strand of hair behind her ear. "When I notice a client developing feelings for me, I wind down the relationship. That's the only correct way to deal with it. At least, that's the way *I* deal with it. I try not to embarrass them in the process and, if they're open to it, hook them up with someone else. It doesn't have to be a big drama." She leaned forward again, tapping her index finger onto the wooden table top. "Now as for the question you didn't ask—well, not in so many words, anyway." She tilted her head. "My conclusion is the following: I think you like Liz."

"Well, yes. I think I said as much." Jessica's hackles went all the way up.

"You sure did." Katherine extended her hand over the table and enveloped Jessica's in hers. "You're like an open book. I'm not saying this to goad you or embarrass you. I'm saying this as your friend. If this is how you feel after a few hours during which—your words—'nothing happened', I would advise you to not see Liz again. I can get you someone else. Someone more like Laurel."

"What?" Jessica shook her head. "No, Kat, you've got it all wrong. Those mimosas must have gone to your head." Jessica pushed a strand of hair behind her ear, but it was too short to remain there and sprang back immediately. Part of the reason why she'd had her hair cut shorter was because it no longer felt right to have long hair. When she went to the hospital to see her oncologist, the waiting room usually held a few people who had not been as fortunate to keep their hair during their treatment.

"I believe I can still hold my liquor." She drew her lips into a soft smile. "You're extra vulnerable right now. You crave someone's arms around you. It's a bitch what you've gone through—and you chose to do it alone, Jess. You didn't tell me you needed surgery. Your emotions were all over the place and you're only now coming back from that. I'm just trying to help. I don't want you to get hurt even more."

"The surgery was almost three months ago. I'm in a much better place right now."

"I can tell you're doing better physically. That's for sure." Katherine squeezed Jessica's hand. Jessica had to admit it felt good on hers. Just like feeling Liz's hand in hers had felt somehow right. "Often, when you feel better after an illness, the brain can trick you into feeling superhuman, like you're up for anything. But you need to give your emotions time to catch up. Falling in love with an escort isn't going to help that process."

Jessica drew her hand away. "For Christ's sake. I'm not falling in love with Liz. I've only met the woman once. All she turned out to be was a nice surprise." Jessica shook her head. "I know you mean well, but your powers of perception are not as finely attuned as you think they are."

Katherine held up her hands. "Fine. I'll drop it." She slanted herself away from Jessica. "Let's change the subject, shall we?"

"Let's." Jessica drank from her mimosa. She barely tasted the alcohol. It slid down so easily. She emptied her glass and poured herself another.

"Are you ready to go back to work?" Katherine asked.

"Oh yes. I'm so tired of doing nothing. That's what killed me after the agency went bankrupt as well. Waking up and having no idea what to do with my day."

"How's Caitlin?" A different kind of smile appeared on Katherine's face.

"She has been so kind to me. Truth be told, I hadn't expected it."

"Even after that disappearing act you pulled on her. Well, on both of us."

"Water under the bridge, Kat. You know why I did it. So does Caitlin. We've all moved on."

Katherine nodded. "When will you be ready to host another dinner party?" She quirked up one side of her mouth.

Jessica shook her head. "That ship has sailed. Caitlin and I are such good friends now."

"What does that say about our friendship then?" There was glee in Katherine's tone.

"It's different with you. Not every friendship is the same."

Katherine gave a brief chuckle then fell silent. "As soon

as you feel up to it, we should go to one of Jo's gigs. You haven't seen her live have you?"

"I've seen plenty of her live." Jessica couldn't help but smile.

"You know what I mean." Katherine smiled with her.

Jessica nodded. "I'll let you know."

Chapter Six

"MORTON'S FINE," Caitlin said. "Very unintrusive." She was referring to the person currently replacing Jessica at ANBC while she was on sick leave.

"You mean he doesn't nag you about getting certain people on your show?" When Jessica had just started her job at the network and had become Caitlin's boss, she had pushed relentlessly for Caitlin to interview reality TV star Kathy Kramer. The show had been a disaster. Jessica had learned her lesson and had since refrained from suggesting guests.

"There's that." Caitlin beamed a wide smile at her. "How are you feeling?" She sipped from her coffee. They were sitting at a table by the window in the Pink Bean.

"Fine." One of the oddest experiences of falling ill was not being able to resort to that standard reply whenever someone asked how she was doing. It was a word so ingrained in everyday life, it was hard to deviate from, even when she was feeling at her worst.

"Really?" Caitlin insisted. "You know you can talk to me."

"Do I not look fine to you?" Jessica painted on a fake, wide grin.

"You do. You look remarkable for someone on sick leave."

"That's why I'm going back to work next week. I've missed bugging you."

"Oh, and how we've missed you." Caitlin put her cup down.

"It does feel a bit strange, though," Jessica said. "It doesn't feel like the same person going back. Honestly, I got lucky. Yes, I had surgery, but it wasn't even that invasive—"

Caitlin held up her hand. "Let me stop you right there." She leaned over the table. "You keep doing this, Jess. You keep claiming you got lucky and that it could have been much worse. But you had a breast removed. You had cancer. That's not what's generally considered 'being lucky.'"

"Not everyone gets to survive," Jessica said.

"That's true, but that doesn't mean you're not allowed to feel shaken up by this whole thing."

"I feel plenty shaken up." Jessica took a deep breath. "I'm just over having to talk about it all the time." She ran a finger over the handle of her coffee cup. "Yet I'm constantly reminded of it. Not only when I can't face myself in the mirror, but just in everyday life. For example, when I think about going back to work. I think in terms of pre- and post-cancer now. I'm not really sure who I am post-cancer, while I knew very well who I was before."

"Let me tell you how your co-workers saw you before cancer," Caitlin said, keeping her voice low.

"No need. They saw me as the big boss's daughter. A bit of a tough bitch who was out to prove she was more than a daddy's girl who took one of the top jobs. Not on merit, but because of nepotism."

"Wow," Caitlin said on a sigh. "Seems to me you've

become even harder on yourself." She shook her head. "That's not what I was going to say at all."

Jessica let her shoulders slump. She inhaled deeply to regroup. "It's like there's this dark cloud following me around. It doesn't always hang over my head, but it moves in and out. When it does move in, things always look so bleak."

"Do you think coming back to work will help?" Caitlin asked.

Jessica nodded vigorously. "God, yes. I need some purpose."

"You won't be working full-time from the get-go, will you?" Caitlin pinned her gaze on Jessica.

"No, but not because I don't want to. They won't let me. My father must have gotten to the HR department. It's very unlike him to meddle with things like that."

"Maybe he realized he could have lost you."

Jessica scoffed. "Edward Porter doesn't let his mind become occupied with futilities like that."

"You'd be surprised," Caitlin said.

"And you're the expert on parents now, are you?" Jessica was well aware of how acerbic she sounded.

"Christ, Jess," Caitlin said. "You have a wall of sarcasm of about this thick around you." Caitlin held her hands ten inches apart. "I know why, so I forgive you, but when you go back to work, not everyone will be as understanding as I am." Caitlin looked at the door and her face lit up.

Jessica followed her gaze. Jo had just walked in. Jessica hadn't seen her often since the night they'd spent together, but every time she did a shiver ran up her spine.

She had orchestrated that night when she, Caitlin, Jo and Katherine had landed in bed together for a reason. It was meant to be a farewell to the Jessica with two naturally-grown breasts. Seeing Jo reminded her very specifically of that, because that night Jo had definitely been the most taken with her breasts. What would she think if she saw them now?

"I'm sorry," Jessica quickly mumbled. Caitlin had sat by her bedside when Jessica hadn't been able to do much and had confided in her about her own sour relationship with her parents.

Caitlin waved her off. "You're forgiven." She pulled up a chair for Jo.

"Hey, Jess," Jo said, and leaned down to kiss Jessica on the cheek. "You're looking well."

"Coffee with Caitlin James will do that to you," Jessica replied. She shot Jo a quick wink, then scanned Caitlin's face to make sure she had definitely been forgiven for her earlier remark.

Jo put an arm around Caitlin's shoulders. "Refills?" Jo glanced around the Pink Bean. "I haven't worked here in months yet it still feels strange to just walk in here," she said.

"Decaf for me, please," Jessica said. "I think this is around the time Amber comes in and I don't want another lecture on the negative effects of caffeine on my body's healing process."

"Even Amber can't tell the difference between regular coffee and decaf by sight alone," Jo said.

Jessica shrugged. "Then I guess her speech worked on me, because I'll have decaf regardless."

"If you really wanted to impress her, you'd have a green tea," Caitlin chimed in.

"And go vegan," Jo added. She glanced at Caitlin. "Another long black for you, babe, so you'll be nicely jacked up for the rest of the day?"

Caitlin patted Jo on the back. "You got it."

Jo headed to the counter and Jessica took the opportunity to lean over the table and say, "Katherine asked about you the other day."

Caitlin pursed her lips together and nodded. "How is she?"

"She wanted to know when I would be throwing another dinner party *like that*." Jessica couldn't help but grin.

Caitlin chuckled. "What did you say?"

"That you and I are friends of a different nature now."

Caitlin nodded. "I'm glad we agree."

They sat in silence for a few moments.

"That doesn't mean we can't have a meal together, of course," Caitlin said after a while. "Do you want to come to ours some time? Bring Katherine?"

"That would be lovely." Jessica couldn't help but think about someone else she would like to bring. After her conversation with Katherine, Jessica had tried not to think about Liz, but trying not to think about someone usually had the opposite result. Jessica's brain was subject to the same laws of psychology. She thought about her evening with Liz often. She tried berating herself by replaying Katherine's words in her head, but she always ended up rebuffing them. What Katherine had claimed was simply too ludicrous.

Jo returned with their cups of coffee.

"Tell us when you're free, darling," Caitlin said, "Jess and Katherine are coming to dinner."

Jo quirked up her eyebrows but didn't say anything.

"Not like that," Caitlin said. "Just dinner."

Jo chuckled. "Of course. What else could we possibly do but eat, drink, and be merry?"

Chapter Seven

JESSICA's first day back at work wasn't going so well. She felt almost as out of place as she had on the day her own company had gone bust and she hadn't told any of her employees yet. Today, she felt like someone placed by her father to oversee the Programming Department, like a mere puppet drilled to report on any unusual goings-on, not someone capable of actually running the department. Caitlin had been right, Morton had done a good job of replacing her. Apart from going through a mailbox with too many emails in it to ever read, Jessica didn't quite know what to do with herself.

Instead of addressing her inbox and getting back into the swing of things, she picked up her phone and scrolled through the apps. Her finger eventually landed on the web browser in which she opened a private window. She logged on to the escort agency's website and let her finger hover over the contact button. Her pulse picked up speed. Katherine had been right about one thing. The entire process at least made Jessica feel very much alive—made her feel something real.

The required action was simple. All she had to do was send a message and request Liz. It could be as brief as 'Liz - this afternoon - my known address'.

But Jessica closed the browser window and threw her phone onto her desk. She had work to do. She shot out of her chair and walked to the window. From her office she could see Darling Harbour. Dozens of tiny people were milling about below, going about their day. They walked as though filled to the brim with a sense of purpose. Something Jessica couldn't possibly fathom.

But what had she expected? That she could just step into her office and, as though she had walked through a magic door, she would feel that drive again?

She didn't feel any purpose, nor magic. It was like she had lost all the drive she had started this new job with not even a year ago. The truth was that while she was on sick leave, Jessica had barely watched ANBC, or any other network TV. The only exception was *The Caitlin James Show*.

She had blamed it on her illness, on not having much appetite for anything. Watching TV had been very low on her list of needs to fulfill, even if it was the only thing to keep her company, especially during the long hours before and after midnight. She had believed this was because TV just reminded her of work, and work reminded her of her advertising agency that she had led into bankruptcy, and the fallout of all of that.

But now that she was back at work, she didn't feel that spark she used to feel anymore. She didn't know if it was because some of her views on life had changed since her diagnosis, or simply because she was, as her father would most likely call it, capricious.

"You're in your forties, yet you behave like one of those entitled millennials," he'd said after he had paid off her employees—his money in return for their silence.

Jessica shook off that thought and tried to empty her mind the way Amber had taught her. Caitlin had brought her on a few visits while she was convalescing, even though they hardly knew each other. Caitlin had barely been able to stop Amber from going through Jessica's kitchen cabinets searching for foods that should be in no cancer survivor's pantry.

Jessica closed off her right nostril with her thumb, breathed in deeply through the other, then pushed her index finger against her left nostril and exhaled through the right one. This was supposed to calm her down. The problem was that Jessica wasn't feeling agitated. It was more a sense of total deflation that absorbed her.

She'd been scared of coming back to work, but also excited. Now that she was here however, the same numbness that had lain over her like a blanket since her surgery had returned—a blanket that she couldn't throw off, no matter how hard she tried.

The only time she'd felt it lift, was on that walk with Liz. And when Liz had pushed her thumbs into the hard knots underneath Jessica's shoulder blades.

Jessica checked her watch. It was almost eleven. She was only supposed to be in half a day. She'd had a big breakfast meeting with the key people in her department earlier that morning. She'd been briefed but, she got the impression, not too much. Even the people she worked with felt like she wasn't fully back yet. She could leave work right now and no one would care. A few people would notice, but they would shrug it off all too easily.

The fact of the matter was that Jessica didn't want to be there. She wanted to walk around the city, preferably with Liz on her arm. Was that really such a bad thing to want? Perhaps it was exactly what she needed. Some time with Liz to recharge and start fresh at work tomorrow. Yes, that was it.

She could come in the next day feeling more alive, ready and able.

She walked to her desk, picked up her phone, and opened the private browser window again. She sent the message.

She paced through her office waiting for a response after the immediate automated one. Was someone calling Liz now to check her availability—and her willingness to see Jessica again? Jessica had been glad for the opportunity to quiz Katherine, but she still had so many questions left. Maybe she could ask Liz. She just wanted to go for a walk, maybe get another one of those shoulder massages, and have a chat.

And feel the warmth of Liz's smile.

She glared at her phone every few seconds, but refused to let herself pick it up until ten minutes had passed. What if Liz didn't want to see her anymore? Or if Katherine had told her about their conversation. Was that even possible? Wouldn't that break the agency's code of conduct?

She picked up her phone and checked her messages on the website. A new one had come in.

Liz will be at your known address at 3:00 p.m.

Jessica balled her fist in a gesture of victory. Instantly, the apathy she had been drenched in all morning fell away. She had four hours to get ready for Liz.

Chapter Eight

JESSICA WAS ready long before Liz rang the doorbell. A little before three, she heard a car pull up in her quiet street. A door opened and closed, then the car drove off. She wondered if the agency had their own car service or if they just used taxis and Ubers.

She opened the door before Liz had a chance to ring the bell. Jessica scanned the street, but her gaze was instantly drawn to Liz.

"Hey." Liz stood there grinning, as though it had always been a foregone conclusion that Jessica would request her services again.

"Hi, please come in." Jessica gave Liz a once-over. She was slightly taken aback by her outfit. Laurel would never have shown up in jeans—no matter how well-fitted—and a plaid shirt. Jessica could distinguish fine clothing from cheap garments made in Asian factories, and the shirt Liz was wearing, unbuttoned over a white, very tight top, didn't look cheap at all, yet the way she wore it made her look so casual. Too casual for the job she was here to do.

Liz slipped inside and as she walked past, Jessica could

smell her perfume. It was fruity and light with a hint of nut. Liz halted in the hallway and put a hand on Jessica's shoulder. "Good to see you again," she said.

"You too." Jessica let her gaze linger on Liz's jeans for an instant and slanted her head.

Liz looked Jessica in the eye. "This is how I dress on a Monday. I took a gamble and thought you'd be okay with that."

Jessica arched up her eyebrows. "It's fine, of course." She tried very hard to not look for any deeper meaning behind Liz's choice of clothing even though it didn't align with her idea of how an escort was supposed to dress.

"How are you?" Liz asked and squeezed Jessica's shoulder again.

"Well." She led them into the living room. "I was hoping we could go for a walk again. The weather's lovely."

Liz stuck out a foot. "Sensible shoes." They were brown leather boots. The color matched Liz's belt. She wore a leather jacket in a slightly darker shade of brown. If Jessica had crossed her in the street looking like this, she wouldn't have only turned around because Liz was a beautiful woman, but because her gaydar would be seriously pinging.

She couldn't wait to walk through the streets of Pott's Point with this woman on her arm.

"Didn't you say you were starting work again this week?" Liz asked.

They had walked to the end of Jessica's street in silence. Jessica wondered if Liz needed some time to read her mood before she initiated conversation. Or perhaps she didn't really know what to say. Conversation skills were surely something she needed in her line of work, but,

Jessica figured, it was hardly her main job. Or maybe it was.

Too many questions were buzzing around in her head again, so she was glad Liz broke the silence, even if it meant she had to talk about work.

"I did, I started today. Only part-time for the first few weeks though. We'll see how it goes."

"How did it go this morning?" Liz was the one to steer them to the right at the end of the street. It didn't matter which direction they walked in. Jessica just wanted to be outside of her house, breathe in some fresh air, and not feel alone while doing so.

Jessica shook her head. "Not an unequivocal success." Her shoulders slumped at the mere memory of how deflated she had felt.

"Isn't that to be expected after a long absence?" Liz asked.

"No, I was expecting the opposite." Jessica glanced at Liz from the corner of her eye.

"Maybe you went back too soon."

"Maybe," Jessica mumbled, but her mind had been put on a different track already. "Have you ever had a corporate job?" she asked.

Liz remained silent for a beat. "I have." Silence again. Jessica didn't say anything, hoping Liz would continue of her own accord. "It was an office job. I would hardly call it corporate. Admin mostly. It didn't suit me very much." She turned to Jessica and smiled. "Come to think of it, it was kind of soul-sucking. And the money wasn't all that good either."

"Soul-sucking?" Jessica repeated.

"It was just dreary, unchallenging, repetitive office work. Some people can thrive in that sort of environment, but I can't."

"Soul-sucking is not a word you would use to describe your current job?" Jessica asked.

"No way." Liz vehemently shook her head. "Quite the opposite I would say."

"Really?"

Liz stopped in her tracks. "It's kind of a strange question."

It was physically impossible for Jessica not to look up to Liz as they stood facing each other.

"Does any of this feel soul-sucking to you?" Liz asked.

"Well, no, but I—"

"You're the client." Liz grinned. "And there's a distinct difference between us in this relationship." She crossed her arms in front of her chest. "That's absolutely true, but I never do a job I don't want to do."

Her words reminded Jessica that, in the end, that was all she was and ever could be to Liz: a job.

Liz uncrossed her arms and touched a finger to Jessica's chin. "I'm out and about on a beautiful spring day with a gorgeous, sophisticated woman. Tell me where the bad deal in that is for me?" She tilted up Jessica's chin.

Jessica averted her eyes. A hot flush crept up her cheeks. Gorgeous? Sophisticated? Technically, Liz was paid to say these things to her, but that didn't mean she had to.

"Shall we continue our walk?" Jessica said.

"Let's go." Liz offered Jessica her arm again, and Jessica gladly hooked hers through.

They walked in silence for a while and Jessica managed to quieten the voice in her head and just enjoy the simple sensation of, as Liz had called it, being out and about. She reveled in the sound of Liz's footsteps next to her, totally in step with her own. In the looks that Liz drew from passersby because of her height and her stunning face.

Jessica let Liz guide the way. Since this was her neighborhood, her walks always took her in the same direction as a force of habit. Liz's meanderings had brought them to the edge of Darlinghurst. Jessica could see the top of Caitlin's building from where she stood.

"Would you like a cup of coffee?" she asked.

"I would love one."

"I know just the place," Jessica said.

―――――

"I'll get the coffees," Liz said after they had walked into the Pink Bean. "You sit down."

"Are you sure?" Again, Jessica was flummoxed by Liz's behavior. Wasn't the client supposed to provide all beverages?

"Of course." Liz shot Jessica a wide grin.

"Okay." Jessica found a table by the window. She looked around, but didn't see anyone familiar. It was the middle of the afternoon.

Jessica's gaze was drawn to Liz's backside as she stood at the counter. She filled out those jeans in the most exquisite way. Jessica couldn't even picture Liz in a dress. She couldn't be totally sure, of course, but she believed Liz wasn't only gay for pay. There was too distinct a feeling she couldn't shake off.

If only she could have ten minutes of unlimited question time. But inside information was much harder to come by than other things when dealing with women like Liz and Katherine. At least that was how they made it look.

"A double espresso for you." Liz arrived at the table. "Planning to stay up late, are you?" She winked at Jessica then sat down opposite and held up her cup. "I'm more a soft-core latte girl myself."

They sipped from their beverages. As Jessica put her cup down, she asked, "How many hours did you exercise today?"

"A grand total of zero," Liz said. "I got an unexpected call."

"Oh yes." Jessica nodded. "A demanding customer."

"Not in the least." Liz smiled softly.

"So…" Jessica was already mentally preparing for a rebuff, but she wanted to ask the question nonetheless. "How does it work when I send a message on the agency's website?"

Liz narrowed her eyes. "Up until now you've been someone who wants to know everything about what I do rather than enjoy my services."

"Right now, that is a very accurate impression of me."

"Okay." Liz nodded. "I'll answer your questions, but I would like to ask you for something in return."

"Sure." Something inside Jessica lit up.

"Two things, actually, because I'm going to need your discretion as well."

"That goes without saying."

Liz gave a curt nod. "You won't let me leave without having given you a shoulder massage again." She plastered a wide smile on her lips.

"How can I say no to a smile like that?" Maybe this was what Jessica had missed most of all. Flirting. Innuendo. The deliciously promising back and forth between her and another woman.

Liz bit her lip. She excelled at the game of seduction whereas Jessica was feeling a little rusty.

"To answer your question, when someone sends a message requesting me and the requested time slot is free in the calendar I share with the agency, I get a call."

"So there's always someone monitoring the messages coming in?"

"Of course. We provide a non-stop service."

"On very short notice as well, it would appear."

"Only the best for our clients. We're as high-end and niche as you can get."

"What does that really mean?" Now this was interesting, unlike the latest ratings analysis of a TV show Jessica didn't much care about.

"It means that there aren't that many women who have the means to pay the prices we charge for 'The Lesbian Experience'."

Jessica rolled her eyes. "That name almost put me off. Who the hell came up with that?"

"Not a lesbian." Liz's cheeks dimpled as she burst into a chuckle. "So despite being put off by our name, what pulled you over the edge?" Liz rested her chin on an upturned palm and regarded Jessica intently.

"A friend of mine who works for The Lesbian Experience."

"Really?"

Jessica nodded.

"You're not going to tell me who?" Liz asked.

"I don't know. I don't want to break any protocol."

"You won't be breaking anything if you say who it is, I assure you."

"To me, she's Katherine. I believe she goes by Lucy at the agency." Jessica felt like she was doing something illicit by mentioning Katherine's real name.

"That just goes to show," Liz said. "We have friends too." She shot Jessica one of her irresistible smiles again.

"Katherine's one of the only friends who has stood by me through all the shit that has happened the past few years. The cancer. My company going bust. The woman I loved leaving me at the worst time. She's one in a million."

"So you didn't meet her through the agency?"

"No. I met her at one of my father's charity balls. She was the plus one of a guest. Turned quite a few heads, as you can imagine. She mainly made my gaydar ping. We got talking and hit it off."

"Interesting." Liz pouted her lips.

"Why are you looking at me like that?" Jessica asked.

"No reason. I'm just trying to picture the scene." She grinned briefly. "That's something I like to do when someone tells me a story."

"When she told me what she did for a living, my interest was... rather piqued," Jessica said. She had never told this to anyone, not even Caitlin. "Do you tell your friends what you do for a living?"

"Not everyone." Liz sat up a little straighter. "I'd like to be all if-they-can't-accept-what-I-do-we're-not-really-friends about it, but that's not how it works. It's not as black and white. Some people just can't deal with what I do. I accept that. I have no choice. But most of my friends know. The closest ones at least. But I never give them any details about my day, of course."

"I hope not."

"We sign very strict non-disclosure agreements. My discretion is literally worth hundreds of thousands of dollars."

"How about your parents?" Jessica asked.

Liz didn't immediately reply. She looked through the window for a brief moment, then back at Jessica. "My mother died nine years ago. She never knew. My father is... Well, he doesn't have a problem with it. He doesn't have a problem with much of anything. He's the very definition of laid back."

"I'm sorry to hear about your mother." Jessica sipped from her cup but her coffee had gone cold.

Liz nodded slowly. She opened her mouth to speak, but then closed it again. She looked away again and only glanced at Jessica after several moments had passed. "I always think I can't say this to other cancer patients, which is bullshit, in the end." She held Jessica's gaze. "My mother died of ovarian cancer."

An ice-cold arrow shot up Jessica's spine. "I'm so sorry," she managed to say.

"Thankfully, I'm not here to talk about my mother." The smile Liz drew her lips into wasn't very convincing.

"You can if you want to. I mean, you don't have to refrain from saying anything because I have—*had* cancer." Jessica stared at the remaining coffee in her cup. "I can handle it, if that's what you're worried about."

"I know you can." Liz startled her by finding Jessica's hand on the table and covering it with hers.

Jessica's gut reaction was to look around and check again whether anyone she knew was at the Pink Bean. Liz might not be dressed the part, but her actions could give certain things away that Jessica would prefer to keep hidden. Then again, that hand felt good on hers, warm and comforting, and she was the one who had wanted to take Liz out.

"Can I speak frankly?" Liz asked, giving Jessica's hand another squeeze.

Jessica nodded slowly. "I guess."

"Yes or no." Liz's smile had become genuine again.

"Yes." The strong tone with which Liz asked the question sent a frisson of excitement through Jessica.

"I think you can handle a hell of a lot more than you think you can at this moment."

Jessica scanned Liz's face. She lost her focus on what Liz had just said for a split second, simply because her features were too mesmerizing. "Maybe," was all Jessica said. "I just don't feel like doing a whole lot."

"I get that, but…" Liz fell silent.

"But what?" Jessica leaned onto the table.

"Look, you don't know me and you don't have any

reason to trust me, but I'd like to take you home and show you what you're capable of."

Jessica's cheeks broke into an instant flush. What was Liz insinuating? "Wh-what do you mean?"

"You'll see when we get there," Liz said and waggled her eyebrows.

Chapter Nine

WHEN THEY ARRIVED at Jessica's house, Liz halted in the hallway and gazed at a painting hanging on the wall. "I probably don't have to tell you," she said, "but this is worth a small fortune."

Jessica stood next to her and looked at the painting with her. "You know more than I do."

Liz looked at her, her brows knitted together. "This is a Robert Barrow. They go for at least a million at auction."

"I hadn't pegged you for an art buff."

"Art historian, actually," Liz said. "The most useless degree you can get at university, but I do recognize a Barrow when I see one."

"You studied Art History?" Jessica took a step back and regarded Liz the way they'd just been studying the painting.

"Is that so surprising?" Liz's smile turned into a lopsided grin.

"I don't know. It surprised *me*." Jessica huffed out an awkward giggle.

Liz leaned against the hallway cabinet, seemingly no longer interested in the painting. "What I'm wondering is, if you have all this money hanging on your walls, why did your company go bust? Why didn't you just pay off the debts and move on?"

Instinctively, Jessica took a step back. "That's a very direct question."

"Is it?" Liz jutted out her bottom lip. "I didn't think it was."

"I'd rather not talk about that if it's all the same to you."

Liz took a step closer. "Your wish is my command."

This made Jessica chuckle. "What did you want to show me?"

"I'd like *you* to start by showing me your bedroom." Liz squared her impressive shoulders.

"I—I'm not sure I want to—"

"Just show me. That's all I ask. I'd like to give you a proper back massage. Nothing more."

Jessica considered this for a moment. She did want to feel Liz's hands on her skin again. She was just worried about what she meant by a *proper* massage. Jessica could hazard a guess, of course.

"Okay," Jessica said and headed up the stairs. Liz followed on her heels.

"Welcome to my boudoir." Jessica opened the bedroom door.

"This should work." Liz scanned the room, then looked at Jessica. "Can you lie on your belly comfortably, or would you prefer a pillow underneath you?"

"I'm fine." It had taken a while, but she could finally sleep on her belly again.

"Do you mind taking off your blouse and lying face down for me? I'll be getting ready in the bathroom while you do so. I won't see anything you don't want me to see. Only your back. Leave your bra on if it makes you feel more secure."

"You don't mess about, do you?" Jessica said.

"Sometimes that's what it takes." Liz flashed her a smile, then pointed at the door next to the bed. "Is that a bathroom?"

Jessica nodded.

"I'll be in there. Just give me a shout when you're ready."

Before she went into the bathroom, Liz stepped closer and cupped Jessica's jaw in her hand. "It's going to be all right, Jess." She said it as though no truer words had ever been spoken. Only Jessica's friends abbreviated her name and it made her feel, for a split second, as though she was in the company of a friend.

Liz dropped her hand and strutted into the bathroom. Jessica stared at the closed door for a few seconds. She took a deep breath. Taking off her blouse was not a problem for her when she was alone and there was no mirror around. She unbuttoned it and hung it over a chair. She debated whether to take off her bra, but that debate quickly fizzled out when she thought of the glimpses she had caught of herself in the mirror, and all the times she had turned away from her mirror image.

She drew the line at her bra. She kept it on and lay on the bed. She let herself sink into the mattress and allowed herself the moment of delightful anticipation. There was nothing to be afraid of. And there was a gorgeous woman getting ready—whatever that entailed—in her bathroom to give her a back massage.

"I'm ready," Jessica said. She didn't know if it was loud enough for Liz to hear, but sure enough, a few moments later, Liz exited the bathroom. She carried a small bottle of oil and a towel and she was no longer wearing the shirt over her top, revealing toned arms. And a smile so disarming, Jessica was sorry she was lying on her belly because it would be taken from her view any moment now.

Liz didn't comment on Jessica still wearing her bra. She proceeded in silence. She covered everything below the fastening of Jessica's bra with the towel, then, gently, Jessica felt Liz straddle her. She didn't rest any of her weight on Jessica but Jessica felt her jeans-clad knees against her sides where the towel didn't cover her completely.

"Actually," Liz said, and pushed herself up carefully. "I'm going to take these off."

Jessica watched Liz slip out of her jeans. The skin she bared looked so smooth, Jessica had to resist the urge to reach out and run a finger over Liz's thigh. But before she knew it, Liz was straddling her again, this time with her bare knees touching the naked skin of Jessica's. Jessica didn't protest or draw Liz's attention to the towel in disarray.

She heard the same squirting sound she'd heard the first evening with Liz, then the rubbing of oily palms together. Next, a pair of warm hands landed on her shoulders. Liz caressed her only lightly, spreading the oil.

"Can I move these out of the way?" she whispered as she hooked a finger underneath Jessica's bra strap.

"Okay." Jessica was hardly going to resist now. And why did her voice sound so hoarse?

Liz lowered her bra straps. Jessica maneuvered her arms out of them one at a time, making sure the cups of her bra remained in place.

Liz gently tucked the straps under the top of the towel. She spread some oil on Jessica's neck and Jessica felt all the tiny hairs on her body stand up. She already had to catch her breath and the massage hadn't even started yet.

As she moved her hand about Jessica's neck and shoulders, Liz's behind sometimes touched down lightly on Jessica's.

Jessica wished she could see Liz's biceps flex as she

worked on her body. If only she could turn around, but that was still out of the question.

"Aah," Jessica moaned when Liz pushed her thumbs into the sensitive spots on her shoulders. Then she simply gave in to the myriad of sensations engulfing her. Relaxation was one of them, but there were many others. She was much more aware of Liz's touch on her skin this time around. Liz's hands moved around much more freely and, Jessica believed, with much more abandon.

Liz's breath sounded steady and controlled. The pressure of her kneading motions gradually increased until Jessica believed she didn't have a single ounce of tension left in her shoulder muscles.

Liz's hands stopped moving and Jessica felt her breath pass along her ear.

"I'm going to move the towel down a little," she said.

She didn't ask. She just told Jessica what she was going to do. Maybe she sensed Jessica would say yes—she'd agree to just about anything at this point.

Soon after, the towel slid down Jessica's back. Liz ran a finger down her spine and the sensation coaxed another moan, albeit of a slightly different nature, from Jessica's throat.

Again, without asking, Liz unfastened her bra. She did it slowly, gently sliding the sides onto the bed. Jessica stiffened a bit in response, but she told herself to take a deep breath. That particular piece of fabric hadn't been hiding anything vital—it just stood in the way of more pleasure.

Liz spread more oil onto Jessica's back and repeated the same process as before. She started by simply caressing Jessica's skin, incrementally upping the pressure, until her fingertips drained Jessica's body of all the tension she'd been keeping inside.

Jessica was so relaxed, she allowed her mind to drift to

where she had fiercely forbidden it to go before. What if Liz had been Laurel? Would more have happened? Would she have shown herself already? And what would it be like to be touched like that by Liz? What was Liz's real name? There were so many boundaries she wanted to cross, but she wouldn't get anywhere if she failed to take on the first hurdle.

When the back massage was finished, Liz leaned over her and pushed Jessica's hair away from her ear. "Any other spots you would like me to get my hands on?" Her voice was sultry and deep.

Jessica took a moment to consider her reply. She had sort of expected the question. She twisted her neck as far as it would go in her current position. "Yes," she said.

Liz nodded and slowly moved off her, as though not to disturb the delicate balance in the atmosphere between them. She lay down on her side, looking at Jessica's face.

"Take all the time you need," she whispered.

Chapter Ten

JESSICA GLANCED into Liz's eyes, as though all the strength she needed for what she was about to do could be found in the depths of them.

She started by pushing herself up with one arm. Her left side—the intact one—would become visible first. She moved her bra from underneath her and tossed it to the side. Ever so slowly, Jessica started to turn on her side to face Liz, covering her chest as best she could with her arm, still limp from the massage. She stopped when she came eye to eye with Liz, who kept her gaze firmly on Jessica's face.

Her right side was covered by the arm she held in front of it.

Liz raised her hand and with the lightest touch imaginable, stroked Jessica's left arm. "You're so brave," she said.

It was all Jessica needed to reach the next level of courage. Those words from Liz.

As she turned onto her back, Liz's hand slipped onto Jessica's belly, and stayed there. The physical connection between them strengthened Jessica's resolve. She was doing this. There was no mirror anywhere near her. She wouldn't even have to see it herself.

Jessica lay on her back, her arms crossed over her chest.

Liz's hand was warm and comforting on her belly. She'd pushed herself onto an elbow and wore a gentle smile on her lips. She looked deep into Jessica's eyes. She started moving her hand. Just her fingers really, wiggling them about a bit. One started tracing a circle around her belly button. Jessica's remaining nipple reacted instantly. It pressed against the flesh of the arm covering her breast.

Then, out of nowhere, or so it seemed to her, she said, "Kiss me, please."

Liz's eyes narrowed, then closed, as she brought her face forward and gently placed her lips on Jessica's. Jessica's body responded by relaxing into the mattress. Another woman's lips on hers. It had been too long. She had pushed too many people away. She'd become afraid of everything, of the smallest, most ridiculous things, as well as the delicious pleasure of kissing another person.

Liz removed her hand from Jessica's belly and brought it to Jessica's neck, her fingers caressing her jaw. Their tongues slipped into each other's mouths and, as they did, Jessica lowered her arms. She freed her chest from the cage she had kept it in. Her nipple stiffened more in response.

She threw an arm around Liz's waist. No matter how good that top looked on her, she wanted to yank it off her. Her other hand she used to draw Liz's face closer toward hers, to drink more of her in. She tasted so good. She smelled divine. Her flesh felt hard and toned underneath Jessica's touch. Jessica was getting so carried away, she nearly forgot about how she got here in the first place. Until they broke from their kiss.

She smiled up at Liz and kept her arms where they were, away from her chest.

Liz caressed her cheek. "You set the pace."

"Seems to me you're rather good at that, actually," Jessica replied.

"In that case, I most certainly wouldn't mind you asking me to kiss you again," Liz said, her voice low and sexy.

Jessica glanced at Liz's shoulder line and the strong arms coming out of the sleeves of her T-shirt. She never wanted Liz to wear anything else again. Then she shut down that line of thought because it reminded her too much of how Liz had come to lie next to her in bed, about to kiss her again.

"Kiss me," Jessica said.

Liz leaned in again and pressed Jessica into the pillow a bit deeper this time. Her body didn't push all the way down onto Jessica's, but it was mere millimeters away. The kiss was less exploratory, more brazen. Liz's fingers cupped Jessica's jaw with a bit more vigor. This woman wasn't about to treat her like a delicate doll—the way Jessica had been treating herself.

Jessica brought her hand underneath Liz's top and reveled in the smooth touch of her skin, before giving in to the urge to take that T-shirt off her. She pushed it upward to make her wishes known. Liz withdrew from the kiss and grinned at her.

"I like the pace you're setting, Jess," she said, found some balance, and proceeded to hoist the T-shirt over her head.

Jessica swallowed hard as she came face to face with Liz's near-naked torso. Bloody hell. What was it she said she did? *T-Rex?* Jessica wondered if she could sign up to watch from the sidelines while Liz worked on her muscles. Whatever it was she was doing, it was working a charm.

Jessica let her finger drift over Liz's skin. She explored slowly, letting the sensations wash over her. It was only after a few minutes of doing so, that she realized she had left her right side totally exposed.

But Jessica didn't stop exploring Liz's skin with her fingers to cover herself up. Feeling Liz's soft flesh against hers was so much more powerful than the fear that kept her from showing herself.

Her hand reached Liz's breast and when she stroked her nipple through the fabric of Liz's bra, it rose to meet her touch.

"This is going to have to come off, I think," she said.

"Why don't you help me with that?" Liz shot her a grin, then maneuvered over Jessica to give her easy access to the clasp of her bra. Jessica unfastened it and guided the bra off Liz's body.

"There we are," she said, her gaze drawn to Liz's breasts. Just like Liz, to Jessica, they looked perfect. Unblemished. Small, tight nipples. A creamy roundness to them she wanted to discover more of. Jessica couldn't bring herself to touch them. While Liz's bra had still covered her breasts, it hadn't been a problem, but now she suddenly felt incapable of bringing her hands to them.

"I used to have beautiful breasts," Jessica said, without the slightest touch of self-pity in her voice. "I was never one of those women who grew up hating my body."

"Do you hate your body now?" Liz asked. She shuffled a little closer and lay down on her side, facing Jessica.

"Hate is a strong word." Jessica sought Liz's hand and intertwined her fingers with hers. "It just feels so out of balance, which makes it feel not right. Makes *me* feel not right."

"You're still a gorgeous woman," Liz said. "Take it from me."

Jessica scoffed.

"You *are*." Liz brought her face closer and kissed Jessica

on the nose. She planted another soft kiss on her cheek, then found her lips. When they broke from the brief kiss, Liz drew a path along Jessica's neck, to her ear. "You're so hot. You turn me on," she whispered. She kissed Jessica's neck again. She planted light kisses along the length of it while her words buzzed around Jessica's head.

You turn me on.

Was it a trick of the trade?

What else could it possibly be?

Liz's kisses trailed down. She kissed the swell of Jessica's left breast, then looked at her. "Is this okay?" she asked.

Jessica hesitated. "Give me a second."

"Of course." Liz let herself fall onto the bed next to Jessica.

"No, stay where you are. Please. Tell me what you see."

Liz quirked up her eyebrows, but then followed Jessica's instructions. She lowered her gaze and looked at Jessica's chest.

"Tell me," Jessica whispered.

Liz cleared her throat. "I see a beautiful breast with a terribly erect nipple." She briefly looked up and smiled at Jessica. "And I see a scar. Like this." With her finger she drew a half-moon in the air. "Like a smile, actually."

"How off-putting is it?" Jessica asked. Her arousal levels had dropped and had been replaced by renewed anxiety.

"It's not off-putting at all, Jess."

"It's hardly a turn on, though."

"It's who you are now. It's a testament to what you've gone through. Of your survival. It's powerful that way." Liz looked at her and cocked her head. "Do you want to see?" She threw in a smile. "Maybe because you've been so afraid to look, you've blown it out of proportion in your head. I'm telling you, it's nothing more than a smile-shaped scar, which will fade away more with time."

Jessica relaxed her neck. All her muscles appeared to have cramped up again. She'd need another massage if she went through with this. But maybe it was better to do this together with Liz, who didn't seem squeamish about looking at her scar. Jessica had even asked her a pretty unfair question and Liz had barely batted an eyelid. She needed someone as strong as Liz by her side to get through this.

Jessica nodded.

"I'll get that hand mirror I saw in the bathroom. I'll be right back."

Jessica followed Liz with her gaze. She was only wearing panties. If Jessica hadn't stopped them, they might be doing much more pleasant things right about now. But how could she even think of that as long as she hadn't seen herself?

Even though she was nervous, Jessica couldn't suppress a smile forming on her lips when Liz exited the bathroom.

"What?" Liz asked, obvious glee in her voice.

"I'm not sure I've ever seen a more beautiful woman in my life." Jessica chuckled to make herself sound a tad less serious, even though she meant every word. "You should be on television."

Liz chuckled with her. "Have I told you I don't have a TV? No Netflix subscription. Nothing. I don't watch television. What would I be doing *on* it?"

Jessica's eyes grew wide. "So you have more time for T-Rex." She gave Liz another once-over, more to stall than anything else. "It really works wonders for you."

Liz giggled. "It's called TRX. Total Resistance Exercise." She hopped onto the bed and put a hand on Jessica's belly again. "Are you ready for this?"

"I'm still flummoxed by your admission that you don't watch any television," Jessica said.

"We can talk about that later all you want," Liz said. She

put the mirror down. "How about you come and lie in my arms and I'll hold the mirror in front of us?"

Jessica inhaled deeply, then let the air flow from her mouth slowly. "Okay."

Liz sat up a bit and opened her arms wide.

Jessica pushed herself up. It was strange to not have any form of top on, not even a towel to protect her chest from view. She lay down in Liz's arms. Her breasts pushed against Jessica's back.

Before reaching for the mirror, Liz wrapped her arms around Jessica and pressed her lips to her cheek. No more words were needed right now.

She held Jessica until Jessica nodded and glanced at the mirror lying next to them.

Liz reached for it and brought it in front of them.

She held it up to their faces first. In the reflection, she blew Jessica an air kiss. Then she slowly started lowering the mirror. Their faces disappeared from view and Jessica closed her eyes, the way she had become accustomed to when standing in front of a mirror.

"Ready when you are," Liz said.

Jessica inhaled, then tried to relax into Liz's body. She opened one eye. The other one opened a sliver regardless of her trying to keep it shut. It made no difference if she looked with one or two eyes, anyway. One blind eye couldn't hide what she didn't want to see. Not if she dared to look in the mirror.

She blinked her eyes open properly. She looked above the mirror first, then let her gaze descend. She focused on her left breast, which, for a woman her age, she had always thought, looked very respectable. Then she finally took in the entire picture. The void on the right. The nothingness, broken only by a dark red scar curving upward.

Her throat tightened. Her breast was really gone. She

had felt it, this strange emptiness where before there had always been something. She had known every time she padded her right bra cup with a prosthesis when dressing. She had known even more so when she hadn't dared to look. But now she *was* looking. The scar didn't remind Jessica of a smile at all. Or perhaps it did look a little like one of those scary clown smiles. A blotch of red on a white surface. Something that wasn't supposed to be there. Something disconcerting no matter which way you looked at it.

She brought her hand to just underneath the scar tissue. Let it rest there for a moment. Then she ran a finger over the flatness of her chest, avoiding the scar at first.

All the while, Liz cradled Jessica with her strong arms, and held the mirror perfectly still.

Jessica's finger crept upward. She ran a fingertip over the outer edge of the scar. It was strangely smooth, but it wasn't the same smoothness as soft skin—of Liz's skin she had touched earlier. The texture was different, ridged in places, and as though it was coated with another kind of protective layer, a film of something she wasn't used to.

This had replaced her breast. It would have to do, at least for now. She could have reconstructive surgery later. Another operation. More scars. They could tattoo on a nipple. Jessica wasn't sure she wanted anyone to wield a scalpel on her body ever again—as long as her life didn't depend on it.

"I've seen enough," she said. "For now," she quickly added because she felt she should.

Liz put the mirror on the bed. "Anytime you need me to hold that mirror, I'll be there."

Jessica ignored the make-believe aspect of Liz's statement. In fact, Liz would be leaving soon. Jessica couldn't bear the thought of that.

She relaxed into Liz's arms. She didn't want to look at

her gorgeous face, nor see her perfect breasts, not for a little while.

Liz wrapped her arms around Jessica again. What they had just done together was, in many ways, much more intimate than having sex. How could Liz possibly go now?

"How are you feeling?" she whispered in Jessica's ear.

"Not very horny." Jessica chuckled. "Which is a damn shame now that I've got you almost naked in my bed."

"The night is young." Liz kissed her lightly on the cheek again. "How about I make us some dinner?"

Jessica huffed out some air. If this wasn't *the girlfriend experience*, she didn't know what was. A walk. A cup of coffee. A massage. And now dinner? All in one day.

Jessica freed herself from Liz's embrace. She looked around for the towel and wrapped it around her chest, then sat in front of Liz on her knees. "Quite honestly, I would love for you to stay a while longer, but I haven't just slipped into a different dimension. I haven't forgotten what this is. I know that what I want is not possible."

"Everything's possible," Liz said with a smile that totally belonged on television.

Jessica tilted her head. "I think we both know that's not true."

"After what just happened, I'm not just going to go, Jess." Liz reached out her hand and put it on Jessica's knee.

"I appreciate that." Jessica put a hand over Liz's. "But—"

"But what?" Liz squeezed Jessica's knee. "I'll stay as long as you want me to."

Jessica knitted her brows together. "Then I'd like—" Just in time, before she said anything too outrageous, she swallowed her words.

"Tell me." Liz scooted closer. "Tell me what you want."

Jessica waved off her question. "Never mind."

Liz pushed herself up. She mirrored Jessica's position

and sat in front of her on her knees. "May I hazard a guess?" She took Jessica's hands in hers.

Jessica couldn't help but stare at Liz's chest. By the time she found the resolve to look up again, she could only say, "Yes."

"I think…" Liz caressed Jessica's palm with her thumb. "You'd like me to stay through the night."

Jessica scoffed.

Liz looked her in the eye. "Did I read that so wrong?"

"You're not a social worker, Liz. I'm very much aware of that."

"I'm not, but that step you just took… I'm not immune to that. It was a big thing. I want to stay. Of course, I won't if you don't want me to."

"You're so different than what I'm used to with Laurel," Jessica said.

"Your entire situation with Laurel was very different." Liz scooted closer on her knees. "Let's be clear, I'm not going to look you in the eye and tell you that I want to stay, solely out of the goodness of my heart. That would be wrong. But I feel things, too. And my gut is telling me to stay."

Jessica grimaced. "I'm glad we cleared that up."

"Let's just start with dinner, shall we?" Liz brought a finger to Jessica's chin.

Jessica looked into her bright smile. Every fiber of her being wanted to say yes to dinner with Liz.

"I'll do the cooking, remember?" Liz's smile transformed into a cocky grin.

"Does that mean you have to get dressed?"

"I can do 'naked chef'. I guess it'll depend on the ingredients I'm cooking with."

"I had a big shopping delivery this morning. There should be something you can work with."

"Great." Liz touched her palm to Jessica's cheek. "What would you normally do for dinner? Do you cook?"

"Sometimes. I used to enjoy cooking because it relaxes me. But, er…" Christ, this was going to make her sound like a spoiled rich girl again. "Well, my father's chef prepares a lot of my food. I have a freezer full of meals made by him. In fact, since my diagnosis, I haven't had a free spot in my freezer. My father even suggested I get an extra one to store all the food he's had prepared for me."

"That's so sweet."

"Maybe in some way." Jessica waved it off. "Let's not talk about my father."

Liz nodded. "So you don't actually need me to cook. I could just grab something from the freezer and pop it in the microwave."

"I'll just have to trust your integrity. And the smells coming from the kitchen."

"Hey, if anything, I'm a hooker with integrity." Liz laughed heartily.

Jessica shook her head. She took Liz's hand in hers and planted a kiss on her palm.

Chapter Eleven

"I HAD an advertising agency for ten years," Jessica said. She looked up from her plate, which contained a bunch of ingredients she didn't even know she had. Pomegranate seeds? She knew they were very trendy these days, but she had no idea how they had appeared on her shopping list. Although it wouldn't take a lot of sleuthing to find out who had decided Jessica needed pomegranate seeds in her diet. It was probably her stepmother, who loved a fad more than anything else. Jessica stuck her fork into a piece of tuna. "This is delicious by the way. Are you a chef as well as an art historian?"

"Okay. Hold up, please." Liz put her cutlery down. "I want to hear more about the advertising agency, but first I'd like to say I'm glad to hear you're enjoying the food. And no, I'm not a chef. I just really like a colorful plate of food. I always go by color when I cook. It must be the art buff in me."

Because of the delightful meal in front of her and Liz's left-field answers to her questions, Jessica was reminded of Katherine's words of the other day again. But for now, she decided to just enjoy the rest of the evening. If she had to break all ties with

Liz as of tomorrow, to protect her own heart, so be it. She still had tonight. She'd make the most of it—something she hadn't done in a good long while. "Do you follow the art world?" Jessica asked, well aware she was steering the conversation in a different direction again. A few minutes ago she'd been willing to talk about her failed business but now Liz was looking all too spectacular again, and was saying the kind of things that on any real date would have Jessica swooning, and Jessica couldn't bear to revisit her failures in front of this woman any longer.

"I collect a little." Liz's eyes lit up. "In my line of work, I get an interesting tip from time to time. A way in behind the scenes of certain galleries. There are many perks." She held Jessica's gaze. "Many," she repeated.

Jessica took a deep breath. She feared a dizzy spell if Liz kept talking like this—and looking in her eyes like that. "Picked up anything interesting lately?" She managed to squeeze the words past the constriction in her throat.

Liz arched up her eyebrows. "I might have." She folded her features into a more serious expression quickly, as though suddenly aware of crossing a boundary. "But let's get back to you. Tell me about your business." She reached for her glass of pinot noir—she had picked the wine as well. Jessica had, literally, only had to show up at her own dinner table. She'd certainly never had the all-inclusive service like the one Liz was offering now.

Jessica responded with a small shake of her head. "You're much more interesting to talk about."

"I assure you that I'm not." Liz leaned away from Jessica. "And you brought it up, which means you want to talk about it. I'm all ears. In fact, I'm rather curious."

Jessica sighed. "It was one big fiasco."

"So you keep saying, but give me some details, please?"

Jessica put down her fork. Her palms had gotten sweaty.

She rubbed them on the napkin in her lap. "It's hard to talk about."

"Surely it's not harder than what you did earlier?" Liz cocked her head.

Jessica leaned over the table. "You know, Liz, there's just something about you that doesn't quite gel with the reason you're here. It's quite disconcerting. It's making me quite unsure how to behave."

Liz nodded slowly. "I'm sorry about that. This is just how I am. I get that Laurel was different but there isn't some sort of standardized procedure to what we do. And in case you're wondering, I'm genuinely interested in you."

"That's what's so unnerving," Jessica said.

Liz stared at her for a few more seconds, then looked around the room. "Hold on." She walked toward a chair by the wall where her bag stood. She fished out her phone and fiddled with it for a bit. She headed back to the table and showed Jessica the screen. "I sent this message to the agency when I came down earlier. Before I started cooking. This means I'm off the clock."

Jessica glared at the message. It was just one word. A cold, sterile one-word sentence. *Done.*

"What does that mean?" Jessica asked.

Liz put her phone on the sideboard behind the table and took her seat across from Jessica again. "It means that, after you were so brave to look at yourself in the mirror for the first time since your surgery, I wanted to stay with you in a different capacity than the one I arrived in."

Jessica scoffed. "And what capacity might that be?"

Liz sucked her bottom lip into her mouth, as though she was giving this some serious thought. "Interested acquaintance, perhaps?" she said after a while.

"I'm still none the wiser." Jessica knew she was massively

on the defensive, but she wanted to make absolutely sure she wasn't misunderstanding anything.

"Okay, it looks like I'm going to have to spell this out for you." She slanted over the table. "I like you, Jessica Porter. I like spending time with you. I didn't much feel like going home. I think we had a bit of a moment earlier and I felt like exploring that more… in a *different capacity*."

Christ. Jessica didn't quite know how to react to that. She wanted to jump up, push Liz's chair back and shower her in all the affection she had saved up since her diagnosis, but something was holding her back. Caution. A gut feeling that something didn't quite add up. "Isn't that terribly unprofessional?" she asked.

Liz smiled. "Maybe," she said.

"I don't really know what to do with that." To prove her point, Jessica sipped from her glass of wine. She couldn't do much else. Her brain couldn't quite compute what was being said. She was afraid of misinterpreting what Liz was saying. In fact, she was sure she was hearing it all wrong.

"I'm sorry, Jess." Liz straightened her posture. "I shouldn't flirt like that. It's unfair."

"It's confusing." Jessica planted her elbows on the table. "To put it bluntly, I paid you to come here. That's what you do. That's the service I asked for. You came. We spent time together. But instead of leaving after my time with you was up, you decided to stay."

"That sounds about right." Liz pulled the sides of her blouse tightly over her chest. "But maybe I should go now." She rose. "I feel like the evening has taken a turn and that I perhaps got the wrong impression. I apologize for that."

The sight of Liz getting up tightened something in Jessica's stomach. "No, please don't leave." Jessica pushed her chair back. "I could use… an *interested acquaintance* right about now."

This brought a small smile to Liz's face. She walked over to where Jessica was sitting and squatted down next to her. "I feel like, under different circumstances, you and I could be friends, Jess." She glanced at her watch. "It's only eight o'clock. Maybe we can create some of those different circumstances tonight."

Jessica scrunched her lips together. "Friends, huh."

"Is that a problem?" Liz asked.

"Well, I have many friends, but I wouldn't dream of doing with them the things I'd like to do with you…"

"Something a bit different than friends then." Liz put her hands on Jessica's knees and pushed herself up. Once up, she brought her hands to the back of Jessica's chair and hovered over her. "Friends who enjoy doing this." She planted a kiss on Jessica's cheek. "Perhaps even this." The next kiss landed on Jessica's lips. "Or this." The next time Liz kissed Jessica, she opened her mouth and licked Jessica's lips with the tip of her tongue. Jessica didn't hesitate. She met Liz's tongue with hers and melted into their kiss.

When they broke apart, Jessica stared up at Liz's triumphant smile. "You seduced me."

"Who's to say it didn't happen the other way around?" Liz said.

Jessica loved Liz's quick wit. The way she had a response at the ready for anything Jessica said. And she adored that smile that, every time it was aimed at Jessica, truly did make her feel as though everything was going to be all right—just as Liz had promised her earlier that evening.

"I am," Jessica said. "And there's no doubt about it." She curved her arms around Liz's neck and pulled her closer so she could kiss her again.

Liz brought her long legs to either side of the chair and straddled Jessica. This time, she didn't hold back. She pushed her chest against Jessica's torso and let her tongue dance freely in her mouth.

"Would you like to go back upstairs?" Liz asked when they came up for air.

"Not yet," Jessica said.

Liz grinned at her. "That's right, you haven't told me about your business yet. Great way to get out of that." She pecked Jessica on the nose.

"I'm still processing what just happened," Jessica said.

Liz stood up from Jessica's lap and pulled a chair close. She took Jessica's hands gently in hers and nodded. "I can imagine it's a bit of a mind fuck."

"You're one big mind fuck. You being here is just… I don't know." Jessica didn't have the words to describe this highly unusual situation.

"How about this." Liz looked at their hands. "You take all the time you need to process but, in the meanwhile, we arrange a proper date." She locked her gaze on Jessica's. "One where you don't pay me at the end of the night."

"It would still be a mind fuck, but I do like the sound of that." She squeezed Liz's hand.

"It's a date then." Liz beamed, giving her a wide smile.

"Does that mean you're leaving now?" Jessica asked.

"Not if you want me to stay." Liz turned her gaze away and stared into the lounge. "How about you show me what's so exciting about watching television. I couldn't help but notice that monstrosity hanging from your wall. Why waste such prime space on a flat screen when you could hang a gorgeous piece of art instead?"

"Art is only entertaining for a few seconds. TV can keep me on the edge of my seat for hours." Jessica thought about how she'd felt about television that very morning. But it had been a long day. And she had a point to prove.

"Oh, the blasphemy." Liz clutched a hand to her chest.

"Art may require you to use a bit more of your imagination, sure, but doesn't that make it more rewarding?"

"More rewarding than an episode of *The Kramers*?" Jessica said. "I think not." She got up and held out her hand to Liz. "Come on, Miss High Brow, it's about time I corrupted you."

Chapter Twelve

LIZ HAD BEEN SHAKING her head for the past five minutes.

"Please, don't hold back on my account," Jessica said.

"I'm perplexed," Liz said. "And I cannot help but wonder what this sort of TV show being so popular says about our society as a whole."

"Oh, so now you want to have a discussion about the effect of *The Kramers* on society?" Jessica grinned.

"All that woman goes on about is how one particular brand of makeup is better than the other. I fail to see the entertainment value in this."

Jessica turned away from the screen. "This has to be one of the strangest days of my life."

"Why? Because it suddenly dawned on you that the company you work for produced this and it has instigated a deep crisis of faith in the TV industry?"

"Hey, you're the one who wanted to watch television."

"Nu-uh." Liz shook her head. "I'm the one who wanted to do very different things." She let her tongue flash over her upper lip.

"What I actually meant to say"—Jessica rolled her eyes

while, really, she couldn't believe how utterly comfortable she felt in Liz's company—"is that watching *The Kramers* with you was not what I thought I would be doing tonight. And I certainly didn't think you'd be all snooty about it."

"But tell me honestly, Jess. How else can one be about this but snooty? It's utter drivel. It makes me happy I don't have a television. In fact, it makes me never want to have one in my life." Liz had a smug smile on her face.

Jessica reached for the remote and switched off the television. "Better?" she asked.

"Much." Liz turned to her and drew her legs onto the couch.

Jessica sunk her teeth into her bottom lip and looked at Liz.

"Pressing matter on your mind?" Liz asked.

Jessica nodded.

"Does it have anything to do with Kathy Kramer? Because I can't help you with that."

"Is Liz your real name?" Jessica asked.

Liz didn't say anything for a few seconds. "It's Nicole Elizabeth Griffith. I never liked Nicole or even Nikki. I've always gone by my middle name. But my name on any official piece of paper would be Nicole Griffith."

"Nicole." Jessica regarded Liz intently. "You really don't strike me as a Nicole."

"That's what I told my mother years ago. Even she called me Liz, notwithstanding the occasional slip-up out of habit."

"Liz is much more glamorous," Jessica said.

"I know. It slips off the tongue so sensually." She chuckled.

"So you don't go by a fake name for, er, work purposes?"

"Nope."

"Is that… safe?"

"Perfectly so." Liz shuffled in her seat. "Look, Jess, the

clients I see are… how to put this. Me knowing their real name, which is something the agency demands, can be much more of an issue for them than them knowing *my* real name. Some girls use a fake name, but I don't like all that fake stuff. I like to provide an authentic experience." She drew her lips into a smile.

"You've certainly got the hang of that."

"But this is really me, Jess."

"Then what's the difference between you at this very moment and you when you're with a client? Say, you about two hours ago?"

"There really isn't much. I like being me. And sometimes I have to make things sound a little more exciting than they are, or I have to smile when I don't much feel like it, but I generally try to avoid those kind of situations."

"You make it sound so… easy."

"I provide a service that many people have the wrong idea about. Do I sleep with other women for money? Yes, that most certainly happens. But you know what? It doesn't even happen all of the time. Often, I'm someone's plus one. Women of a certain age really hate going to functions on their own. A lot of the time, I spend a few hours with someone just to brighten up their day."

"Like with me?" Jessica asked.

"Exactly."

"So, it's not weird that we… haven't done anything?"

Liz shook her head. "Of course not, although what happened today was highly unusual. We were definitely intimately involved. Much more so than if we'd had actual sex." She reached out her hand and touched Jessica's thigh. "'Weird' is really not a word that should come up."

"Well, Nicole," Jessica said, "I'll have to take your word for that." She snickered.

Liz shook her head again, but much more forcefully this

time. "If you start calling me Nicole, I can't be held responsible for the consequences." Her hand snuck up from Jessica's thigh to her belly, where she pinched her in the side.

"Ouch," Jessica squealed. "Have some respect for a cancer survivor's body, will you?"

Liz withdrew her hand and found her gaze. "I think someone just made a huge leap forward."

"How do you mean?"

"You just made a very lame cancer joke." Liz drew up her brow.

"Lame? How very dare you." Jessica mimicked Liz's earlier hand motion and pinched her in the side.

Liz held up her arms. "I surrender," she said in a dramatic voice. "Have mercy."

Jessica retracted her hand and glanced at Liz, who sat there with a wide grin plastered on her lips. "You know what would be a massive ratings hit?" Jessica straightened her posture. "*The Nicole Elizabeth Griffith Show.*" She witnessed Liz's grin evaporate. "That smile. The wit. The wisdom. The intriguing life you lead."

"Oh sure, I can hear the voice-over already. Liz is about to visit a high-profile client. Jessica Porter really needs a seeing to today, so it would appear."

"I concede," Jessica said. "The format is dead in the water already." She snuck another glance at Liz, then looked away. She couldn't remember the last time she'd had so much fun.

Chapter Thirteen

"EARTH TO JESSICA. EARTH TO JESSICA," Caitlin said while she waved her fork in the air. "Are you so preoccupied with work already? You've only just come back."

Jessica had invited Caitlin to lunch after her second half day back at ANBC. She hadn't fared much better than the day before—and she was doubly distracted by the prospect of her date with Liz that evening.

"It's not work," Jessica said, surprising herself with the amount of glee in her voice. "I have a date tonight."

Caitlin's eyes grew wide. "A date?" She put down her fork. "How did you swing that?"

"What do you mean *how*? Some might consider me a most eligible bachelorette."

"Oh, I don't doubt it, Ms. Porter, but you haven't exactly been busy in any social circles now, have you? I'm just wondering where you met this dateable woman." Caitlin leaned back in her chair.

"She's a friend of a friend." Jessica wasn't going to tell Caitlin how she'd met Liz. "And I really, really like her."

Memories of last night flooded her mind again. They'd sat in the couch for a while longer, chatting and chuckling, until Jessica had gotten visibly tired and Liz had left. She'd kissed Jessica chastely on the cheek and had invited her to her place for their date the next day.

Jessica couldn't believe she was actually going to Liz's home tonight. She glanced at her watch. Only six more hours of unbearable anticipation to get through.

"Very mysterious," Caitlin said. "Is the friend anyone I know?"

"I'll tell you all about it later, okay? I shouldn't have brought it up. I'm probably massively jinxing it just by talking about it."

"Sure. Let's meet here again tomorrow so you can give me all the details." Caitlin flashed a smile.

"I'm a little nervous," Jessica said. "It's been a while since I last went on a proper date."

"If it's meant to be, it'll work out."

"It's… rather complicated…" Jessica waved off her own statement. "But no need to get into that now." While she was excited about seeing Liz again, and it had, indeed, been ages since she'd gone on a date, it was hard to ignore Liz's profession and its ramifications. When it all came down to it, Jessica should know better than to fall for a call girl. "How's your show going?"

"Do you mean to say you haven't been watching?" Caitlin asked, her tone mock-serious.

"Of course I have. I never miss an episode of *The Caitlin James Show*. How could I? Best hour of my week." Jessica shot Caitlin a grin.

"Then you will know we're doing fine. No complaints. Production-wise, it's like a well-oiled machine by now. Thank goodness we have a wide variety of guests who can keep things interesting. Speaking of, as much as I love having my compatriots on the show, I've been working on a more international wish list. I may need your connections if I want to make some of it come true."

"If by that you mean my father's connections, I'm not sure I can help," Jessica said on a sigh.

Caitlin narrowed her eyes and regarded Jessica intently. "Where's that annoying enthusiasm you hit me over the head with after you just started this job, Jess? Remember the good old days when you made me interview Kathy Kramer? I did that for you. I'm just cashing in my favor, that's all."

"I think that enthusiasm was cut out of me along with the cancer." She let her hands fall into her lap. "I can't seem to muster much of it for anything job-related these days."

Caitlin pursed her lips together for a brief moment before she said, "Did you come back to work too early? There's no shame in that. You only took three months off and what you went through was so life-changing."

"I want to work. I want to do something. It's just this job… I don't know. The thought of jumping back in hasn't exactly lit me up."

"I guess that's to be expected. I would just give it some time. Work half days for a while. Get your head back into the game. Go on a few dates. Pick your life back up again."

"That's the thing. I'm not so sure there's that much of my pre-cancer life I want to pick back up. This job…" She shrugged. "I'm grateful for the chance my father gave me after my business went under, but it's not like I had many choices back then. Not if I wanted to work. I think a lot of my enthusiasm from back then was due to the simple fact that I was able to work again after I… crawled out of depression. The energy that came with that just propelled me forward. I don't seem to have that same kind of energy right now. If anything, I feel much more like when I was still suffering from depression. Like this numbness is hanging over me." *Except last night when I was giggling with Liz.*

"Have you been seeing…" Caitlin tapped a finger on the table. "What's her name again?"

"Mrs. Buchman," Jessica said. "No. I haven't seen her for a while. I don't feel like seeing her. I don't feel like rehashing all my emotions concerning cancer again. I just want to stop thinking about it and get on with my life, but I can't seem to be able to."

Caitlin leaned over the table. "I wish I could help you."

"You have helped." There was that tremor in Jessica's voice again—she never used to have that before her surgery. It was as though having cancer had pushed her feelings to a place inside her from where they could well up at the most inopportune moments. "You're helping now by being here," Jessica managed to say. "By listening to me."

"I wish I could do more." Caitlin reached out her hand over the table.

Jessica accepted the display of affection and grabbed hold of Caitlin's fingers. "I thought I could face it alone. That's why I pulled that disappearing act." She shook her head. "I was so wrong."

"The point is that you're not alone." Caitlin squeezed back. "You have me and Jo. You have Katherine. You have your family. You have your friend who introduced you to a woman you're going on a date with."

Jessica nodded. She'd just been starting to find her feet again after her depression when she'd gotten the cancer diagnosis. Even though the surgery had been successful, and Jessica had a good prognosis for full remission, she felt like she had taken too many steps backward. As though the healing of one disease had undone some of the healing of the previous one.

"Her name's Liz." Jessica held up a finger of her free hand. "But you can't tell anyone about this, okay?"

"My lips are sealed. The name Liz is locked up inside of me." Caitlin turned on her TV smile. It was infectious and Jessica couldn't help but mirror it—or maybe it was just the mention of Liz's name.

"Quite frankly, she's the most gorgeous woman I've ever laid eyes on." Jessica felt herself go soft inside. She let go of Caitlin's hand and leaned back, allowing images of Liz to fill her mind. "But it's not just that. She's so easy to be around. We really hit it off the other night. She… pushed me in all the right ways. And now I can't stop thinking about her."

"That's a lot of information," Caitlin said. "I need a few moments to process." She stared at Jessica as though trying to read more information off her face. "So you've spent significant time with this woman already?"

Jessica nodded.

"But you're not going to tell me about it?"

"I can't. It's… delicate."

Caitlin's eyes grew wide. "*Delicate?* Is she married? Famous and in the closet? Part of the upper echelons of society?" She chuckled.

"None of that."

"Come on, Jess. You'll have to give me something. The suspense is killing me." Caitlin brought a hand to her throat and pretended to suffocate.

"I want to tell you. God, I do. But you have to promise me that you won't judge."

Caitlin cocked her head. "Do you even know me?" She waved her hand theatrically. "Yoohoo, it's me, Caitlin James! Rattler of the bourgeoisie mind. Upsetter of many a traditional thinker."

"Even so." Jessica's voice had gone down a notch. "I still think you might judge."

"Only one way to find out." Caitlin fixed her gaze on Jessica.

"Liz is… a friend of Katherine's." She looked Caitlin in the eye. "And by friend, I mean colleague."

"I see." Caitlin slowly nodded. "Just for the record, I'm not judging. I'm just processing the facts."

"Take your time," Jessica said. "I sure as hell haven't processed them yet."

"So Katherine introduced you to her colleague and you hit it off?" Caitlin asked. She wasn't born yesterday. Someone like Caitlin would put two and two together quickly.

"I, um, booked Liz's services." Jessica chuckled nervously. "Nothing happened. We just talked and walked around. Had dinner." She paused. "Well, then I booked her again and showed her my scar."

"Still not judging, but I must admit I'm a little surprised."

"Anyway, how I met her is beside the point. The fact is that I met her and that I like her and I think she likes me too, but of course Katherine thinks I'm crazy. I can't talk to her about this."

"I have to ask this. I wouldn't be a good friend if I didn't." Caitlin looked away for a moment. "You don't think Liz is leading you on?"

"No," Jessica said curtly.

"Okay," Caitlin replied.

"I know how this sounds," Jessica said. "Like I've lost my mind after my surgery." Jessica shook her head. "Even *I* thought I had for a minute. But I haven't. Honestly, Caitlin, you should meet her, then you'd understand."

"I'd love to. Bring her to dinner next weekend."

"Let's not get too ahead of ourselves. I need to see how the date goes first," Jessica said, even though the prospect appealed to her very much.

"Of course. I just don't want you to think that Liz is not welcome at ours."

"I'd never think that. You invited Katherine, remember?"

"Bring Liz. You've got me all curious now," Caitlin said.

"If I bring Liz, I'll have to tell Katherine first." Jessica rested her chin on her upturned palms. "It's not going to go down well."

"Don't tell her. Just show up." Caitlin grinned.

"All that drama in your gorgeous penthouse." Jessica chuckled.

"Drama and a view, what's better than that?" Caitlin quipped.

"I'll let you know," Jessica said.

"I'm here for you, Jess. You can talk to me about anything, and that includes Liz." She glanced at Jessica with a funny look in her eyes. "But… how do you feel about Liz's profession?"

"Isn't that the million-dollar question," Jessica said. "I have rather complicated feelings toward it. And I'm not so naive to think it won't stand in the way of a straightforward romance." She shook her head. "Even though I really shouldn't be using the word romance. It's just a date."

"It's more than a date. I can tell by the way you talk about her."

"I haven't felt like this in such a long time, but, you know, I can never be quite sure it isn't the cancer talking. Why am I feeling like this? Because she was so kind to me? Because I was blinded by her beauty? Is it all even real?" Jessica sighed. "I really don't know."

"Time will tell. And if there's one thing you can always count on it's for time to pass."

"Thanks." Jessica looked at her friend. "One good thing has come from me taking this job at ANBC. Meeting you.

I'm serious. And I'm allowed to be corny because, well, you know…"

"If only you'd been this corny when we first met." Caitlin sent her a big smile.

Jessica glanced at her as warmth spread through her chest.

Chapter Fourteen

JESSICA HAD DRESSED CASUALLY for the date. They weren't going to a fancy restaurant, after all. She showed up at Liz's door at her Bondi Beach address, in a beige pair of trousers and a navy shirt on top. She'd brought two bottles of Pinot Noir. She rang the bell and, for a split second, wondered if the people living across the hall knew what Liz did for a living. Jessica pushed the thought away and then the door swung open.

"Hello, hello." Liz gave her a big smile. "Welcome to my humble abode." She threw her arms wide for Jessica to step into.

It was an awkward hug because Jessica was holding the bag with the bottles of wine and, even more so, the familiarity with which they had left things the previous night wasn't there yet. It couldn't possibly be.

"Sit. Make yourself comfortable," Liz said. Her voice sounded a little different—as though she too was a little nervous.

Jessica looked around Liz's living room. The last of the light outside slanted in through big windows.

Liz took the bottles of wine from the bag Jessica had handed her and examined the labels. "We'll be having excellent red tonight then." She put one bottle on the dining table and brought the other one into the sitting area.

"What a lovely place," Jessica said. Totally different from Katherine's home, she thought. But she really should stop comparing Liz to Katherine—or Laurel. People in the same profession didn't live carbon copies of each other's lives. "Do you own it?"

"No." Liz carried over two wine glasses. "I'm not really one for owning property. I like the freedom that comes with renting."

"And the sky-high Sydney rent?"

Liz waved her arm around. "The square footage of this place isn't huge. And I get by." She winked at Jessica. "My landlady is very nice, actually."

Something tightened in Jessica's stomach. What did that mean? That Liz paid rent with other means than just money? She pushed the thought out of her mind. She couldn't spend the evening with ideas like that swarming around in her head.

Jessica sat down. "Your decor is very Scandi-chic," she said.

"Is it?" Liz looked around her living room as though reassessing it. "If by that you mean most of my furniture is from Ikea, you're half right." She chuckled.

Liz poured them a glass of wine and handed one to Jessica. She looked into her eyes as she did. "I'm glad you're here," she said.

"Me too." One gaze into Liz's eyes and Jessica was ready to forget most thoughts she had walked in here with. "I didn't mean to imply that your furniture is from Ikea. I actually meant—"

Liz silenced her with a grin. "It's fine. I'm not sensitive

about my furniture." She sat next to Jessica and drew one knee up onto the couch so that it touched the side of Jessica's thigh. "Let me try this wine you brought." She made a performance of pushing her nose into the glass, taking a sip and swirling the wine around in her mouth. "All I can say is that it's exquisite, Ms. Porter," she exclaimed. "You have great taste."

"So do you." Jessica noticed the Xiao Mei Chong on the wall across from where she was sitting. "How long have you had that?"

"Almost ten years." Liz gazed at the painting as well. "Bought it for less than two grand."

Jessica's eyes grew wide. "Wow. It must be worth several times that now." She looked at Liz. "Do you have any other gems like that?"

"I'll give you a tour later." She grinned at Jessica. Clearly Liz's mind was not on art. "If only I had more wall space."

"Feel free to hang any excess art at my house," Jessica blurted out before she realized how presumptuous that sounded.

Liz glanced at her in silence. "It's my dream to open an art gallery someday. After I've retired."

"Retired," Jessica repeated. "Do you have a set retirement age in your… business?"

Liz shook her head while she chuckled. "Not really. But most of my colleagues quit soon after forty."

"Is that your plan as well?" Jessica sipped from the wine. Excellent as it may be, she was too distracted waiting for Liz's reply to pay much attention to its taste.

"Yes. Although it depends. Starting an art gallery requires a fair bit of capital. Barring any unforeseen circumstances, I should have the money in a few years."

"Is it terribly indiscreet to ask how old you are?" Jessica

shuffled around. "You probably already know that I'm forty-five."

"I'm thirty-nine. It's not a secret. I've never understood why women are so coy about their age."

Jessica shrugged. "Just another thing pushed upon us by women's magazines."

"Doesn't your father own a few of the worst offenders?" Liz asked. "If you're sick of TV, maybe you can go into the women's magazines business and shake things up a little. You'd be doing many women a favor." Liz pushed a strand of dark hair behind her ear.

"Hm." Jessica bunched her lips together. "No, TV is higher on my work wish list than magazines, I'm afraid."

"How about going back to advertising?" Liz asked.

"I've thought about it, but my name isn't going to inspire a lot of confidence in possible clients after what happened." She took another sip of wine.

"Is this where you finally tell me about it?" Liz's voice was sweet. "Full disclosure. I tried to google it, but didn't find a thing."

"Never underestimate the reach of Edward Porter when it comes to keeping his reputation untarnished. And to be clear, that reputation extends to anything that could reflect badly on him, including his daughter's illness."

"You were ill?" Liz asked. Her knee still rested against Jessica's thigh.

"I suffered from the disease so many women my age suffer from. We try to do too much while also trying to prove that we're up for the job, which costs us double the effort as men because we need to first convince ourselves that we're not imposters. Then we have to convince all the people around us." She sighed. "Most days, I started work from home at 6 a.m., putting in a few hours before going to the office, and I didn't stop until midnight. It was pure madness when I look back on it. These days, I'm not sure what I was trying to prove. I'm pretty certain it didn't help with keeping my body cancer free."

"Oh, no, please don't blame yourself for that." There was a twinge of agitation in Liz's voice. "My mother used to say things like that as well. If only I hadn't done this or that —the list was endless. But it's so pointless."

Jessica shook her head. "You can't help it though."

Liz just nodded.

"I burned out completely. I sank into a deep depression. My managing skills took a nose dive. I lost us one big client, which was like the first in a line of very well-aligned dominos. The business went under in less than a year."

"I'm so sorry to hear that." Liz put a hand on Jessica's knee.

"Maybe it happened for a reason. Clearly, I couldn't go on the way I had been. I was ignoring all the warning signs." Jessica looked into her wine glass. "Of course, my father stepped in to take care of everything. He made sure my employees got handsome severance packages and he paid off my debtors. In theory, the business never officially folded, but in my head, it did." She looked up again. "He hasn't really treated me the same since." She pulled up one shoulder. "I guess I've always been a disappointment to him."

"Is it the classic story of you not wanting to take over his empire?" Liz's tone was free of judgment.

"In a way, but it's a bit more complicated than that." She leaned back into the couch. "But maybe we can keep that story for another time." She narrowed her eyes. "I want to know more about you."

"I have very few secrets," Liz said and threw her arms wide as if to illustrate her point.

"Really?" Jessica drew her lips into a skeptical pout. "I mean, I do hope you have some."

"Well, yes, professional discretion is paramount. That's a given."

"How did your parents react to you coming out?" Jessica asked.

Liz gave a small shrug. "Not much at all. It wasn't a shock nor a surprise. I guess they knew much sooner than I did. And my father is, well… he simply doesn't care about any of that. Maybe my mother was a bit worried about my future, but if she was, she didn't really show it. It was the most undramatic non-event. The way all coming-outs should be, really."

"*Should* be, yes. But not all parents are like yours, unfortunately," Jessica said on a sigh.

"Oh, that's—" Liz was interrupted by the loud ring of her phone. It lay vibrating wildly on the arm rest of the couch. She shot up and grabbed it to look at the screen. "I'm sorry, I really need to take this."

Jessica nodded.

Liz exited the living room and only took the call when she was in the other room and had closed the door behind her.

Jessica looked around the living room, but her attention focused on the sound of Liz's voice next door. It could be anyone calling her, but Jessica tried to think of whom of her friends or family she would allow to interrupt a date with a phone call. She concluded that, barring very few exceptions, she wouldn't pick up. Liz said she *had to* take this call. It pushed Jessica's thoughts in a direction she would rather steer clear of, but that was easier said than done.

"Sorry about that." Liz entered the living room again, all smiles. She put her phone on a bookshelf against the furthest wall. "I promise we won't be disturbed again." She sat down next to Jessica, but this time, left a little more space between their bodies so they didn't touch. "I believe you were about to tell me about your coming out?"

Jessica gained some time by drinking from her wine. "Can I ask you something instead of telling you my depressing coming out story?"

"Of course." Liz's smile was a bit tight, as though she already knew perfectly well what Jessica wanted to ask her.

"That call you just took… Was that the agency?"

Liz's smile grew even more thin-lipped. "It was."

Jessica tried to look into Liz's eyes but she couldn't. She had to look away.

"Is that a problem?" Liz asked.

"I honestly don't know," Jessica said. "I guess I have a bit of a problem with it, otherwise I wouldn't bring it up."

Liz shook her head. "It's normal for you to react this way, but I will tell you that I'm way past defending what I do for a living. I'm fine with what I do."

"Have you had, er, many relationships since you started?"

Liz chuckled. "No, not really. Because, guess what? Most women seem to have a really big problem with my profession. Me being so unapologetic about it doesn't help matters much."

Jessica didn't know what to say to that. She could hardly be holier than thou about it. She had met Liz because she had hired her. But Liz getting that call gave her a very different feeling—it made her feel that, even on their first real date, she already had to share Liz.

"Look." Liz shuffled a little closer. "Even though I will never apologize for what I do, I do understand it's difficult for other people to accept. This may be the so-called oldest profession in the world, but it comes with more preconceptions and judgement than anything else." Liz looked at Jessica's knee first before she put her hand back where it had been before she had received the call. "If you don't want this date to continue—and I'll understand if that's the case—there will be no hard feelings, I promise. Although I will be disappointed, of course." She cocked her head and shot Jessica a quick grin. "For the record, I like you a lot and I would very much like for it to continue." Her thumb pushed into Jessica's thigh. "We're going to need very clear communication from the beginning, which may take away a bit of the magic, but, let's be honest, I think we're going to have to bypass some of that either way simply because of how we met."

Jessica couldn't help herself. The warmth she'd felt when sitting in front of the TV with Liz the other day remained inside her so vividly—because it contrasted so heavily with how she'd been feeling for months. She put her own hand over Liz's. "I like you more than a lot," she said. "And I totally agree about the very clear communication. Does that mean I can ask questions freely?"

"Yes, as long as you don't ask for details about my clients, because you know I can't give those."

Jessica nodded her understanding. "That phone call you just got," she asked, "was that to set up a date?"

"Yes." Liz drew her lips into a half pout.

Jessica took her time to absorb the information. "A regular?" she asked after a while.

"You could say that." Liz glanced around then reached for her glass on the coffee table, all the while keeping her hand beneath Jessica's.

"For when?"

"Friday evening."

"Do you often… work on weekends?"

Liz nodded. "Yes."

"How many dates do you go on in an average week?" Jessica was starting to feel like a journalist researching a long article about the subject.

"No one week is the same, but…" Liz paused to think. "Never more than three."

"Is that your own choice or something the agency imposes?"

"My own choice." A small smile was starting to form around Liz's lips.

"You said the woman you got the call about is a regular. Does that mean a weekly standing appointment?"

Liz shook her head. "No. That's not a service I provide."

"But if someone was to request you every week, you wouldn't say no?"

Liz chuckled. "If someone did that, it would cost them a hell of a lot of money."

"So? Money is no issue for these women, I presume."

"I think I get where you're going with this and we do have guidelines about this. Most of it we handle on instinct, and if I start to sense that a regular pattern is occurring for any other reason than the service I provide, then I take measures. I become unavailable for the client for a while. But this hardly ever happens. Yes, people are easy to fool in the short term, but long term is something else entirely. Most people know what they're buying—and it's not love, just temporary affection."

"Isn't it against some guideline for you to have invited me to your home for an actual date?"

"Not if you no longer book me." Liz drew up her eyebrows. "Is that going to be a problem?"

Jessica burst into a chuckle. "It shouldn't be, no."

"Good." Liz squeezed her knee. "I wouldn't take your money, anyway." She found Jessica's gaze and their eyes met.

Jessica tried to determine the color of Liz's eyes. They were lighter than most brown eyes she'd seen, but they also had specks of green in them.

"Enough with the twenty questions now?" Liz asked. "Are you hungry?"

"Sure." Jessica could do with a break from receiving all those candid answers. She needed some time to digest what she'd already learned. She wasn't hungry in the least, however.

"Let's eat." Liz didn't get up immediately. Her hand remained tucked underneath Jessica's for a few more seconds as they looked into each other eyes.

In her glance, Jessica saw much more than answers to the many questions she had. She was faced with feelings she perhaps shouldn't have—not if she wanted to keep her life simple while she was only just beginning to build it back up. But Liz was already a big part of the rebuilding of her existence, and what was fun about a simple life, anyway?

Chapter Fifteen

"MY FATHER WAS VERY disappointed when I came out. In the true sense of the word," Jessica said, when they'd nearly finished eating. "He wasn't angry or blaming himself or any of the other classic reactions. It was like something I was doing *to* him. By the time I could make him understand that this was how I was born, too much had been broken between us. And we weren't exactly close before."

"And your mother?" Liz asked.

"My mother. Gosh." Jessica huffed out some air. "By the time I came out, I hadn't seen my mother in ten years. I called her because, for some reason, I thought she should know. She sounded as if she didn't care much either way."

"That's a rough deal."

Jessica shrugged. "By then, I didn't care much what my mother thought of me. She and my father divorced when I was five. I stayed with my father. It wasn't my choice. I was never asked. It was just decided for me. But it was definitely the better choice. Anyone who has ever claimed that maternal instinct comes naturally to any woman who has given birth is very, very wrong. Some people are simply emotionally unfit to be parents. My mother is one of those people."

"Jesus, Jess." Liz put her fork down. "That sounds so horrible."

"It's fine. I didn't have a bad childhood. I had the most fabulous nanny. The same one until I turned thirteen. Her name was Emily. She raised me single-handedly. And guess what? She didn't take it as a personal affront at all when I told her I was a lesbian." Jessica put her cutlery down as well. "Parenting is so much more than being someone's mother or father. Emily was so much more of a parent to me than my real parents. I did have one stepmother once who took a bit of an interest, but that marriage didn't last very long and after a while you learn to not get attached to new people in your life too quickly."

"What happened after you turned thirteen? Why did Emily stop being your nanny?"

"My father decided I was becoming too much of a brat and sent me to boarding school."

"Is that where you became a lesbian?" Liz asked, her voice serious but her eyes filled with glee.

Jessica burst out laughing. "Of course. No cliché has gone unexplored in my poor little rich girl's life." She glanced at Liz from under her lashes. "Boarding school wasn't too bad. In fact, it was good for me. I was on many a sports team." She waggled her eyebrows. "It helps."

"I bet it does." Liz winked at her. "Do you still see Emily?"

"She passed away three years ago." Jessica's throat still constricted at the thought of Emily no longer being there.

"I'm so sorry to hear that." Liz sighed. She paused for a bit until she asked her next question. "Did you call your mother when you got your cancer diagnosis?"

Jessica shook her head. "I had no reason to. She wasn't

going to offer me much comfort, was she? And my father was already acting totally out of control. His only child having cancer and there was nothing his money could do about it. Another notch on the disappointment belt."

"Surely he wasn't disappointed because you fell ill."

"I'm pretty sure he was, although, this time, he didn't say as much. Not like when my company went bust or I came out. Or I wasn't born as a boy. Or at the very least wasn't a more respectable heir."

"Sounds like there's some bad blood there."

Jessica shrugged. "It's better now. He's been quite different, actually. He's pushing seventy-five. I guess that's an age that makes you think about things a little differently."

"Maybe. He's not thinking about retiring yet?"

"He'll die working. He'll never stop. Actually, I think it would be bad for him to stop. What would he do? He loves what he does now, so why stop?"

"I do agree. If you enjoy your work, why retire?"

"Does that mean you don't always enjoy your work? You *are* thinking of retiring?" Jessica didn't feel like talking about her family any longer.

"My case is different. Some jobs are not meant to be done for life. Imagine me dying on the job." Her lips formed into a smile, but it wasn't reflected in her eyes.

"That would be a tough one."

"Without wanting to romanticize my job, I do enjoy it. It's very sociable and I like to be around people. It puts me in touch with some very interesting characters. And I have much more sex than most."

"If you put it like that." Jessica took a quick drink.

"But just like any profession, there are down sides. No job is all plus sides. Life isn't like that. We all have to make compromises."

Jessica peered into her wine glass. Another pressing question had taken hold of her, but she didn't know how to ask it.

"Come on then," Liz said. "Out with it. I'm ready for a second round of twenty questions, although I would appreciate it if we could keep it to only ten this time." She pushed her plate a little farther on the table and leaned her elbows on the tabletop.

"It's a silly question, really."

"Did no one ever teach you that there's no such thing as a silly question?" Liz asked.

"No, I was raised on real talk and that's just bullshit. At least that's what my father would say."

"Well, I'm sure your question is perfectly valid. Come on. Let me have it."

"Okay." Jessica took her wine glass in her hands. It made her feel less vulnerable. "When you're with a client. In bed. Do you ever, er…"

"Yes?" Liz asked.

"You know. Come." A hot flush crept up Jessica's cheeks.

"Sure." Liz sent her a smile. "It really depends on the situation. Some women really get off on that. If the vibe between us is right, I do sometimes let go. Although mostly I do have to fake it. There are so many different scenarios. But it has happened, although it's definitely not part of my job description." Her smile widened. "Now can I ask you a question?"

"It would be pretty rude to say no at this point." Jessica mirrored Liz's smile.

"What happened when you had Laurel over? Did you insist on making her come?"

The previous blush had scarcely faded before Jessica's cheeks were again engulfed in hotness. "Well, er, I didn't insist," she stammered. "But I did try. Although I'll never know whether she faked it or not."

"Interesting." Liz sat there nodding as though she had just uncovered a hidden truth about Jessica.

"It's really not that interesting."

"Oh, it is." Under the table, Jessica felt Liz's shin slide against hers. "Can I interest you in some dessert? I make the lightest chocolate mousse you'll ever taste," she said.

"That's a bold claim to make." Jessica let her leg lean into Liz's. She was glad for the break in their conversation. Her cheeks needed some urgent cooling off.

"I've just realized I may have said that to the wrong person. Does your father have a pastry chef?"

"Nope. Edward Porter is not a dessert man."

"Well, then. Let's see if I can impress you."

"This was delicious, by the way." Jessica grabbed her plate and started to rise.

"No, no, no. Please remain seated. Or stretch your legs, if you like. But there's no need to help." Liz quickly rose, and took the plate from Jessica's hand. "The kitchen is a right old mess. I want you as far away from there as possible."

"Ah, that explains it." Jessica sat down again and leaned back in her chair. "I'll stay in the safe zone then."

"If you want to feel useful, you can always pour us some more wine," Liz said and disappeared into the kitchen.

Jessica refilled their glasses and rehashed all the things that had been said. No matter the oddity of the subjects, Liz was still so easy to talk to. She had so much confidence, she made up for what Jessica lacked right now.

"Has the person who invented the dishwasher ever received a Nobel Prize?" Liz sauntered back into the living room. "Because no greater service has ever been done to humankind." She carried two low glasses filled to the brim with chocolate mousse. "Here you go, Madam. Did you want coffee or tea with that?"

"Wine will be fine," Jessica said.

"Here's to a wonderful date." Liz picked up her wine glass.

Jessica joined her in the toast. It might be an unusual date, but that didn't make Jessica feel any less special when she was in Liz's company.

Chapter Sixteen

THEY WERE BACK on the couch, steadily working their way through the second bottle of wine. Jessica was contemplating calling in sick at work the next day. It was only her third day back, but no one would bat an eyelid if she did. Someone would probably tell her father—he had spies in all departments—and then she'd have to deal with him. She actually preferred him a bit more aloof than the worried persona he had adopted since she'd gotten sick.

"I can't believe I have to go to work tomorrow." Jessica heeled off her shoes and stretched her legs onto the ottoman. "You also made me eat too much. I need to lie down."

"Don't get too comfortable." Liz scooted next to her and stretched her legs as well. "I still need to give you a tour of the premises."

"Ah yes, your art collection. Maybe we can save it for next time. Yours will make mine look like child's play, anyway."

"Are you kidding? You have a Robert Barrow hanging in your hallway. Not even in the living room; in the hallway of all places."

"For that welcoming feeling."

"More like intimidating." Liz leaned into her.

"Only if you're in the know."

Jessica felt Liz nod next to her. "So," she said after a beat. "The hour is getting late and the lady is getting tired." She put a hand on Jessica's thigh. "Can I put you down for a second date or do you need to get back to me on that?"

"Is this your way of sending me home?" Jessica asked.

"Goodness, no." Liz turned to her. "You just look as though you might fall asleep any minute now."

Jessica sighed. "My stamina needs a little work. It has taken a bit of a hit lately." She tried to square her shoulders. "But it's just a post-dinner slump. I'll get a second wind in a bit."

"Pity we can't watch some of *The Kramers* to pass the time," Liz joked.

"Exactly what I was going to say." Jessica slid her hand underneath Liz's and intertwined their fingers. "Whatever will we do to make time go faster?"

"Seeing as this is, technically, our first date, our options are limited, I guess." Liz grinned.

"Although we have seen each other half naked," Jessica said.

"And we've kissed and watched television together," Liz replied.

Jessica's breath stalled in her throat. She was glad she and Liz had only kissed while Liz was on the clock, so to speak. Liz had shown her the message she had sent to the agency. It had sent a clear message to Jessica as well.

"I've introduced you to the wonderful world that is my job." Jessica rotated a little so she could see Liz's face better. "You do realize we're now living in a time dubbed *Peak TV*."

"Aren't we the lucky ones," Liz said.

Jessica snickered. "You can be so snobbish."

"Moi?" Liz put a hand to her chest. "With my Scandi-chic furniture?"

Jessica slapped her on the thigh. "Enough already. I was nervous when I first arrived. Have some mercy."

Liz leaned in a little closer and whispered, "Are you begging for mercy already?"

Jessica swiveled her head and looked Liz straight in the eye. She had a smile on her lips, but her eyes told a different story. Jessica wanted to bridge the few inches between their faces and feel Liz's lips on hers again, but something was holding her back. The exact same thing that had been holding her back for a long time. Fear.

"Too much, too soon?" Liz asked and squeezed Jessica's hand.

Jessica shook her head while she sank her teeth into her bottom lip.

"Good." Liz's voice had dropped an octave. She *did* have the guts to bridge the tiny distance between them and pressed her lips softly against Jessica's. She withdrew for a split second until their lips met again the next moment.

Liz slid her fingers from between Jessica's and brought her hand to Jessica's cheek. She touched the back of her fingers against the spot where Jessica had blushed so fever-ishly earlier. The touch made Jessica flush again, but she didn't care this time around. She pushed her cheek against Liz's hand while she pressed her lips against Liz's. It was the only logical outcome. Jessica wanted Liz. There had never been any doubt about that.

And Liz wanted Jessica too. That much was obvious by the way her tongue slipped between Jessica's lips, by the way her body twisted to meet as much of Jessica's as possible.

"Let me get a bit more comfortable," Liz said when they

came up for air. She pushed herself up and crawled onto Jessica's lap, planting her knees on either side of Jessica. "Hi," she said, when they were face-to-face again.

"Hi." Jessica's voice was hoarse and deep.

Liz kissed her again, palming Jessica's cheeks with both hands. The kiss was deep and impossible to misinterpret.

"I want you," Liz said, when they broke from the kiss. She was panting slightly and something had changed in her eyes again. She looked as though she had them firmly on the prize—there was no doubt the prize was Jessica.

"I want you too," Jessica managed to say.

Liz smiled at her. "Come," she said. She climbed off Jessica and held out her hand. "Let me show you my boudoir."

Jessica giggled as she extended her hand and let Liz pull her out of the couch. Liz slung an arm around her and held her tightly as she led Jessica into the bedroom. Jessica had no eyes at all for anything on the walls. She only felt Liz's arm around her and her own heart beating away in her chest.

"Welcome," Liz said, and closed the door behind them. They stood in complete darkness. "Oops, sorry about that." Liz let go and stumbled around. A few seconds later a lamp on the bedside table lit up the room. "Not as suave as I had hoped to be." Liz grabbed Jessica's hand again.

The sudden illumination drew Jessica's glance to the wall behind the lamp. A large black and white photo hung above Liz's bed, portraying a stark naked woman from the back. The woman flexed her muscles and boasted an impressive shoulder line. Jessica couldn't explain how, but even though she couldn't see her face, and wasn't that familiar with her naked shoulder line yet, she knew it was Liz.

"Is there a particular reason you have a naked picture of yourself hanging above your bed?" Jessica asked.

"There are many." Liz stood next to her and looked at the picture with Jessica. "The main one being this type of reaction." She put her hand in the small of Jessica's back. "How did you know it was me?"

"Something about it is just so quintessentially you."

"Ah, must be the impressive posterior chain." Liz let her hand drop and gently slapped Jessica's bottom.

"It's rather intimidating, actually. For women like me who are not exactly in their prime." Jessica pushed her behind into Liz's hand regardless.

"Believe it or not, but not many women make it into my boudoir," Liz said. "In fact, you're the first since I hung that up. I'm still kind of testing it out." Liz followed up with a chuckle.

"So you'll get me to fill in a survey later on the effects it had?" Jessica leaned against Liz's side. She felt so solid and strong.

"That's exactly right." Liz's hand sneaked up again and slid under the hem of Jessica's blouse.

"Who took that picture? It's hardly a candid shot."

"A friend of mine who dabbles in amateur photography."

"Impressive for an amateur."

Liz's fingertips traced a line up Jessica's spine. "Do you mean even more so than the subject of the picture?"

"God no." The hair on the back of Jessica's neck stood up. "Nothing's more impressive than that."

Liz slipped behind her and moved both her hands underneath Jessica's blouse, coming to rest on her belly. Her lips found Jessica's neck and traced a path up to her ear.

"I want you," Liz repeated her words from earlier in the living room. "So much." She withdrew her hands from Jessica's belly and she kissed her neck again, then started to unbutton her blouse. It was obviously a skill she had perfected because mere seconds later, Jessica's blouse slid off her shoulders.

Liz brought her hands to Jessica's hips and gestured for her to turn around. Jessica stood facing Liz in her bra, but she wasn't engulfed with the familiar trepidation. Liz had already seen her and, more importantly, Jessica had seen herself. Yes, she was missing something, but she didn't look like the monster she had made up in her head. In fact, when Liz stood in front of her like that, lust brimming in her eyes, her chest rising and falling rapidly, Jessica didn't think about the prosthesis in one cup of her bra much at all.

Liz took hold of the hem of her own white-and-blue boat-neck top and hoisted it over her head. Jessica was now faced with a real-life bra-clad Liz. Together with that picture above the bed, it made her pulse pick up speed.

Liz brought her hand to Jessica's cheek again and caressed it. Jessica was glad there was no mirror in front of her so she couldn't see how pink her cheeks were.

"You're beautiful," Liz said. Her hand slipped to the back of Jessica's head and she pulled her in for another kiss. It was even more insistent than the last intense one they had shared in the living room. Liz was clearly also very skilled at ratcheting up the tension.

"Do you think I should also hang a naked picture of myself in my bedroom?" Jessica asked when they broke from the kiss, a grin on her face.

"I most certainly do." Liz didn't waste any time and kissed her again. Her hands drifted up Jessica's sides and all the hairs on her skin rose up in excitement. When Liz's hands were on their way down, they halted at the button of Jessica's pants. Liz snapped it open and, in what seemed like one movement, the zipper beneath it as well.

"I want you naked," Liz said, then hesitated for the first time. "As naked as you're comfortable with."

Jessica reached for the button of Liz's jeans and flipped it open. "I'm comfortable with you."

That was what it all came down to in the end. The immense sense of comfort Liz had given her, just by being herself, and being there.

"I'm happy to hear that." Liz pushed Jessica's pants down her hips. She waited for Jessica to do the same to hers.

Jessica wrapped her arms around Liz and drew her nearer to the bed. She took advantage of the situation to unhook Liz's bra.

"Can I take yours off?" Liz whispered in her ears.

Jessica nodded, her chin bumping against Liz's shoulder.

"Okay," Liz said. Before she undid Jessica's bra, she held her close for a while longer. Only after a few more moments of holding her in her strong arms, did she undo Jessica's bra. Jessica held the cups against her while she watched Liz slip her arms out of hers and throw it on a chair behind her.

She swallowed hard at the sight of Liz's naked torso. At the view of her perfect breasts.

Jessica slowly let her bra drop away from her, careful to keep the prosthesis in its cup. She folded it up and gave it to Liz to place down.

Liz laid Jessica's bra on the seat of the chair, treating it with much more care than her own. "Come here," she said.

Jessica stepped into her embrace again and she felt safe and at ease—as at ease as a woman as aroused as her could possibly feel.

Liz kissed her on the cheek and soon Jessica met her lips. As they kissed, Liz walked them to the bed, until Jessica felt the edge bump against the back of her knees.

Liz pushed Jessica onto the bed and crawled on it with her. For Jessica, it felt natural to let Liz take the lead. Liz didn't seem to mind much either. She was probably used to initiating, but no—Jessica willed her thoughts not to go there. This had nothing to do with Liz's profession.

They maneuvered until they were both fully supported by the bed, then Liz pressed her body against Jessica's side.

"Is there anything I'm not allowed to do? Certain spots I'm not allowed to touch?" Liz asked in a soft voice. Her hand rested on Jessica's belly.

Nobody Jessica had ever been in bed with had asked her that question. "I don't mind you touching my breast, but I'm not sure how I'll react to you touching my scar."

"Understood." Liz smiled at her.

Jessica thought it only polite to return the question. "Is there anything I shouldn't—" It sounded so strange, but maybe this was how it should always be. All lines of communication wide open.

"With you, I have zero no-go zones." Liz flashed her a grin, then leaned down to kiss her. She kissed Jessica for a long time, while her hand roamed across her belly and her sides, steering clear of Jessica's chest.

When they finally broke from the kiss, Liz slid half on top of her, pushing her knee between Jessica's legs. She refocused her attention on Jessica's neck, kissing it softly and slowly in a straight line from Jessica's ear to her shoulder. The gentle kisses drove Jessica crazy—and made her forget about how she was lying on her back, totally exposed.

When Liz kissed her like that, and her entire body became one tingling mass, Jessica could almost forget she'd ever had surgery.

Liz moved on to the other side of her neck as Jessica lay squirming underneath her.

Jessica ran her fingers through Liz's straight black hair. It was short in the back and long-ish in the front, so her bangs always threatened to fall into her eyes. She had the most adorable habit of brushing away a strand of hair. And her hair was so soft. As was her skin, although the muscles underneath had nothing of that softness.

Jessica's fingers explored Liz's back. She'd seen it with flexed muscles in that picture above their heads. To now hold that powerful body against hers was a thrill.

Liz kissed a path down from Jessica's neck. Her lips touched down on Jessica's collar bone, then dove south along her left breast. Liz didn't linger but instead started kissing Jessica's belly. It wasn't exactly flabby—Jessica had the good fortune of skinny genes in her family—but it was hardly toned either. Unlike Liz's hard stomach. Maybe she should go to TRX with her.

Liz's tongue dipped into her belly button and the fire that had been steadily building underneath Jessica's skin grew stronger and hotter. Jessica felt she might burst out of her skin soon if Liz kept this up. And she wasn't going to stop any time soon.

It had been a long time since Jessica had really made love to a woman. She'd only met Liz last week, yet she felt like they were making *love*. Liz had helped her take some steps Jessica wasn't sure she could have taken with anyone else—or on her own.

When Liz had shown up on her doorstep instead of Laurel, Jessica's initial disappointment had quickly been replaced by something else entirely. The undeniable chemistry between them.

Jessica felt that chemistry flow through her as Liz kissed her way down from her belly button. She pictured Liz's supple lips touching down on her skin every time their softness sent another pang of arousal up her spine. Soon her thoughts drifted to Liz's tongue, which had felt so heavenly in her mouth, and would feel even more heavenly elsewhere very quickly if Liz kept up this pace.

Jessica shuddered in anticipation. She couldn't believe

how much she wanted this—how much she wanted Liz. And how much Liz wanted her. After she'd just had surgery, feeling sorry for herself in the hospital, she could never have dreamed of anything like this happening to her again. Yet, here she lay. And Liz's lips were closing in.

Liz gently pulled off Jessica's underwear. She pushed Jessica's legs apart and kissed Jessica's inner thigh. Jessica dug her fingers deeper into the flesh of Liz's shoulders. She wished she could feel more of her—she wished she could see her face.

Liz stopped kissing her and looked up. "Are you okay?" she asked.

Jessica gave a quick nod. Liz smiled in response, then resumed her kissing action. She took her time bestowing kiss after kiss on the sensitive skin there and every single one drove up Jessica's level of excitement.

Going to bed with Liz wasn't only exciting because of how she was falling for her, so quickly and unstoppably, but also because of what she did for a living. Jessica could try and deny it as much as she wanted—and she would if asked point blank—but it was extra arousing. Not so much Liz's skill, but all the other implications of her job. The emotional intelligence she had to display. The sensitivity and extreme communication she had to employ. Jessica tried to fight it, but Liz was planting kisses on her thigh—closing in on her wildly pulsing clit—and it was the truth of it. Not a simple truth, but a complex, slightly unnerving one.

Then Liz's tongue touched down on her clit and Jessica stopped thinking altogether. From the moment Liz had given her that first neck massage, this was what Jessica had wanted. This beautiful, smart, strong woman licking her clit. Now it was happening and it met her every expectation.

Jessica buried her fingers in Liz's soft hair. Her entire body felt like a live wire—her clit the spark. She threw her head back and looked at the wall behind her, at the picture of Liz's impressive backside. Then she looked down and saw the part of Liz's back that was curved upward while she was licking her.

It didn't get much better than this. Not after going through a vicious depression, destroying her business, and losing her right breast. For some reason she would never be able to explain, Jessica brought her hand to where her breast used to be. First, she found the void. Then the scar. She planted her hand down on the flattened part of her torso and let it lie there. Her other hand remained in Liz's hair.

For a few moments, Liz stopped licking her clit. Jessica looked down and stared straight into Liz's eyes.

Liz didn't smile, but gave Jessica an altogether different kind of look. One that shivered up Jessica's spine before lodging itself in her heart, in a spot beneath her flesh not far from where her hand was resting on her chest. It was as though Liz had sensed that Jessica had taken the next step and wanted to take time to mark the moment—wanted Jessica to know that she was with her every step of the way.

Liz's head disappeared between Jessica's legs again and her piercing glance was gone. Jessica let her head fall back, kept one hand on her scar, and brought the other one to her left breast, which she cupped gently in her palm. Even though she was in the throes of being sexually pleasured, it wasn't a sexual act. It was one of acceptance.

Liz upped the ante of her licking action. Hot waves of excitement coursed through Jessica's body. This could have happened when they'd first met, but it wouldn't have been the same. It was good that things had played out the way they had. Now, she could meet her orgasm without any reservations. This was right. Liz was right for her. Nothing else mattered.

The back of Jessica's head dug deeper into the pillow.

The burst of heat in the pit of her stomach became unbearable. As she exploded into orgasm, and the blackness behind her eyelids turned into a kaleidoscope of color, an image emerged. Liz looking at her like she had done earlier. Nothing but complete understanding in her glance.

Chapter Seventeen

"MORNING," Jessica said. She'd only just opened her eyes and was already met with Liz's gaze on hers.

"Morning, gorgeous." Liz kissed her on the cheek and pressed her naked body against hers.

"Please tell me it's not past eight o'clock yet," Jessica said on a sigh.

"It's just gone seven," Liz said. "Plenty of time to call in sick."

Jessica brought her hands over her eyes. "I really shouldn't. It's irresponsible. It sends the wrong kind of message."

"Come on, Jess. You only live once. And what's the worst that can happen? A Kramer might feel a little less special for a minute or so?"

"God, I hope one day I get the opportunity to introduce you to Kathy Kramer." Jessica crawled deeper into Liz's embrace.

"Tell me, honestly, as a woman who's had cancer and who appreciates the value of every minute of her life... Wouldn't you rather spend the morning with me? If you didn't, you'd miss my super-delicious scrambled eggs, which take time and dedication to prepare."

"Well, I couldn't possibly miss out on your eggs, of course. That would most obviously be a crime against humankind." Jessica removed her hands from over her eyes. "You really are keeping me off the straight and narrow."

"I've never been very interested in the straight and narrow. It's so boring there." Liz's hand stole up Jessica's belly. "And you're too scrumptious to keep to such a boring path."

"I'm sure the HR department at ANBC will agree."

"How about this as a compromise, then." Liz turned on her side and supported her chin on an upturned palm. "Instead of working this morning, you work this afternoon. Sheer brilliance, don't you think?"

"There's just no end to your brilliance." Jessica snickered.

"So, what do you say? Am I allowed to take you hostage in my bed for the morning?"

"Don't you have a TRX class or something?"

"I can do TRX right here." Liz maneuvered under the sheets until she hovered over Jessica. She performed a push-up, lowering herself until her entire front touched Jessica, then pushed herself back up. She repeated the process three times until she collapsed onto Jessica. "Looks like I don't have the strength today, anyway. I'll need to stay in bed to recuperate."

"And the woman is a comedian as well. Where will it end, indeed?" Jessica couldn't suppress a grin from appearing on her lips. She felt so carefree with Liz. But could she really not turn up for work? Without feeling guilty? Because that was bugging her most of all. Maybe she should take a page out of Liz's book. And Liz was right. What was one more morning off work, when you'd had a mastectomy? What if *she* used cancer as an excuse, instead of the cancer using her and turning her into a fearful wallflower?

"I hope it will end with you in this bed for a long time to come," Liz said.

"Okay, fine. I've been officially charmed. You'll need to get your naked body out of bed for a moment and run into the living room to fetch my phone, though," Jessica said.

"Oh really?" Liz, who was still lying half on top of her, slipped off. "Is this how it's going to be?"

"Looks like it. You just told me to enjoy life and to definitely not stay on the straight and narrow. I'm just taking my first steps."

"And I'm not even allowed to wear a robe?" Liz asked.

"Absolutely not." Jessica stuck an arm out from under the duvet. "It's not cold, so that can't be the problem. I hardly think bashfulness is either."

Liz batted her lashes. "For a woman with a naked picture of herself above her bed, I can be extremely bashful."

"Come on." Jessica held up the duvet, letting the warmth escape. "It's up to you."

"Yes, Ma'am." Liz sprang to her feet and gave her behind a little wiggle as she exited the room. She must have sprinted because she was back in a flash, clutching Jessica's purse in front of her chest. "Here you go, Ms. Porter." She handed Jessica the purse and crawled back underneath the covers.

"Thanks." Jessica kissed Liz on the cheek. "Your reward is coming shortly." She fished her phone out of her purse and looked at the screen. "It's not even seven thirty yet. It's too early to call."

"You tricked me." Liz started tickling her. "You have to pay."

Liz's hands were so cold that Jessica dropped the phone.

"Stop it," she squealed. "I'll email my assistant. She'll take care of it."

Liz stopped tickling her. "Go on. You have two minutes before my hands are all over you again."

Jessica shook her head. She composed a quick email and sent it before she could change her mind.

"How does it feel?" Liz asked.

Jessica put the phone away and turned to Liz. "You make it sound as though skiving off work is the most daring thing I've ever done."

Liz waggled her eyebrows. "Do tell. What is the most daring thing you've ever done?"

Jessica should have known Liz would call her bluff. She was that kind of person. Jessica racked her brain. She wasn't sure she could share the most daring experience she'd had. But this was Liz. She felt she could tell her just about anything—after having revealed her scar—and making love to her.

"I'll have you know I had a foursome once." She tried to look smug, but guessed she probably just looked ridiculous, what with words like that coming from her mouth—they didn't quite fit.

"What? Hold the presses!" Liz sat up. "Give me all the details, please."

Jessica chuckled. "I can't give you all the details. That would be breaking the confidence of those involved."

"Really? Were they women of whom one would not suspect they would be involved in such an activity? Like one Jessica Porter?"

Jessica thought about that. "No, actually not at all. It was definitely the most daring and unexpected experience for me, even though I was the one who set it up."

Liz looked at her expectantly and Jessica told her the story of how, not long after she received her cancer diagnosis, she organized a dinner party at her home with Katherine, Caitlin, and Jo. And how one thing had led to another.

"Caitlin James?" Liz asked, after Jessica had finished her story. "You slept with Caitlin James?"

"You sound impressed." Jessica couldn't suppress a smile.

"Let's just say there aren't many Australians who are so vocal and eloquent about some very important topics. I don't admire many people, but I definitely admire her."

Jessica glanced at Liz, but didn't say anything.

Liz cocked her head in response.

"I talked to Caitlin about you and... if you play your cards right, you might very well be invited to dinner at hers and Jo's on Saturday."

"Hm," Liz said. "Please remind me, which card game is it again that we're playing?" She sneaked her finger up Jessica's thigh gently, then started tickling her again.

"Stop, stop. It's too early for this," Jessica groaned.

"Does that mean the invitation is now official?" Liz stared at her with hope in her eyes.

"I'd love for you to join us. Although I'll need to tell Katherine first." Jessica's shoulders slumped.

"Katherine?" Liz knitted her brows together. "Wait, that dinner party you just told me about... and this upcoming one. Are they of the *same kind*?" She put emphasis on the last two words.

"What? No. We're all friends now. That was a one-time thing. A goodbye-to-my-right-breast tumble in the hay. Caitlin and I have gotten way too close to repeat that. She really stood by me after I had my surgery. Everything's different now between us." Jessica put a hand on Liz's wrist. "Besides, I don't want to share you."

"In that case I'd be very happy to join you," Liz said.

"You're free?" Jessica asked, unsure whether she was successfully hiding the trepidation in her voice.

"Even if I wasn't, I'd make sure I was." Liz smiled at her. "So what's the deal with Katherine?"

"She gave me a speech about how utterly stupid it would be for me to develop feelings for you."

"You told Katherine about me as well?" Liz waggled her eyebrows. They were long and very expressive. "My name has been rolling off some tongues, it seems." She chuckled.

"I just told her that you replaced Laurel. I didn't tell her anything. She just assumed."

"Did she now?" Liz scooted a little closer to Jessica. "She has the sixth sense. It probably makes her very good at what she does."

"She wasn't very understanding about it."

"That makes perfect sense to me." Liz shot her an apologetic smile. "She wouldn't be a very good friend if she encouraged you to have the hots for the likes of me."

It was Jessica's turn to arch up her eyebrows.

"Let's face it. The reason Laurel left is either that she was ready for retirement or she met someone who couldn't deal with what she was doing for a living. That's the reality of this job," Liz said. "Katherine knows these things. She wants to save you from getting hurt. It's normal. She's just trying to be a good friend to you. Something you can hardly hold against her."

"Yet here I am. In bed with you." Jessica couldn't quite believe what she was hearing. "And I don't need saving."

"Hey." Liz swung an arm across Jessica's belly and held her close. "This is going to come up. Your friends will have questions. Although, perhaps, we're getting just a tad ahead of ourselves."

Jessica relaxed her shoulders and let herself fall into the mattress a little deeper. She hadn't gotten that much sleep and she was still tired—her body stiff in places she didn't even know it could be.

"Didn't you promise me your super-delicious scrambled eggs?" she said.

"I sure did." Liz kissed her on the tip of the nose. "Do we need to talk about this more?"

Jessica shook her head. "Not now. It's not even eight and someone kept me up most of the night."

"Really? I wonder who that was?" Liz grinned at her again—that irresistible disarming grin. She wondered how many women got wet just at the sight of it?

"The same woman who promised me eggs for breakfast."

"Ah, you mean the same woman who made you dinner?"

"And gave me a few orgasms in between." Jessica felt herself relax again.

"Christ, what a woman."

Jessica nodded. "The kind that truly deserves a picture of herself above her own bed." She chuckled.

"I know all about that kind." Liz nuzzled her neck and, instantly, Jessica was flooded with memories of last night again.

Chapter Eighteen

"ALL YOU NEED IS patience and a generous dollop of butter," Liz said. She cracked a couple of eggs into a bowl and started whisking. She wore a tight tank top and Jessica was entranced by the slight flex in her biceps as she spun the fork around.

Liz was the kind of woman Jessica could look at for days on end. Study the ripple of her muscles, the smoothness of her skin. She looked at least ten years younger than her age.

"What's your secret?" Jessica motioned with her hand to cover the entire length of Liz's body. "How come you look like this at thirty-nine?"

Liz looked up from her eggs. "I treat my body the way certain gay men treat theirs." She winked. "I save my calories for alcohol."

Jessica chuckled.

"I'm serious," Liz said. "And this being Bondi, my TRX class is usually a bunch of gay guys and me."

"Sounds like fun."

"It's a hoot afterward." She poured the eggs into the pan.

"Now, no more distractions, please. It's all in the attention you give the scramble."

"These eggs are so hyped. I hope you're not setting me up for disappointment," Jessica joked.

"I've never had one negative review of my eggs, so best brace yourself."

Jessica watched Liz as she stirred the eggs. "Are you doing anything special to them? It doesn't look any different than ordinary scrambled eggs."

"Shh," Liz said. "I need to focus and you're very distracting."

Jessica watched her in silence. Below the black tank top, Liz was wearing a stripy pair of pajama bottoms. She looked so scrumptious, Jessica would rather have another piece of her than those eggs she was scrambling.

She got up from her chair and stood behind Liz, wrapping her arms around her, and letting her hands slip underneath Liz's tank top.

"What did I tell you?" Liz said, but her voice sounded mellow and she leaned into Jessica's embrace. "Besides, if you're going to spend the morning here, you need to eat because you'll need your strength." Liz pushed her behind against Jessica's groin. She wasn't wearing any underwear beneath her pajama bottoms and Jessica let one hand slide inside her pants to cup her ass cheek.

"Okay, that's the eggs ruined." Liz switched off the gas and put the pan on another hob. She turned around, removing Jessica's arm from her trousers. "When I'm cooking, I become highly combustible, so you'd better fuck me now." There was no smile on her face, only determination. Lust glimmered in her eyes. She reached for Jessica's forearm and slid Jessica's hand back into her pants. "Please finish what you started." The words seemed to come from deep inside her throat.

"But I'm hungry," Jessica said. Her hand swept past Liz's pubic hair, straight for the prize.

"You should have thought of that before you got handsy with me." Liz grinned at her. "Anyway, I've got just the thing to still your most acute hunger." She pushed her pants down.

At the sight of her own hand between Liz's legs, Jessica's pulse picked up speed.

"Fuck me," Liz said, and she said it in such a way that Jessica couldn't do anything else—not that she had any other plans.

Jessica kissed Liz on the lips. Those soft, soft lips that could draw into the most gorgeous smile. What had she called it? A TV smile. The country would be a better place if Liz's smile was broadcast to its people on a regular basis, of this Jessica was convinced.

With her finger, she stroked along Liz's nether lips. She remembered the sight of them from last night. Everything about Liz was just so excruciatingly beautiful. No exceptions.

Liz stepped out of her pajama bottoms, then she spread her legs wider. Jessica took advantage of the better access to slip the tip of her finger a little higher up Liz's lips, to gauge for wetness. She was surprised to be met with a copious amount.

"How is this even possible?" she whispered in Liz's ear when they broke from their kiss.

"Must have been whisking the eggs." Liz shot her a quick grin, then pulled her back in for a kiss.

Jessica slipped her finger higher inside of Liz. Automatically, memories of last night blasted her mind. Her hand on her scar as Liz made her come. The ultimate act of accepting that this was who she was now. A woman with one remaining breast. It felt as though Liz had given her that gift of acceptance. For that reason, as Jessica slipped another one of her fingers inside Liz, she was able to easily shove aside any worries about not being the only one to do this to Liz in the weeks, perhaps even months or years, to come.

Liz clutched Jessica's shoulder with one hand. They broke from the kiss and Jessica scanned her face. A small smile played on her lips. Jessica moved slowly inside of her. Liz seemed to be enjoying the rhythm.

"I want you to make me come like this," Liz whispered. "Just by fucking me with your fingers."

Jessica smiled at her. That was a new one. Liz was still so new to her. Jessica wasn't all that acquainted with her body yet. And she was fucking her against the stove, of which at least one hob was still hot from Liz's attempt at making eggs.

But if Jessica had learned one thing in her forty-five years on this planet, it was to fake it until she made it. She narrowed her eyes and tried to empty her mind. Over-thinking it wasn't going to help—that would only make her feel like she was taking some sort of exam. *Make the call girl come.* Wait. Was that why Liz was talking to her like that? No. *Stop it.* Jessica had two fingers inside the most gorgeous woman she had—truly—ever seen. A woman who had just begged her to make her come. A woman who already meant so much to her.

Liz started meeting her thrusts while grinding herself onto Jessica's fingers, giving Jessica the impression that she'd be taking care of her own climax. Jessica's fingers were just the instrument she needed to get there. Jessica hoped something more than an instrument was needed. Perhaps the connection between them. And the look in Jessica's eyes as she fucked Liz.

Liz kept her eyes open throughout. Her teeth sank into her bottom lip as Jessica's fingers and Liz's pussy seemed to melt from two separate body parts, from two different human beings, into one entity. They moved together. Jessica could feel Liz's growing arousal shoot up through her fingers. She felt it tingle inside of her. She lost herself in the lust she saw in Liz's eyes. Because that was what had gotten her this far along the way. The fact that Liz wanted her. It was in her every word, in her every glance. It was reflected back perfectly at Jessica now as she looked into Liz's eyes. Those pools of kindness mixed with kinkiness. Jessica couldn't get enough of them. Certainly not now when her fingers were being swallowed by the heat of Liz's pussy.

"Oh, Jess," Liz moaned. Her fingers dug deeper into Jessica's shoulder muscles. So deeply, Jessica guessed they would leave a mark, but she didn't mind a mark left by Liz. Liz stopped grinding and her eyes fell shut while she shivered and let out a few deep-throated sighs.

She breathed out heavily through her nose as her limbs relaxed and Jessica withdrew her fingers.

"You can forget about those eggs now," Liz said. "Unless you enjoy eating rubber." She pulled Jessica into a hug and kissed her on the mouth.

Chapter Nineteen

JESSICA PACED AROUND her living room. She stopped at the window and looked out across the street. No sign of Katherine yet. She'd invited her over for two reasons. To tell her about Liz. And to get the scolding she knew she was going to get. She needed it. It was Friday evening and Liz was *working* and the thought of it was doing Jessica's head in. She didn't know what to do with herself. She didn't know what to think. She tried to keep certain images from popping up in her head, but it didn't work. She'd wandered around her living room unstoppably since 7 p.m.—the time Liz had *gone to work*.

Jessica was still standing by the window when a car pulled up. It was Katherine's white Audi. Jessica took a deep breath and headed for the front door.

She opened it before Katherine had a chance to ring the bell.

Before she hugged Jessica, she said, "Are you okay, Jess? You haven't had any bad news, have you?" Katherine pulled her into a tight hug.

"I'm fine. Come in." She ushered Katherine into the

living room. They sat down but Jessica immediately stood up again. "Drink?" she asked.

Katherine narrowed her eyes and regarded her. "Something's going on. What is it?"

"I'll tell you over a drink, shall I?" Jessica said.

"Sure. I'll have some of that wine you're drinking."

Jessica had opened a bottle right after she'd called Katherine and asked her to meet. She'd gone through nearly half of it on her own.

She tried to take a discreet deep breath as she poured Katherine some wine.

"Okay," she said. "You're going to think I've lost my mind and I actually very much think I am losing my mind." She fidgeted with the sleeve of her sweater. "Just for the record."

Katherine slanted her head. "Let me guess," she said. "You've only gone and fallen in love with an escort."

Jessica sighed. "We just really clicked."

"Oh, I'm sure you did." Katherine drank from the wine Jessica had just poured her. "I'm not going to judge you for falling for her, but don't expect this to be a walk in the park either."

Jessica sighed. "I know it's not. I'm going mad because, er, right at this moment Liz is with a client. Honestly, if you weren't here, I'm not sure what I would be doing."

Katherine put down her glass. "Look, Jess, I wish there was a manual for this, but there isn't. If you're going to do this with Liz—have a relationship with her—you're going to have to tell her how you feel, but you're also going to have to learn to respect what she does and that she chose this job." She looked longingly at her glass again. "Believe me, I know it's hard."

"If I'm going to be like this three times a week…" Jessica said.

"You're freaking out right now. It's normal. You probably have all sorts of images in your head."

"Not only that, but I have a pit the size of a cannonball in my stomach. If I see her tomorrow, what am I going to say to her? How am I going to behave? I mean… I'm jealous. That's really what it comes down to."

"Oh, Jess. Of all the women in Sydney." Katherine shot her a smile.

"She just… made me feel something so real, so undeniable. We had fun, you know. Genuine fun. She made me giggle when I didn't think I had much reason to." She pulled up her shoulders. "I just love being around her. I love how she makes me feel when I'm with her. And she seems to feel the same way."

"All of that, eh?" Katherine said warily.

"And then some. I just wonder what she sees in me."

Katherine held up her hand. "Oh no, none of that, please. It's well established you're a catch."

"The hell I am."

"I'm not even going to discuss that. Honestly, you can take that up with Mrs. Buchman. I've wasted enough of my breath on trying to convince you of that."

Jessica waved off Katherine's remark. "I invited Liz to Caitlin's." While she had her hand up, she gestured for Katherine to swallow her upcoming remark. "Don't worry, it was Caitlin who extended the invitation. She knows what Liz does. I told her."

"I look forward to getting to know her better then." Katherine cocked her head. "And to seeing the two of you together."

"Have you and her ever, er, worked together?"

Katherine chuckled. "Please, Jess, don't ask *me* these questions. Ask them of Liz. Start a conversation. Whatever it is you and she are starting, it's not going to be easy, but it sure as hell won't be boring either. You'll always have plenty to talk about."

"Thank goodness we'll have conversation then."

"Conversation is a lot to have."

They sat pondering this for a moment.

"I thought you'd be more cross with me," Jessica said. "That you'd go off the deep end like last time."

"That was hardly me going off the deep end. Either way, it needed to be said. This isn't a fairytale you're walking into."

"Maybe not, but she's as gorgeous as any fairy princess." A smile appeared on her lips. "I guess when you look like that, you might as well…" Jessica brought a hand to her mouth. Had she really said that out loud?

Katherine either hadn't heard or had decided to ignore Jessica's last remark. She didn't say anything and Jessica couldn't bear the silence hanging between them.

"Do you think it's possible… I mean, do you know women who do what you do and are in a successful relationship?" Jessica asked.

Katherine reached for her wine glass again. She drank before speaking. "Don't you think it's time you actually started using the words invented for *what it is I do*? I'm an escort, Jess. Some would call me a hooker, or a call girl, a prostitute or a sex worker."

"There's no need to be crass," Jessica blurted out.

"It's not crass. It's a job."

Jessica let her head fall back. "I'm sorry," she said when she looked back up. "I didn't mean to offend you. It was just all so much easier before I met Liz."

"To answer your question. Yes, it is possible, but not common. But there are always exceptions to the rule."

"Liz wants to start an art gallery," Jessica said. "I have

money." She regretted it as soon as the words had left her mouth.

"Please don't try to save her. Liz doesn't need saving. Please take the advice I'm about to give you very seriously. Don't offer her money. One of the core reasons any of us do this job is because of the independence it gives us. We don't need some rich girl swooping in with bags of money. We make our own way." She took a quick sip. "I can only speak for myself, of course."

"You don't have to tell me you can't buy happiness with money," Jessica said. "My father's been trying that all his life and he isn't exactly the happiest person I know."

"Would this include you as well?" Katherine asked.

"Well, I certainly know," Jessica said wistfully. "I've experienced it firsthand. But money is supposed to make some things easier." Of course, the simple equation of her having money and Liz saving money to open her own art gallery didn't work in real life. Jessica knew that much as well.

"You're going to need to have a cold hard look in the mirror and ask yourself if being with Liz is what you really want. It's going to come at a price. Are you willing to pay?"

"There's no way I'm letting her go because she's an... escort." She barely managed to squeeze the last word past her lips. "She makes me feel too good—too much—for that."

"Think about it for a bit longer, anyway. Because this is the early stage, when you're still giddy with hormones which make a lot of things a lot easier to handle."

"I showed her my scar, Kat. Somehow, she got me to do that. Before I hadn't even dared to look at myself in the mirror."

"You did?" Katherine's eyes grew wide.

Jessica nodded. "It was such a special moment, but when you look at it in another way... I mean, I *had* booked her. It could also be something totally different. Like a paid-for emotion or something."

"There's no such thing as a paid-for emotion," Katherine said matter-of-factly.

"You know what I mean." Jessica looked at her friend. She probably had a lesson or two to learn from her. Maybe Katherine was right and she should be learning them from the woman she was falling in love with instead.

"I know what you're getting at, but I think it's a pretty safe bet that what you felt when you showed yourself to Liz was as real as it gets. There's no way that didn't evoke some very real emotions in her. It might very well be why she's falling in love with you. Vulnerability can be a beautiful thing."

Out of nowhere, a tear pushed itself out of the corner of Jessica's eye. "Oh, fuck." She quickly wiped it away. "I haven't cried since…" She had to think. "Since before the surgery."

"Oh, Jess." Katherine stood and came to sit next to her in the couch. "Why are you rich people so hard on yourselves?"

"I don't think it's necessarily a privilege of the privileged," she joked. She didn't want any more tears leaking from her eyes.

"From what I gather, what happened between you and Liz was a beautiful thing. You opened yourself up to her emotionally and that's not an easy thing to do. No matter how difficult things might be, you'll always have that." Katherine put her arms around Jessica. "I think you should have a good cry on my shoulder now. I'm your friend, remember?" She rubbed a finger over the fabric of her blouse. "This old thing can take it."

Jessica shook her head. "I don't want to cry."

"If you're sure." Katherine pulled her a little closer. "Either way, I'm here."

Jessica put her head on Katherine's shoulder. She swallowed the rest of her tears and thanked her lucky stars Katherine had come over. But, of course, she couldn't call a friend every time Liz went to see a client. If this was going to last, she'd need to find a different coping mechanism.

Chapter Twenty

"HEY GORGEOUS." Liz kissed Jessica on the cheek. It was a lingering kiss and Jessica inhaled Liz's scent deeply.

They had a few hours before they were expected at Caitlin and Jo's. Jessica was glad they had some time together. After last night's agitation, she felt she needed to get used to being around Liz again. It seemed to be a recurring thing. She always managed to feel completely at ease with Liz, but only after a while. Before she could reach that stage, she always had to take on a certain hurdle—it wasn't much of a secret to Jessica what the problem was.

They headed into the sitting room and sat down. Liz had proposed to meet at the Pink Bean, but Jessica had asked her to come over to her house instead. She needed to say a few things and wasn't sure a Saturday afternoon at the Pink Bean was the best location for it—not that there was any best location to have this particular conversation.

"I missed you." Liz apparently didn't have any hurdles to overcome because she started pushing Jessica down into the couch. "A lot." She went straight for her neck.

"Please, stop," Jessica said, in a more forceful tone than she wanted to.

Liz sat up and looked at her. "What's going on? I figured you didn't want to meet me in the coffee shop because..." She waggled her eyebrows. "You know."

Jessica scoffed.

"What?" Liz asked.

"You really don't know?" Jessica asked.

Liz sighed. She adjusted her position and sat down properly, crossing one knee over the other.

"I have an informed guess." She fixed her gaze on Jessica. "Talk to me."

Jessica huffed out some air. "Talk, talk, talk," she said. "Some things just aren't that easy to talk about. Some things, I simply don't have the vocabulary for."

"Well, I *do*, Jess." Liz turned in the couch, drawing one leg up. "You're jealous. It's to be expected."

"I—I just have no idea how to deal with this—how to be around you."

"Ask me what you want to know. I'll tell you. I can't tell you who I was with, but I can tell you what happened. Is that what you want to know?"

Jessica considered this, but the ball in the pit of her stomach only seemed to grow at the thought of actually knowing what Liz and her client had been up to. She shook her head. "No, I guess that, for starters, I just want to know if with... your client, it was the same as with me."

"Of course it wasn't. How could it possibly be?"

"I was your client," Jessica said.

"For about five minutes, Jess. I think we both knew there was something else going on between us pretty quickly." Liz looked away for a moment, then fixed her gaze on Jessica again. "People meet under all sorts of circumstances and this happens to be how we met. I've never fallen for a client before and I didn't fall for you because you were a client. But what you have to understand is that I no longer justify what I do, because doing that would mean a few things. For starters, it would mean that it *needs* justifying. In the end, I could give you all the justification I wanted, it wouldn't change how you felt. I can understand how you feel, that's not what I'm saying, but this is something you're going to have to get over. I'll help you in any way I can, but this is me. This is what I do and what I'm going to be doing for the foreseeable future. Either you learn to live with it or you don't."

"I'm sorry," Jessica said. "I didn't think it was going to be this hard."

"It's okay. You'll get used to it."

Jessica wasn't so sure of that. How could she possibly get used to the woman she was falling in love with sleeping with other people? But then again, what choice did she have? Stop falling in love? If this couldn't stop her, nothing would.

"Maybe we need some sort of protocol," Jessica said, even though she didn't really know where she was going with this suggestion. "Some cooling off period after you've had a date with a client."

Liz shook her head. "How about this instead." She shuffled closer but didn't touch Jessica. "I just don't tell you when I'm working. That way you can't freak out about it."

"I'm not sure that's going to work. I'll know regardless of you telling me."

"Oh really? Have you been bestowed with the gift of knowing what I'm up to when we're not together?"

"If you're not free in the evening, I won't be able to conclude otherwise than that you're on a date."

"That's your conclusion to draw, but I do have other evening activities. Gym. Friends. Art show openings. Believe it or not, I have a life. A good one. One I'd introduce you to, if I felt you were up to it."

"That's a bit unfair." Jessica shuffled in her seat. "You can't blame me for how I feel."

"I don't blame you. I just wish we could move past this." Liz held out her hand.

Jessica looked at it. Suddenly, holding each other's hand had taken on a deeper meaning. If she put her hand in Liz's, it meant she was at least willing to give that a try. That she was willing to consider moving past it.

She extended her hand and touched Liz's. Immediately, the softness of it struck her again, but the knot in her stomach remained.

"Shall I impart some hooker wisdom on you?" Liz shot her a soft smile.

"Please do," Jessica said. That smile was making her melt already.

"It's all a balancing act. Basically, life is a balancing act. We're all just looking for the same thing. It's not so much about happiness as about a steadier feeling of contentment. That's the balance. But every time the pendulum swings one way, be it to the side of extreme happiness or extreme sadness, or any other off-balance emotion, it needs to swing all the way back to the other side if it ever wants to reach the middle again." With the finger of her free hand, Liz made a swinging motion, then halted in a spot in the air that was supposed to be the middle. "One doesn't exist without the other. You want to be with me." Her finger went up in the air. "But for that to happen you'll have to accept certain parts of me, which will be a challenge." Her finger arched to the other side of where it had previously stopped. "But hopefully we'll meet each other here at some point." Her finger curved through the air and stopped at Liz's self-chosen point of balance.

"Wow." Jessica chuckled because she didn't really know how else to react. "Very deep for a hooker, indeed."

"See, you're starting to swing the other way already. You just made a hooker joke." Liz's smile grew—it resembled the arc she had drawn in the air.

Chapter Twenty-One

"I HAVE BROUGHT A FAN GIRL," Jessica said before she introduced Liz to Caitlin. "Brace yourself."

"I can keep my cool," Liz said, and held out her hand to Caitlin. "Unlike some."

Jessica saw her wink at Caitlin. Caitlin responded with a big smile followed by ignoring Liz's extended hand and drawing her into a hug instead.

"This is my partner Jo," she said, and put a hand on Jo's shoulder.

"I've heard a lot about you," Liz said and, following Caitlin's lead, threw her arms around Jo.

"Very nice to meet you," Jo said.

As Jessica kissed Jo hello, she wondered if Caitlin had told her about what Liz did for a living. Then she remembered what Katherine had told her the other day. She should stop referring to Liz's profession in roundabout ways—even in her own head—if she was ever going to accept it, which, truth be told, Jessica wasn't so sure she could.

"Katherine texted she's going to be late," Caitlin said. "It's just us for now. Do come through."

Jessica had been at Caitlin and Jo's before, but she let Liz take in the place in her own time. And it was a hell of a place to take in. Jessica remembered the very first time she'd been invited here. She'd like to believe that she'd set up that four-some all by herself, but Caitlin had propositioned her first. In this very place.

The memory of that evening, strangely, put Jessica more at ease. Perhaps because it reminded her of Caitlin's extreme lack of judgement when it came to certain things. If she could take Liz as her date somewhere for the first time, it was here. Jessica didn't want to think ahead to the moment when she would introduce Liz to her father. His first question to anyone was, without exception, "What do you do for a living?"

They all sat in the living room. Liz cast a glance at Caitlin and Jo's impressive bookshelf. Jo poured champagne without asking if everyone wanted to have the same drink.

Jessica took a sip immediately, just to calm her nerves. Wasn't this going a little too fast? It was the worst time to wonder about this, because the invitation had been accepted and they were already sitting on Caitlin and Jo's couch, but she wondered nonetheless. Should she be introducing Liz to her friends already? It had seemed logical after their first week together, but that was before Liz had been with a client. Those few hours had changed a lot for Jessica.

She tried to hold on to the sweet memories she and Liz had already created, and how important those memories already were in her life. But was it really worth all this insecurity?

Earlier at home, Liz had wanted to make love, but Jessica couldn't even consider it. Even though Liz looked as scrumptious as ever, and her smile was confident and inviting, her body just as strong-looking as always. There was a mental barrier Jessica wasn't able to overcome.

She needed to find a way to relax. Or perhaps Caitlin and Jo would help. After all, Jessica had been as relaxed as she could possibly be around them. Yet the thought of that didn't seem to help. Instead, it blended together in her brain as one big mess of strange memories and too high expectations and a question that made its way forward through all the fog in her mind: since when had sex become so important? Since when was it allowed to influence her thoughts and conversations so much? Christ, Jessica should get a grip.

"Are you okay, Jess?" Jo asked.

All three of them were holding up their glass. Jessica had missed the toast.

"Yes." She tried to sound assured. "Cheers. Thanks for having us."

———

Katherine arrived and Caitlin had served dinner not long after. The fact that she was in charge of the main course didn't seem to stop Caitlin from knocking back quite a few glasses of champagne, making Jessica wonder whether she was nervous about something.

Liz, Katherine, Jo and Caitlin seemed to be having a great time, with conversation flowing easily and sometimes, apparently, hilariously, between them. Jessica didn't seem to get half of the jokes and innuendo. Not tonight.

"I'm not sure what my life would be like without my gays," Liz said. "No offense to anyone present, of course, but lesbians can be so bloody uptight."

"None taken," Caitlin was the first to say. "I'm pretty sure you don't mean me."

"Nor me," Katherine chimed in. "I can't really afford to be."

Jo clutched a hand to her chest. "What? I'm the uptight

one then?" She shook her head. "I guess I used to be, but I'd like to believe I've unwound quite a bit since shacking up with Caitlin. Who wouldn't? What with the things she makes me do." She grinned and blew Caitlin a kiss.

Caitlin shot Jo a wink.

"You're awfully quiet tonight, Jess," Caitlin said. "Are you all right?" She leaned over the table. "You're sworn to complete openness when it comes to your health, with both Kat and me. You scared us too much when you disappeared on us three months ago." She looked at Liz. "Has she told you about that?"

"She has." Liz put a hand in the small of Jessica's back. Jessica hated herself for flinching. She hoped Liz hadn't noticed, but Liz noticed everything. To make up for it, she pushed her back into the palm of Liz's hand, only to feel her retract it abruptly.

"I'm fine. I promise you. I had an appointment with my oncologist last Thursday. Everything's going according to plan. I just had a bit of a weird week with going back to work."

"Understandable," Jo said. She was such a sweetheart. And she was about to get her PhD. Now *that* was respectable. You could take that information home and boast about it to your parents.

"I hope you don't think I meant that you're uptight, Jess." Liz was sitting next to her and turned toward her. She gave Jessica a look she couldn't quite decipher.

"Of course not," Jessica quickly said.

"It's not every day you have dinner with two call girls," Caitlin said, which was such a typical thing for her to say.

Jessica froze. She took a deep breath and tried to relax. Everyone else at the table seemed to find this amusing. It was easy enough for Caitlin to say. Her girlfriend was the very picture of wholesomeness. Although even Jo was chuckling away happily.

Jessica realized she had been talking to the wrong people about this. Katherine and Caitlin were much more open-minded than she was. She needed someone to confide in about this who would have an equally hard time dealing with it. But, of course, that would make the conversation so much harder to have. What would be the benefit in the end? Jessica's unease would just be strengthened.

By the time Jessica snapped out of the tailspin of her thoughts, the conversation had progressed. She looked to her left, where Liz was sitting. Was it her imagination or had Liz moved her chair away from her? Either way, whether there was more physical distance between them or not, Jessica felt a huge emotional divide opening up.

"It's just another double standard in today's society," Josephine was saying. "I'm guilty of it as well. It takes work to get past that sort of thing." She cleared her throat. "I was all up in arms when I found out that Katherine was a sex worker, *after* I slept with her, I must add." She shot Caitlin a look.

"Understandably so," Caitlin said. "I should have told you." She glanced at Jessica.

"I should have said something," Jessica said. "It wasn't fair."

"Well, yes. Information is always paramount," Jo said. "But my point is that I got over it very quickly. Once I knew what Katherine's situation was, it didn't matter to me that much."

"Wait," Liz said. "There's something I'm missing here." She glanced at Jessica. "You told me that the four of you got it on and that you set it up as some sort of pre-mastectomy 'treat'."

Jessica nodded. It sounded so silly when put like that.

"So why did Kat's job matter? Wasn't it just four friends getting together?" She narrowed her eyes. "Or did you book Katherine to spice up your evening? And didn't tell Caitlin and Jo?"

"That's right. Jess sprang that one on us well and good," Caitlin said. "I worked it out pretty quickly, but Jo didn't."

Liz raised her eyebrows and leaned back in her chair. Jessica felt the distance between them loom even larger than before.

Jessica wanted nothing more than to change the topic of conversation. She glanced at Josephine. "Jo, how's your thesis coming along?"

"Oh no, we don't mention the T-word on a Saturday evening," Caitlin said. "It's crunch time for Jo." She drew Jo close to her by the shoulder. "But she needs to relax tonight." She kissed Jo on the cheek making a big smacking sound.

"It's a bit stressful at the moment," Jo said. She leaned into Caitlin's embrace. Their closeness made the gap between Jessica and Liz appear even greater.

"Is work totally not allowed as a topic?" Liz asked. She looked at Jessica pointedly while doing so—as though she was setting all the rules.

"No, of course not." Jessica tried a smile. She fought the urge to scoot her chair a little closer to Liz's—to bridge that growing distance between them. She wished they hadn't come here. That they'd just stayed home and enjoyed each other's company. "We can talk about anything."

"Good, because I'm about to have a fan girl moment." Liz turned to Caitlin. "You once wrote something about sex workers. I read it just after I had made the decision to join The Lesbian Experience and it made me feel so much better about myself and my decision." Liz tapped a finger against her chin. "I'm trying to remember the exact words. I can usually recite them by heart, but I think I've had a bit too much of this." She pointed at her empty glass.

"Sex work isn't always a manifestation of exploitation, abuse, or a dysfunctional power dynamic. It can be empowering and a viable way to make a living," Katherine said.

"Yes, that's it." Liz smiled at Katherine, who sat opposite her. "That was some sturdy hooker pep talk. But not just that. You made me feel as though we mattered just as much as anyone else. That what we do is equally important and viable as any other services provided for money. It was very significant to read for me at the time."

"There are so many different kinds of sex work," Caitlin said. "What you and Katherine do is light years away from what ninety-nine percent of the population think it is. And of course sex work can also be exploitative. It can put the people who do it in a very vulnerable position. They face violence and degrading circumstances every single day. It has never been my objective to sugarcoat things and to make it look like it's all sunshine and roses, because it's not. But when it's your own choice and you have a very clear reason for doing it—and that reason is mostly money—then it shouldn't be automatically judged."

"If you don't mind me asking," Jo said. "Have either of you ever worked with men?"

Both Liz and Katherine shook their heads vigorously.

"We provide The Lesbian Experience only," Katherine said.

"I'm sure there are plenty of men who'd like to put themselves right in the middle of that," Caitlin said.

Liz rolled her eyes. "Been there, *not* done that."

Jessica glanced at Liz. There was so much she didn't know—so much she would never know.

"Alana has a knack for sniffing out weird situations," Katherine said.

"Alana is the owner of the agency," Liz explained. "Sometimes she does make mistakes, though." Liz grinned at Jessica. "But hey, if she weren't human and prone to mistakes just like the rest of us, I would never have met Jess." She shot Jessica the most endearing smile. "Nor would I be sitting at Caitlin James and Josephine Greenwood's dinner table."

"Alana really screwed that one up," Katherine said. "That should never have happened."

Liz shrugged. "Maybe it happened for a reason."

Jessica tried to smile, but her lips remained in a pout. A cock-up at an escort agency. That was her and Liz's origin story. She could just imagine the faces of her family members when she told them.

"Maybe," Jessica said. Then the ugliest thought she'd had so far crossed her mind. Why, after all the hardship she had gone through during the past year, when she'd finally met someone she really liked, did the object of her affection have to be a hooker?

Chapter Twenty-Two

"CAN I COME IN?" Liz asked, when they reached Jessica's house. They had walked back in silence from Caitlin's apartment in Darlinghurst. It was only a fifteen-minute walk. All throughout, Jessica had tried to focus on the memory of the first walks she and Liz had taken. The unexpectedly pleasant meanderings though her neighborhood. But her mind had been persistent and had not allowed her to dwell on those innocent dates they'd had.

"Of course." Jessica opened the door and let them in. Liz was in no state to drive home and Jessica guessed it was implied that she would stay the night.

"I don't just want to assume," Liz said. She seemed to have a particular liking for champagne and had happily guzzled up anything Caitlin had much too generously poured. Since her surgery, Jessica seemed to have gone off champagne and she'd only drank a few sips to be polite.

When Jessica closed the door behind them, Liz immediately pushed Jessica's back against it. "I've been waiting to do this all night," she said. She wasn't so drunk that she slurred her words. She just looked pleasantly tipsy, really, yet her very demeanor was getting on Jessica's nerves.

Liz nibbled on her neck, then traced a path of wet kisses to Jessica's cheek, to land on her lips.

Jessica didn't open her mouth to let Liz's tongue slip in.

Liz withdrew and looked at her. "Not in the mood?" she asked.

"Not really."

"What's wrong?" Liz scrutinized her face and Jessica could barely stand Liz's gaze on her.

"Nothing. I'm just tired."

"Would you rather I went home?" Liz took a step back. "I can call a taxi."

Jessica sighed. "I don't know."

"If you don't know then I should probably go."

Jessica didn't say anything because she was afraid confirming would lead to something she might regret, but she couldn't deny that she wanted Liz to go home. She tried to remember Liz's words about the swinging pendulum, but her brain was too tired and foggy.

Liz brought her hands to her hips. "You're not going to say anything?"

"I don't know what to say. Okay? I have no idea."

"How about you say what's going through your mind right this second." Liz's voice was no longer smooth, nor calm.

"I—I just don't want to—" Jessica stopped. "Why don't you come in and we'll talk about it." She moved farther into the hallway past Liz.

"Talk some more? I'm not in the mood for that, Jess. It's late. We can talk tomorrow." Liz's shoulders sagged.

"I just can't be with you right now. I need some time to… I don't know, to process, I guess."

"If you're so afraid to say it, then why don't I pick up

your slack, huh?" Liz squared her shoulders. "Don't think I didn't notice you were ashamed of me."

"I wasn't ashamed of you." The high pitch in Jessica's voice betrayed her lie.

"Come on, Jess. Be honest. It's the only way," Liz pleaded.

"I'm sorry." She sighed. "All I seem to be doing is apologizing for how I feel. It's making me so ill at ease. I don't want to feel this way. I don't want our first weeks together to be like this, yet they are. Somehow, I feel like it's all my fault. Like I'm the one who can't handle it, while I don't think I've done anything wrong."

"You haven't done anything wrong, but neither have I." Liz took a step back. "It's too late for this. We've already had this conversation once earlier today. I don't think I can have it twice."

"Neither can I. There's nothing new to say, anyway." Jessica felt herself deflate. It had been a long day. In fact, she hadn't been able to relax fully since last night before 7 p.m.

"Maybe there is." Liz pulled her leather jacket a little tighter around her shoulders. "Maybe we should end this now. Before it gets even more painful."

"What? No," Jessica blurted out. "I don't want to end things. I'm just asking for a bit more time."

"Take all the time you need and while you do, don't invite me over if you don't want to see me. Don't take me to dinner with your friends if you're not having a good time because you're too embarrassed about what I do. It's humiliating for me. I hope you can see that."

"Won't you come in? Let's have that chat, anyway." Panic gripped like a cold fist around Jessica's heart.

"I can't give you an ultimatum, Jess. That wouldn't be fair. But I simply cannot be with someone who doesn't really want to be with me."

"But I do want to be with you. How can you even think that I don't?"

"Part of you does, yes. I do believe that. But what do you want? For us to hide inside your house forever? For me to be your stealthy lover? This was dinner with Katherine and Caitlin. You won't find anyone more open-minded than those two. And already you couldn't deal. What are you going to say when someone at work asks what your new girl-friend does for a living?"

"I'm certainly not going to tell them she's a hooker," Jessica blurted out.

"Exactly," Liz said. "That's what I thought."

"What? You want me to tell people what you do? That's just ridiculous? Like it's something to be proud of."

Jessica watched Liz lose composure in front of her eyes. Her knees seemed to buckle a little and her shoulders slumped.

"I'd best be going now." Liz turned around.

"Wait, Liz, please." Jessica rushed to her side. "Let's get you a cab first. Stay until it gets here." Jessica reached for her purse. She didn't dare touch Liz. She knew she'd gone too far.

"I'll wait outside. It shouldn't be a problem to get one." There was a trembling undertone to Liz's voice.

Jessica leapt to the door and stood in front of it. "I'm sorry. I shouldn't have said that."

"That's right." Liz straightened her spine a little. "I'm a human being. Just like you, Jess. Why can't you see that?"

"I *can*. Liz, please. I don't want to lose you. We only just met," Jessica pleaded.

Liz shook her head. "I'm willing to be understanding and I'm willing to have all the conversations you need to under-stand me and what I do and the reasons why I do it, but I draw the line at the obvious mortification you feel because of being with me." She sighed. "This is supposed to be the fun time, Jess. You can't even bear to touch me. It's obvious we're not right for each other."

"We can't just end things in the middle of the night in my hallway. We need to discuss this in the daylight, after a good night's sleep."

"I don't." Liz stepped closer to the door and grabbed the handle. "Please move, Jess. I want to leave."

"But—" Jessica had no more arguments. Everything she could say now would be a repeat of what she'd already said, and she'd said all the wrong things.

Liz might also very well be right. Jessica couldn't do this. They were too different and wanted different things. But if that was the case, why wasn't Jessica being flooded with relief because she was off the hook? Why did it feel like someone was punching her repeatedly in the gut instead?

Jessica moved away from the door. What else could she do? As torn and empty as she felt at the depressing prospect of never seeing Liz again, she'd done all the begging she could do. And she couldn't in good faith ask Liz again to stay and say they'd work it all out.

Liz opened the door and before she left, she turned around to look at Jessica. "You know, when we were talking about double standards at dinner earlier, I really hoped some message was getting across to you. Clearly, it didn't." She paused. "Bye, Jess," Liz said, and the sadness in her voice felt like the most painful punch to Jessica's gut yet.

Jessica stared at the closed door for a while longer. When a tear showed up in the corner of her eye, she quickly brushed it away. She didn't deserve to cry over this. She deserved the pain, but not the relief of tears.

Chapter Twenty-Three

JESSICA HAD BARELY SLEPT. She hadn't wanted to call Katherine in the middle of the night, but she had counted the hours until she could. It was only eight on a Sunday morning, but Jessica had to talk to someone. She'd been cooped up in her house in silence for far too long. Her heart might explode out of her chest with pent-up regret if she didn't talk to someone soon.

She dialed Katherine's number and tapped her finger on the kitchen counter while it rang. Katherine didn't pick up. Jessica could hardly blame her. Her phone was probably on silent. She had wondered if she and Liz were ever allowed to put their phone on silent—if even on Sunday mornings they should be reachable for the agency. Clearly not.

Or maybe Katherine was screening her calls. Maybe she'd been woken by the phone, had seen it was only Jessica calling, and had rolled over in bed.

Jessica made a cup of extra strong espresso and took it into the living room. She'd barely sat down when her phone rang. For a split second, she hoped it was Liz. She could have changed her mind overnight and wanted to spend Sunday together.

"Hey, Jess," Katherine sounded very chirpy for a Sunday morning. "Sorry I didn't pick up. I was in the shower."

"You're up early," Jessica said.

"So are you," Katherine replied. "It's my turn to host brunch. You know how hard the gays are to impress."

Jessica had heard about Katherine's brunches, but she'd never attended one. She didn't know that many gay men, to be honest. "I guess," she said.

"What's going on? Why are you calling me so early?"

Jessica sighed. "I wanted to ask if you were free for breakfast, but you're not, so let's get together some other time."

"There are so many red flags in what you just said. I don't even know where to start."

"Liz and I broke up. Last night after we got back from dinner. I was being a right ass. I could use one of your pep talks."

"Come to brunch," Katherine said without hesitation. "It'll take your mind off things at the very least."

"I'm not sure I'm in the mood for that."

"Of course you're not in the mood, but it beats moping at home. Come a little early, we can have a chat while you help me scramble the eggs." This made Jessica think of the eggs Liz had tried to scramble for her only a few days ago, when everything still seemed so full of hope.

"Okay, I'll happily join you." She paused. "Liz isn't going to be there, is she?"

"No," Katherine says. "Just you, me, and five fabulous gays."

———

"Basically what you're saying is that you can't be with Liz," Katherine stated matter-of-factly. Jessica wasn't being much help preparing brunch, but she had stopped by a bakery and bought a dozen fresh rolls and a pavlova for dessert.

"That's not really what I said."

"Maybe not in so many words, but I can read between the lines, Jess." Katherine stopped what she was doing and turned to Jessica, her hands on her sides. "Tell me honestly. Have you ever had a problem with our friendship?"

"What? No. You know that."

"What if I don't believe you?" There was a sudden edge to Katherine's voice.

"Come on, Kat. I've known you for many years," Jessica replied sharply. "There's a big difference between being friends with someone and dating them."

"You have to understand that Liz and I can't be apologetic about what we do. Certainly not with potential love interests. That would put us in a position of weakness and well, let's be honest, life's already no fairytale for the likes of us. We get judged all the time. By our clients. By our friends, even the ones who know us well, because of preconceived notions. By our family, if we ever find the courage to tell them. By everyone who even gets an inkling of what we do. I think it's normal Liz reacted the way she did, although I do think she could have been a bit more understanding about your feelings. It's a tricky one."

"I don't blame her for how she reacted at all. I think I might have been channeling my father last night. Or I was subconsciously, and very much prematurely, dreading his possible reaction. Long before I would even think about taking Liz home. But my mind can't help going there."

"I asked you to really think about being with Liz. It's not easy. Not everyone can do it. In fact, I dare say most people can't deal with it. There's no shame in being one of those people."

Jessica shook her head. "But I don't want to be one of those people."

"Maybe you don't get to choose." Kat cocked her head. "You're Edward Porter's daughter, after all."

"Ouch." Jessica blew out some air.

"The truth hurts." Katherine apparently really meant what she'd just said.

"You think I'm someone who can't be with a woman who's a sex worker?"

"I think there's a definite possibility of that being the case."

"But what does it take? If you got the opportunity to dream up the ideal partner for yourself, what would you want them to be like?"

Katherine chuckled. "Jesus, Jess. It's Sunday morning. Can I get back to you on that?"

Jessica chuckled with her. "Sure. First thing on Monday would be fine."

"Should I stop by your office or can I phone you?" Katherine joked.

"You make it sound so black and white, though," Jessica said. "Like I'm one and can't possibly become the other."

"If the boys weren't arriving in"—she checked her watch —"fifteen minutes, I'd remind you of the story of Katherine and Suki. But I have some trays to artfully arrange and I think you remember that story, so." Katherine turned around and got back to work.

Jessica had never known Katherine's ex Suki. She'd only heard about her. She remembered that things hadn't worked out well. Then the bell rang.

"Oh, shoot. Someone's here already." Katherine quickly rinsed her hands.

"I'll get it." Jessica painted on a smile—the one she'd used since she was a child and her mother had left—and headed for the front door.

———

The gay brunch Jessica had ended up at could not have been more different from the lesbian dinner party she had attended the night before. It seemed like not one serious word came out of these men's mouths. Jessica had been formally introduced to all five of them, and she had done her very best to remember their names, but it turned out they all addressed each other as darling or sweetie which made it impossible for her to know who was addressing whom and—even more so—who was mocking whom.

She was, however, beginning to understand why Katherine enjoyed their company so much.

"I'll sleep when I'm forty," a lanky guy with a beard—Jessica thought his name was Richard—said while he suppressed a yawn.

"You're thirty-nine, darling," someone else said.

"Oh fine." He reached for his mimosa. "I'll cut my alcohol intake in half then. I'll see. When the day comes."

"Maybe you should try cutting your Grindr time in half instead," Alan—Jessica had remembered his name—said.

Richard held a hand in front of his mouth and pretended to look upset. "What are you insinuating?"

"Yes, sweetie, what are you trying to say?" Alan's partner said. "There are plenty of boys looking for daddies on Grindr. Richard's got a lot of work ahead of him."

Katherine rolled her eyes. "You guys are so lucky. The closest thing to Grindr us poor lesbians get is the RSPCA website."

"Oh you shameless thief," Rocco, an impressively

muscled man with not a hair on his head said. "You totally stole that joke from Margaret Cho."

"I confess, but she has a point, though," Katherine said.

"There's a new lesbian at work. Well, I think she's one, at least," Chris, Rocco's equally-muscled partner, said. "I just get that feeling about her and the other day, she winked at me—you know, one of those winks of recognition—when she walked past my office. I'll try to find out if she's single for you, Kat. You never know…"

"That would be the day," Katherine said. "When one of you guys sets me up with a woman. You talk a good game, boys, but nothing, I repeat, *nothing* has ever come of it. While you and Rocco would never have met if it weren't for me."

"We owe you for that forever," Rocco said. "You'll be the best man at our wedding." He blew Kat a kiss. "But we don't hang with the lezzies that much." He looked at Jessica. "What about you, honey? Kat doesn't tickle your fancy?"

Jessica had just taken a sip from her mimosa and nearly spat out the liquid all over her plate.

"Jess and I are friends," Katherine said. "Besides, she's hurting. She needs cheering up, not being asked whether I tickle her fancy or not." Katherine winked at her.

"What's going on, sweetie?" Chris asked. "Did a mean lesbian trample all over your tender heart?"

Jessica shook her head. "Nah. I did it to myself, really."

"And here I was thinking it was all so much easier for the lesbos," Richard said. "Meet, move in, watch Netflix, happy monogamy, followed by a bout of lesbian bed death here and there, but basically domestic bliss for the rest of your lives."

"Wow," Katherine said. "You've really outdone yourself with the clichés this time, Rich. You failed to mention the U-Haul, though."

"And the macramé," Peter said.

Jessica chuckled. It was the first real laugh she'd managed since last night.

"I'll have you know," Katherine said, "that Jess and I know a lesbian couple who practice non-monogamy successfully."

"Ooh," Rocco said. "What's their secret? Do tell. I'm genuinely interested."

Katherine shrugged. "What's the secret of any relationship?" She looked at Jessica as if she held the answer. "Communication, I guess. I really wouldn't know with my track record."

"You just haven't met the right woman yet," Peter said.

"I've thought about this," Jessica said, "having been single for quite some time, and I disagree with the silly notion that there's only one person out there for everyone. I think that's bullshit. At least, in my life, among the people I know best, I haven't seen much evidence of that. Let's not forget that divorce rates are soaring."

"And that's not going to go down any time soon," Rocco said, "now that the gays are starting to get married." He apparently thought this was very funny and slapped himself on the thigh.

"I disagree with you, Jess. But maybe that's just the romantic in me," Katherine said.

"Well, maybe if you'd asked me yesterday, I would have had a different opinion." As they did every other minute, Jessica's thoughts drifted to Liz again. What was she doing right now? If things had gone differently last night, what would they have been doing together? *What if? What if? What if?*

"Are you going to keep us in suspense much longer," Peter said. "Or are you going to tell us what happened with you and that woman who left you so bitter you don't believe in love any longer?"

"That's putting it a bit dramatically," Jessica said. "I do believe in love. I'm just not a fan of the overly romanticized take on it. It can be bloody hard sometimes to fall in love." She sipped from her mimosa.

"We're still waiting for your story." Peter leaned back in his chair.

"Don't feel as though you have to entertain them with your heartache, Jess. They can go home and watch *Queer Eye* if they want some drama."

"Ooh girl, you've got the 'tude today," Rocco said.

"It's really just a matter of irreconcilable differences," Jessica said. "This woman and I, we're just too different."

"But you at least had a good tumble in the hay with her?" Chris asked.

"Oh yeah." Some glee had sneaked into Jessica's voice. "Quite the tumble."

"You go, girl." Chris held up his hand for a high five.

Flabbergasted, Jessica looked at it, then slapped her palm against his.

"This is not about sex." Rocco told his partner off. "Can't you see Jessica's in distress about this."

"At least she got something out of it," Chris said.

"You know just as well as I do that it's different for lesbians," Rocco said.

"Oh, please," Chris said. "Here we go again." He waved off Rocco's remark. "Kat, darling, back me up here."

"But what Rocco just said is so true," Katherine said in a mock-serious tone. "I have no idea what you guys are doing in my house. I'm a lesbian and you're gay men. We have the least in common of all the possible sexual orientations." She snickered.

"Kat's not a representative lesbian," Rocco said. "She has more sex than the five of us combined." He turned to the other men. "No offense, darlings."

"Let's not go overboard," Katherine said. "For that to be even remotely true, I'd need to be having sex multiple times every single day."

Richard brought a hand to his mouth. "Do you mean to say that you don't? You've just shattered my entire image of you."

Katherine shook her head. "I'm way too exclusive for that."

Jessica couldn't believe what she was hearing. These were not the conversations about sex she was used to. In fact, she wasn't used to many conversations about sex at all. But these men and Katherine talked about it as if it was just any other hobby or pastime.

Chris held up his hand to high five Katherine this time. Jessica took another sip from her mimosa and looked them all over. They all looked happy enough, chattering away on a Sunday morning. Being themselves didn't allow room for being ashamed and their self-respect clearly didn't depend on what anyone else thought of them.

As the day progressed, Jessica's admiration for them grew, and by the time she left Katherine's house, she felt as though the uptightness she'd been accused of earlier had vastly diminished just by being in the company of people who could be just as judgmental as herself when it came to superficial things, but who had learned to be free of judgment where it really mattered.

Chapter Twenty-Four

"NICOLAS IS COMING to see you at ten," Jennifer said. "And your father called. He asked that you call him back as soon as possible."

"Why did he call the office?" Jessica asked, although she could hardly expect Jennifer to have the answer to the question.

"I'm not sure." Jennifer took a step closer to Jessica's desk. "Can I get you anything? A strong coffee, perhaps? If you don't mind me saying so, you look a little pale."

"I didn't sleep well," Jessica said. "But I'll be fine. I'll gladly have that coffee, though." She gazed into Jennifer's worried face. "Is there anything else I should know?" What she really wanted to ask was: do you really need me here?

When she'd walked into the building half an hour earlier, she'd been flooded with even more dread than the week before at the prospect of working there for the foreseeable future.

Jessica had spent the better part of Sunday afternoon watching television, and it had been an excellent distraction —and perfect background noise for sleeping off her post-brunch buzz. But watching TV and working in TV were two very different things. And she couldn't stop thinking about a certain person who didn't even own a television set.

"No," Jennifer said. "I'll bring you a strong cup of coffee straight away."

Jessica sank into her chair. She didn't feel like calling her father. He'd want to ask how her weekend went. And these days, when he asked this particular question, he actually listened to the answer. He sometimes even asked a follow-up question.

Jessica could easily lie to him, but she didn't want to. Just over a week ago, she'd met Liz. The previous Monday, exactly one week ago, she'd booked her services again. As a direct consequence, Jessica had come to life again. Liz had done that. It had all happened so quickly. It might as well not have happened. Maybe she could shake off Liz's passage in her life as some crazy fever dream. Attribute it to late-stage complications after surgery.

Jessica scoffed. Was she really so afraid that she would be willing to ignore the best thing that had happened to her in years?

A knock came on the door and Jennifer brought in her coffee.

"Thanks. You're a life saver," Jessica said. She took a sip and was grateful she had made at least one meaningful contribution to the Programming Department during her short time heading it: procuring a state-of-the-art coffee machine for the break room.

Instead of calling her father, Jessica dialed Caitlin's extension. She hoped she had arrived at the office already.

———

"Morning, Boss," Caitlin said. "I rushed down as soon as you called. What's the Monday morning emergency?"

"Please close the door."

"Ooh, sounds ominous," Caitlin joked.

Jessica checked her watch. She had a bit of time before her meeting with Nicolas Morton.

Caitlin sat down. "Who would you like me to invite on my show? Grannie Kramer?" She sat there beaming a wide smile.

"This isn't about work."

Caitlin pursed her lips together. "I figured as much."

"Liz and I have... well, I'd say broken up but we weren't really ever together, were we?"

"I did pick up on some tension between you. The way I understood it from you, Katherine might have been a problem at the dinner, but, er, it turned out to be someone else."

"I'm sorry for behaving the way I did. It was pathetic, really. It ruined a perfectly good night."

Caitlin shrugged. "We all have bad nights. Don't worry about it."

Jessica chuckled. "Are you letting me off the hook so easily because I had cancer? It's not a free-for-all insult-who-you-want card, you know."

"I'm your friend, Jess. I'm simply not half or even a quarter as hard on you as you are on yourself. Give yourself a break." Caitlin linked her hands behind her neck and rested her head back. "My life became so much easier when I started forgiving myself for everything. It's the only way."

"You're Caitlin James," Jessica said, and remembered how Liz had fawned over her at dinner last Saturday—before it all went south. "What could you possibly have to forgive yourself for?"

Caitlin shook her head. "Every single person on this

planet has plenty of things to forgive themselves for. It can be small things or huge things. But some people prefer to hang on to their mistakes and their pain and be all victim-y about it."

"Do you mean me?" Jessica asked.

Caitlin sat up. "You've been through a rough time, Jess. It was never going to be easy to pick yourself back up, but you're doing it. So you said some things to Liz, or you made her feel bad and as though things between you couldn't work... so what? Right this minute, millions of people are making similar mistakes. It doesn't mean things can't work out. I'm sure Liz has had to endure far worse than what you've thrown at her. If you feel like you screwed up, get over it, and get her back."

Jessica's phone started ringing. It was Jennifer.

"Sorry," she said to Caitlin and picked up.

"I have your father on the line for you," Jennifer said.

"Oh Christ," Jessica said. She looked at Caitlin. "I'm going to have to take this."

Caitlin shot up out of her chair. "Call me later," she said, and scooted out the door.

Jessica took a deep breath and said, "Hello, Daddy."

"How's my favorite daughter?" her father said.

"I'm your only daughter," Jessica replied, as always.

"Still my favorite." Jessica knew he was in a good mood if he continued the joke—no matter how silly it was.

"How are you?" she asked.

"I'm good, as always. How are you?"

"Well," Jessica said.

"Well enough to come to the Porter gala next weekend?"

Jessica had completely forgotten about that, even though it was a yearly event and her presence was non-negotiable. She'd had other things on her mind lately. But she knew that turning up meant a lot to her father.

"Of course. I'll be there with bells on."

"Great." Her father paused. She could hear his breath in her ear while he was trying to find the words to say whatever he was going to say next. It was an odd thing. Edward Porter usually wasn't one to beat about the bush. His only child getting cancer had changed more about him than Jessica allowed herself to consider. But when she was faced with it like this, it was hard to ignore.

"Yes?" she asked.

"It's just that, um, an acquaintance of Christine has seen you with someone and, I guess, we were both wondering if you'd be coming to the gala alone or bringing a plus one?"

"Seen me with someone?" Jessica's heart started racing.

"Walking down the street, apparently. That's what I've been told."

Jessica relaxed. "People walk down the street with other people all the time, Daddy."

"Well, yes, of course. Sure they do. But this person who spotted you apparently told Christine that you looked as though you were very close."

"Erm, excuse me, but is this Edward Porter on the other end of the line or an impersonator pulling a prank on me?"

"You know what your stepmother's like," her father said. "She wouldn't let me off the hook until I asked you."

"Ah, good to know Christine still wears the trousers at home."

"What should I tell her?"

"The truth. That I was walking down the street with a friend. Getting some air during my convalescence. Doctor's orders and all that."

"And you'll be coming to the gala alone?" her father asked.

"Yes. Alone," Jessica confirmed, but not without a pang

of regret shooting through her. This was the same gala where, four years ago, she'd met Katherine.

"She was just a friend then?" Her father took her by surprise with that question.

"Yes, Daddy. Just a friend." Right now, Liz wasn't even her friend. In fact, Liz had never been her friend. Jessica had fallen hard and fast for her, but friendship had nothing to do with it.

"Okay," he said. "Don't work too hard."

Jessica shook her head, well aware her father couldn't see her response to more evidence of his changed behavior.

"The same goes for you," she said.

"Do you know what?" her father said. "I might actually take your advice."

————

On Tuesday afternoon Jessica found herself at home, not knowing what to do with herself. She logged onto The Lesbian Experience website and surfed to Liz's profile. In the picture that came with it, her face was obscured to protect her privacy, but her lingerie-clad body was on full display. Jessica remembered the picture hanging above Liz's bed. Then she remembered Liz's actual body all over hers. Liz's finger tracing her scar. Liz's lips on her nipple.

She read through Liz's profile again. It was all fairly vague but pretty accurate at the same time.

Liz likes to go to the gym and keep fit. Liz likes to visit art galleries and go to the opera. She has a fair complexion and short black hair.

That information wasn't too up-to-date. *Liz has bangs that fall into her eyes all the time,* Jessica corrected the profile in her head. *And she tucks it behind her ears with the cutest gesture you'll ever see.*

Jessica scrolled down and stopped at the section titled *Specialties*.

First time lesbian experiences. Liz will make you feel totally at ease. Her warmth will disarm you and she will create that special kind of atmosphere in which you can fully relax and discover what you really like.

Liz would be perfect for that. In her head, Jessica added another special skill: helping cancer survivors accept their changed bodies. She figured that wouldn't do well on the agency's website.

She scrolled down to the next section: *Most beautiful feature*: *bedroom eyes*.

Goodness, Liz's eyes.

Jessica closed the website. She didn't want to read about Liz's features on the internet. She wanted to see them in real life. Caitlin's words rang in her head. *Get over it and get her back.*

Jessica wished it were that simple. Yes, she had been insensitive and prejudiced and judgmental, but not without good reason.

In the end, it all boiled down to the choice she had to make. She got up from the couch and looked out the window. Someone had seen her walking around the streets of Pott's Point with Liz on her arm. Jessica had no idea who and she had no intention of asking her stepmother.

She put on her jacket and went for a walk—on her own. She walked all the way to the Pink Bean, retracing the route she and Liz had taken only last week.

She ordered a coffee and sat by the window, gazing out, watching the people going by. Foot traffic was high and every single time she caught the profile of a tall woman with dark hair, her heart skipped a beat.

But what would Liz be doing in this neighborhood, anyway? Come to think of it, she could have a client in

Darlinghurst. She may need a cup of coffee after and hop into that coffee shop she discovered the previous week.

Jessica shook her head. Had she really fought her way out of depression and beat cancer to feel like this? To glance at strangers in the street and hope they would be the woman who had made her feel the most alive in years? Was it really a case of love versus virtue? Because Jessica wasn't all that interested in virtue anymore.

"Hi, Jessica," a voice came from behind her. "So good to see you."

Jessica looked up and saw Sheryl standing by the table.

"How are you?" Sheryl asked.

Jessica didn't know what to say. Politeness required her to answer that she was doing fine, and physically she *was* doing well, but emotionally, she was about to fall apart.

"Can I sit?" Sheryl asked when Jessica didn't reply.

"Of course. And I'm fine, by the way." Jessica tried a smile.

"Are you?" Sheryl glanced at her with the most piercing gaze.

"Yep."

"Not back at work yet?" Sheryl asked.

"Only half days for now."

"Ah, so you're a lady of leisure in the afternoon." Sheryl narrowed her eyes and examined Jessica's face. She was about to say something—or ask a question Jessica was pretty sure she wouldn't want to answer—when Kristin showed up at their table. She put her hand on Sheryl's shoulder. It was a simple gesture, but it held so much meaning. It reminded Jessica of what she'd said at Katherine's brunch the day before. The harsh words she had spoken about love. Yet, right in front of her nose, she was presented with the very image of love. Two women who had been together for decades. Two women to whom the simple gesture of laying a hand on each other's shoulder meant very little and so much at the same time.

Jessica had turned forty-five and she'd never been the recipient of such a tiny gesture. She had, however, very much been on the receiving end of a very grand gesture. Liz's kindness, which not only shone in her eyes every time she looked at Jessica, but had been so blatantly on display when she'd coaxed Jessica to look at herself in the mirror.

"It's lovely to see you both," Jessica said. Neither Sheryl nor Kristin would ever know how truly she meant it. "But I have somewhere to be." She pushed herself out of her chair, shot the two women a smile, and went on her way.

Chapter Twenty-Five

JESSICA LOOKED out of the window of her car and gazed at the entrance of Liz's building. She'd rung the bell earlier, but nobody had answered. Either Liz wasn't home or she was ignoring her.

On the drive over to Bondi, Jessica had considered turning around quite a few times, but something had kept her foot firmly on the gas pedal and had kept her hands from turning the steering wheel. She knew exactly what that something was. The feeling Liz had given her. Jessica missed it. She missed it when she got up in the morning and faced herself in the mirror. When she glanced at her face as well as her scar. She could so easily go back to ignoring the flatness of her chest where her right breast used to be. All she had to do was turn away from the mirror or raise her glance upward a bit. But she didn't want to go back to that space where she'd lingered before she'd met Liz.

She, very simply, wanted Liz back. The alternative was feeling like she'd missed out on one of the greatest opportunities of her life, and Jessica couldn't live with that. She needed Liz to give her another chance. If only she would come home already.

Maybe she shouldn't stay in her car, ogling Liz's building like a stalker. The beach was only a few blocks away. She could go for a walk and come back later. Or she could just give Liz a call.

But Jessica found that she couldn't move. Something kept her in the car, her gaze glued to the building's entrance, waiting for the gorgeous sight of Liz to pop up in her field of vision.

———

Jessica had been sitting in her car for more than an hour, focusing on Liz's building while sipping from a bottle of water. Now she really had to use the toilet. Liz could be anywhere. She could be away for a few more hours. Maybe she had an appointment away from Sydney. An overnight in an exotic location. She had read on the agency's website that the women working there could be booked for those sort of things.

She squirmed in her seat, pressing her legs together. There was a coffee shop on the corner of the street. She could go there.

She got out of her car. It felt good to stretch her legs. She glanced around the street. She hoped Liz wouldn't arrive just then. Jessica needed to take care of her biological emergency first.

When she exited the coffee shop, a paper cup in hand, Jessica leaned against her car and scanned the street one last time. Her stake-out plan hadn't worked. She walked over to Liz's building and rang the bell one more time, on the off chance she'd arrived home while Jessica was using the facilities, but nobody answered the door.

While she drank her coffee, Jessica walked the few blocks to the beach. She threw the empty cup in a trash can and fished her phone out of her pocket. Somehow, turning up at Liz's had felt like the grand gesture she needed to make. Calling her up had seemed at the same time not enough and also harder to do. But it was her only option if she wanted to speak to Liz today. And she did.

Jessica dialed Liz's number and every time it rang, her heartbeat picked up speed. It rang seven times before it went to voicemail. Jessica listened to Liz's voicemail message. When the beep came, she found herself speechless so she hung up.

She looked at the ocean and breathed in deeply. Liz not picking up didn't necessarily mean that she didn't want to speak to her. Maybe she was driving. Or she'd just missed the call.

Or she was with a client.

Jessica forced herself to focus on the last option. Liz could very well be with a client. Say that she was, what would Jessica do if she knew this for certain? Say Liz forgave her, they made up, and Jessica was in her apartment waiting for her to come home. Could she live with that? The answer to that question was the crux of it all.

But Jessica couldn't give a hard no or yes. Imagining it wasn't the same as actually experiencing it. Besides, she had come here this afternoon because she had felt that she didn't have a choice. Liz had been placed on her path for a reason. It had hit her—like a shudder all the way into her bones—when she'd seen Sheryl and Kristin simply standing together. What was virtue worth without love? It wasn't a choice. It was just another example of Jessica being afraid to live her life to the fullest.

Chapter Twenty-Six

AFTER SHE WALKED BACK to her car, Jessica decided to give ringing Liz's bell one last try. She'd been gone for a good twenty minutes. Plenty of time for Liz to have come home—and not picked up her phone.

Jessica pressed her finger to the bell. It could very well be the last time she did so. But at least she had tried. Or maybe she would come back tomorrow. She didn't know.

The buzz of the intercom crackled, snapping Jessica out of her spiral of self-pity. "Yes?" Liz's voice said.

"Liz, hi. It's me." Didn't Liz have a video intercom system? "Jessica."

"Yes. I can see you. What do you want?"

Jessica hoped she was looking into the camera. "I would really like to speak with you. Can I come up?"

"You've sure been persistent enough," Liz said, and buzzed her in without further ado.

Jessica pushed open the door and called the elevator. What did Liz mean about her having been persistent? And what on earth was Jessica going to say to her? Would sorry be enough? She breathed deeply in and out while the elevator took her to Liz's floor. When she stood in the hallway, she found Liz's door ajar. She pushed it open and stepped inside the apartment.

Jessica didn't see Liz, so she figured she must be waiting for her inside. She closed the front door and headed into the living room.

Liz was looking out of the window, her arms crossed in front of her.

"Hi," Jessica said.

Liz didn't turn around.

"You're lucky you didn't get a parking ticket," Liz said. "I was surprised you didn't pay for your parking, I must say. It just seems like something you would always do."

"What? I'm not sure—"

"Your car's been parked across the street for two hours."

"You were home all this time?" Jessica was confused.

Still with her back to Jessica, Liz nodded.

"Why didn't you answer?"

"Why would I?" Liz finally turned around.

Jessica didn't know what to say to that. "I'm sorry." She felt it best to launch directly into an apology. "You have no reason to. I just... really wanted to see you."

"Why's that?" Liz uncrossed her arms and leaned against the window sill.

"To apologize for, um, not treating you with the respect you deserve. For putting my own insecurities above... everything else."

Liz sighed, but didn't say anything.

Jessica took a step closer. "I'm not here to give you a big declaration of love, but I am here to ask for another chance."

"What's changed?" Liz was wearing a very loose t-shirt and the sleeve had just slipped off her impressive right shoulder, baring it. "Don't tell me *you* have, because I don't think that's possible in just three days."

"Meeting you has changed me, though. I think you know that too." Jessica stopped herself from taking another step closer.

Liz shook her head. "The only thing I do know is that I don't know all that much about you. And what I do know about you, I don't care for that much."

"You can be really harsh sometimes," Jessica said.

"Likewise," Liz said. She glared at Jessica but something in her face had softened.

"I'm here, Liz," Jessica said. "I'm here because it's the only place I want to be. Nothing else is of interest to me. You made me feel things..." She shook her head. "I can't even begin to tell you."

"How do you propose I react to this?" Liz held up her hand. "Don't give me your dream scenario, just give me an honest assessment. If you were in my shoes, what would you do?"

Jessica couldn't stop a small smile from forming on her lips. "That's an impossible question and you know it."

Liz pursed her lips together. She looked at her watch ostentatiously. "What if I told you I had to meet a client in an hour. How would you react to that?"

"I would say..." Jessica racked her brain. So much seemed to depend on her reply. She looked at Liz, at how she stood there, the light from outside like a halo around her, her shoulder bare. Her eyes were challenging Jessica, but they conveyed kindness as well.

"Well," Liz said when Jessica remained silent, "what's it going to be?"

Jessica locked her gaze on Liz's. She had stopped racking her brain. The answer to Liz's question wasn't to be found in her logical mind, anyway. It had to come from her gut. "I would say," she repeated. "Care to practice on me?"

Liz burst out into a chuckle. "Oh really?" She brought her hands to her sides. "That's what you would say?"

"I just said it, didn't I?" Jessica shuffled closer.

Liz regarded her from under her eyelashes. "Very well." She sank her front teeth into her bottom lip. "Come here." She reached out her hand.

Jessica looked at it before she took hold of it. She tried to keep a calm expression on her face, but on the inside, nerves were tearing through her.

Liz gently tugged Jessica toward her. They stood inches apart. Jessica could smell Liz's perfume and the scent had the same effect on her as a kiss from Liz's lips would. Just to stand so close to her was enough to make Jessica's knees tremble.

Liz brought her hands to Jessica's waist and spun her around. She pushed Jessica's backside against the window sill and pressed her lower body against Jessica's.

"Did you mean what you just said?"

Jessica couldn't speak so she just nodded.

"I need you to say it. Do you stand by it?"

"I—I do," Jessica stammered.

"Do you give me permission to put what you just said to the test?" Liz's voice was solemn and serious.

Jessica nodded again. If this meant Liz was going to put her hands all over her, she wanted nothing more.

"Say it," Liz whispered.

Jessica swallowed and looked into Liz's eyes. "I give you permission."

"Good." Liz leaned in as though she was going to kiss Jessica, but then deviated from her path, and planted a kiss on Jessica's neck. She was going straight for Jessica's soft spot. She traced a wet path along Jessica's neck and Jessica was glad she had the window sill for support. When Liz kissed her like that, she needed all the support she could get.

Liz stopped kissing her neck abruptly. Jessica opened her eyes and gazed at her. Liz stood there with a triumphant grin on her face. She brought her hands to the hemline of her t-shirt and pulled it over her head.

"I saw you staring at my shoulder earlier," she said.

Jessica's gaze was pulled away from Liz's face to her bra-clad breasts and that impressively square shoulder line. Her clit started pulsing between her legs. If this was Liz's idea of foreplay today, she was up for it.

"Now." Liz pressed herself against Jessica again. "As we're standing in front of the window, I'm not going to take off my bra." Her smile transformed into a grin.

This made Jessica acutely aware that they were standing in front of said window. She had stared at this window for a good long while that afternoon and not once spotted Liz in her apartment. Maybe because she thought she wasn't home, but still. She had her back to the street below. She could work with this. And with the sensation of Liz's breasts pressing into her. Liz's knee spreading her legs apart. Liz's breath traveling over her skin.

Liz brought a finger to Jessica's face and traced her jawline with it. She dragged it all the way underneath her chin and let it travel upward to her cheekbone, then down past her cheek to end up dancing along her lips.

Liz's finger stopped in the middle of Jessica's bottom lip. Liz held Jessica's gaze then slowly pushed her finger inside Jessica's mouth.

Jessica sucked Liz's finger inside. She twirled her tongue around it as though it was the last thing her tongue would ever touch.

While her finger remained in Jessica's mouth, Liz leaned to her side and whispered in her ear, "Remember, this is a test." She paused. "I need to know that you want me to touch you. That you really, really want it." While she bit gently into Jessica's earlobe, she flipped open the button of her jeans with her free hand. "I'm going to need you to come for me," she whispered. "Do you think you can do that?"

Jessica's mouth was too filled with Liz's finger to speak so she just nodded. The way her clit was buzzing in her panties, she figured she wouldn't have any problem with that at all.

Liz stopped speaking. She unzipped Jessica's jeans. She stood straighter so she came face to face with Jessica again. She withdrew her finger from between Jessica's lips and slipped her hand inside Jessica's panties.

A split second later, Liz's wet finger was circling Jessica's clit.

She gasped for air at the first contact. Liz's touch was light but deft. She kept her gaze on Jessica and Jessica lost herself in Liz's bedroom eyes. There was no doubt in her mind that she would pass this test with flying colors. She wanted Liz and she would show her just how much.

Jessica wrapped her fingers around the ledge of the window sill. Liz's other hand cupped her jaw and Jessica pushed her head against it. It was the only physical contact between them. Liz's hand against her cheek, and her wet finger circling Jessica's clit. But beneath the surface, so much more was going on. Jessica was surrendering to Liz. She was saying, by means of her body's reaction, that she accepted Liz and the choices she had made in her life. The choices she'd be making in the future and the life she had chosen to live.

Liz's circling motions grew faster, as did the rhythm of Jessica's breath. She felt in perfect sync with Liz, this woman who had been so unspeakably kind to her. Who had brought her back to life. How could she even have considered not wanting to see her anymore? Especially when this burgeoning ecstasy flowing through her was a big part of what being with Liz meant.

Jessica might have hired Laurel in the past. She had always justified it to herself as an act of self-care. Something to take away the loneliness, if just for an hour or two. The joy of an orgasm shared with another woman. It seemed to be something Jessica craved. But it receded into nothingness compared to what she was experiencing now. This exquisite woman's hands on her. This was an act way beyond self-care. This was Jessica opening herself up to the possibility of love—and accepting, along with slowly coming to terms with the changes to her body, that she was worthy of it.

"Oh, Liz," she moaned. It was as though saying Liz's name sent extra bursts of delicious lightning from Liz's finger to her clit. "Liz," Jessica repeated.

She closed her eyes as warmth exploded inside of her. She let her cheek drop all the way against Liz's waiting hand. Jessica's legs shook and she gasped for more air. "Oh, Liz," she said on a sigh, and sank deeper against the window sill.

She opened her eyes and stared into Liz's eyes. That small, triumphant grin was back on her lips. Liz's hand didn't retreat. She kept it inside Jessica's panties. Liz tilted her head as though studying Jessica's face, gauging her expression for something. Had Jessica not passed the test? Either way, she'd like to sit down, or at least collapse into Liz's arms, kiss her all over—and repay the favor.

Liz's tongue flicked over her lips. Jessica felt Liz's hand stir in her panties. She wasn't retreating though. Oh no. She was parting Jessica's nether lips and then, oh so easily, she slipped inside Jessica.

"Oh," Jessica exclaimed.

"Come for me again," Liz said.

"Wh—I—" Jessica wasn't capable of actually saying words, although she did want to protest. Was this still part of the test? She wasn't sure she could do this. She'd just come at

Liz's fingertip already. What more could possibly be expected of her?

Liz thrust inside of her gently—easily. Jessica must be soaking wet.

"You can do it," Liz said, not a shimmer of doubt in her voice. "I'll make sure of that." This time, when she leaned in, she did kiss Jessica on the lips. As her finger stroked high inside of Jessica, her tongue slipped inside Jessica's mouth, and Jessica started to believe what Liz had just said.

She threw her arms around Liz's neck. Jessica knew she had passed the test already. In fact, there'd never been any test. There had been her and Liz looking at each other, knowing that something inside of them made them belong together.

Jessica had no idea what magic Liz's finger was working inside of her. She thought she'd spent all her arousal on the first orgasm, but maybe it had just made her more excited. Liz's finger was insistent and it felt like so much more of Liz was inside of her. Jessica felt Liz's arm working as she fucked her, she felt Liz's naked shoulder rub against her as her finger thrust inside her. Her tongue was soft against hers. Its touch delicate, unlike the touch inside her pussy. Liz had ramped up the rhythm another notch and, for the second time that afternoon, Jessica let go.

She was able to surrender again because it was Liz doing these things to her. Liz, who had been at the center of her world since she'd met her. As she came, Jessica knew she had reached yet another level of feeling alive, of being her true self. She would always be the Jessica Porter who had suffered from depression and cancer and acute uptightness, but she would also be Nicole Elizabeth Griffith's girl, and that changed everything.

After Liz had withdrawn her hand, she smirked at Jessica

and said, "I just wanted to reward your persistence with some of my own."

Jessica chuckled. "Let me catch my breath and I'll show you how much more I have in me." She drew Liz closer again and kissed her on the lips.

Chapter Twenty-Seven

"I'm NOT REALLY MEETING a client today," Liz said.

Jessica lay with her head on Liz's naked chest. "I figured as much."

"I'm meeting someone tomorrow, though," Liz said.

"Okay." Jessica pushed herself up. "But what are you doing on Saturday?"

"Hopefully not going to another disastrous dinner party with you." Liz smiled at her.

"I have an even better proposal." Jessica leaned on her elbow. "Will you come to the annual Edward Porter Charity Gala with me?"

Liz's eyes grew wide. "You want to introduce me to your family?"

"Nah, I'll save that ordeal for later. We can just show up and not talk to them."

Liz shook her head. "You're so strange sometimes."

"I guess that beats being harsh."

"I was being harsh on you, I admit that," Liz said. "But for your information, I already wanted to plunge my hand down your panties while you were still in the elevator."

"Must be because you were watching me through the window all afternoon. All that desperation on display. Must have been very arousing."

"Once you were up here, you'd already passed the test."

"So, what do you say?"

"To what? Meeting your family?" Liz asked.

"It's just my father, stepmother, and a few distant cousins. It's only called the Edward Porter Gala because of my dad's grandiosity. It's more a business networking thing than anything else."

"I thought it was for charity?"

"It is. Attending the dinner alone costs a fortune, and there's also an auction. It's especially for people who want to remain in my father's good graces."

"You make it sound like so much fun."

"I have to go. My father—well, my stepmother really, has been organizing this event for nine years straight and I've never once taken a date."

"How come?" Liz extended her hand and stroked Jessica's arm. "A woman like you?"

"For the longest time, my schedule was way too packed for something as frivolous as a date. When I did find myself with some unexpected time on my hands, I was too depressed to attract another woman."

"Is that why you hired Laurel? Because you didn't have time to find a date?"

Jessica sighed. "Among other reasons, I guess."

"What were the other reasons?" Liz kept stroking Jessica's arm.

Jessica arched up her eyebrows. She rolled onto her side to be more comfortable. "After I met Katherine and she told me what she did, I got really curious. And, well, I was a woman in my prime, yet nobody was touching me. Plus there was the sheer excitement of it all."

"So you made the call to the agency?"

Jessica nodded. "Yes, the first time I called, they asked me a bunch of questions."

"You weren't ordering pizza, after all," Liz said.

Jessica nodded. "The first time I set a date with Laurel, I cancelled an hour before she was supposed to arrive. I was too nervous. I couldn't go through with it."

"That happens all the time. The thought of hiring an escort can be very exciting, but actually meeting someone is another ballgame."

"In the end, I was too curious to let the thought go completely," Jessica continued. "I did go through with the second appointment." A smile appeared on Jessica's face at the memory. "Laurel was so nice. So natural. A lot like you. It takes something special to put people at ease like that."

Liz didn't say anything for a while. Then she looked at Jessica, her hand still on her arm. "The only reason I will ever give up this job is for me. Can you understand why I can't do it for someone else? Where that would leave me in the power dynamic of a relationship?"

"I'm trying to." Jessica put her hand over Liz's. "I can hardly sweep into your life—as a client, no less—and expect you to change everything about it for me."

"This job is my independence. In a few years, it will sponsor my dream. I'm so close, I can already imagine it. The Liz Griffith Gallery."

"My father is a big art collector as well," Jessica said. "My stepmother pretends to be, but she never had... I don't really know what it is you need in order to know what's going to be big or not."

"Knowledge. Patience. Willingness to do research. A degree in Art History helps as well."

"Christine has none of those things."

"Your father does?"

Jessica thought for a while. "Apart from the degree… yes, I think he does."

"Then I can't wait to meet him," Liz said. "But…I'm going to say something that's extremely contentious in my line of work. Something I've lost and gained dates over in equal measure." She smirked at Jessica. "I don't wear dresses." She waggled her eyebrows. "I look pretty dashing in a tux, though."

"Oh, I'm sure you do." Jessica leaned in to kiss her. She didn't want to think about Liz seeing a client tomorrow, or anyone who might recognize her at the gala. Instead she lost herself in the tender touch of Liz's lips, how her tongue slipped into her mouth, so assuredly, and focused only on this moment. She didn't yet know how else to deal with anything that might come her way, but she had dealt with plenty of things in the past. And look where she was now. Naked, in the arms of a gorgeous, intelligent, art-loving woman who, no doubt, would be the tux-wearing belle of the ball.

Chapter Twenty-Eight

IN THE BACK of the car, on the way to the gala, Jessica couldn't keep her eyes off Liz.

Liz hadn't lied. She indeed looked stunning in a tux, oozing equal portions of feminine and masculine energy at the same time. Jessica had only to glance at her and a slew of butterflies rose up in her stomach. But those butterflies were not only amorous hormones acting up. If they were only that, she would have been able to keep her knee from bouncing up and down the way it was.

Liz put her hand on Jessica's jittery leg.

"I've been to quite a few of these," Liz said. "So no need to worry about my dreadful posh events etiquette."

Jessica chuckled. "It's not you I'm worried about. It's my father. He's been so different lately." In her head, Jessica again went over the phone call she'd made to her father a few days earlier. He'd been strangely speechless when she'd told him she would, after all, be bringing someone to the gala. As though he was fighting back a tear. "I'm wondering if I should speak to his doctor."

"Why?" Liz asked. "Because his daughter's illness has

miraculously put him in touch with his emotions?" She shook her head. "It's a gift. Not something to worry about."

"It's disconcerting when you've known him your whole life."

"Maybe you should speak to his wife. See how she feels about it." Liz nudged her knee against Jessica's.

"Goodness no. Let's leave Christine out of it."

"I'm even more curious to meet them now."

Jessica sighed. "Maybe this was the wrong occasion. I should have introduced you to them privately."

"But you didn't want to go to the gala alone," Liz said matter-of-factly.

"Correct."

"And your father sounded over the moon that you're bringing me," Liz continued.

Jessica nodded.

"Well, perhaps not me specifically." Liz threw in a chuckle. "You're quite sure Christine has never hired a lesbian escort for some harmless fun on a weekday afternoon?"

Jessica slapped Liz on the thigh playfully. "Stop it." She had to suppress a giggle, though.

"I do predict I won't be the only working girl or boy at this event. People with enough money to spare, to casually spend five grand on a charity dinner, enjoy having some eye candy on their arm."

"Not even I can deny that." Jessica flashed her a smile.

The car stopped.

"We've arrived," the driver said. He got out and opened the door.

———

Jessica's father did a double-take as she and Liz approached. Perhaps he hadn't expected his daughter to turn up alongside a woman in a tuxedo. He quickly regrouped and threw his arms wide. He hugged them both. Then looked Jessica up and down.

"You look smashing, dear," he said. "As always."

Then he grinned at Liz. "You make a stunning pair."

"Thanks, Daddy," Jessica said. She glanced at Christine, who stood next to her father, doing her very best to not look too uncomfortable. At least she was trying.

"You must come to dinner next week. No excuses," her father said and winked at them, once again reminding Jessica that he was not the same man she'd known before her surgery.

When she'd suffered from depression, he had shown his fatherly love in the way she was accustomed to: throwing money around and making sure all the bad press went away quickly.

"I would love to, Mr. Porter," Liz said. "It's a real pleasure to be here."

Jessica was pulled from her thoughts by Liz being overly formal. She looked around. While she and Liz had greeted her father and Christine, a group of people had formed around them. It was clear that most of them wanted to say hello to her father and stepmother.

"We'll talk more later," Jessica said. She pulled Liz aside.

Before she had a chance to step away, her father put a hand on Jessica's shoulder and shot her the kind of joyful smile she wasn't used to seeing on his face.

"How many marks out of ten for that?" Liz asked when they'd moved away. "For impressing your old man upon first meeting him?" She leaned in and whispered in Jessica's ear. "For your information, I can now officially confirm that your stepmother has never availed of my services."

A waiter waltzed by with a tray of champagne glasses. They each took one.

"Will you tell me when you see someone who has?" Jessica asked.

Liz painted a smile on her lips and shook her head. "No can do, and you know it."

———

"Shall I bid on this?" Jessica asked. The auction was on its last legs and she had yet to make her first bid.

"A two-night stay at The Belgrave Spa and Resort in Katoomba, all expenses paid," the auctioneer repeated. "After you've paid for them in advance, of course." He paused. "Can I start the bidding at three thousand dollars? Any takers?"

Seven people raised their hands.

Jessica looked at Liz. "Do you want to go on a weekend getaway with me?"

"I most definitely do."

Jessica joined the bidding. The price quickly went up to six thousand dollars, until it was just her and one last tenacious bidder left.

She craned her neck to check out her competition. "Who is that woman?" she said under her breath, not expecting an answer.

"A tough cookie with very deep pockets," Liz said. "You may want to brace yourself for a real bidding war."

Jessica's eyes grew wide. "You know her?"

Liz nodded.

"Do we have six and a half?" the auctioneer said.

The woman raised her hand. Jessica quickly followed suit.

"You may also want to set yourself a top price you don't want to go over before this gets out of hand," Liz said.

Jessica shook her head. "No bloody way. My pockets are equally deep. I'll show her."

"Jess, I'll take you on a weekend to Katoomba. It's not worth this kind of money nor... competition," Liz said.

"It is to me." Jessica kept raising her hand.

"The Belgrave sure is popular," the auctioneer joked. "But let's remind ourselves that all proceeds of this auction go to Sydney Children's Hospital," he said. "Do we have a bid of ten thousand dollars?"

The woman raised her hand.

Liz put her hand on Jessica's knee. "Let it go." She raised her eyebrows.

"Going once," the auctioneer said.

Jessica looked at Liz. What point was she trying to prove, anyway? That she had more money than this woman she believed had hired Liz's services? What could that possibly accomplish?

The auctioneer looked straight at her. "Twice." He tilted his head.

Jessica glanced in the direction of the woman who was about to outbid her. She was staring straight ahead of her, as though she had no eye for anyone else.

Liz squeezed her knee and whispered, "Just let it go."

"Sold," the auctioneer said. "The two-day getaway in Katoomba is going to Mrs. Robinson. Congratulations. Thank you on behalf of Sydney Children's Hospital and enjoy."

"I was just driving up the price," Jessica said. "Doing my bit for charity."

"You could just make a donation if it's that important to you," Liz said.

Jessica examined Liz's face. She had to know. She leaned

toward Liz and asked, "Is that Mrs. Robinson a client of yours? Is that why she was being so tenacious?"

"Don't ask me that," Liz replied, and by saying nothing she had just said everything.

"She's probably jealous because I'm here with you," Jessica continued.

"Jess, I'm serious," Liz said. "You really have to let this go. Okay?" Her voice was firm.

Jessica nodded, but she couldn't help throwing another glance at Mrs. Robinson. Jessica guessed she was in her early fifties. She'd need to ask her father what he knew about her.

Or, as Liz had suggested, she could just let it go.

They sat through another few bidding wars, none of which Jessica felt inclined to participate in, until the auction ended and the dancing started.

People got up from their seats and either danced or milled about to start conversations with acquaintances. Jessica's father was in his element and she was glad he had this evening. She was, for the first time in a long while, happy for him.

Just as Liz had convinced Jessica to have a dance with her, and they were about to get up, Mrs. Robinson appeared next to their table.

Jessica was too flabbergasted to say anything.

"Congratulations," Liz said, and extended her hand. "You drive a hard bargain."

Mrs. Robinson took Liz's hand in hers and held it for far too long according to the etiquette Jessica was raised with.

"You're Edward's daughter, aren't you?" she asked Jessica. She finally let go of Liz's hand but didn't offer to shake Jessica's. Mrs. Robinson probably believed Jessica had hired Liz for the night, as her plus one.

"Yes." Jessica kept her tone clipped. She didn't have it in

her to be friendly to this woman. "Enjoy your stay in Katoomba. It's beautiful there this time of year."

"Oh, I know, dear." She painted a wicked smile on her lips. "And I'm not the only one." She shot Liz a quick wink and turned on her heels.

"Bloody hell," Jessica said. "What was that?"

Liz came to stand in front of her and put her hands on Jessica's shoulders. "Let's dance," she said.

"I'm not sure I know how to let this go," Jessica said.

"It's very simple," Liz said and kissed her on the cheek. "Dance with me."

"Dance with you?" Jessica arched up her eyebrows. "And that's going to solve everything?"

"It won't, but it will at least take your mind off things. Turn some heads. Make you feel some joy in here." She touched her chest.

Jessica nodded and allowed Liz to lead her to the dance floor. *This is the real test*, she thought. There might be many more to come.

Then she looked at Liz who stood there waiting in her impeccable tux and with her warm, inviting smile, hand outstretched. There was no way Liz would ever look at the likes of Mrs. Robinson like that. This particular intensity in her glance was reserved solely for the woman Liz was obviously falling in love with.

For Jessica.

Jessica stepped into Liz's embrace and Liz's warm strength seeped into her as they slow-danced to an old song. Jessica didn't remember the song title, but it must have been requested by her father because she remembered him playing it at home when she was younger.

"You understand me," the lyrics went. "You're you and that's why I love you."

Liz pulled her closer and Jessica melted into her embrace.

423

She pushed the thought of Mrs. Robinson from her mind and concluded that if she wanted to pass the test, all she had to do was let go. Life was what it was. It certainly wasn't a fairytale. Yet here Jessica was, dancing with her fairytale princess in a tuxedo.

Epilogue

"DARLING." Jessica's father pulled her into a tight hug. "Congratulations."

Liz stood next to her and she was next in line for a Daddy Porter hug. Jessica hadn't told her father what Liz did for a living. She and Liz had discussed it, but when it came down to it, it wasn't any of his business. And this art gallery they'd opened together provided Liz with the perfect cover.

"Elizabeth," Jessica's father said, and threw his arms wide for Liz.

Jessica watched their embrace with a combination of delight and wonder. At least her father had shown some of his old personality when Jessica had told him she was quitting her job at ANBC. She had given him a few days to compose himself after delivering the news—a few days he had sorely needed. But compose himself, he had.

"Don't let anyone else buy anything before I do," Jessica's father said. "I want to make the first official purchase."

"You'd best start browsing straight away then," Liz said.

"I'll need you to give me a tour," Jessica's father said.

"Come on then." Liz winked at Jessica and took her father by the arm.

Jessica watched them walk toward a painting together and wondered how her father would react if he found out that Liz worked for an escort agency. It was not unthinkable that he already knew. He could have had someone do a background check on Liz. But even if he knew, he hadn't said anything. And he and Liz seemed to get on like a house on fire.

"Jess, hello." Jessica was snapped out of her reverie by more guests arriving. It was Katherine and her gaggle of gays. Kisses and congratulations were exchanged, glasses of champagne distributed.

When most of the invitees had arrived, Katherine and Jessica stood chatting in a corner of the gallery, overlooking the crowd.

"It's a real problem in our industry," Katherine said.

"What is?" Jessica asked.

"Clients falling in love with escorts." She looked at Jessica. "It comes with the territory of offering a lesbian experience, I guess."

"Says the woman who gave me such a hard time about having feelings for the woman I'd hired."

"I did so with good reason, Jess. Clients fall for us all the time. Things can get really tricky if it's not mutual."

Jessica chuckled. "So when you made that joke about the RSPCA being the closest thing to Grindr for lesbians, you actually meant to say escort agencies."

"The RSPCA is cheaper though."

"And you get a pet *and* a girlfriend at the same time."

"Double whammy," Katherine said.

"Remember when I asked you if a client had ever fallen for you?" Jessica found her friend's glance.

Katherine nodded.

"How about the other way around? Have you ever fallen for a client?"

"What's with all the questions? Don't you have some guests to entertain?" Katherine smiled good-naturedly.

"Just curious, as it seems to be quite a common occurrence."

Katherine shook her head. "I haven't. I guess I'm more the kind of girl who looks for romance in other places."

"How about art gallery openings?" Jessica asked.

"Sure," Katherine said. They both let their gaze wander over the crowd. "Meanwhile, I'll just keep on having my fun."

"What's your retirement dream?" Jessica asked. "Liz wanted to open an art gallery. Do you have something you're saving for?"

"I might have," Katherine said.

Jessica turned to her. "How long have I known you?" She put her hands on her hips. "You've never told me about your dream?"

"You never asked."

"It never really occurred to me," Jessica said. "Don't keep me in suspense. What is it?"

"A coffee shop," Katherine said. "Rocco and I have been talking about it for years. He believes in the black gold as much as I do. When I retire, that's what I would like to do. Start our very own coffee shop."

"Well then, please allow me to introduce you to two people who know all about coffee shops." Jessica took Katherine by the hand and led her to where Kristin and Sheryl were standing.

———

"Your father bought two works," Liz said.

427

Jessica rolled her eyes, even though she was grateful.

"He really doesn't come across as the man you described to me when we first met."

"That's because he's a different man. It only took me losing a breast to change him into a human being." Jessica curved her arm around Liz's waist. "What do you think? Successful opening?"

"Spectacular," Liz said. "Art is big business and your father's crowd knows it." She smiled at Jessica. "I'm so glad we've been able to put your privilege to good use."

Jessica snickered. "No more poor little rich girl for me. I'm owning it."

Liz pressed her side against Jessica's. "I'm really happy," she said. "This is just… perfect."

They overlooked the gallery, which was empty apart from a few people from the catering company cleaning up.

"I'm happy too," Jessica said.

"I bet I can make you a tiny bit happier," Liz said. "There's something in my back pocket for you."

A tingle rushed up Jessica's spine. "For me?" She turned Liz around. She felt inside and found a small envelope.

"Open it," Liz said.

Jessica tore at the flap, which was glued shut too tightly for her liking. When she managed to open it, she pulled out a card that said: The Belgrave Spa and Resort in Katoomba is delighted to invite you for a two-night stay.

A smile appeared on Jessica's face.

"And guess what?" Liz folded her arms around Jessica's neck. "It didn't cost me ten grand."

"Let's hope Mrs. Robinson isn't there at the same time," Jessica said. "I don't want you working when we're there."

Liz chuckled. "I never confirmed that so you can keep your assumptions to yourself."

"How about when you retire. Will you be able to confirm some things to me then?"

"Nope. Some things I'll have to take to my grave. Like how we met."

"What are you talking about? We met at an art gallery. An artist we both like had a show. It was love at first sight. It made us want to start an art gallery together not long after. And here we are, six months later."

"Keep telling yourself that," Liz said. "But I'll always know the truth."

"So will I," Jessica said. "The escort agency screwed up and there you were."

"The perfect story for any dinner party." Liz grinned.

"Yep." Jessica nodded. "We can easily shock people with that for the rest of our lives."

Liz leaned in and kissed her on the lips. "How about you take me home now? I'm not used to the kind of job where I have to be on my feet for so long."

Jessica shook her head and suppressed a giggle. "Come on then." She took Liz by the hand. "I'll have you on your back in no time."

MORE THAN WORDS

PINK BEAN SERIES - BOOK 9

To everyone who's lost someone.

Chapter One

KAT

"THIS IS the perfect location for a third Pink Bean," Kristin says, standing in front of the large shop window. "I can picture it already." She turns around to face Rocco and me and reaches out her hand. "And I'm very happy to be in business with both of you." I let Rocco shake her hand first.

Just as I'm about to touch my palm against Kristin's, my phone starts vibrating in the back pocket of my jeans. I sigh because I can so easily guess who it's going to be—Alana, trying to convince me, once again, to reconsider quitting The Lesbian Experience.

"This is a job perfectly suited for working part-time," she said yesterday, when I was silly enough to pick up. "Even one appointment per week would be good."

"Do you have to get that?" Kristin asks and quickly lets go of my hand.

"Let me check." I slip my phone out of my pocket. A picture of Liz appears on the screen. Relief washes over me and I pick up. Even though we used to be colleagues at the agency, I know she won't try to convince me to take another

435

client. She knows that once you're done with being an escort, you're done. That door has been closed once and for all.

"Hi Lizzie," I greet my friend. We've gotten much closer now that we're no longer co-workers—although we never actually, in the true sense of the word, collaborated.

"I'm in my old hood," Liz says. "I thought I'd drop in."

"Rocco and I are with Kristin at the venue for the new Pink Bean. Swing by here." I give her the address. When I hang up, Rocco's telling Kristin all about his interior design plans—again. His arm swoops through the air and his voice shines with enthusiasm. We've been talking about this for so long—although I'm not sure either one of us ever sincerely believed our dreams would come true. Then we met Kristin and everything started going really fast.

"Liz is stopping by," I say when a silence falls in their conversation.

Rocco checks his watch. "Auntie Hera should be here soon as well."

We make our way into the empty shop.

"If only we had a working coffee machine already," Kristin says, a smile on her face.

"My aunt will have the renovations done in no time. She's not one of those builders who say yes to a deadline only to push it back time and time again. I'm also her favorite nephew and she can't pull that shit with me." Rocco puts his hands on his hips.

"Family connections can work in your favor as well as against you," Kristin says.

Ever since we started talking to her about a possible third Pink Bean branch, she's been uttering words of advice like that. She doesn't talk a mile a minute, but she's been invaluable in helping us make our dream a reality. And as a silent partner she has invested enough money so that Rocco and I can devote all our energy to getting this off the ground as quickly as possible.

He waves her off. When they talk to each other, Rocco so flamboyant and Kristin so measured in her movements, the contrast always makes me smile. They're so different, yet they seem to hit it off. Then again, Rocco is the kind of person who hits it off with almost everyone he meets. He wags a finger at her.

Kristin peers at it as though it's a gesture not many people have ever had the balls to aim at her.

"Not when it comes to my aunt. Nu-uh," he says. "She's a woman of her word if ever there was one."

"A woman after my own heart then." Kristin gives him a small smile. I don't think she's capable of anything more generous, as though her genetics don't allow her wide grins.

"After we've talked with Hera, we can set an opening date," I say, my voice brimming with excitement.

When Jessica first introduced me to Kristin, I misjudged her as the kind of person who would take great offense at my then-profession. But looks can be deceiving—something I should know all about—and Kristin embraced the idea of the new coffee shop from the start. It helped that she already had a partnership going with two women who run a Pink Bean branch, slash feminist book shop, in Newtown.

"We'll see," Kristin says. "I know she's your aunt, Rocco, but it will also depend on the budget."

Rocco waves her off again. Kristin looks at his fluttering hand as though, if he waves it at her one more time, she might very well slap it away. "This is even better than mates' rates, Kristin. This is family."

Even I'm curious about meeting Rocco's aunt. I've known him for a long time, but I've never met her. However, I do know all about her long-term partner Samantha suddenly dying of a cerebral hemorrhage last year. Rocco may have cried about it when he was with me but I'm sure he was a rock for his aunt. He's that kind of guy. As camp as they come, yet with a heart of gold underneath. I love him to bits for both those elements of his personality.

A woman on a pale blue racing bicycle stops in front of the window, catching all of our attention. From her lanky form, I can tell it's Liz. She takes off her helmet and straps it to the handlebar of her bike. She waves at us through the window.

"I can't believe there's going to be a Pink Bean in bloody Bondi," she says as she steps inside. "Now that I no longer live here."

"Sorry, darling," Rocco says. "But this is where it's happening. You shouldn't have been such a lez and moved in with your girlfriend after two dates."

The three lesbians surrounding him protest loudly, telling him off for his inane utterance of clichés. While Liz admires the space, I see a bright red flatbed truck pull up outside. The driver manages to maneuver it into a tight spot, impressing me with their parking skills.

Rocco claps his hands together. "Hera's here."

We all watch Hera as she descends from the truck. She stands looking at the building for a split second, just long enough for me to take her in. She's tall with short cropped dark hair that is greying slightly at the temples. Her jeans are faded and marred with paint spots. The T-shirt she's wearing is loose and shapeless, but from its sleeves, a pair of bulky biceps protrude. Hera pushes her tortoiseshell glasses up her nose and heads inside.

Chapter Two

HERA

Rocco introduces me to Kristin, Liz, and Katherine. I've heard him talk about Katherine before. I know what she used to do for a living.

I've always had a soft spot for Rocco, as he's my only nephew, but I was still hesitant to take on this project. Especially when he told me he would be carrying out the 'interior design' of the coffee shop.

I glance around and conclude it's a good space. It's light and airy so it won't feel cramped.

"The counter will go here," Rocco says, not wasting any time. He's like an overexcited puppy. It makes me want to pet him to calm him down a little bit, but I'd better not embarrass him in front of his business associates. I know he and Katherine will be running the show, with Katherine putting in most of the money—apparently being a hooker allows you to save up quite a sum of cash.

Kristin will be lending her brand name and expertise, and is also investing a percentage of the money. What Rocco lacks in cash, he can sure make up for in sheer enthusiasm, I know that much. I'm secretly proud of him for doing this, for making his dream come true. Life can be so short, he's right to make the most of it.

"Rocco has drawn up some plans," Katherine says. "Which I'm sure he'll share with you."

I point at the backpack slung over my shoulders. "I've studied the plans already." I lock my gaze on Katherine's for an instant. Her eyes are dark and intense. I can see why a woman like her could hire out her... *services*. I quickly push the thought away. I'm here to help Rocco make his dream come true, not to judge his business associate. He's old enough to make his own decisions. I'm just the builder. I come in, do the work, and leave. "I'm here to get a feel for the place." I glance away from Katherine. "What you've planned for it shouldn't be a problem, from a builder's point of view." I have to admit that, though striking as she is, Katherine looks quite different than I pictured. She's much curvier than my idea of a high-class escort—but what do I know? She wears her curves well, however, and maybe that's where the secret lies.

And if I'm going to do this job, I really need to get over Rocco's friend's profession—or former profession, as he has assured me.

"You'd best not tell your mother who you're hanging out with," I told him when he first told me about Katherine's job. "She won't understand."

Rocco had shaken his head in that way he has, adding an exaggerated eye roll and hiss, and said, "Seems to me the one who doesn't understand is sitting right across from me."

When he offered me this job, I took it because I needed it. Not so much from a monetary point of view—although at the time Australia wouldn't let us legally marry, Samantha had made me the only beneficiary of her life insurance policy—but because I needed the distraction.

I need to work, need to do something with my hands to

chase the ever-growing cobwebs from my mind. If I have to work for an ex-prostitute, so be it. I've always considered myself an open-minded woman, but I have my limits. Trading sex for money is something that falls out of the boundaries of my comprehension.

"When can you start, Auntie?" Rocco asks. "And how long do you think it will take?"

Kristin steps forward. "We will also need a quote from you, Hera. On paper."

"Of course." I nod at her. I like her. She seems to know what she's doing, unlike Rocco who's been wagging his tail over this coffee shop for months now.

"You're opening up a coffee shop called the Pink Bean?" I asked him, incredulously, when he first told me. "You're not pulling my leg?"

He looked at me with his eyebrows all arched up. "Because we're all gay, hence the coffee beans are supposedly pink," he said, looking much more innocent than I knew him to be.

"Sure, dear," I said. "If that's what you want to believe."

I'm glad Rocco and Katherine have Kristin on their side for this venture. It makes me feel as though I won't be working on something that's bound to go bust in a few months' time.

"I'll get you the quote, on paper, by the end of the week," I say. "I can start as soon as all parties are agreed. I don't have any other jobs going at the moment." I don't explain why. I'm sure Rocco has told them all about how his aunt has become a sad, grieving widow. "The job is pretty straightforward." I give Rocco a quick pat on the biceps. "If we put all this vanity muscle to use, Rocco can be a great little helper if he wants to be. It should only take a few weeks. Let me have a proper think about it and I'll give you a better idea of the time I'll need when I send over the quote."

"Sounds great," Katherine says.

"This place is going to be amazing," the lanky, toned woman, whose name I've already forgotten, says.

"I'll do my best," I say.

Rocco puts his arm around me. "I know you will." He cocks his head. "When Chris and I redid our apartment, Hera tore down the walls as if it was nothing." He grins at me.

Katherine extends her hand. "I look forward to working with you."

I have no choice but to shake her hand. We stand around chatting for a few more minutes, after which I do another run of the place, inspecting its nooks and crannies.

By the time I'm back in my truck, already doing calculations for the quote in my head, I'm glad for this opportunity. It's time to get out of my house and start living in the real world again.

Chapter Three

KAT

I PROMISED Rocco I'd be at our future coffee shop for Hera's first day, not only so that we could both be present but also to mark the occasion that it is. But I also told him that I'm no good with my hands, which earned me quite the look from him.

"My skills have always lain elsewhere," I said to him.

"Of course, darling," he replied, throwing in a big fat wink.

Hera has arrived and she has barely given me the time of day so I just stand around, doing nothing. There are things to arrange, of course, but I'd reserved today to welcome Hera —and to help where I could.

She's pressing her fingertips against a wall, as though gauging its strength, but what do I know? For some reason, Rocco gets away with pretending he does know. She bends over and Rocco does the same. I find myself staring at their backsides. I already know Rocco's bum is pert and tight—he spends enough time in the gym doing squats, then telling me all about them. Hera's behind is but a tiny bulge in her jeans.

She has impressive arms, but the rest of her is lean in that sinewy, coiled way, probably from being a builder all her life.

She murmurs something to Rocco that I can't make out. When they straighten up, I ask, "Can I get you anything? Some water? Or coffee, perhaps?"

Hera points at the flask she brought in earlier. She does seem very self-sufficient. She doesn't respond verbally, which irks me a little.

"I'll have a coffee," Rocco says. "If only to give the competition some extra business before we seduce all their customers away."

"Have some of mine," Hera says. "I have plenty in my flask." Her voice is low but smooth.

"Thanks, but no thanks, Auntie." Rocco screws up his face. "I'll go for the real deal."

Hera just shakes her head.

"One flat white coming right up." I know Rocco's preferred hot beverage.

"Rocco, why don't you run along. Let me get a better feel for the place on my own without you two hovering about." Her tone's quite brusque, but Rocco doesn't seem to take offense. Maybe that's just Hera's way. Or maybe he's happy to get out of here already. He might have bulging biceps, but that doesn't make him the ideal builder's apprentice. They're, quite literally, just for show.

"Chris is coming by later," he says when we walk out. "He took the afternoon off."

"That's nice of him."

"It's not every day something like this happens in his partner's life."

I bump my shoulder into his. We're about the same height, something I've always teased him about, but today's not the day for that.

We walk in silence for a bit, until I say, "I get the feeling that Hera doesn't like me very much, even though we've only just met."

Rocco stays quiet.

"Or maybe it's more that she doesn't approve of me for some reason. Did you happen to tell your aunt what I used to do for a living?"

Rocco halts and turns to me. "I did. But it was a long time ago. Should I not have?"

I shake my head. "No, it's all right. I just get the impression she can't deal with it very well. Some people can't help but be judgmental about it."

"Ah, you know, she's old school. Religious upbringing and all that. There are some things she just doesn't understand."

"So I gathered." I start walking again, Rocco follows.

"You can't take it personally, Kat. She's had such a rough time. This is her first job since Sam died. She may be a bit rusty in the social skills department but her social skills are not why we hired her, anyway."

"It's fine. I don't need to be friends with the the builder." I sigh. "In fact, there's not much point in me being there at all while Hera's working. You can oversee things perfectly well on your own."

"Do you want me to talk to her?" Rocco asks.

"No, that's all right. Just let her get on with the job. The sooner it's done—"

"The sooner we're in business, K.Jo." Rocco almost shrieks.

"I know." As we approach the coffee shop we've been frequenting ever since we found the venue for our own, I stop in my tracks and look at it. It's much smaller than ours, but the front window is fully collapsible, opening up the space and bringing the outside in.

This place is closer to the beach and the pavement in front is much wider. Rocco and I wanted a window like this one, but, according to Kristin, it would be money wasted because of our location. She advised us to focus on coziness instead of trying to merge with the world outside and, instead, make it a place people want to retreat into, for a brief break from the real world.

"I still can't believe we're going to have our very own coffee shop," I muse.

"I know. It's quite the change, isn't it?"

We head inside and order our coffees. Rocco decides to give Hera all the time alone she needs and we take one of the tables by the open window.

"What's most baffling is that it's actually happening. That we're building something from nothing, from a silly idea we once came up with while under the influence of your way-too-strong mimosas." Rocco grins at me.

"As Kristin said, coffee is black gold and the gold rush is long from being over." I stare into my cup, remembering a long talk I had with Kristin about the almost inexplicable draw of a cup of coffee. How it can be so disappointing sometimes, when not well-made, and so intoxicatingly delicious when it is.

"You don't miss the old job too much?" Rocco inquires.

"I wouldn't say I miss it per se but it is strange not to be doing it anymore." I glance at him. "If it were up to Alana, I'd still be seeing at least one client a week."

"Good to know you're still sought after." Rocco sips from his flat white. "This is bloody good coffee." He looks behind him at the counter. "We need to figure out their blend so we can copy it."

I smile at him and, while we savor our coffee in silence, I think about my old job. I do miss it sometimes. But my decision has been made, and this is my new life now.

"Before I forget," Rocco says. "I promised Steve I'd teach

two spin classes the day after tomorrow. Can you be there for Hera?"

"You're the one who can't let go of your old profession," I joke.

"I miss the endorphins." He sits up straight and pats his belly. "And my six-pack is starting to disappear." He locks his gaze on me. "There's not going to be a problem between you and Hera, is there?"

I shake my head. After all, I'm used to people judging me by what I do—or did—for a living. "I'm sure she won't need me much anyway."

Chapter Four

HERA

"I'm sorry, Rocco," I say. "It's just something I have a problem with. It's a gut thing. I can't simply change how I feel about her."

"Just try to be courteous. Do your gallant butch routine. It can't be that hard to pretend."

"I believe I'm plenty courteous with Katherine." I do my best to say her name with a straight face. "Has she said anything?"

"No, but I've noticed how you are around her and it bugs me." Rocco knows he can be frank with me. After all, he has seen me at my lowest. "You're both lesbians, for crying out loud. If even the lesbians can't get along with each other, what's the world coming to?"

"Like you get along with every gay man." I glance at him over the rim of my glasses. I do love winding him up, although the fact that he has noticed my instant dislike of Katherine startles me. He's not usually one to pick up on things like that.

"Well no, but Kat's so lovely, if only you'll give her a chance."

"A chance at what?" I take a bite from my sandwich, while Rocco picks at his salad. I ponder his question further while I chew. I have no desire to befriend an ex-hooker. I don't say this out loud to my nephew, of course. For some reason, he's quite taken with this woman—and has been for a good long while.

"I'm just the builder," I repeat. "I don't have to become friends with everyone I work with. In fact, it's rather uncommon that I do."

"I'm just asking for courteousness, that's all." Rocco puts away the Tupperware box that held his salad. "You've been locked in your house for so long. I thought you might have forgotten how to be nice to other people."

"I go out," I say, noting that my tone sounds defensive.

"Uh-huh. Sure," Rocco says. "I'm not saying you should start dating, but good things can happen when you're nice to people."

My hackles go up. He's pushing it. "First of all, I won't be dating anyone anytime soon. You can interpret 'soon' as 'ever again' if you want." I expel a sigh. "And second, you can be friends with Katherine all you want, and not give a damn about her being a prostitute, but, to me, things like that say something about someone's personality and moral fiber and I'm perfectly entitled to not fawn over her for that reason."

Rocco holds up his hands. "All right. All right. Point taken." He tilts his head. "But you're going to be alone with her tomorrow, so please behave and don't act all superior."

"Have you ever known me to act superior to anyone?"

"You know what I mean."

I shake my head. "What I don't get is why any woman would choose a profession like that. Was she starving? She sure doesn't look like it."

"Let's not get into this any further. I won't pretend I can

change your mind about Kat, even though she's genuinely one of the loveliest, most kind-hearted people I know." Rocco glances at me. "It's just that... for someone who had to stand up to so much prejudice when she first came out, you can be really narrow-minded." Rocco's the one to shake his head now. "It's hard to understand."

"One has nothing to do with the other. Being gay is not a choice, we both know that. Whereas you deliberately have to make the choice to sell your body for money."

"It's just sex." Rocco throws up his hands in desperation. "Why are lesbians so bloody uptight about sex?"

"Your lesbian friend Katherine doesn't appear to be."

"Just... be nice to her, please. That's all I ask. I know you have it in you, Auntie." He bats his lashes at me, the way he used to do as a boy.

"I promise I'll try." I can't help but smile when he looks at me that way.

———

"Do you need me to stick around?" Katherine asks. It's the first time we're alone and she keeps pushing a strand of dark hair behind her ear.

"It appears I forgot my coffee flask this morning." Rocco's words echo in my mind and I'm doing my best to not see her as a hooker, but as any other woman—and my nephew's business partner. "Would it be terribly rude to ask you to get me a coffee from that place you always disappear to?" I throw in a smile and everything.

"No flask today," Kat says. "Whatever happened?"

"I had trouble falling asleep last night," I blurt out. "I snoozed through my alarm this morning and had to rush out the door."

"Are the renovations keeping you awake?" Kat makes

intense eye-contact when she speaks—probably a trick from her former life.

"No, nothing like that. I have bouts of insomnia. I'm not a very good sleeper on the best of nights."

"Hence the flask." She sends me a wide smile now.

"You figured me out." I find myself smiling back.

"A long black?" Katherine asks.

"Sorry?"

"Your beverage of choice? I've seen you drink your coffee black, so shall I bring you that?"

"Oh, right. Yes, that would be lovely." I shrug. "It's quite ironic that I'm renovating a future coffee shop and don't know the first thing about all the modern coffee drinks. I'm used to just drinking plain old coffee."

"Plain old coffee is the new hype. We'll have that on offer as well, if you were to swing by when this place is up and running."

I roll my eyes. "And pay five dollars for a cup."

Katherine gives a slight shake of the head. "The builder drinks for free, of course." She throws in another one of her smiles. I feel like she's working me. Is this how she used to break the ice with… what to call them? *Her clients?*

"That's very generous of you." I promised to be nice, but I just can't separate Katherine from what she used to do. I wish Rocco hadn't told me. I might have found her perfectly lovely if he hadn't.

"Anyway. A long black coming up." Katherine turns to leave and I only exhale once she's left the premises. There's an energy about her that unsettles me. I hope Rocco is able to free himself from his old job soon so he's the one I have to deal with while I'm working here, not Katherine.

Chapter Five

KAT

HERA STRIKES me as the kind of woman who hides her true self—her natural beauty—underneath a layer of dust and those wide, dark-colored T-shirts she's always wearing. Or maybe she just likes to be comfortable.

Before I walk back in, two disposable coffee cups in hand, I look at her through the window. She's mixing something in a large bucket. Maybe I should ask her about the building process as a way of having her open up to me a little more. But why bother? It's obvious she doesn't like me. I learned long ago to not be perturbed by that. Yet, with her, it's different. Because she's Rocco's aunt and, also, because she represents an important step in this new life I'm trying out.

When I walk inside, the radio is blasting an old Genesis song really loudly and Hera is swaying her hips while she stirs the contents of the bucket with a thick wooden stick. There's rhythm to her sway and she seems completely absorbed by the music.

I don't want to disturb her but I don't want her to have to drink a cold cup of coffee either. I clear my throat and she instantly goes back to her usual guarded ways. The sway of her hips instantly stops and she stands there stiffly, as though she'll never sway to any piece of music ever again.

"Coffee delivery." I walk up to her. She does have bags under her eyes. The rest of her skin is olive, while the area underneath her eyes is purple like a bruise.

"Ah, thanks." She takes the cup, then turns to lower the volume of the radio. "I could do with sitting down for a minute." She heads over to the corner where we've placed a couple of old chairs.

"Can I sit with you?" I ask.

"It's your place," she says matter-of-factly.

I follow and sit next to her, casting my gaze about. She and Rocco have taken down a wall and I can already imagine how it's going to look when it's finished.

"Not too bad for a drink with a silly name," Hera says.

"So, no need to worry next time you forget your flask."

"How much did that set you back?" she asks.

"Five bucks," I say. "Your estimate was bang on."

"I'll settle up with you later." She exhales a lungful of air.

"Don't worry about it. Consider it part of your payment." I gaze at her slouching shape in the chair. "You look like you need a nap more than a cup of coffee."

She pushes her glasses up and pinches the bridge of her nose. "As I said, I only got a few hours of shut-eye last night. And this is my first job in a while. It all takes some getting used to." She straightens her posture. "This won't affect my work, of course. No need to worry about that."

"I'm not worried. You're Rocco's family so I trust you implicitly."

Hera arches her eyebrows. "That's a bit naive, don't you think? I could be the worst builder and yet you'd still trust me just because I'm your friend's aunt?"

"But you're *not* the worst," I say, locking my gaze on hers. "And Rocco knows that."

She presses her lips together. "He didn't just hire me because he thinks I'm good at my job," she says. "I was also a bit of a charity case." Hera glances away, as though she has said too much.

"Rocco and I are pretty close. Well, very close, actually. I know your partner passed away unexpectedly."

"Hm," is all Hera says. "It's good to be out of the house. I reckon I only have a few more years of this job in me. I'm getting on." She chuckles. "Christ, I'm really not selling myself, am I?" She brings her gaze back to me. Something sparkles in it—something I haven't seen in her eyes before. "Please disregard this conversation and consider Hera Walker for all your future renovation work." She sends me her version of a winning smile—which almost does its job of winning me over.

I grin at her. For the first time, I feel as though Hera doesn't see me as Katherine the ex-escort, but just as the person she happens to be having coffee with. Something uncoils in my gut. "As a matter of fact, I've been wanting to redo my kitchen for ages. How are you with refitting kitchens?"

"As good as they come, of course." The smile hasn't been wiped off Hera's face. Maybe the long black I brought her is a couple of notches stronger than what she's used to drinking from her flask. She tips her head back and drains her cup. "Thanks for this. I feel as good as new." She jumps up. "Time to get back to it."

"Can I help you in any way?"

Hera gives me a once over. "Let's be honest," she says, "those manicured fingers were not made for helping me." She stares at my hands, which are wrapped around my coffee cup. "There's really no need for you to stick around at all. I'm going to plaster that wall over there and I can manage on my own perfectly."

"I'll leave you to it then."

Hera already has her back to me and she just raises a hand. It's as though the five minutes we just spent chatting, breaking some of that persistent ice between us, never even happened.

Chapter Six

HERA

I sink into Jill's sofa with a loud sigh. I considered cancelling, but decided against it at the last minute.

"That was quite the sigh," Jill says. "Tell me all about it."

"I'm knackered. I have this job going." I let my head fall back. "In fact, I could fall asleep right now." I snap my head back up. "But I pay you too much for that to happen."

"How's the job going?" Jill gazes at me with her pale blue eyes. When I first started seeing her, I never thought she'd look at me in such a confrontational manner. As though she wants to unearth the depths of my soul just by looking at me. Maybe she does.

"Fine. It's not too big but also not too small. The perfect kind of project to get back to it, really. And I'm working for Rocco, which makes it extra pleasant."

"That's good." Jill doesn't say anything else. She's definitely the kind of therapist who lets silences linger in the hopes she'll get me talking. I fall for it every time, even though I know what she's doing—she lets me think for myself. I *am* here to talk, of course, and at least, these days, I can do so without falling apart. I've gone through many a box of tissues in this office.

"Rocco's business partner's another kettle of fish, though," I blurt out. Most of the time, I don't even look at Jill when I'm talking, but fix my gaze on a painting behind her. It's abstract. Just a blob of colors really. Nothing I would ever consider art, not that I know much about it. Yet this very painting has now become a sort of solace. I've looked at it through oceans of tears and, like today, through hooded eyelids because I can barely keep them open.

Jill just nods.

"Her name's Katherine. They've been friends forever and Rocco told me long ago that she was a hooker. Although he prefers the term *escort*. 'She works for a lesbian escort agency that caters only to women.' That's how he put it. As if that made it more acceptable. As long as I never had to meet her, I didn't give it that much thought, but now I see this woman almost every day, I find her choice of career so… revolting."

"Interesting choice of word," Jill says.

"But it *is*." I throw my hands in the air. "At least to me it is. But I'm old, and Rocco says I'm way too uptight about sex."

This earns me a raised eyebrow from Jill. I've talked about sex with her before, about Sam and our sex life—it's one of the main reasons I first sought Jill's help. But this is the first time I've uttered the word in a good long while.

"Is that why being around her bugs you so much?" Jill asks. Before I found Jill, I had tried out a few other therapists, all of whom had a very monotone voice, as though any inflection could cause me psychological harm. Jill's voice, however, is full of life.

"How do you mean?" I ask.

"I think you know what I mean, Hera." Typical Jill. I've

been coming here for more than two years now. She probably knows me better than I know myself.

"Because she represents something I'm no longer interested in?" I almost scoff when I say it.

"For instance," Jill says.

I shake my head vehemently.

"You said it yourself." Jill doesn't shy away from painting the occasional smug smile on her face. I've always liked that she lets her personality shine through in our sessions, but right now, it bugs me as much as having to see Katherine nearly every day.

"Okay, I must have brought her up for a reason." I look at Jill with a hopeful glint in my eye. "What's your take on prostitution?"

"My take on it doesn't matter one bit." Jill told me this from the very beginning. *This is not a friendship, even though, inevitably, sometimes it will feel like one, but it's important that you're aware of the difference.* She tilts her head. "I can tell there's something going on with you, Hera. How about we try and figure out what that is instead of you asking me questions like that?"

"Fine." I know nothing about Jill's personal life, yet she knows all about my inner workings. It's a strange but comforting situation to walk into once a week, although it wasn't always that way. "I just can't be myself around her. She's a beautiful woman. I can see the appeal, but I just can't get over the fact that she… did those things in exchange for money."

"Would you like to name those 'things'?" Jill asks.

"Goodness, no." I jerk my head to the side.

"Okay. Then tell me what it's like to be back at work." I've been seeing Jill long enough to know she's not going to let me off the hook about Katherine this easily despite the change of subject matter.

"It's good, though exhausting. I feel I've grown ten years older since Sam died instead of the one since she's been gone. Everything I lift seems heavier. It's hardly a desk job, is it? But it is a satisfactory one. There's nothing like transforming a building, seeing it come to life again in front of my very eyes. I've missed that."

"If you haven't lifted anything heavy for that long, even the lightest load will feel like a ton. But you'll get used to it again, Hera. You keep on building." She cocks her head. "I can see the change in you so clearly."

"I have Rocco to thank for that. In fact, when I do the gratitude meditations you've advised me to do, it's mostly him I feel thankful toward."

"There's no one else?"

"Well, sure, there's Hilda. But it's different with her. Rocco just has this easy way about him. Even when I was at my most depressed, when I looked at him, with all his energy and bottomless zest for life, I had to acknowledge there would always be something else other than the despair I was feeling. He's just so... bubbly, even though I hate that word to describe a person." I shrug. "What does it mean to have a bubbly personality? I always thought it was the opposite of my own."

"And that would be?" Jill's lips quirk into a small smile.

"Cranky, and getting more so the older I get."

"You're not that cranky. Not all the time, anyway," Jill says. "You were grieving. There's a big difference."

"I guess." Something comes to me. "Maybe that's what I see in Katherine as well. That effortless bubbliness, or whatever you want to call it. That's probably why they get along so well, because they recognize that in each other, that same drive to always get the most out of life."

"Yet in Rocco you admire it and in Katherine it bugs you?"

"Well, yes, because Rocco's my nephew and she's... an escort."

"You didn't have to take that job if you knew it was going to annoy you so much to be around her."

"But I didn't know. It was only when I met her that I felt she was getting under my skin—in a bad way."

"You hadn't expected to react to her the way you did?"

"No. She's actually really nice. If I didn't know, I certainly wouldn't be able to tell just by looking at her. She's very... classy. Upmarket, I guess."

Jill nods. "And that offends you?"

"No." I shake my head for emphasis. "I don't know."

"Could it be that you actually like her, Hera? But you're annoyed with yourself because you can't allow yourself to do so because she's an escort."

"Actually she's no longer an escort," I blurt out. Why does it feel like I'm coming to Katherine's defense in the privacy of my therapist's office? Nothing of this makes any sense.

"Okay, my bad," Jill says, then goes silent again.

"At least it's good to feel something, even if only annoyance." I do look Jill in the eye now. "Remember when I first came here? I was such a mess. And then, with your help, I was starting to pull myself together, and then Sam died on me. Just when everything was looking up." I'm not saying this to garner Jill's pity—she made it very clear from the start that her pity would never be up for grabs—only to summarize. To make things clear, once again, in my head.

"As I said before, Hera, I can see the difference in you." Before I let my glance skitter away from Jill I consider that it might not be friendship we have between us, but it's something very meaningful nonetheless.

Chapter Seven

KAT

"Jess is running late," Liz says. On Kristin's suggestion, I'm spending some time at the other Pink Bean location in Newtown. Rocco's busy with Hera so I've asked Jess and Liz to meet me here. With getting the coffee shop up and running, I haven't seen enough of them—especially Jessica. I also want to get their take on the atmosphere. "She had an appointment with her surgeon and he's always late."

"Is she considering reconstructive surgery?" I ask.

Liz just shakes her head. Maybe she doesn't want to talk about it. She looks around. "What a cozy place." She narrows her eyes and peers into the book shop part of Pink Bean Two, as Kristin refers to it. "Look at that Caitlin James display over there." She paints a grin on her lips.

"Must be good for business." I let my glance wander around to look for any changes that have happened since my last visit. "We won't have a bookshop attached to our branch, but this is definitely the vibe I'm going for."

Liz quirks up her eyebrows. "Does Rocco agree with that?"

"Oh, we'll just dot some golden accessories around the

place—pineapples and bananas are all the rage these days—and he'll be happy." I smile at the memory of Rocco showing me a picture of a golden, half-peeled banana of which the fruit was also a lamp.

"How's it going with his aunt, the builder?"

I roll my eyes. "Let's just say I've been made aware that my presence at the site isn't required every single day."

"Ah, it's like that."

"Hera doesn't appear to be the most sex-positive of people."

"Rocco told her about you?" Liz asks.

I nod. "It's no big deal. And I know she's had a really rough time lately."

"That's no excuse for bad manners, Kat."

I wave her off. "It's fine. I mean, we might both have said goodbye to our old jobs, but it will always be a part of us. And there will always be people who can't deal with it. We've always known that." Liz and I quit the agency around the same time a few months ago.

"Hm." Liz sends me a conspiratorial smile. "How about I get us some coffees?"

"That would be lovely. I'm going to have a little browse in the book shop."

Liz heads to the counter. I venture into the book shop area of the Pink Bean. The woman behind the counter, who has her nose in a book, briefly looks up to give me a nod. She's wearing the same type of glasses that Hera does—the kind that seems much more suited to a bookshop than a building site.

I don't introduce myself just yet, although I guess that the woman must be Annie. Kristin has told me about her and her wife Jane Quinn, the lesbian romance writer. They were away when I first visited the Newtown Pink Bean, so I'm quite keen on meeting them today. But before I engage Annie in conversation, I want to walk around in silence for a bit, get a better feel for the place, and revel in what my own future will look like.

There's a display of Jane Quinn books and I'm drawn to them because of the connection they have to the very shop I'm in. I pick up one of the books and run my gaze over the back cover. I'm more of a non-fiction girl myself, but the premise sounds interesting.

Annie clears her throat. "Do let me know if I can help you with anything," she says. She has the calm and easy demeanor of someone who has been manning this book shop for decades.

I send her a smile. "Actually, I should introduce myself. I'm Katherine Jones."

"I thought you might be," Annie says. "Kristin said you would be stopping by today. It's lovely to meet you."

"Likewise." I walk toward the counter and offer her my hand. "Sorry for not introducing myself earlier. I just wanted to soak up the vibe before we started chatting."

Annie nods as if she completely understands. Then she fixes her gaze on the Jane Quinn book I'm still holding. "How about I call Jane to come down so we can all have a chat?" She looks at her watch. "She's still writing right now, so a little bit of patience might be required." Annie suddenly looks right past me.

"Is this Katherine?" a voice comes from behind me.

I turn and stare into the face of a very pleasant-looking woman, who also, unmistakably, makes my gaydar ping. I seem to have ended up in lesbian coffee slash book shop heaven.

"Mia Miller," the younger woman says. "I work with Kristin."

"Ah yes, of course." I've heard all about Mia. Kristin

never told me she was such a fox, however—Kristin isn't really one to indulge in frivolities like that.

———

Fifteen minutes later Jess has arrived and, instead of having a quiet conversation with my two friends, we're joined by Mia and Annie, with Annie promising that Jane will be there soon as well.

"Don't be alarmed," Mia says, "this time of day is always a little quiet, but it's the welcome kind of quiet between the morning and lunchtime rush." She paints on a wide smile and brushes her hair from her forehead with a gesture so assured, it makes something flutter in my stomach. Maybe I should invite Mia for a one-on-one conversation, as Kristin has suggested a few times already. I'm sure she can impart more than a few nuggets of wisdom pertaining to running a successful coffee shop.

"This gives us the time to chat," Annie says, as she adjusts her glasses on the bridge of her nose. She bears an uncanny resemblance to one of my favorite clients who went by the name of Mrs. Robinson. And I think that maybe I'm the one who has trouble flicking the switch, who finds it a hard transition from the life I used to live—the life that only a very few truly understood—to this atmosphere of utter normalcy I currently find myself standing in. Maybe that's what Hera has been picking up on—and reacting to with overt hostility.

Mia plays with a ring on her finger, a gesture I know well. I've seen dozens of women touch their wedding rings like that, as a means to ground themselves after they've been with me, to ready themselves to step back into the real world. It would be a small miracle if a woman like Mia wasn't involved with someone.

"When's the opening planned?" Mia asks.

"In a few weeks. The building's being renovated as we speak and the builder doesn't appear to be a flake." I throw in a smile. "We should be up and running soon."

"Kristin's building herself quite the empire," Jessica says.

"And yet she's always wanting to scale back her hours." Mia rolls her eyes. "Which she always does, only to start a new venture not long after."

"She's only a silent partner," I say. "But her advice has been invaluable." It was Kristin who got the ball rolling for Rocco and me and if it hadn't been for meeting her at the opening of Liz and Jess's gallery, we wouldn't be where we are now—a few weeks away from opening.

"Are you hiring staff from the get-go or planning to do everything yourself?" Mia asks. "It's you and another person, isn't it?"

"Yes," I nod. "My best friend Rocco and me. It'll just be us for starters."

Mia nods. "My advice—don't wait too long to hire people to help. I understand the urge to save on wages, but service and self-care are key." She tilts her head. "What industry were you in before?"

Jess instantly shuffles in her seat.

I find Liz's eyes and revel in the complicity in her gaze. We have a line for this—a different one for different occasions. Annie and Mia are people we'll run into again so I give them the version best-suited for that category.

"I was a travel agent," I say. "Taking care of people's every need."

Mia nods again. She seems to be taking this very seriously. "That's good. You're used to dealing with people."

"Oh yes." She has no idea.

When I started at the escort agency, Alana's first words of advice to me were to never openly tell strangers what I do, to always resist the urge because it's not about my sense of self or how empowered I might feel—it's about the others and how society has forced upon them the notion that paying for sex is always, unequivocally, wrong. "It's not how you want to start off a relationship, darling," Alana would say. "Any kind of relationship."

A group of women arrives in the shop and Annie gets up to help the ones drifting to the book shop, while Mia keeps an eye on the coffee shop counter. When the line grows too long, she excuses herself to help the person making and serving the drinks. I observe them for a few minutes, working in tandem, in quiet understanding, and wonder if Rocco and I can ever become a well-oiled machine like that. For starters, we will never be able to work together in silence, because Rocco can't keep his mouth shut for two consecutive seconds.

"They're lovely," Jess says gesturing towards Mia and her colleague, pulling me from my daydreams in which I picture my near future.

I look my friend in the eye. "How was your appointment?"

"Pointless," she says with a smirk. "You know surgeons. Always trying to sell you some more surgery."

"Reconstruction?" I ask.

She nods. "Liz says she doesn't mind bestowing all her attention on just my left breast."

Liz smiles at Jess and I'm so happy they've found each other. I resigned myself a long time ago to a life of single-hood, so much so that I've pretty much closed myself off to the possibility of the kind of love they share. But, now that I'm an ex-call girl, that primal urge to bond has been rearing its head once more.

Chapter Eight

HERA

It's the last day of the Pink Bean renovations and I had forgotten all about final-day melancholy. This was a pretty quick, not very invasive job. Nevertheless, now that the work is almost done, and I have the satisfaction of casting my glance over the results of my hard graft, I'm overcome with a sense of sadness.

It was pleasant to work alongside Rocco. Although the boy doesn't have any natural aptitude for this kind of work, his enthusiasm for his and Katherine's coffee shop made him execute the tasks I set for him with unseen zeal. His partner Chris often dropped by and helped out as well and I've grown fond of the companionship that has developed between the three of us. It feels good to live my life among real people again, instead of rehashing old memories of people who are no longer here.

I've barely seen Katherine the past few days, which has helped with my mood. She might be a sight for sore eyes but, as long as I didn't see her, I didn't have to confront my ambivalence toward her. I do prefer it that way, in this transitional part of my life where I'm trying to be less of a hermit and more of everything I used to be.

But, today, probably because it's the last day, Katherine's here. She isn't dressed for a building site. To me—and really, what do I know?—she looks more like she's ready for an appointment with a client.

I've been going over the conversation I had with Jill about Katherine in my head for days now. When plastering walls, the mind tends to wander.

I've concluded that my gut reaction was the right one—it usually is. She may look all dolled up today, red lipstick and matching nails, and smell like a million bucks, there's still something unseemly about her. Something I can't get over.

Rocco can have a go at me about it for as long as he likes, and Jill can question my motives all she wants, but, at the end of the day, I believe I'm entitled to how I feel about Katherine. And I'd rather keep my distance than have another conversation with that woman.

"You've done a wonderful job, Hera," Katherine says. She has walked up to me and stands so close her perfume wafts up into my nose.

"Thanks. It's what I do, so." I run a hand through my hair. It's getting too long. I make a mental note to get out my clippers tonight after I've showered. After this job is totally done. And I have to start thinking about the next one.

"I was serious about you having a look at my kitchen." Katherine looks me straight in the eye and smiles at me a little too broadly. "Can I call you some time?"

"Sure. Rocco has my number." I'm pretty sure I won't be picking up the phone.

She tilts her head and sends me a funny look. Is it a flirty one? I've no idea. I haven't flirted with a woman in years. Any desire for that died along with Sam. And I certainly have no desire to be buttered up by some professional flirting from the likes of Katherine.

"You'll come to the opening, won't you?"

"Rocco wouldn't speak to me for weeks if I failed to show up."

"He adores you," Katherine says, and something about it, maybe the way she says it, jars me to the point that I feel my limbs stiffen.

I shrug, hoping to end this conversation, this inane chit-chat. Before Katherine has the chance to open her mouth again, I point at the ceiling. "I have a couple of holes to fill up there before the painter can get to work."

"Of course."

I get back to it, positioning the ladder, and putting the tools I need within reach, but Katherine doesn't move. I feel her stare on me.

Before I climb the ladder I try to give her a look which I hope conveys that I don't appreciate being watched like that.

"I do admire a strong woman," she says, and smiles with lips that are too red for this place. All the walls are still bright white, there's dust everywhere, and I'm dressed in jeans and a T-shirt with a couple of holes running down the side, yet here Katherine stands, all smiles, in impossibly glam attire, with her red lips and red fingernails. She doesn't fit in here or, at the very least, her presence irks me. But I can hardly ask her to leave.

I start climbing the ladder but, for some reason, it sways and I lose my balance for a second. I'm only two rungs up and I try to regain my footing, but it's hard to refocus when you have two dark eyes boring into you like that.

"Damn it," I mutter under my breath as I, very inelegantly, jump off the ladder and have to take a step back to stabilize myself. I look down and notice a piece of cardboard under one of the legs of the ladder.

"Are you all right?" Katherine has the audacity to grab me by the arm. I shrug her hand off me immediately.

"If you could just leave me to finish my work in peace," I snap.

"Sure." She withdraws her hand while our gazes meet. Hers is soft and caring. Mine, I hope, is thunderous and menacing. I want her as far away from me as possible.

I kick away the unbalancing scrap of cardboard and reposition the ladder, using all my concentration this time, not allowing Katherine-the-ex-call girl to mess up my focus, cursing myself inwardly because it's stupid little mistakes like not properly securing a ladder that cause the most accidents in my line of work.

Before I attempt to climb up again, I make sure Katherine is far enough away. She's walking away from the ladder, her back to me, her hips swaying like she's on a bloody catwalk instead of a building site. The airs and graces of this woman. And what kind of clientele will she attract to this place? This coffee shop that has been my nephew's dream for so long. I do hope word doesn't get out about her previous job. Although, truth be told, Rocco's friends would probably be drawn to her for that very reason. They probably all know and coo around her as though she's the Queen of Sheba, while all she is… I halt my train of thought. Getting worked up while ascending a ladder is never a good idea. I take a deep breath and focus on the holes that need filling.

Chapter Nine

KAT

"ONE MORE WEEK," I say.

Rocco stands facing me and claps his hands together. "I know, *K.Jo*, can you believe it?"

We've been counting down the days forever, or so it seems, yet it still feels good. And it only gets better as the number of days decreases.

Rocco gives a big, exaggerated sigh. "The painters will be out in two days and then, *finally*, I can work my magic." He jumps up and down, which is always a funny sight because he's such a short muscle queen. He bulges his right biceps. "And with all the stuff Auntie Hera made me carry, I think I've grown some extra muscle to put into it." He turns to watch Hera, who's standing on top of the ladder she nearly fell from earlier.

Both her arms are up, one against the ceiling to steady herself, the other applying some sort of putty to smooth out the last dents. Her T-shirt has ridden up and I can make out the skin of her belly.

"Your aunt really doesn't like me, does she? I thought I

could charm my way into her good graces, but I get the feeling it hasn't worked."

"I bet that doesn't happen to you a lot." Rocco bumps his hip into mine lightly. "That you can't charm someone into liking you." He flutters his lashes at me. "This place will be teeming with lesbians wanting to bask in some of your irresistible K.Jo charm, girl. For that alone, this coffee shop will be a gold mine."

I chuckle. "As long as they don't know about my previous career. That has a tendency to turn people against me." I nod at Hera. "I've asked her to remodel my kitchen, by the way."

"Ooh, someone's not ready to throw in the towel just yet." He winks at me. "Is it really so important to you that my aunt likes you?"

I shake my head. "My kitchen just really needs a do-over and you know how hard it is to find a builder you can trust. I've seen Hera at work. She's thorough, fast, and reliable. She may not like me, but I'm convinced she'll do a good job regardless. That's all."

Rocco nods. "As long as you don't get any romantic ideas in your head about her. That ship has sailed for Auntie Hera and not even a woman of your quality and grace could ever change her mind about that."

I huff out some air. "Romantic? Are you crazy?" My turn to slam my hip against his. "The woman practically has to force herself to say hello to me."

"Just saying," Rocco says, in that nonchalant way of his. He probably didn't mean anything by it. He's the kind to blurt out silly things like that.

I look over at Hera again. She has descended from the ladder and is casting her gaze about the place. I can't fault her work ethic. She worked long days and has delivered on time. As far as I can tell, her job's done, and it's only mid-day.

"I think Hera's finished."

"Yay." Rocco does a simultaneous hand-clap and jump. "Can it be true, Auntie?" he yells. "Have you finished?"

"Just a few bits and bobs," Hera says in her usual low growl.

"Shall we take her to lunch to celebrate?" Rocco asks.

"You take your aunt to lunch. I get the feeling she wouldn't enjoy her meal all that much if she had to share a table with me."

"Oh, come on, Kat, be the bigger person," he pleads. "Do it for me, your best friend and business partner. I want to have lunch with my two favorite girls."

"Your mother wouldn't be very pleased if she heard that," I reply.

"My mother didn't just renovate our coffee shop in record time. She's probably at home filing her nails."

"Ask Hera if she wants me to come. If she does, I will. If she doesn't, you'll have to respect her decision."

"Will do, darling." Rocco shimmies over to Hera, who has started gathering her tools.

I watch them as he whispers to her. Hera glances at me and I give her a smile, because why not try to get her to thaw a little more? Rocco's probably emotionally blackmailing her and, hard as nails she may be with me, it's so obvious she has a massive soft spot for him—and can't say no to him.

Rocco turns to me and gives me a thumbs-up. I'm not sure whether I should be delighted that he was able to make a tiny bit of an inroad on my behalf, or deflated at the prospect of having Hera stare at me with nothing but contempt for the duration of a meal. Although, I could really have sworn that contempt's not all I've spotted in her gaze.

I think things are far more complicated than that.

Chapter Ten

HERA

I'M NOT SURE HOW, or why, I find myself having lunch with Katherine. Ah yes, my darling nephew. From the moment my sister Hilda had suspicions her son might be gay, she urged me to spend time with him. Hence, Rocco and I have been growing closer since he was ten years old and Hilda found him strutting around the house in her high heels with her lipstick plastered clumsily onto his lips.

I was the one to assure him that there was absolutely nothing wrong with him and that he was no less a person than anyone else. Conversations like that tend to create a bond.

Once again, I found myself unable to say no to him. So here I am. Rocco's sitting across from me and Katherine's seated next to him. Even though Rocco's been helping me apply the final touches to the coffee shop, and loading all my dusty gear into my truck, he still looks as though he's fresh from the shower. Foreseeing as he is, he always has a freshly ironed T-shirt in his car. I guess when you have the conviction to iron your T-shirts, it's only a small step to always having a spare at hand.

Rocco and I have gone for meals dressed the way we are countless times, but it has never made me feel out of sorts. That's who he is and this, faded jeans and spotty well-worn T-shirt, is who I am.

It's Katherine's presence that is unsettling me again. While we peer at the menu, I decide my best bet to make it through this lunch is to opt for silence.

"This occasion calls for a good bottle of wine," Rocco exclaims. "K.Jo, you do the honors and choose." He looks up at me. "She has exquisite taste."

"I bet she does," I say, before I can even stop myself. I can't stop the corners of my mouth from drawing down either. Being near this woman puts my teeth on edge. Thank goodness it's Wednesday and I have a session with Jill later today. Although I may not mention Katherine at all. The job's done. It's time to put her out of my mind once and for all.

Katherine glares at me over the menu she's holding. She doesn't say anything, just gives me a look I quickly turn away from.

A waiter comes around and we place our order. Katherine orders a New Zealand pinot gris. I sneaked a peek at the wine list myself, even though my opinion wasn't called for, and I probably would have picked that one as well.

Rocco, an expert at keeping conversations going if ever there was one, has barely had time to open his mouth when the wine is delivered to our table.

Katherine only makes a small display of tasting it and quickly approves it. Once we've all been poured a glass, Rocco holds up his.

"To you, Auntie. We're so happy with the work you've done. You hear such horror stories of builders who only do a half-assed job or never meet a project's deadline, but you finished half a day early, and definitely didn't do a half-assed job. Thank you for being so reliable." He turns to Katherine and offers her the widest smile. "You're in business with a very reliable breed," he says.

"Thank you both." Katherine winks at Rocco then holds her glass out to me. Her red fingernails stand out to me again. What is it about her nails and makeup that gets under my skin so much? "For everything."

"With all this praise, you'd start thinking I did this job for free. You are paying me, aren't you?" I joke while quickly lifting my glass a fraction. I don't hold it out any farther to clink rims with them for fear my hand may be trembling too much.

"Of course, the usual family rate," Rocco says.

"What's your next job?" Katherine asks.

If she's going to ask me direct questions, it'll be hard to stick to silence.

"I'm not sure yet. When you've been out of commission for a while people forget about you." I shrug. "It's normal when you've had to say no a couple of times. But word will spread soon enough. Builders are always needed and there are never enough of us to make people's renovation dreams come true. It's how the world turns."

"Sounds like a very good profession to be in," Katherine says. "What made you become a builder? I guess it's more common now for a woman to choose that profession, but I can imagine that back in the day, it must have caused some looks."

"I still get plenty of looks." I take a sip from the wine, which is light and crisp and just the way I like it. "But I worked with my father for a long time before I took over his business when he retired. You tend to run into the same people a lot." I lean back in my chair. "Clients are something else, of course. The majority hardly bat an eyelid when a woman turns up on their doorstep, but some really can't deal with it. And then there are those who don't notice I'm a woman at all." I throw in a chuckle.

"We all have to live in this world," Katherine says. "Which is rife with prejudice." She locks her gaze on mine for an instant. Is she trying to send me a message?

"That may be so, Kat," Rocco interjects. I'm surprised he's managed to let us speak for this long without intervening. "But Auntie Hera made sure I was ready to face any prejudice when it was time to come out. Plus, she made my coming out to my parents a piece of cake."

I wave off Rocco's comment. "Your mother knew long before you did."

"And in all fairness, darling," Katherine adds, "you've worked in a gym for most of your professional life. Being gay is practically a requirement for an instructor in a Bondi gym." She gives him a smile that lights up her face.

"What is this?" Rocco says. "I was trying to have a genuine heartfelt moment and all I get is the lezzers ganging up on me." He sighs dramatically. "I've always vehemently fought what Auntie Hera has told me all my life. That of all the variations of gender and orientation, gay men and lesbian women have the least in common, except the battles we've had to fight side by side. Right now, for the first time ever, I'm starting to believe you were right." He paints on a smirk.

I can't help but laugh at his silly indignation. Rocco has always had a knack for making a point in the most dramatic fashion. He gets that from his mother, for sure. Sometimes, when he was at my house as an adolescent, it was like being around my teenage sister all over again.

"Then I guess we should toast Hera once again," Katherine says. "For encouraging you to become such a fabulous and unapologetic gay."

"What's there to apologize for anyway?" Rocco says, before taking a sip of wine.

"Absolutely nothing, when it comes to your sexual preference, at least." I glance at Katherine. It was quite fun to gang up on my nephew for a minute, to jest with another woman like that.

"What do you mean by that exactly?" Katherine asks. Her gaze is glued to mine. "By the 'at least' in what you just said?"

Chapter Eleven

KAT

"I'M NOT sure I know what you're getting at," Hera says.

"I think it's wonderful that you've been such a great role model for Rocco and I appreciate that coming out was much harder a mere decade ago, let alone thirty years ago. But how can you sit here basking in Rocco's praise about you being so supportive when, all the while, you're judging me?"

Damn. I didn't mean to have a go at Hera. She hardly deserves it. In fact, apart from the clear judgment she's been casting on me since the very first moment we met, I can so clearly tell she and Rocco are cut from the same good-natured cloth. But it's perhaps that one glaring discrepancy in her personality that gets to me. Moreover, this is supposed to be a happy occasion. Us thanking her for a job well done, and celebrating another milestone in our journey toward our coffee shop dream. Yet Hera can't help but ruin the moment with her snide little remarks. If she thinks she can just keep dropping them into conversation, and hope Rocco and I won't notice, she has another thing coming. Granted, Rocco probably doesn't notice, but I do. I'm too finely attuned to throwaway remarks like that venomous 'at least' that sprang from her lips.

I might be able to understand people's reactions to what I do—we all live in the same world, governed by the same old conservative societal rules, after all—but that doesn't mean I have to let everyone walk over me, least of all someone like Hera, who knows better than most what it feels like to have public opinion against you.

"Because one has nothing to do with the other," Hera says, casually, as if it's the most sense-making sentence ever spoken.

"Now, now, ladies," Rocco says. "Look, lunch is coming. I understand we're all a little *hangry*, what with all the hard work we've been doing. But salvation's on the way."

Our dishes are brought to the table and, as I glance at Hera, I can almost see the wave of relief that washes over her. If she thinks she's off the hook, she is, however, sorely mistaken. But I'll let her have a few bites of her lamb chops first.

"Delicious," Rocco says. "How's your salmon, Kat?"

"Good." My tone's clipped. Too clipped. I look at Hera, and how she hesitantly cuts off a chunk of lamb. I'm probably radiating combativeness. I need to defuse the situation. "I'm sorry, Hera," I say. "I was feeling a little under attack and my claws came out. It's a gut reaction."

Hera waves her fork in the air. "You and I may not agree on certain things, but we have the boy to consider." She nods at Rocco. "He's lived such a charmed life, let's not break the spell."

"Oh, great," Rocco says. "For the record, yes, I want you two to get along for my sake, but that doesn't mean you have to gang up on me and spout half-truths about me to do so."

"Make your choice already," Hera says. "I've told you many times. You can't have everything you want in life." I realize I actually haven't seen her smile yet, not the kind of genuine smile she draws her lips into right now. It lights up her face and transforms her into another person. Maybe that's who she was before Sam died. Or maybe that's the kind of person she is when she's not having lunch with former escorts.

"Tell me honestly, though, Hera." I put my cutlery down. "Would you really take on the job of remodeling my kitchen? Or were you just nodding your head to get rid of me?"

Hera inhales deeply. "Truth be told, I had no intention of actually taking on the job." That's all she says.

"*Had*?" I ask.

"I don't think I deserve the way you just spoke to me, but, then again, I don't think you deserve the way I've been speaking to you either. So let's call a truce and see where we go."

"That would be nice." I pick up my knife and fork again.

"Hallelujah. Praise the lord," Rocco says. "I've been thinking about your kitchen, Kat," he continues. "Shall I run a few ideas by you?"

"Let's see how the coffee shop looks first. Then we can talk again."

"Oh, you'll be dazzled, girl. It'll be so pretty; you'll want to spend every waking hour in the place." He quirks up his eyebrows.

"I'm very excited for you two," Hera says, "in case that wasn't clear. And very honored to have been able to help build your dream."

"Come in any time for that coffee on the house." I look Hera in the eye while I remember the only half-decent conversation we've had—those five minutes we spent chatting in the garden chairs in the corner of the Pink Bean.

"I will." This time, she aims her real smile at me, and something inside me shifts.

Chapter Twelve

HERA

"Have you thought more about what we discussed last time?" Jill asks, not beating about the bush.

"I always think about what we discuss. Isn't that the point?"

Jill sends me a smile followed by a gentle nod. "The job at your nephew's coffee shop is done?"

"Yep. As great as it was to work for him, I'm glad it's behind me."

Jill doesn't say anything. No surprise there.

"I'm very grateful that he asked me to do this. I missed work much more than I was willing to admit. It's great to be out there again."

Jill nods.

I wasn't going to discuss Katherine any more, yet I feel compelled to. "The three of us had lunch today and, um, some things were said." It's as though I can feel the pang of anguish that burst inside of me when Katherine spoke to me the way she did all over again. It took me by surprise so much; I didn't have the wherewithal to come up with a proper reply.

"Such as?" Jill asks.

"She basically accused me of being a bigot."

Jill draws up her eyebrows.

"I may have let a few things slip. It's hard not to…"

"When you feel such contempt for someone?" Jill leans forward and places her elbows on her knees, regarding me. I know this pose. I'd best be careful what I say next, although, judging from the pose, Jill has already figured me out. It sometimes irks me how she reads me so easily, and draws conclusions about me long before I can.

"Contempt?" I meet her gaze.

"That's how I understand it. Being accused of bigotry is usually the result of displaying contempt."

"I wouldn't go as far as calling it contempt."

"What's contempt other than lack of respect for another human being?" Jill's coming on a bit strong today. It's unlike her.

I narrow my eyes as I remember her words from the very beginning of our sessions together: we are not friends. Yet I ask, "Everything all right with you?"

"Of course." She leans back in her chair.

"If you say so."

"Don't deflect, Hera."

"I always believed it wasn't your place to judge and I just felt rather judged by you."

Jill nods and purses her lips. "That wasn't my intention. I apologize."

"Apology accepted." I've lost my train of thought and am not immediately sure how to continue.

Jill re-crosses her legs. "I've been thinking about last week's session as well."

"Have you?" In all the time I've been seeing Jill, it's the first time she's said something like that. I imagine she must think about her clients, but this is the first time she's put it like this.

"What you told me about Katherine piqued my curiosity so I did some research on lesbian escort agencies." Jill states this so matter-of-factly, as though it's something people research all the time. Maybe they do.

"Did you now." Despite my disgust for the profession, my curiosity is piqued as well.

"It's an intriguing subject," Jill says.

"Maybe. In a way."

"You're not curious at all about how it all works?"

"No." I shake my head for emphasis. "But I am curious about *your* curiosity."

"So you don't mind if I share some of my findings?"

"Of course not."

Jill clears her throat. "I came across an interview with the owner of a lesbian escort agency in England. In Manchester or somewhere like that. It was very enlightening." She pauses a moment before continuing. "I understand where the mind goes when you hear the word 'escort' and the associations it immediately conjures up. Exploitation. Illegality. Human trafficking. The unsavoriness of paying for something as intimate as sex. But that's not all it is. Especially not when it comes to escorts who only work with female clients."

"I can imagine that's the picture the madam of any brothel wants to paint," I deadpan.

"For some of the clients, it's the only intimacy they experience—the only form of intimacy they have access to."

"How can you even call it intimacy?" I ask.

"Because that's what it is, no matter the exchange of money. It's a service. Touch is so important. Imagine never being touched again."

"I can imagine it very well. In fact, it's my preference," I blurt out.

489

Jill nods. She probably has me exactly where she wants me again.

"You may think it's your preference, Hera, but the majority of people need this basic intimacy. Leave them unfulfilled for too long and people just wither away."

"I haven't been touched in quite some time and I'm doing just fine. No urges to call on the services of an escort agency just yet, thank you very much." I know I sound defensive, and this is the last place for me to be in defense mode, but Jill's pushing my buttons—and she knows it.

"So, you can look me in the eye and honestly tell me that you haven't imagined touching Katherine?"

My eyes go wide. "I'm really worried now, Jill. It sounds to me as though you're starting to lose your mind."

"I can assure you I'm completely sane." Her gaze on me is piercing.

"I admitted before that I think she's an attractive woman. Way too glossy for me though. Why is all that make-up required, anyway? Isn't that catering to the male gaze?"

"I vividly recall you telling me that Sam liked her lipstick and mascara."

"She did, but… that's different." My voice breaks a little. "That was Sam." Just like that, the void her death left me in envelops me again.

Jill doesn't say anything for a few minutes and nor do I for fear my voice will break even more.

"Could it be,"—Jill's voice is so soft, I can barely make it out over the hum of traffic outside—"that Katherine somehow reminds you of Sam?"

I shake my head with vigor. "God, no. Sam was an entirely different person than Katherine. For starters, she wasn't a prostitute!" My voice shoots up.

"I mean physically. The way she dressed and how she

liked to put on make-up, pretty herself up before you took her out on a date?" Jill insists.

"No," I repeat.

"Okay," Jill says. "But will you think about it? We can come back to this next week."

"I can usually guess where you're trying to go with something," I say, "but the direction of this conversation is leaving me completely stumped." I shake my head again. "Katherine has nothing to do with Sam. And Sam's dead."

"Will you see her again?" Jill asks. For a split second, I think she's referring to Sam and I'm ready to declare her mental—again. Then I realize she's talking about Katherine.

"At the opening of the Pink Bean. I thought about making an excuse not to go, but Rocco will never stand for that, so I guess I'll be going."

"I think it's good that you'll see her again," Jill says. "But let's move on, for now."

Chapter Thirteen

KAT

"This is it, K.Jo," Rocco says. He stands in between Chris and me and squeezes both our hands. I'm happy for him that he gets to share this with his partner. Not for the first time since I quit the agency, I feel a twinge of something, a sadness, at not having a significant other to share such a momentous occasion with. "We're about to open for business."

I glance around our coffee shop. One wall is made up out of a huge vintage shelf unit. Books fill the open spaces, easily accessible for our customers to peruse while they have their coffee. Plant baskets hang from the ceiling, adding a green touch.

I've been to Rocco and Chris's home often enough to know that Rocco has great interior design taste, but I'm blown away by the intimate atmosphere he's been able to create. I'm proud that he's my partner in this venture—and he'll have a way with the customers, for sure.

"Let's do it. Let's open that door, darling." He gives my hand another squeeze and kisses me on the cheek.

I head to the door and unlock it, then open it wide.

We've invited our friends and families for a first-day opening party. We've had a sign outside for the past week announcing it so we're hoping some people from the neighborhood will drop in as well.

Kristin has graciously lent us some of her staff from the Pink Bean in Darlinghurst, so Rocco and I can mingle instead of making coffee. Our real test will be tomorrow. Today, we celebrate.

I glance out the window and spot a familiar red truck parked in front of the shop. Hera's. Has she been waiting for the door to open? How eager. She looks to the side, out of the open car window and our eyes meet. I give her a smile. She's not dressed in her usual worse-for-wear T-shirt, but has donned a bright white shirt with a very stiff collar. From where I'm standing, it looks brand new, as though she bought it for the occasion.

She sends me a small smile back, then gets out of the car, a bunch of flowers in her hand.

"Hi." I'm not sure how I feel at seeing her again; all I know is that I feel something. Probably just nerves because she's the first person to arrive. "You're very punctual."

"Yeah." She shoves the flowers into my chest. "I figured it'd be best to get here before the crowd does."

"Thanks, Hera. These are lovely." I hold the flowers away from me to admire them.

"Congratulations," she says. Her mouth closes, then opens again, but no more words come out. She gives me a quick, rather cold pat on the shoulder, and heads inside to greet Rocco, who's squealing and jumping up and down in delight.

I walk to the back room where I put the flowers in some water. This is just the storage room, but even here Rocco has worked his magic and made the shelves look pretty by applying some funky wallpaper to them.

"It's all in the details, Kat," he said. "And if you can choose between having a smile on your face when you get something from the shelf or not, wouldn't you always opt for the smile?" He'd beamed a wide smile at me then.

When I come out of the storage room into the coffee shop, Hera's still the only one there. It's not even two o'clock yet—the official time we put on the invitation. I join Rocco, Chris and Hera.

"It's really gorgeous, Rocco," Hera says, and I can hear the pride in her voice.

"Can I get you a coffee?" I ask. "Or something stronger, to mark the occasion?" I smile at Hera. She looks different after she's gone all soft as a result of her nephew's accomplishments.

"A glass of champers for Auntie Hera, of course!" Rocco shouts. "I'll get it." He heads behind the counter, to the large fridge which, for the occasion, is stocked with bottles of bubbly. Chris follows him, leaving me alone with Hera.

"Are you on your next job?" I ask, to fill the silence.

She nods. "A remodel just a few blocks away from here, actually."

"Ah, will we be seeing you around for a few cups of black coffee then?"

"Maybe. If I forget my flask," she says matter-of-factly.

I can't help but chuckle. This is one of the happiest days of my life and just a minute ago, Hera herself was radiating happiness for Rocco, but a few moments alone with me seems to have returned her to her usual self—at least the self she has chosen to be when she is around me.

"What's so funny?" she asks.

"You really don't like me, do you?"

"It's nothing personal. Really," Hera says.

"That's a good one. Of course it's personal. It usually is when you don't like someone."

"Maybe you're used to everyone liking you all the time, but I'm not. It's not a big deal." Hera turns away from me a little.

"Maybe you can recommend someone else to renovate my kitchen then," I say, my tone a little menacing. I'm fine with not being liked by everyone—which only puts me at an even keel with the rest of the human population—but I'm not fine with Hera raining on my parade, today of all days.

"Sure."

Rocco and Chris return, each with two glasses of sparkling wine in their hands. They hand one to both me and Hera.

"To the Pink Bean," Rocco says.

"To the Pink Bean," I repeat, pride swelling inside me.

Hera and Chris join us in a toast. I decide to forget about Hera's negative vibes. This is my and Rocco's day. This is our dream, one that has come true well ahead of the vague planning we always entertained between us, sometimes more as a way to fill conversation than anything else. Then Jessica introduced me to Kristin and now here we are.

I check my watch. It's a few minutes past two and there's movement outside. A few people walk past the window. They're all women.

"The guys had better arrive soon before I wither away from too much estrogen around me," Rocco says.

Chris bursts out into a chuckle. Hera's face remains expressionless.

Kristin's the first to walk in. She has seen the place already, of course, but she still takes a moment to admire it— for the sake of her company.

Sheryl heads straight toward us and throws her arms wide. "Congratulations, Kat, it's so gorgeous."

While she hugs me, I take in the women who have walked in with her. "Caitlin and Jo are here."

"Yes, and be warned, Caitlin's on a mission," Sheryl says, as she lets go of me.

"What kind of mission?" I ask.

"You'll see." Sheryl winks at me and greets Rocco.

We are all introduced and I try to remember all the names—Micky, Robin, Amber, Martha—but more people walk in and soon all the names I've heard are a blur and our party's on.

———

"I know your gut reaction will probably be to give me an immediate no," Caitlin says. "But try to respond, not react." She beams a sly smile at me.

"She's been spending too much time with Amber," Josephine says. "Too much meditation isn't always a good thing." She kisses Caitlin on the cheek.

"What is it you're trying to lure me into?" I ask.

"I would be extremely honored if you'd be a guest on my show," Caitlin says. "I'm so sick and tired of interviewing 'famous' Australians. You, on the other hand, would make the most fascinating guest."

"Me?" I hold a hand to my chest.

"Don't be coy now, Kat. Of course you would be. You're so open and completely unapologetic about being an escort. The things you have to say would blow people's minds."

Caitlin was right. My first instinct is to give her a resounding no. "I'm flattered you would think so, but I'm also a very private person."

"I understand that." Caitlin's eyes sparkle. She has come here with her pitch prepared—and what better time to ask me than on such a merry occasion? "But the time is so right for this, Kat. I've been pushing and pushing for more radical feminist guests, and the shows have proven successful enough for me to keep on pushing. To me, you represent the epitome of feminism. I would love to get the chance to put that on display in front of a national television audience."

Jo jabs Caitlin in the arm. "I told her not to do this today," she says to me. "This is so not the time or the place."

"I'm not asking you to reply straight away. In fact, I don't want you to. I just wanted to broach the subject," Caitlin says. "So you could think about it."

"Darling." I see my friend Richard approach from the side.

"I'll leave you to the socializing now," Caitlin says. "I'll be in touch." She lightly pats my arm before turning away from me.

Richard draws me into a hug, then kisses me on the cheeks. In the far corner, I spot Liz. I wonder what she would say if Caitlin asked her for an interview. I make a mental note to speak to her in private as soon as I can.

Chapter Fourteen

HERA

"I THINK I'm going to leave," I say to Hilda.

"No, no, no," Hilda says. "I don't get to see enough of you. Besides, you've had too much bubbly. You need some more coffee before you can drive."

"I wasn't going to drive." I fish my phone out of my jeans pocket. "I was going to be very modern and get an Uber."

"I'll be damned. My sister in an Uber." She narrows her eyes. "I thought you'd feel right at home here, though, what with all the lesbians." She casts her gaze about the place. "Some of them are really hot." She bumps a shoulder into mine. "And earlier, in the restroom, I was queuing to wash my hands alongside Caitlin James." She gives a little shriek. "I just love her."

It figures that someone like Katherine would be friends with an ultra-feminist like Caitlin James, with all her talk about open relationships and sexuality. I hardly think she's a friend of Rocco's—he would have mentioned it if he was friends with the likes of Caitlin James.

"She's all right," I mumble.

"What's with the sourpuss attitude?" Hilda asks. "Ever

since I got here, you've been in a foul mood. Aren't you happy for Rocco?"

"Of course I am, Hilda. I know he's wanted this for such a long time. I even considered investing in his dream, but then, well, you know."

"You wish Sam were here to see this." Her voice is solemn.

I nod.

"I wish she were here too. She'd fit right in. She would have absolutely loved this."

I catch a glimpse of Katherine and think about what Jill asked me to consider. In our last session, I managed to avoid the subject of Katherine altogether, because I suffered one of those all too familiar falling-apart days—even though it had been months since the last one.

I picture Samantha next to me. Sometimes, when I'm alone in the house, it's as though I can still smell her. Out of nowhere, I catch a whiff of her favorite perfume, and it always knocks me for six.

"If you're taking an Uber anyway," Hilda says, "how about another glass of that champers. Not too bad for a coffee shop, I would say." She shoots me a big grin and goes in search of more. I don't even have the chance to decline. That's my sister's way with me. I've had more than fifty years to get used to it. It would feel off if she were to ask me gently if I wanted another glass of sparkling wine. Like just after Sam died, and she suddenly started speaking to me in a soft, deferential voice I didn't recognize. For a moment, I thought I had lost my sister as well as my partner.

I glance around the place. Rocco has done a great job with the interior. I get a feeling this place will be successful and I guess, for that, he also has Katherine to thank. There go my thoughts again, drifting to Katherine. Where is she now?

She seems to be fond of the color red—today she's wearing a bright red blouse. It makes her stand out. I don't even need to search for her in the crowd. She's talking to the woman who was here on the first day of my job. What was her name? Liz, I think. They're deep in conversation so I take the opportunity to watch them discreetly. Katherine shakes her head, then she tilts it and brings her fingers to her cheek, tapping just below her cheekbone in exactly the same way Sam used to do. Damn it. Maybe Jill was right.

I look away from Katherine and her friend and try to find Hilda. She has two glasses in her hands, but she has also managed to engage Caitlin James in conversation. I guess I'll have to be patient. This is one of the highlights of her day—maybe her life—so I won't interrupt her just because I'm thirsty. Besides, I'm old enough to procure my own drink.

I head to the counter and, without asking, a young woman offers me a glass. I eagerly accept it.

Before I have the chance to turn around, someone bumps rather clumsily against my hip.

"Alyssa, can I have another bottle please, darling?" I recognize Katherine's voice.

Alyssa nods and goes to fetch the bottle.

I glance to my side and it seems that Katherine only now notices how rudely she has bumped into me.

"Don't mind me." I turn the snark all the way up in my voice.

"Oh, sorry, Hera. I didn't hurt you, did I?" She looks me straight in the eye. There's not a hint of apology in her glance nor in her voice. In fact, her eyes are a little glazed over.

"Of course not," I reply.

"I can tell you're rather tough." She glances at my hips, as though that's where the evidence of my toughness can be found. She looks back up and locks her gaze on my drink.

"I'm glad you're letting your hair down a bit, Hera. We all need to have some fun." She smiles now—a smile I don't know what to do with.

Luckily, Alyssa returns and hands an open bottle of sparkling wine to Katherine. "You don't need a top-up?" she asks.

"No, thanks."

"Talk to you later," Katherine says and *sashays away*—an expression I've learned from Rocco.

I stand by the counter a while longer, waiting for Hilda to return and tell me all about her conversation with Caitlin James. I regret that I was so cold with Katherine when I first arrived. Tonight, on this happy occasion, for the first time, I can see her for who she really is—just a woman living her life. And experiencing great pleasure from doing so. Even though she has disappeared into the crowd in front of me, I swear I can hear her laugh bubbling up over the noise.

I could do with some of that pleasure, I conclude. It's been too long.

Chapter Fifteen

KAT

It's the first operating weekday of our Pink Bean and Kristin has just left. Rocco's wiping the spout of the milk frother for the umpteenth time today. It seems to be his nervous tic. According to Kristin, we've sold a decent number of coffees for a first morning. Now that she's left, and it's just me and Rocco in the shop, it feels like our very first minutes of complete independence.

"It's strange," I say to Rocco. "All this time we've dreamed of this, and now here we are, and I don't really know what to do with myself."

"Why do you think I've been keeping that machine squeaky clean?" he says.

"It's just nerves, isn't it?"

"How about a nice cappuccino to help you with those?" Rocco grins at me.

"I wish we were still serving bubbly," I joke.

"That was quite a party."

Someone walks by the window and we both stiffen. We're not used to this yet. I consider both Rocco and myself very good with people, but it doesn't feel natural yet to have people walk into our coffee shop. We're still adjusting to the new reality of our lives. This morning, apart from being exhilarated, I was so nervous, I thought I might say yes if Alana called me again. But she has stopped calling now.

A man walks in and Rocco and I paint on big smiles.

"Hi there," Rocco says. Somehow, even on this very first morning, it has become the natural order of things for him to greet the male customers.

I try to make myself look useful by grabbing a cloth and wiping the tables I've already wiped a dozen times. Everything's in order. Everything's set up so that we can serve customers easily and swiftly. Now all we need are the customers.

Rocco and the man continue their chat. I sit at a table in the corner and, out of habit, pull my phone out of my pocket. I notice I've received a message. It's from Caitlin asking me not to forget about her proposal.

I haven't forgotten. In fact, I've had quite some time to think about it, but no matter how I twist and turn her offer of being a guest on *The Caitlin James Show*, I can't conclude that it's my task to convince the nation that sex work has its virtues.

Another person walks by the window, drawing my attention. A familiar figure. Tall and broad-shouldered. Short hair. Faded black T-shirt. Hera. I can hardly believe it. Maybe she has forgotten her flask again.

She walks in and Rocco's face lights up. I'd best go say hi. I never thought she'd actually show up.

It takes me back to the very first time she came here, when all the work still had to be done—and I was oblivious to the fact she had already made up her mind about me being a lesser person than her.

"Hi." I send Hera a smile nonetheless. "Long black?"

"Katherine," Hera says, as though stating a fact instead

of my name. A fact she has no choice but to accept. Then, out of nowhere, she returns my smile. "I would love a cup of coffee."

"You're in luck," Rocco says. "We happen to be in the coffee business."

"I'll get it," I say.

"No, no, no," Rocco tuts. "Auntie Hera's first official coffee in the Bondi Pink Bean will be prepared by her favorite person in Sydney, perhaps even on this planet." He flashes a smile and turns around to make it, leaving me to chit-chat with Hera. At least she has given me a smile to work with.

"How's the——" I start, at the same time as she starts to say something.

"You first," Hera says, accompanying her words by opening her palm.

"Just wondering how the new job's going."

"Fine. It'll take a few weeks, so you might see more of me."

Is that another smile? Has Rocco's aunt had a personality transplant? She has been friendlier to me in the last few minutes than all the times I ran into her while she was working here.

"Here you go." Rocco plants a big mug on the counter. "That should keep you going for a while."

The guy who came in earlier heads back to the counter.

"That one's mine as well," Rocco whispers, then paints on his widest grin.

"He's having the time of his life." Hera's gaze softens.

"It's all still so new and exciting." I glance over at Rocco as he chats with the customer.

"How are you adjusting?" Hera asks, surprising me again.

I gaze at her from under my lashes. She did apologize

after that little spat we had at the restaurant, but this is something else altogether. Instead of judging me, she's treating me like an acquaintance she's actually fond of.

"Very well, although I'm still not used to getting up so early."

"Nothing as gorgeous as the crack of dawn." Hera looks at me over the rim of her mug, making eye-contact.

Her eyes are light brown and her glasses have slipped off the bridge of her nose again. It can't be comfortable to wear them while tearing down walls.

"I still need to be convinced of that." I return her gaze. "Once we're truly up and running, I may let Rocco do the morning shift."

Hera looks behind her for an instant. Rocco's still chattering away.

"I wanted to say sorry again for, well, you know." She puts her mug down and looks me straight in the eye again. "For being such a bigot. You were absolutely right. I have no business judging you." Her voice is crisp, her words crystal clear.

I tilt my head. "Why the sudden change of heart?"

A blush blooms on Hera's cheeks. She shuffles a bit and reaches for her coffee mug again. Her mouth briefly opens but she doesn't say anything.

"Apology accepted," I say. As much as I'd love to make her squirm some more, it's important for me to acknowledge her message. Without thinking, I place my hand on her arm. It's what I do. I trade in touch—a habit that's hard to break. Her biceps are hard against my palm.

Hera drains her cup. "I have to get back to the job." She seems to suddenly have lost the ability to meet my gaze. "Tell Rocco I'm expecting him for dinner tonight no later than seven."

"Sure." I watch Hera swagger off. There's nothing feminine about her gait. Her long-legged strides are all about function, about getting from one place to the next without fancy.

I'm happy she apologized, but I can't shake the impression there are other things left unsaid between us. I hope she stops by again soon.

Chapter Sixteen

HERA

"Caitlin James asked Kat to be on her show," Rocco says. "In fact, she's as good as stalking her."

"She'd make a good guest," Hilda says, "with the life she's lived."

They both look at me as though it's vital I contribute to this conversation.

"Are you sure you want your business partner to go on national TV and announce that she was an escort for a decade? It can't possibly be good for business," I say.

Rocco leans back as though he hadn't yet considered this. He glares at me.

Maybe I've read him wrong.

"Why did you even apologize to Kat if this is still how you feel about her?" Rocco asks, waving his fork around.

"Apologized for what?" Hilda asks.

"Auntie Hera could not deal. She could not deal *at all*." Rocco says it with all the theatrics of an opera singer.

"It is a little unusual that she was a sex worker," Hilda says. She winks at Rocco. "And not everyone's as open-minded as your mother."

"Which is exactly why Kat should do the interview," Rocco says. "How will public opinion ever change if no one ever talks about it?" He shrugs. "Anyway, she doesn't want to do it… yet."

"Why not?" I inquire.

Rocco scrunches up his lips. "She doesn't feel it's her job to be the spokesperson for a profession she's left." He taps a finger against the stubble on his chin. "And, actually, she may also be protecting the Pink Bean. Although, as far as I know, Kristin didn't seem to have a problem with it at all."

"If she doesn't want to do it, she doesn't want to do it." I put down my fork. "Not everyone's after their fifteen minutes of fame." I quite admire Katherine for wanting to keep a low profile—or is that my bigotry speaking again? It's hard to tell the difference, even for me.

"You tell Caitlin James," Hilda says, "that if she's after an interview with the average woman in the street, she can call me."

"Mother, how dare you," Rocco exclaims. "You are by no means average with me as your son."

We all burst out laughing and the topic of Katherine being a guest on Caitlin James' show is forgotten, although, throughout the rest of the evening my mind keeps drifting to Katherine. To how she looked at me so quizzically this morning after I apologized. As though she was onto something I have no clue of yet myself.

———

The next day I find myself at the Pink Bean again, even though I've not forgotten my flask. When I walk in, there are two people ahead of me and I have time to study Katherine as she interacts with the customers. Her long chestnut hair is tied up in a ponytail and my gaze is drawn to her fingers.

Her customary nail polish is a different shade of red than at the opening party, but red nonetheless. I guess I already know what her favorite color is.

Rocco comes bounding through the back door. He waves at me as soon as he sees me and motions for me to bypass the queue. I shake my head.

"Hello." Katherine flashes me a big smile when it's my turn. "Always lovely to see returning customers. Same as usual?"

I nod. My conviction, that it's ridiculous to pay twice as much for a cup of coffee as what it would cost me to brew an entire flask at home, has been dwarfed by my desire to help my nephew. Or so I like to tell myself.

"Coming right up." As Katherine turns around to prepare my coffee, Rocco hands me a mug already.

"I know how she likes it. Why else would Auntie Hera be back already?" He sends me a big fat wink.

I put the mug down—the coffee is, indeed, delicious— and deposit five dollars on the counter. None of that payWave contactless credit card use for me.

"A promise is a promise," Katherine says, and slides the coins back in my direction.

"I know you're good on your promise, but it makes me feel uncomfortable not to pay." I pick up the coins and hand them back to her.

"You built this place, Hera." Katherine doesn't take the money.

"And you paid me for my efforts. That's how the world works." I look her in the eye. There's a sparkle in her gaze that makes me think she's enjoying this tiny standoff between us.

"Take the money already, Kat," Rocco whispers. "It's not as if Auntie Hera spends her fortune on clothes or anything fancy like that."

I chuckle and refocus my gaze on Katherine. "He's absolutely right."

"Fine." Katherine sighs. "But you get a free refill." She grins at me. Although I'm relieved she's giving in, I'd like to stand face-to-face with her and haggle over something insignificant a little longer.

"If you insist," I say.

"I do." Her red-painted lips widen into a warm smile.

"Thanks." I deposit the money in her palm, take my coffee, and find a spot to sit in the corner.

While I enjoy my beverage, my glance is pulled back to the counter again and again, and I ask myself when I started being unable to keep my eyes off Katherine.

A few minutes later, she stops by my table. "Ready for that refill?" She has her hands on her hips.

"I really ought to get back to work."

She plants her hand on the back of the chair opposite me. "Do you mind if I sit for a moment?"

"Of course not."

She glances directly at me and, before saying anything, sucks her bottom lip between her teeth. The sight of it moves something inside me, in a spot where nothing much has moved in years.

"Would you consider it terribly untoward if I asked you to dinner? At my place." She cocks her head. "You know, so you can have a look at my kitchen. Tell me what you think."

I burst into a chuckle while a sensation I can't identify courses through me. "I don't think it would be untoward at all. It would be work."

"Are you free this weekend? Say, Sunday?"

I nod. I'm usually free.

"Any food allergies I should take into consideration?"

"Nope. I'm old school like that."

This elicits another smile from Katherine. "I figured you

would be." She rises. "It's a date then. I'll text you the time and address."

I watch her walk off, all sass and delicious curves. Only then does it hit me what she just said. It's a *date*.

For me, it will just be work.

Chapter Seventeen

KAT

"*You* could do it," I say to Liz. "If you think it's so important. You look like a model and a movie star rolled into one."

"I wasn't asked," Liz says matter-of-factly.

"I wonder why that is." I scan Liz's face. "Jessica's no longer Caitlin's boss, so it can't be that."

"Jess's father still is, though, so let's not pretend it doesn't have anything to do with that." Liz draws up her eyebrows.

"So I'm the next best thing."

Liz shakes her head. "I think Caitlin has a bit of a soft spot for you."

An involuntary smile quirks up my lips. "I bet she does." I remember that night we shared fondly. "So tell me this. Will Caitlin James allow me to divulge the details of her own escapades with a call girl on her show?"

"Good point." Liz pulls up her shoulders. "I have no idea."

"You're just the messenger." I plant my elbows on the table.

Liz shakes her head. "No, I just stopped by for a coffee with my friend, really." She flashes me one of her winning smiles. "I honestly don't think Caitlin would have a problem talking about her own experiences. She does that all the time these days. And wouldn't you agree that hers is a voice that needs to be heard?"

"I do agree with that, but we should all be careful not to throw oil on the flame of the far-right, ultra-conservative populist discourse."

Liz makes a throw-away gesture with her hand. "Oh, please. Those people have long ago made up their minds about us." She leans over the table. "Look, I get it, Kat. It's a matter of privacy."

"Not just for me. I went on very public dates with women. What if their friends, or worse, their enemies, see me talking about being an escort on TV and put two and two together?"

"Fair point."

"Surely Caitlin must have thought about all these things. She's as sharp as they come."

"She's getting more and more radical, I guess."

"Just tell her no again from me when you see her." I shuffle in my seat. "Can we talk about something else now?"

"Sure." Liz eyes me quizzically. "Not tired of the coffee business already, are you? You can say what you want about being a high-end call girl, but the hours are pretty good." She waggles her eyebrows.

I pause. I'm not even sure I want to bring this up. But I can't really talk about it with Rocco. "What are your thoughts on Hera?"

"The bigoted builder?" Liz asks.

I chuckle and nod.

"Why do you ask?"

"I'd like her to remodel my kitchen."

"And?" Liz inclines her head.

"So I asked her to dinner at mine. Tomorrow."

"Because you want her to remodel your kitchen?"

"Is that so strange?"

"Nope." Liz shakes her head. "It's crystal clear to me. You have the hots for the bigoted builder."

I snort out a nervous laugh. Do I? I guess I can kid myself all I want, but I wouldn't have asked Hera to dinner if I wasn't at least a tiny bit attracted to her.

"She did apologize. Twice."

"We should do a double date. Jess can tell her all the ins and outs of dating a call girl."

"Let's not get ahead of ourselves. So far, she's been quite reluctant to even refit my kitchen."

"But she has agreed to come to dinner?"

"She has." I straighten my back. "And I have the tiniest of hunches that she kind of likes me back." An involuntary smile spreads over my lips.

"There's no underestimating a hooker's instinct. Speaking of. Is Alana still on your case?"

I shake my head. "She has given up all hope."

Liz glances around the coffee shop. "You have this now."

"I know. You know what's weird though? Free time in the evenings. Half the time, I have no clue what to do with myself."

"I know something you can do next Thursday." She reaches into her bag and hands me an invitation to an opening night at the Griffith-Porter gallery. "Bring the bigoted builder, if you like."

"Can we stop referring to Hera like that as of now, please?" I study the invitation. "Alyssa Myles. Is that the Pink Bean's Alyssa?"

"The one and only." Liz taps a fingertip on the table. "She's very talented. You should see her stuff. It's going to blow your mind."

"Really?" I study the invitation in more detail.

"It just goes to show, Kat. Most of us have hidden talents." She sends me a wink. "I mean, who knew you could make your own coffee?"

"I'd be delighted to attend." I ignore Liz's remark.

"Caitlin will be there, though, so beware."

"It'll give me a chance to tell her no once and for all." I put the invitation down. "Tell me, Lizzie…" I don't really know how to ask this, but Liz is the only one I can ask. "What's it like being in a long-term relationship after retiring from the job?"

"It has its challenges," Liz says in a serious tone before breaking out into a huge smile. "But more than that, it's simply wonderful."

"Jess is a wonderful woman."

"She sure is. Now *you* tell me something, Katherine Jones… Might you be on the prowl?"

"I might very well be." I smile at Liz. I want what she has with Jess. It seemed so unlikely when they first met, yet look at them now.

Chapter Eighteen

HERA

I GLANCE at myself in the mirror and run my hand over my hair. I trimmed the edges and I find myself worrying over something I usually never worry about—my hair looks a little uneven on the sides. Sam used to do this for me. She'd take the clippers in her steady hand and make me look as good as new again.

There's a picture of us on the mantle next to the bedroom mirror. It shows us in our thirties, brimming with health and as careless as we could be. Sam wasn't supposed to die four days after her fiftieth birthday. She sure as hell wasn't supposed to die without giving me the chance to say goodbye.

"What do you think, babe?" I ask her picture. "Can I go out with hair like this?"

I try to imagine what she would say but the situation makes it hard. In my gut, I know this isn't just me having a look at someone's kitchen for a possible remodel job. If that were the case, I wouldn't even have combed my hair. I wouldn't be standing in front of the mirror stressing out about something that can only be noticed if examined closely.

"It's just a job," Sam might say. And if she were still alive, then it would just be that. But now that she's been dead for more than a year, it's something else.

I turn around, facing away from the mirror and the picture of Sam and me. Jill's going to have a field day when I tell her about this next Wednesday. I can already predict her questions. I push those thoughts from my mind as well and walk to the closet. I guess a T-shirt is out of the question. Or is it? I'm not one for great sartorial debates but I realize that what I wear will send a message. If I turn up at Katherine's in one of my work T-shirts—freshly washed because it's a Sunday after all—it will tell her that this is nothing more than a work appointment. But most potential clients don't cook me dinner so I should at least make some effort to reciprocate the gesture. And then there's the small matter of what I want to project.

I've warmed to her since we first met and I can almost be myself around her without constant images of her... of her what? How does it even work when you're an escort? Maybe I should ask her tonight. But no, best steer clear of that inflammatory topic. She's Rocco's friend and business partner and she and I might become friends, but never anything more than that. That's probably the most important message to send. I accept who she is, but we can never have anything between us. Not only because she used to be a call girl, but because Sam's sudden death plunged me into such a pit of despair. I'd rather be alone for the rest of my life than experience the loss of a partner again.

That's decided then. I reach for a navy-blue V-neck T-shirt and pull it over my head. That should convey the message.

When I ring the doorbell at Katherine's, I wish I'd worn a shirt. But at least I've brought a bottle of good wine. While I wait, I run my finger over the nick in my hair. I hear the lock being turned and hope she won't be all dolled up—although all dolled up seems to be Katherine's default mode.

As soon as the door opens, she sends me a wide smile.

"Hi," she says, and ushers me inside. She briefly puts a hand on my shoulder and I'm happy she doesn't kiss me hello. That would be very un-work-like. Maybe we have the exact same idea about tonight. I hand her the wine while I force myself to relax a little. Then I glance around.

Katherine's apartment is gigantic even though it's just on the outskirts of Bondi on the right side to get to the city center. It must be worth a small fortune.

"Crikey." I stifle a remark about how the escort business must be very profitable. I don't want to start off the night that way. And of course it's profitable. Why else would a woman like Katherine bother? "Nice place."

"Thanks." Katherine briefly glances at the label on the wine bottle, then puts it on the table. "Do make yourself comfortable." She points at the largest sectional sofa I've ever seen and a thought pops into my head. Did she use to 'entertain' here? Did unspeakable acts happen on the very sofa she's pointing at? Surely there must be some sort of protocol —and a smart woman like Katherine wouldn't jeopardize her privacy like that.

"Shall I have a look at the kitchen first?" I ask.

Katherine cocks her head. "It's a bit of a mess at the moment. I promise you that I can actually cook, but I tend to make a right mess when doing so. I'm a bit like Nigella that way, except that I have to clean it up myself." Her eyes light up as she smiles.

"Is it going to be less of a mess at any point during the evening?" I ask.

She quirks up one corner of her mouth. "I'm afraid it will only get worse."

"Then I'd best have a look now, don't you think?"

She nods and I follow her to the kitchen. I take the opportunity to eye her from behind. She's dressed in some sort of red jumpsuit that flows around her body as she walks.

"It does look like a bomb went off in here," I say when I enter the kitchen.

"What can I say?" Katherine puts her hands on her hips the way I've seen her do a few times. "I'm a messy cook. It's my style."

I glance around the kitchen, trying to ignore the chaos of dirty pots and pans. The cabinets and work surfaces look almost new, no scuffs or scratches visible anywhere. And the appliances are all top-of-the-range as far as I can see.

"I'm not really sure why you asked me here. This kitchen doesn't need to be refitted."

"Maybe it doesn't need to be, but I *want* it done. Would that be okay with you, Hera?" She narrows her eyes.

"How old are your appliances?"

"We can keep the appliances; I just want a different feel. All this marble is so cold. I want it to be warmer, more inviting, I guess."

"You should have asked Rocco to re-design it for you then."

"I will. After all, he's made the Pink Bean look very special. But first I wanted to ask you whether what I have in mind is possible."

She proceeds to explain that she wants the cooker on the other side, by the window, and the breakfast bar removed altogether.

I've been in this business long enough to know that it's

people like Katherine, with their surplus funds and permanent need to change their interiors, who bring in the most money. During my career, I've torn down houses that were in ship-shape condition just because the owner had a recurring dream about it being totally different.

"Everything's possible, of course. But it's going to be a two-person job. I can't get rid of all this marble on my own. And I'm certainly not going to smash it to speed things up. It's too beautiful for that."

"You want to recycle my marble?" Katherine asks, hands on hips.

"I most certainly do." For a split second, I'm not sure it's actually the marble of her kitchen we're talking about. I feel a bit light-headed—I need some food in me.

"Fair enough." Katherine steps closer. "Does that mean you'll take the job?"

"Why don't you send me some pictures tomorrow, when all this mess has been cleared, and I'll have another think about it?" I lock my gaze on hers.

"You're a hard woman to get a straight yes out of, do you know that?"

"I simply don't want to make any promises I can't keep."

Katherine nods. Did she just give me a once-over? I wonder what she makes of my T-shirt. If she thinks anything of it at all, even after raking her gaze from the crown of my head to the tips of my toes, she doesn't let on. She does the mysterious sphinx smile well.

"Can I pour you some wine now?"

"Please do," I say and follow her back into the living room.

Chapter Nineteen

KAT

I WANTED this to be a date and so it feels like a date, although Hera certainly didn't dress the part. She looks every inch the builder I met at the Pink Bean a few weeks ago. A woman who is here to assess my kitchen first, and eat my food second. Most likely a woman for whom getting to know me better is the least of her priorities. It looks like I will have to deploy all the tricks in my charm toolbox tonight.

As I pour us each a glass of wine, I remind myself that this is not a paid-for appointment. This is my home and I've invited Hera for a meal because I'm so intrigued by her—although that may just be code for finding her butch and rather blunt ways a challenge as well as quite a turn-on.

"I'm glad you came," I say after I've sat down next to her, angling my body toward her. I send her a wide smile that, again, makes me feel self-conscious. I haven't been on a proper date for far too long—if tonight is even that.

"Just a heads-up," Hera says. "I have an early start tomorrow."

I can't help but burst into a chuckle. "No problem.

Dinner will be served pronto." I take a drink from the wine she brought. It's a good choice.

Hera looks into her glass, then up at me for a fraction of a second, before her glance skitters away again. "I'm… quite direct in my ways and I wouldn't want you to get the wrong idea about me."

"What idea would that be?"

"I don't know what Rocco has told you about me, but I'm not… looking for anything just because I'm single."

"Wow. You really are quite direct." I hear Hera's words but I have trouble believing them fully. Next to me sits a woman with her guard fully up, no doubt about that, but there's something else going on. Something even someone as direct as Hera can't put into words.

"I wouldn't want there to be any misunderstandings between us." Hera drinks again.

"Great way to kill the flirty vibe I was trying to nurture here." I tilt my head. "And I haven't even served you my wooing dish yet."

Hera chuckles. "You have certainly succeeded in making me very curious about it now." She holds out her glass of wine. "Friends?" she asks.

I bring my glass to hers. "A small miracle in its own right," I joke.

Hera doesn't say anything, so I decide I can play it naughty for a little longer.

"Is that why you're here then?" I ask. "To atone for your initial bigotry?"

Hera swallows hard. "And I thought *I* was direct."

"Two can play that game." I draw up my knee and it almost touches her hip.

"I've apologized for that so I thought that was behind us."

"Is it really, though?" I ask even though it's a futile question. It's a question Hera doesn't even need to answer because I can read her reply in her body.

"If it's not, then I would certainly like to put it behind us once and for all," she says.

"Does that mean you don't want to talk about it anymore or that you've fully accepted my past as a call girl?" I wouldn't have needled her so much if she hadn't tried to thwart my intentions from the get-go. What else am I going to do throughout this evening?

"It's not something for me to fully accept. In fact, it's not really any of my business."

"Would it help you if we did talk about it? If you knew more about it instead of getting hung up on all the images in your head? Most of which are, I dare suspect, based on false beliefs."

"Oh, so you can read my mind now? Very impressive." Hera shuffles in her seat and when she sits still again her hip is a few inches farther removed from my pulled-up knee.

"You're the one who toasted to us being friends earlier. I'd say, so far, the beginning of our friendship is rather shaky. I also have no intention of befriending someone who's always judging me."

Hera shakes her head. "I'm not judging you, Katherine. I'm here, aren't I? All the things you're saying to me, that you're projecting onto me, they're all in your head." She pauses but doesn't give me a chance to reply. "Yes, I was a bigot and judged you on what you used to do instead of how you were with me, which was always very pleasant. As I said before, and *meant*, I apologize for that. So why the need to drag it up again? Seems to me that you're the one who has a problem with it. Not me."

I have to put my glass down because my hand has started shaking too much. I can't remember when I last got a dressing-down like this. The hardest fact for me to grasp is that

Hera is probably right. I'm the one with the chip on my shoulder tonight.

"Okay." I rise from the sofa. "Do you mind if I take a minute before I reply? Meanwhile, I'll get dinner ready."

Hera looks up at me, her gaze not flinching this time. "Take all the time you need. I'm not going anywhere."

———

"It has been harder than I thought," I say, after we've sat down for our meal. "I've always been so headstrong about my profession and I've always been able to defend my choice but, now that I've quit, there seems to be this... I'm not sure how to articulate it. A vacuum of sorts. Like I'm no longer the person I used to be. And I still get very defensive when anyone tries to slag me off, or even hints at it."

"I, um, talked about you with my therapist," Hera says.

I nearly drop my fork. Not only at Hera's candid admission that she has discussed me with another person, but that she's in therapy. "Really?" I quickly compose myself.

"Sam and I were going through a bit of a rough spot when I started therapy. Anyway, that has nothing to do with what I'm trying to say." She waves her fork about. "Jill, my therapist, said some things about your profession that made me think. Obviously, it's very hard for me to imagine how you must feel, but I can definitely empathize with you feeling like you've lost the identity you've been clinging to for a big part of your life."

Warmth blooms in my chest. "She must be really good. Your therapist."

Hera nods almost reverently. "She's helped me a lot. Especially after Sam passed away so suddenly. But also before, when she made me realize that every single one of us is always busy reinventing ourselves and that going through a rough patch comes with the territory of change."

"You're a very wise builder, Hera." I grin at her. "You should put some of your words of wisdom on tiles like they used to do, and put them up in people's houses."

"I can do one for your kitchen, if you like." She grins at me.

"I think I'd like that very much." Hera can say what she wants about not being interested in anything romantic. Or maybe she's the kind who doesn't realize she's flirting.

"I'll have to consult Jill and see what I can come up with. No extra charge." She gazes into my eyes ever so briefly then redirects her attention to her plate. "This lamb is delicious, by the way."

"I'm glad you like it." I decide to seize the moment. "Are you interested in art at all?" I ask.

"Not hugely," Hera says matter-of-factly.

"Alyssa, the woman who was working at the Pink Bean opening, has a show in Liz and Jess's gallery. It opens on Thursday night and I've been invited. I was wondering if you'd like to, perhaps, join me?" My insides coil into a tight ball. I feel like I may have overplayed my hand—if I had a hand at all.

"Is Rocco going?" Hera asks.

I purse my lips. "I'm not sure. Liz invited me."

"Why don't you take him instead of me? I think he would appreciate it more. Art openings are really not my scene."

"What is your scene, if I may ask?"

"I don't have much of one, I guess. I prefer a simple, quiet life."

"Liz told me Alyssa is 'mind-blowingly' talented. Are you sure you want to miss that?" I quirk up an eyebrow in anticipation of her response.

"Please don't see this as a rejection, but when I come home from work, I'm usually knackered. I love what I do, but I haven't done heavy labor in quite some time and I turned fifty last year. What time does it even start?"

"Seven-ish, I guess." She's giving me an opening. "I can check right now. The invite's in the kitchen."

"If you can guarantee I'll be in bed by ten, I might be swayed."

"I hereby solemnly swear you'll be tucked in at nine fifty-nine. I'll drive you home myself."

"You're going to drive me?" Hera's voice drips with disbelief. "Do you mean you won't drink anything at all?"

"If I'm driving you, then that will be the case."

"How about I drive *you*?" She tilts her head. "That suits me more."

"Are you doubting my driving skills?"

"I doubt everyone's driving skills."

"Except your own?"

"I have nothing to doubt about my own." Hera's lips curve into a smile. If this isn't flirting, I surely must have lost the hang of it years ago.

"Come on, Hera. I'll pick you up and drive you home. Give me a chance to at least prove that I can negotiate a car through Sydney traffic."

"All of that so I will redo your kitchen?"

"And perhaps give me the number of your therapist." I reflect Hera's smile right back at her.

"I'll never give it to you. It would be a conflict of interest."

"Why?" I put my cutlery down because I'm done with my lamb—the evening has taken that kind of turn.

"Because I'm already seeing her."

"And that means none of your friends are allowed to see her?" I straighten my back.

"I think so. There must be some sort of code."

I shake my head. "I'm sure there's a code of ethics, but I'm also pretty sure there would be no mention of friends seeing the same therapist. How could there ever be enough of them if not?"

Hera leans back. "It would make me feel uncomfortable, I guess."

I pause. Hera has polished off most of her dish. "I have to respect that, then."

"I can ask Jill for a recommendation."

I nod while I sink my teeth into my bottom lip. "So, can I pick you up on Thursday then?"

Hera doesn't say anything, just nods her confirmation.

I refill our wine glasses—she hasn't said anything about driving herself home tonight so she must trust certain taxi drivers' abilities—and hold mine up to her the way she did at the beginning of the evening. "Friends," I repeat her words, although, to me, at this stage of the night, they have a very different meaning.

"Friends," Hera says, and clinks the rim of her glass against mine. "The kind you see on those silly TV shows, you know, who go to art galleries together." Out of nowhere, she sends me a wink that, if I hadn't been seated, would knock me to my knees.

Chapter Twenty

HERA

JILL SITS there with a slight smile. I haven't even said anything apart from hello. I'm still not sure why I mentioned her to Katherine, why I divulged that particular piece of very private information about myself. I know very well that these days it's almost trendy to discuss one's mental health issues—like a badge of honor—but I'm not in the habit of discussing this part of my life.

"I'm waiting for you to start," Jill says. "I sense you may have a thing or two to talk about. Something exciting."

I shake my head. When I saw my sister yesterday, a woman I've known my entire life, she didn't bat an eyelid. She just chattered away like always, not noticing anything different about my demeanor. Or maybe I've gotten too used to hiding my inner life from her.

Jill picks up on the slightest change in me instantly, though, and it's a comforting as well as disturbing thought.

I'm not one to launch straight into a conversation about my feelings, however. I need my engine to rev up, my lips to form a few unrevealing words first. "It's been an interesting week."

Jill nods and gives me time to continue. Her office is not a place for verbal fireworks—which is probably one of the reasons I've kept on coming here for so long.

"I've, um, agreed to work on Katherine's kitchen."

"That does sound interesting." Jill narrows her eyes.

"I still have a while to go on my current job, though, but…" My engine seems all revved up already. I haven't been to the Pink Bean all week, even though I really wanted to go. But Katherine must have told Rocco about asking me to the art gallery tomorrow and I know what Rocco's like. I couldn't face his inquisitive looks, not quite yet. "I went to her home. She invited me to dinner and then…" I pause to collect myself, as though I still have trouble believing any of this myself. "She asked me to this art thing tomorrow night, even though I made it very clear I'm not looking for, well, you know, anything like that. Anything she might be offering." I'm slightly out of breath after pushing all these words from my mouth too quickly.

"And what do you think she might be offering?" Jill asks.

"For some reason I fail to understand, I think she might be… interested in me."

"And you're not interested in her?" There's that smile again, more defiant this time. As though she already knows the very thing about me that I'm not willing to acknowledge myself.

"I like her and I think I made it clear we can be friends, but no, I'm not really interested in anyone. I can't be."

"Even though you clearly *are* very interested in her." Jill draws up her eyebrows.

"As a friend. Yes. I mean it was nice to be in her company. She's very easy to talk to." And easy to look at, I add in my head.

"As a friend," Jill repeats my words.

"I know what you're thinking." I may as well call her

bluff. "Just like you always assume you know what I'm thinking." The smile I send her isn't half as assured as the one she keeps shooting in my direction. "Yes, I like her. I admit it, but I certainly did my best to not give her the wrong idea about me. You know that I'm not up to a relationship, and that's regardless of the fact that Katherine used to be a call girl."

"Let me ask you this then." Jill rests her elbows on her knees. "Do you think you deserve credit for wanting to be friends with her?"

I chuckle and shake my head. "Of course not."

"Since you just very boldly claimed to know what I'm thinking, do you mind if I tell you what I am actually thinking? Or would you like to tell me first?" Her smile has softened.

"Go ahead."

"You're different today from any time I've ever seen you in all the years you've been coming here. There's a lightness to you that you just can't hide, no matter how much you'd like to."

"I haven't made a new friend in a while," I say matter-of-factly but, as I say it, it's as though I can feel the lightness Jill just talked about glowing inside me.

Jill nods. "Tell me about the art gallery thing then." Jill points at the abstract painting—that comforting blob of color—on the wall behind her. "I'm quite interested in all things art."

"Katherine's friend Liz and her partner Jessica own an art gallery somewhere in Potts Point. They're showing art by one of the baristas who works in the Pink Bean coffee shop in Darlinghurst."

"Would this be the Griffith-Porter gallery?" Jill sits up a little straighter.

"I think so, yes."

"I go to all their openings. I love the work they exhibit.

It's always right up my alley and surprisingly affordable, considering Jessica's pedigree."

Jill has lost me and… did she just infer that she might be going to the same event? "Do you mean you'll be there tomorrow?"

"I had planned to go, barring any emergencies. I usually don't work on Thursday evenings."

I shuffle nervously in my seat.

"Does that make you uncomfortable?" Jill asks.

I purse my lips. "I think it's logical that it would. I'll be there with Katherine and I'd feel… watched."

"Sydney is a big city, but that doesn't mean I don't sometimes run into clients in social situations. Don't worry about it. I'm very discreet."

"I actually told Katherine about you."

Jill draws her eyebrows all the way up. "You did?"

"It came up in conversation."

"You must really like her then."

"Actually… I was meant to ask you for a recommendation. I think Katherine might be looking for a therapist."

"And you didn't feel comfortable referring her to me?" She nods. "I get that." She pauses. "I'll email you some names."

"Thanks." Now that I know Jill will be there tomorrow, my gut instinct is to cancel the whole ordeal. I have no interest in over-priced paintings and ninety-nine percent of the art I've ever seen has confounded me more than garnered any of my genuine attention.

"Please don't cancel your date with Katherine because I'll be there," Jill says quite sternly. "You now know beforehand so it won't come as a surprise."

"How does it work when you run into clients?"

"It depends. Some people don't acknowledge me at all, with some I just exchange a knowing glance. Others may even introduce me as their therapist, while most seem comfortable referring to me as an old friend. It's never really a big deal."

I sigh. "Maybe not to you."

"I can't make you promise me anything, Hera, but I urge you to not make a problem out of this." She locks her gaze on mine. "Cultivate your friendship with Katherine. It'll be so good for you."

I find it impossible to hold her gaze for very long because, even though my brain is telling me I should absolutely not go, my heart knows that Jill is right. Getting to know Katherine has already been better for me than I could ever have imagined.

Chapter Twenty-One

KAT

WHEN I RING Hera's bell, I can't help but wonder what she'll be wearing. She did put on a shirt for the Pink Bean opening, but maybe her professional pride played a part in that.

Her house is in Bronte and looks immaculate from the outside, with flower pots gracing the window sills.

When the front door swings open I say, "Your carriage has arrived, my lady."

Hera grins at me, then looks over my shoulder. "Don't tell me you're taking me somewhere in that white thing over there." She shakes her head.

Before I reply I take in her attire. Not only has she donned the same kind of pristine white shirt that she wore at the Pink Bean opening, but she's wearing a light gray blazer over it.

"I thought red was more your color," Hera says. "But here you are, with a white car and a blue, what do you call it..." She points at my jumpsuit.

"I like all the colors of the rainbow."

Hera nods. "Have you eaten?" she asks.

"Do I look like a woman who forgets to eat?" I bring my hands to my hips.

Her cheeks turn pink. "I—I meant, do you want to come in or head off straight away?"

"I'd love to come in." I pause for a moment. "How did you know the white car was mine?"

"I know the cars in my street. None of them are white." She steps back to let me into a narrow hallway.

Hera opens the first door on the right and ushers me into the living room. I take in the wooden cabinets along the wall, the worn leather sofa and matching armchairs that stand upon a thick patchwork carpet. The room is decidedly small —especially compared to my open plan home—but it somehow feels cozy, rather than cramped. Like you'd want to curl up in the sofa with a mug of cocoa and a book, and forget about the outside world. I imagine it served as a safe haven for Hera after her partner died.

"You have a lovely home," I say as my gaze settles on her.

"Do you want to see my kitchen for inspiration?" She grins at me.

I want to see everything, I want to say, but don't.

"Would you like some water?" she asks and gestures at the sofa. "Sit for a second. I'd like to, uh, discuss something with you before we leave."

I settle in one of the armchairs and wait for Hera to return with a glass of water for the designated driver.

"Don't freak out," she says, after she has sat down in the chair opposite mine. "But Jill, my therapist, is going to be there tonight."

"Really?" I tilt my head and, just in time, refrain from making a joke that might not be received very well.

"It's a coincidence. I didn't ask her to come or anything." Hera gives a nervous chuckle that is very unlike her.

"Why would you?"

"I'm just a little bit annoyed by it."

I can't help a smile from spreading to my lips. "Because you talked about me with her? And now there's a good chance she'll meet me?"

Hera nods.

For a woman who has been on her guard since we met, she can be surprisingly open about things. I doubt she realizes what kind of signals she's been sending me. Whether she's aware or not, I'm receiving them loud and clear.

"Would this evening be more comfortable for you if I let you drive?" I give her my warmest smile.

She smiles back. Her eyes sparkle at me. "No way, I want to see you in action. If I don't like it, I'll just take a taxi back."

"I promised you'd be home before ten and I'm a girl who keeps her promises." I narrow my eyes. "Always."

"Let's be on our way then." Hera rises. "If you can talk and drive at the same time, maybe you can tell me some things I really need to know about art on the way."

———

"It's not really about the art," I whisper in Hera's ear. "It's more like a social gathering, but don't tell Liz I said that."

"I actually really like this." We're standing in front of a dreamlike depiction of the Sydney Opera House. "Don't ask me to explain why, but it speaks to me."

"You don't need to explain. And I agree, these are really good."

"Hello stranger." I feel an arm on my shoulder.

"Caitlin." I turn to her. "You remember Hera? Rocco's aunt?"

"Yes, of course. Lovely to see you again." Hera flinches a little as Caitlin kisses her on the cheek. "I have a bone to pick with you, Kat. I get the feeling you've been dodging my calls."

"I asked Liz to give you my message. Clearly you haven't received it."

"I have, but I've thought of a different angle." She looks over at Hera. "I don't want to monopolize you tonight, but if I come over to the Pink Bean next week, do you think we can talk?"

"A different angle?"

Caitlin gives a slight nod. "I'll tell you all about it over one of your delicious coffees. Let's say Monday?"

A waiter comes by with a tray of champagne flutes. Caitlin and Hera both grab one while I ask for a glass of water.

"Sure. Monday it is."

"I've bought two already." Caitlin nods at the paintings. "They're stunning." She cocks up her eyebrows. "Obviously I've known for a while that many a barista has a hidden talent."

"Speaking of," I ask. "Where's Jo?"

"At a gig." Someone comes along who taps Caitlin on the shoulder and she excuses herself.

"My sister said to refer Caitlin to her if she's so desperate for an interviewee," Hera says with a smirk on her face.

"Hilda?" I laugh. "She'd be an excellent guest, as would her son, by the way."

As if he has heard our conversation, a dramatic voice booms from behind us. "K.Jo!"

"Brace yourself." I find myself whispering in Hera's ear again, breathing in her scent as I do. "The gays have arrived."

Richard squints at Hera and me. "Wait," he says. "Is there something I should know?" He looks at his partner

Alan. "Has Rocco been keeping crucial lesbian intel from us?"

I try to wave off his comments as discreetly as possible— I'd like Hera to stay for a while.

"Lovely to see you, Hera." Richard winks at her.

"Don't mind him," I say. "You know over-excited is his default mode."

"Evening," a voice I don't recognize comes from the side.

"Jill." Hera snaps to attention—as though the head-master has just arrived to break up a raucous assembly.

"We're going to circulate," Richard says. "Catch you later."

"Bye, darling," I say absent-mindedly, as I focus my attention on Jill.

"This is Katherine," Hera says, her voice stiff.

"Lovely to meet you." Jill extends her hand and smiles warmly at me as she looks straight into my eyes—maybe she's trying to assess whether I will end up hurting her client. "I won't keep you, but I just wanted to say hello." She aims her smile at Hera now. "Have a lovely evening." With that, she saunters off and dissolves into the crowd.

I turn my body fully toward Hera. "That's done then." I glance at her empty glass of Champagne. "How about another tipple?"

"I can't believe she just came up to us. She promised me she'd be discreet."

"If first impressions are worth anything, I'd conclude she makes for an excellent therapist." I put a hand on Hera's shoulder. "I guess she doesn't let you get away with much."

"She's wonderful, actually."

Is Hera leaning into my hand?

"Ah, just what the doctor ordered." I grab a glass of Champagne off a passing tray and give it to Hera.

"What kind of doctor are you to prescribe me this?" Hera's voice has relaxed again.

"One without a degree but with a lot of wisdom from the streets." I glance at Hera as she takes a sip. I wish there wasn't a crowd of people around us—I wish we could continue this conversation somewhere a little quieter. From the corner of my eye, I see Kristin approaching. I remove my hand from Hera's shoulder again. "Here comes our silent investor. Lucky I'm not drinking. She can't help but inquire about 'some numbers' every time she sees me."

Kristin and Sheryl arrive and, as expected, Kristin immediately engages me in conversation about the Pink Bean. I try to give her most of my attention, but I can't help glancing at Hera as she chats with Sheryl. She nods thoughtfully and from this angle, with her chin turn downward like that, she looks so together, so every inch the woman I've come to know—serene though always a touch reluctant—that I feel something flutter inside my rib cage.

Chapter Twenty-Two

HERA

KATHERINE KNOWS MOST PEOPLE HERE, which is good. The way she's been busy talking to this and that person, tonight can hardly be construed as a date. I've had my fill of chit-chat for one evening and, as Katherine gets swallowed by the crowd more and more, I gravitate to the edge of it. I end up near the painting of the Opera House again and examine it in more detail.

"How about I replace the one you've been looking at above my head for years with that one." I instantly recognize Jill's voice.

"I think you might be too late." I point at the little red dot that's been stuck over the price.

"Oh well, guess you'll have to make do with the same old abstract then."

"Just as I've made do with you for so long," I blurt out. I've not gone as easy on the free champers as someone who has to wake up at six the next morning should.

"It's quite helpful for me to see you in a social situation," Jill says. "It gives me more context to work with."

I turn to face the crowd. Even though she's not wearing

red tonight, it's always easy to spot Katherine. "What do you think of that particular piece of context then?"

"We only exchanged a few brief words, but Katherine seems thoroughly lovely. Very warm and engaging."

"To be continued next Wednesday, I guess." It must be the Champagne, but I can't tear my gaze away from Katherine. There's something so magnetic about her.

"You bet," Jill says, and snaps me out of my thoughts about Katherine.

This is *not* a date—apart from Katherine driving me home later. Earlier, I was impressed with her driving skills. She's very assertive yet polite in traffic, which is a trait not given to many. Of course, she may very well curse like a sailor when she's alone in the car.

"I'm about to say my goodbyes, Hera. It was great seeing you," Jill says.

"You're leaving already?" I'm a little jealous of Jill. I wish I could slip out discreetly with her, but then I couldn't keep watching Katherine as she mingles effortlessly.

"I've seen what I've come here to see. I'm not one to linger." Jill turns to me. "Saying good night at these things is always a little awkward, isn't it?" She tilts her head. "Peck on the cheek for your shrink?"

"Go on then." I grab Jill by the shoulders and kiss her on the cheeks—a whole new way of saying goodbye to her—but I've had enough Champagne to not feel too self-conscious about crossing the invisible boundary we've always had between us.

"See you soon," Jill says. "Have a little fun tonight."

Jill leaves me standing there on my own, my gaze, once again, only drawn to one person.

"Where did Jill disappear to?" Katherine asks me as we walk to the car. It's only quarter past nine so she has plenty of time to get me home before my self-imposed curfew.

"She slunk off while you were being the belle of the ball. Isn't Alyssa a colleague of yours in a way?" I ask. "Did you ask her if you could steal her thunder on her big night?"

"I did no such thing." Katherine gives a loud cackle. She slides her arm into mine. Her body radiates heat onto me. "How dare you even insinuate something like that." She presses herself against me. She might not have had a drop of alcohol, but she must be one of those people who get intoxicated by the company of others, who come alive under their gaze.

"I was just giving you my objective observations of the night."

"Does that mean you were keeping an eye on me, Hera Walker?"

Jill's last words ring in my ear. *Have a little fun tonight.* "Some people have a knack for drawing the eye."

"Some people certainly do." She leans into me again, finding my ear, the way she has done several times this evening already. "Some of whom, well, one in particular I must say, looks rather stunning in a gray blazer."

Unfamiliar heat swells inside me. I wish Katherine would keep her distance but, at the same time, I wouldn't mind her lips staying close to my ear for a while longer.

"You mean Richard? That did look like a rather well-tailored blazer." We have arrived at the car but Katherine doesn't let go of my arm yet.

"Deflections, deflections," Katherine says while squeezing my biceps. "Goodness." She rubs her thumb over my upper arm. "I think I just found something else to compliment you on."

"The clock's ticking." I grin at her so broadly, she must

know how much I'm actually enjoying the way she's talking to me.

"Oh yes. The lady has a curfew." She lets go of me, unlocks the car, and holds the passenger door open—another brand-new experience for me.

Once in the car, Katherine concentrates on the road. Traffic's still pretty dense. I trust her driving more now that we're on the way back and I let my head fall back against my seat, enjoying the buzz of the alcohol and the warm, exciting glow of sitting next to Katherine.

"I'm glad I came," I say. My inhibitions have been lowered by the alcohol so I don't stop myself from saying exactly what I want to say—and doing exactly what I want to do.

I put my hand on her knee.

Katherine glimpses sideways for a second and flashes me an encouraging smile.

We drive the rest of the route to my house in silence, my hand firmly pressed to her knee.

———

When Katherine parks the car, I withdraw my hand. She's a swift, confident parker and the car is neatly in its spot in no time. My bedtime might be fast approaching but, even though I have a million reservations—and about a dozen reasons to bolt out of this car—I don't want to.

"Thanks for being my plus one." Katherine smiles again, but her smile tells a different story now. It tells me what I've known for a while. "I promised to tuck you in, so…" She unbuckles her seat belt.

I chuckle, then swallow hard. I hesitate. I'm almost overcome with the urge to lean in and kiss her, but I'm a woman in her fifties. I don't kiss girls in cars.

"All right then. Come inside," I say.

Katherine stands only an inch away from me as I unlock the front door. Once inside the house, I'm keenly aware—possibly helped by all the Champagne I knocked back—that I might never feel like this again. As though the exact circumstances that have been created—me being a little tipsy, being encouraged by Jill, and being intoxicated by just enough booze *and* Katherine's irresistible glow—might never happen again and I have to do something to mark the occasion.

I have to kiss her.

We're still in the hallway when I turn to her. I take her hands in mine and look her in the eye.

"You are such a remarkable woman."

Katherine doesn't say anything. She just stands there looking so incredibly alluring, with her hair a little wild, and her lips a glossy red. I take a step closer and bridge the distance between us. I tilt my head and inhale her scent—again. My level of intoxication grows. All throughout the night, it hasn't been the Champagne that has been clouding my judgment. It's Katherine. With her self-assured, inviting ways. The curve of her hips. The sway in her step. How she greets people with a warmness that's been lacking in my life. I'm drunk on Katherine and, despite all my reservations, I have to kiss her. There's no other way.

I press my lips to hers, only for a brief moment at first. During the split second when I pull my lips back from hers, already brimming with desire to touch them against Katherine's again, I realize there will be no way back from this. No way back from her body heat and the promise it holds. I kiss her again. I have to. My knees buckle when I first feel her tongue slip into my mouth.

Katherine frees her hands from my grasp and brings them to my chin. When we break from the kiss—still chaste, still exploring—she looks into my eyes and, ever so slowly, sucks her bottom lip into her mouth, her tongue flashing over it before it disappears. I forget everything I've made her stand for in my head. Desire explodes inside me. This will not end with a kiss. It's like a lid has been lifted and all the feelings I've denied myself for years, all the things I've tried to talk about with Jill but could never really find the words for—burst through the opening they've now found. The opening Katherine represents.

I walk us to the nearest wall and push her against it. When our lips meet again, our tongues do the same, and it's the kind of kiss that makes time stand still for its duration. I push my entire body against Katherine's, wanting to absorb her heat, her humanity, her very essence.

She wraps her arms around my neck and pulls me closer —although there's nowhere closer for me to go. Her hands are in my hair, my own hands begin to caress her neck, then drift lower.

"I want you," I whisper in her ear. In my own mind, it sounds more like *I need you*. I need Katherine. She quenches a thirst I haven't allowed myself to quench for far too long. I need to touch her. Need to feel a warm body against my skin, in my hands.

"Time for me to tuck you in?" she asks.

Chapter Twenty-Three

KAT

HERA LEADS me up the stairs. I have no eyes for the decoration of her bedroom—I only have eyes for her. I seem to want her more in this moment because of how she treated me when we first met. My desire has a certain I-knew-it quality about it.

Even more surprising than Hera kissing me—although I did feel the possibility of it in the air when she put her hand on my knee in the car—is how it makes me feel. Maybe this is what I need to shake my old self off completely. To move on from who I used to be and what I used to do. The more she kisses me, the more I shed my former skin—the barrier I had to create to draw a line between what was real and what wasn't.

I used to always be sure. I used to always calculate my next move for maximum result, but with Hera, there's none of that. Besides, I think she might be in charge. Letting me drive her was one thing—I get the feeling she won't go as far as letting me top her.

She shrugs off her blazer and throws it onto a chair. She

switches on a lamp on the bedside table and it casts her in a seductive glow. She comes closer again.

Here is the woman I need. As I think it, I can't explain why, but the knowledge burns inside me like something that's been true forever. Like it's inevitable—part of nature's laws.

Then I have no more time for any thoughts at all because when Hera comes for me again, with the same intensity as she kissed me with downstairs, there's no room for anything else.

For the longest time, I haven't allowed my body to just be flesh brimming with desire. For years, I had to keep my mind in charge of the tiniest act my body performed. My body was my instrument, my livelihood. And now Hera's here to take all that away. And she doesn't know it, she may never know it, but she does it effortlessly. And I wonder if this is what I saw in her, even all those weeks ago when she didn't like me. I wonder if I didn't see this in her the first time she stepped out of her bright red truck outside the Pink Bean. That I could meet her needs the way she could meet mine. It's been vibrating in the air between us since the beginning, even when we were too occupied with all the other nonsense to even realize.

She tugs at the zipper of my jumpsuit. It's a bit tricky to open—one of the reasons I never wore it on the job—so I turn around in her embrace to give her better access. When I have my back to her, she doesn't fumble with the zipper though. She brushes my ponytail aside and kisses the back of my neck. Even if I can't see her face, I can feel her intention. Her desire comes through the touch of her lips against my skin.

A small moan escapes me. God, I want more. I want it all. I want to unearth the depths of Hera Walker. I press my behind against her to make my own intentions known. But Hera takes her time kissing my neck, as though she wants to cover every inch of it. Her tongue skates along the nape of my neck and the hot sensation blasts through me as though she's already touching me between my legs.

I haven't been kissed like this for ages. Another need of mine reflected in Hera's. Her hands slide around my waist, press me harder against her. Then they venture up and rest underneath my breasts. Her hands inch up and I throw my head back, onto her shoulder, in a gesture of complete surrender.

I revel in the fact that she's so completely in charge; it reminds me that I have no responsibilities here. Not tonight. Not in this bedroom with the faint light of a small bedside lamp and Hera's breath catching in my ear. I'm someone else in her arms.

Her hands cup my breasts and the entire expanse of my skin breaks out in goosebumps. There might be layers of fabric between us, but her hands on my breasts like that, almost audaciously, carry me into an area of intimacy I've avoided since I started working for Alana. You can't bring sensations like this to a job. It's as if Hera reads my body, as though her hands on my breasts signify much more than an erotic gesture—much more than foreplay. She's getting to know me, without words, finding the real me. Seeing me in the semi-darkness of her room.

Her hands squeeze me intimately and my nipples push against the fabric of my bra. They burn against it, wanting to tear holes through it, wanting to be touched by her desperately. Her lips skate along my neck and her kisses are no longer measured. They're wet and her tongue is in play and I can feel Hera's desire—her need—for me in the press of her body against mine. Her hands slide from my breasts to my back and she pushes me away from her. She zips me out of my one-piece item of clothing as though she deals with extremely aroused women in jumpsuits on a daily basis.

I kick off my shoes and stand in front of her in my underwear. On display, which is nothing I'm not used to. Hera's gaze is burning, like I've seen many a client's do, but this is different. I'm not the one to pounce. I don't try to get her white shirt off her. I could try but I sense that she's the kind of woman who likes to strip off her own clothes.

I suck my bottom lip between my teeth again, the way I did earlier, downstairs, when I could so easily tell how crazy that was driving her, how it made that wall around her crumble. The wall may not come all the way down tonight, but there are huge gaps in it already. The first brick was removed long before Hera put a hand on my knee in the car.

She unbuttons her shirt but doesn't take it off. Briefly, I can make out the olive skin of her belly, as she rushes toward me again, as though our separation has already lasted long enough. Her hands are in my hair, tugging at the band that's holding up my ponytail. As my hair cascades down, she looks at me as though she's just spotted the world's most beautiful hidden waterfall. The desire in her eyes is the kind no money can ever buy.

She kisses me again and walks me toward the bed as she does. Her mouth is hungrier on mine, her tongue more insistent than before. The backs of my knees hit the bed and she pushes me down, flanking me. I sense some movement in her legs as she kicks off her shoes, then presses her warm, warm body against mine. She kisses me again, all intention and heat, then pauses and gazes at me from above. No words are needed now. I don't have any of my own and if I did, I wouldn't say them, because I wouldn't want to break the magic spell of this moment. The warmth in Hera's eyes, mixed with the desire demonstrated through her actions meeting my own, is plenty to rev up my engine some more. My clit already aches for her touch. I want her strong, sturdy builder's fingers inside me. God, I want them so much. But I need to go at her pace. I need to give her this moment. Mine will come later because, even though I'm fully in the throes of my own desire, a part of me already can't wait to see Hera yield under my own touch.

She kisses me again and it's a kiss that doesn't stop for minutes. While her lips are locked on mine, Hera draws a line with her finger from my chin, over my neck, to my breast. It dips underneath the cup of my bra, finding my nipple. I bring a hand underneath Hera's shirt, my fingertips scratching the skin of her back. As her body presses into me, so does her belt buckle, but I restrain myself and don't try to undo it and get it off her. If it leaves a mark, it's one I will look at with nothing but fond memories.

Hera pushes herself up, the side of her shirt covering my belly. Her finger withdraws from my bra as she finds her balance, then she brings both her hands behind my back to take off my bra. She doesn't say anything but I can see the wonder in her eyes when my breasts are bared to her. As though she had resigned herself to never seeing another woman's breasts in the flesh again. I could be wrong—I could be reading Hera all wrong—but that's how it feels to me in that moment. Like I'm a miracle Hera never even dreamed to hope for ever again.

I glance down as Hera comes for me, both her hands on my breasts. There's hunger in her grasp, something untamable. Her true nature coming through that carefully constructed wall, pushing through, telling her that this part of her still exists. This particular moment of wonder I've seen many times and, every single time, it fills me with hope and gratitude and I marvel at how humans can deny themselves something so essential. But, no matter how adept we become at ignoring our needs, they always find a way to shine through again. It's no different with Hera and the eagerness in her grasp is reflected in the pulsing of my clit.

And anyone who has ever tried to argue with me that what I did was just sell my body, sell the naked act of sex in exchange for money, has never witnessed a moment like this.

I need to snap myself out of this train of thought. Hera looks up at me briefly, as if she knows I'm on my own personal journey as well, and I send her a small smile of encouragement, to let her know that I'm with her here, all the way.

She leans her head down and while her hands try to contain my ample breasts, she sucks my nipple between her lips.

"Oh," I moan, and rake my fingers through her short hair. Hera licks and sucks and, then, bites down gently. My body sizzles with the heat that's being generated between us. Her lips sear against my nipple, erasing all the memories that have no relevance tonight. Because tonight, I'm here with Hera, and this is more real than anything I've ever known. It holds more promise and gives me hope that, maybe I too, can be destined for love.

Hera's wildness increases. Her lips on my other breast are less restrained. She pushes me all the way down, her hands sliding from my chest over my arms to my hands. She intertwines her fingers with mine, then kisses my breasts again. Her tongue flicks over my nipples, her teeth graze against my flesh. Then, she finally makes her way down.

I can't help but squirm against the sheets. My legs are already spread for her, but I'm still wearing my panties. Not for long though. From Hera's breathing, I can tell she's past the patient, teasing stage. I can tell she wants to lick my clit as much as I want her to lick it. She aches for me the way I ache for her. And even though, on my way over, and throughout the hours we spent at the gallery, I didn't even allow my mind to entertain the possibility of this for a fraction of a second, maybe the hope brimmed somewhere inside me nonetheless.

Hera kisses my inner thigh, inching ever closer to my panties, which have become a nuisance now. The last frontier before I give myself to her completely. And I want to give myself, I'm ready. I want to give myself in a way I haven't in a very long time. No holds barred and, also, without a whiff of transaction to it.

Hera kisses my belly, just above my panties. I push myself toward her—my way of giving permission, or, perhaps, of telling her to get those wretched panties off me already. I want to be naked for her, show myself unrestrained, meet her growing wildness, her desire to please me, with everything I have—as my truest self.

Hera's losing it as much as I am. She tugs at my panties now, showing her unbridled self to me in the process. We're matched, I think, in this moment of desire, of nothing else but our need for each other, perfectly cast in the roles we're in.

Hera sits between my legs, looking down at me. I only see the crown of her head but her gaze on me there is enough to set my skin on fire. She bows down, her body folding in on itself, and then, at last, I feel her breath on my swollen lips.

She kisses my inner thigh again but without the barrier of my underwear between us, the sensation is much more urgent, much more paralyzing. Because now I am at her mercy. I want her to do this to me.

Her lips reach my clit. She kisses it tentatively, but only for a split second. Then her tongue comes out to play and I'm lost. I disappear in the joy her touch brings me and it's no longer just her tongue on my clit that I feel, it's all her intentions, and all my own desires bursting through my flesh, straining under the surface of my skin. I'm as alive as I've ever been as I allow this very sensation, this surrender to another person completely, back into my life.

And god, I want her to fuck me, but I'm so aroused, my desire is so acute, that I'm not sure my body has the patience to hold out. And why would it wait, when it has waited all this time? Surely, this is not a one-night thing between us. It can't be. Most likely, it won't even be a one-orgasm night. What with the way my flesh is coming alive, and desire is crystallizing into pleasure on my skin. Hera licks and sucks my clit into her mouth. I rock my pelvis up to her, to her eager, able mouth; I press my hands into her hair pushing her as close to me as I can bear. And then I come because there's no sense in waiting, in denying myself this burst of pleasure, this wave of nothingness and everything that takes me, and tethers me to her in a way I someday hope to adequately convey to her. But for now, I collapse under her touch. I free myself from who I was and become someone else with her—as we are always a slightly different version of ourselves with different people.

I cave in under the pressure of her tongue, of how it feels to be naked in front of her, opened up, vulnerable but safe in the knowledge that she knows what to do with me.

"Oh Christ," I groan, and pull Hera toward me hurriedly. I look into her eyes briefly and before I pull her in for a kiss, I wonder if that was the beginning of a tear in her eye.

Chapter Twenty-Four

HERA

I WRAP MYSELF AROUND KATHERINE, feeling nothing but honored that she's allowed me to drink her in like that, to take from her so freely the thing I wanted the most. For the privilege of burying myself between her legs.

She pulls me close to her and I rest my cheek on her chest. God, those beautiful, luxurious breasts. I fear I may never get enough of them. I wouldn't mind lying like this for the rest of the night. But first, I fear, there's a conversation to be had.

"Do you feel all tucked in now?" Katherine whispers above my head.

I nod, her breasts swaying with my movement. I don't feel like lifting myself toward her, like facing her. I need this moment of quiet bliss, of her hand gently twirling through my hair, of the up-and-down of her chest beneath my cheek.

But I don't want to take too many liberties either. And what do I really know about what a woman like Katherine's thinking? All I do know is that she just came under my touch, and the power of that is unrivaled in what my life has become since Sam's death.

Katherine's hand wanders down my back, her finger tracing a line down my spine over the fabric of my shirt. She cranes herself toward me and kisses the top of my head. "I know it's way past your bedtime now," she says, "but let me give you something that will make you sleep like a baby." Her body shudders underneath me as she chuckles.

Her hand has traveled up again and her fingers dig into my shoulder.

"Hera," she whispers. "I'd very much like to kiss you again."

The prospect of Katherine kissing me is too alluring to resist. I push myself away from her chest and peer into her dark eyes. She looks like a different person lying in my bed like this. Her hair is wild, her gaze is full of something I haven't seen in it yet. And she's naked, of course. And newly recovered from a quick, inevitable orgasm.

She looks a bit like Sam.

I quickly push the thought from my mind because it feels so wrong to bring the memory of Sam into this situation.

"Come here," Katherine whispers, and pulls me close to her. I can still smell her on my lips and my mind drifts back to that glorious moment when my tongue met her clit for the very first time.

She kisses me, her lips hot and silvery against mine, and I lose myself in this kiss, the way I've been losing myself since I pushed her against the wall downstairs.

"Can I take this off you?" Katherine asks, taking the collar of my shirt between her fingers. "I feel a bit naked next to you."

"Let me." I sit up and shoulder off my shirt. "Better?"

"It's a start," she says, "but I'm still feeling a little under-dressed." She throws in a smile. "Or do you sleep in those jeans?" She quirks up an eyebrow.

I don't immediately react.

Katherine tilts her head and, in the low light of the room, finds my gaze. "Are you all right?" she asks. Her voice is gentle, not a hint of insistence in it.

"I'm perfectly fine." I try to sound light. "What just happened between us was magic as far as I'm concerned, but... erm, I'm not sure I can reciprocate in the same way."

Katherine narrows her eyes. I can see her swallow hard. "Do you mean you feel uncomfortable getting undressed in front of me or... do you mean that you prefer not to be touched?"

"Both," is the only word I can push past my throat.

"Come here." She opens her arms wide.

I scoot closer to her again, and to be held by her with so much skin on skin contact is divine in its own way, but it does nothing to change my mind about what I want.

"Here's a suggestion," she whispers. "Show me the way to the bathroom and while I'm gone, you can undress and wait for me under the covers." She kisses the edge of my ear. "If you want me to stay, of course. Do you want me to?"

"I'd like that very much," I quickly confirm.

"I'd like that too." She slides down until we are face-to-face. "I happen to quite like you."

"You're just saying that so I give you a good price for redoing your kitchen."

Her lips curl into a half-smile. "You see right through me." She plants a kiss on the tip of my nose. "Where's the bathroom?" she asks.

I show her the way and fall onto the bed after she has left the room. I ask myself if this is some sort of defining moment for the rest of my life, but I don't have time to answer that question—no matter how valid or silly it may be—while Katherine's in the bathroom. I promised I'd undress while she was out of the bedroom, so I'd best get on with it.

I step out of my jeans and dispose of my underwear,

throwing it in the laundry basket in the corner. While I'm at it, I hang my shirt on the back of a chair and find Katherine's discarded clothing. I fold it, underwear included, and put it on the same chair.

I feel no need to hastily duck underneath the covers because this is not really about being naked. I'm too old to have many qualms about my body—and your partner suddenly dying rather puts having a patch of cellulite on your thigh into perspective. It's only when the door to the bedroom opens that I throw the duvet back, inviting Katherine underneath it with me.

Her gaze flits over my body and when she meets me in bed, gluing herself to me immediately, I see desire glimmer in her eyes.

"Do you want to talk?" she asks, her face so close to mine that her breath warms my cheeks.

"Do you feel like we need to talk?" I ask.

She chuckles and I feel her breasts—nipples all perked up —shake against my skin. "I guess that means no."

"Look." I create a fraction of distance between us. "It's not that I don't know how to do all of this anymore, because I do—"

"I noticed," Katherine says with a loopy grin on her face.

"Emotionally, I mean. Well, not just emotionally, but…" I'm not sure I have the words to explain this. Not now, after a night out—after going down on Katherine. "Maybe we can talk tomorrow?"

"Can I ask you one question?" Katherine's face is more earnest now.

"Of course."

"Is it your intention to make a pillow princess out of me?"

I can't tell if she's being serious or not, until she bursts into a giggle.

"I'm not going to lie," she says. "After the life I've lived, I could probably get used to that." This makes her laugh so hard, her entire body rocks.

I can't help but laugh with her. Jill will have some work to do after so recklessly advising me to have some fun.

"For your information, my alarm clock goes off at five-thirty," I say.

"Looks like I won't be getting my eight hours of beauty sleep then." Katherine pushes herself against me. "Heads-up, my complexion might be a bit off in the morning."

"I look forward to meeting the early-morning you." I kiss her on the cheek. No matter how the evening has ended, it was still one of the most amazing nights of my life. "Do you want to be little spoon or big spoon?"

"I wouldn't for a second consider being the outer spoon, Hera," Katherine says, and turns around in my embrace, so I can pull her backside close to me.

Chapter Twenty-Five

KAT

I WAKE UP, it seems, only a few minutes after I fell asleep. Hera's clock radio crackles way too loudly in my ear. Hera. Memories of last night flood my brain and I blink open my eyes.

"Sorry about that." Hera leans over me and gives the alarm a good whack. She breaks into a smile while she squints. "Are you related to Katherine Jones?" she asks. "You kind of look like her, but also not quite like her."

"Whatever happened to good morning, my love?" I groan.

"Morning." Hera leans in and kisses me on the lips. "Did you get some sleep?"

"Not enough."

"Don't you have to open the Pink Bean?" she asks, an amused smile playing on her lips.

"Rocco's opening this morning. I told him I had a big night planned."

"What, getting his aunt into bed by ten?"

Hera looks a thousand times more relaxed than last night, when she didn't want me to touch her. It makes me wonder if I should make a move now. But it's early and I think it's a safe bet to leave the making of moves to Hera for now. "Which I did, by the way. Mission accomplished."

"Did you tell him you were taking me out?"

"No, but I'm pretty sure he knows by now. The gay gossip mill never stops turning. I'm willing to bet Richard texted him within minutes of seeing us together." I pause. "Do I need to watch what I tell him?"

"Heavens, no. He has certainly never watched what he's told me about his love life. All the things he didn't want to discuss with his mother, he has always, very graphically, discussed with me." Hera scrunches up her face.

"Are you giving me permission to tell him I spent the night with you?"

"He's your best friend, Kat." It's the first time Hera has called me Kat. "And I trust you know where to draw the line." She cranes her neck and looks at the clock. "I really need to get going. But feel free to linger."

"How about I make you some breakfast while you shower?" I bat my lashes.

"I must have died and gone to heaven." Hera pulls me in for one last hug, and I soak up all her warmth. I'm not sure when I'll get the chance to savor it again.

———

By the time I arrive at the Pink Bean, it's almost ten. I've stopped by my apartment to change my clothes and make myself presentable.

Rocco's busy and just gives me a look. I jump right in and work alongside him, only exchanging coffee-related words with him until the queue in front of the counter has dissolved.

"You sure took your sweet time this morning, K.Jo." He steps back and crosses his arms in front of his chest.

I try to disarm him with a smile. "I'm so sorry, darling. One of those mornings."

"I'm not going to be all coy with you about this. Hera is my aunt, Kat. Why didn't you tell me you were going out with her?"

"I thought you were sulking because I was late."

"I can handle a crowd." He leans against the counter.

"I didn't want to make a big deal of it beforehand. To be completely honest, I sort of expected Hera to cancel on me last-minute."

He takes a step closer. "I'm just… very ambivalent about this," he whispers. "She might not look it, but Hera's fragile."

"I can handle fragile."

"Oh, I'm sure you can, but, on top of that, you're mixing business with pleasure. What if things go wrong between you? Who will be caught in the middle then?"

"I think you might be getting a little ahead of yourself." I can understand Rocco's defensive attitude up to a point, but I hadn't expected him to come down on me so ferociously—even though, most days, ferocious seems to be his default mode.

"Just…" The door swings open. He leans in and hisses, "Don't hurt her, Kat. I swear to you." Rocco greets the customer and I'm left standing there baffled. Maybe the Walkers are a much more complicated bunch than I thought they were. I've known Rocco for years and he has never spoken to me so disrespectfully.

"For your information," I say, once the customer has left, "Hera and I had a lovely time. Maybe, instead of throwing a hissy fit, you could be happy for us?"

"I'm not throwing a hissy fit. But we are here together every day and you didn't breathe a word of it."

"Because it's delicate. She *is* your aunt and I know you adore her."

"She doesn't have many people. I can't help but be protective of her. She's only just now started coming out of her shell again. You weren't there when she…" He falls silent.

"Look at it this way." I try a smile. "If your beloved aunt's going to go on a date with someone, wouldn't you prefer it to be with your best friend instead of someone you don't know the first thing about?"

Rocco just stands there, nodding slowly. "That's the thing, Kat. I'm not so sure."

"Excuse me?" I have to restrain my indignation—I sure hope Rocco didn't mean what I think he meant by that— because the door opens again. My heart skips a beat because it's Hera walking in. She has some plaster on her cheek, and her hair is all dusty, but she looks scrumptious just the same.

"Hi." She saunters up to the counter and sends me a big smile, then glances over at Rocco, who still has a pout on his face. "I'm not sure which vibe you're going for today, but I sense some tension in the air," she says matter-of-factly. "I sure hope I'm not the cause of it." She sends me a wink.

"Long black, Auntie?" Rocco asks, not acknowledging what Hera has just said.

"Yes, please."

"On it." He turns away and starts preparing the coffee.

"Some of us are not having the best morning." I lean over the counter and kiss Hera on the cheek.

"Does he have a stick up his ass over us?" Hera asks.

"I think, perhaps, he feels a bit left out," I say.

"I can hear you, you know," Rocco says.

"Good to know there's nothing wrong with your hearing then," I quip. "Only your loyalty to your best friend."

"Rocco," Hera says. "Come sit with me for a minute."
She winks at me again. "I'll sort him out," she whispers.

Rocco takes her coffee to the table furthest away from the counter. I'm still shocked by what he might have implied about me but, now that Hera's here, I trust he'll see things differently soon enough.

Chapter Twenty-Six

HERA

I LOOK AT MY NEPHEW. Even though he's a grown man, I can still see the child in him.

"Great coffee." I look around the place. "Good number of people in here, as well." I take a sip. From the moment I left my house this morning, with Katherine still inside, I knew I wouldn't be able to stay away from the Pink Bean today. I knew I had to see her again as quickly as possible.

Rocco chuckles half-heartedly. "I don't need a talking-to in case that's what the two of you are thinking."

"I wouldn't dream of giving you one." I lean over the table. "Instead, let me tell you all you want to know." A warm tingle spreads through me as I remember the sequence of events. "Kat invited me to hers last Sunday to have a look at her kitchen. We had a lovely meal. Then she invited me to Alyssa's art show at the Griffith-Porter gallery, and we had a great time." I suppress a giggle. 'Great time' sounds like the understatement of the century.

"I know all about the great time you had. Richard sent me a picture of you and Kat at the gallery." He sighs. "I'm not upset because I didn't know. Although I probably should have known, what with the way I'm always up in Kat's business. Nor is it that she didn't tell me about your dinner, which I've only just found about. In fact, it's great that you get along now." He briefly purses his lips. "Let's be honest, that never really looked as if it was ever going to happen, did it?"

I shrug and take another sip from my coffee.

"It's just that… now that I'm faced with the two of you together, it's really weird for me. That's the only way I can describe it." He looks over his shoulder. "From the way you were making eyes at each other, I guess you'll be seeing each other again."

"I sure hope so." I lean back and glance over at Katherine. She looks like the other version of herself again, all made-up and ready for the daytime. Already, I like all versions of her. "I know I didn't give her a chance in the beginning. I was clearly wrong. She's… pretty amazing."

"It's really strange for me to hear you say those words?" Rocco slants over the table. "Not only because you're my aunt, and I've only ever known you to be with Sam, but also, well, because of the things you said about her when you started the renovation work here."

I nod. "I fully accept that." I'm not sure what else I can say. All throughout last night, from the moment Katherine showed up at my door, I've not given much thought to what she used to do.

"That's it?" Rocco asks.

"I guess so."

"I was a bit mean to her earlier." He sits up straight again. "No one needs to convince me that Kat's amazing. I've known that forever."

"Now I know it too." I shoot him a wide grin.

"Chris couldn't believe it either."

"How about you and Chris come over for dinner at mine soon?"

"That would be nice." He narrows his eyes. "If Chris hadn't had this work thing last night, I would most likely have been at the gallery myself, you know."

"Good thing you like a nice surprise then." I smirk at him.

He shakes his head. "It's really not as funny as you think it is." He has a grin on his lips regardless of what he just said.

"You're right." I drain the last of my coffee. After I put my cup down, I say, "I'm very serious about this." I look Rocco in the eye. I can tell from his slightly frustrated facial expression that there are things he wants to share with me, but has decided against. Some things are better left unspoken. "I need to get back to work. I'll give you a call soon." I get up and stand next to him. I put an arm on his shoulder and give it a little squeeze. "Thanks for looking out for me," I say, "but I'm plenty old enough to look out for myself."

———

"What are you doing this weekend?" I ask Kat, after we've had the same old squabble again about me paying for my coffee.

"No plans," she says coyly.

"Would you like to make some plans with me?" I ask.

"I thought you'd never ask." She bats her lashes. "Come to the back for a minute." She beckons me behind the counter.

I follow her into a small storage room, which is, completely according to my expectations, neatly organized along the principles of Rocco—he once explained them to me but being rather chaotic myself, I've long forgotten them.

She closes the door behind us and presses me against it. Her breasts push against mine and I feel the same heat as last night course through me.

"Maybe some more of this?" she whispers in my ear, before kissing my neck.

"Who can say no to that?" I push her away from me slightly. "You'll have dust all over your dress if you keep this up."

"Goodness," she coos, "imagine what Rocco will have to say about that."

"He's under the mistaken impression I can't fend for myself—or deal with a woman as wonderful as you." I gaze into Katherine's dark-brown eyes, wishing I didn't have a job to go back to.

"I'd best not give him all the details about last night then." Kat rubs herself against me again, clearly not caring which state it will leave her clothes in.

"You can tease him a little, though." I pull her in close. "He deserves it." Before I kiss her, I ask. "Tonight?"

She nods her confirmation and then our lips meet, and it's so easy to forget we're in the storage room of the Pink Bean, when Katherine is pressed against me like this, and all I want to do is tear that dress off of her. But I can wait until tonight.

Chapter Twenty-Seven

KAT

"Before you get any wild ideas in your head," I say to Hera after she's let me in and we're standing in the living room, a little more awkwardly than I had anticipated, "I have to open the Pink Bean tomorrow."

Hera regards me intently. "I'll make sure you get your beauty sleep."

I sigh. "I'm really feeling it." I bridge the small distance between us. "Even though my new job is not nearly as emotionally taxing, my work hours are much longer. And I don't get to have any more naps." I run a finger up her bare arm. Hera's freshly showered and is wearing a clean T-shirt. "I've always been a strong believer in the power of the nap." I grin at her.

"Would you like to take a nap while I make us some dinner?" Hera puts her hands on my hips.

"That's the problem. When I'm with you, I don't feel like napping at all."

Hera nods. "What do you feel like then?"

"I feel like doing this." I drag my fingers higher up her arm, underneath her sleeve, and witness how her skin breaks out in goosebumps. Hera might not know it yet, but I've come here to seduce her. I have full faith in my powers of seduction—after all, they were my bread and butter for years. "And this." My other hand softly brushes Hera's neck, just above the edge of her T-shirt.

I hope Hera was only joking when I asked her, in jest, if she intended to make a pillow princess out of me. I need to taste her, feel her on my fingers. Find out what she looks like after she has come.

"You're not hungry?" she asks, her breath catching in her throat.

"Only for you," I say, knowing full well how cheesy that sounds.

"I seem to have quite an appetite for you as well." Hera still has her hands on my hips and she tugs me to her. Before she kisses me, her lips curl into a small smile. She brings her hands to my back and holds me close, before going to work on my zipper. She must be really hungry then.

I let her strip me but I've come with my own agenda today. I'll let her take the reins for a while—it obviously excites her—before I make my own move.

She has my dress in a puddle on the floor in no time and has already progressed to the clasp of my bra. Before I know it, I'm standing in Hera's living room in just my underpants.

"Whatever happened to offering a girl a drink?" I ask.

"I'm not old-fashioned that way." Hera grins at me. "Also, it's a miracle I made it out of the site alive today, or without causing an accident. In fact, it should be illegal for me to go to work when under the influence of Katherine Jones."

I burst into a chuckle. Hera's desire for me is no match for my intentions. She comes alive when she has her hands on me and, in turn, it excites me beyond belief. But I will, at the very least, need her to take her T-shirt off before she goes any further. I start hoisting it over her chest, but she doesn't let me. Instead, she pulls it off herself.

She's wearing a sports bra so white, it must be brand new. It contrasts with her olive skin and I need to look away from her chest, into the bottomless pools of desire in her eyes, to stop myself from stripping her of that bra right there and then.

She presses herself against my side and launches an onslaught of kisses on my neck, while her hand already delves down. She briefly strokes my belly, her mouth meandering to my breast. As she sucks my nipple between her lips, her finger skates over my panties. I know what Hera means when she says that, all day long, she's been distracted to the point of it being dangerous. After she left the Pink Bean, I spent every free minute daydreaming about something very much like the situation I'm in—although the roles were quite reversed.

But as I stand here, it's impossible not to go with the flow Hera's creating. Her determination is sexy. The clench of her teeth on my nipples is so light in its grasp but so firm in its intention, I soon want her to rip my panties off me and slide a finger inside me. God, how I want to feel her inside me.

Her finger circles my clit, while her lips are fastened around my nipple—as though she couldn't let go of it even if she wanted to. I glance down at her strong neck, the muscles moving beneath her skin, straining to please me. Everything in her body working toward the same goal.

When she does finally let go, and she looks at me, her face is flushed, the lust in her glance multiplied.

"Come," she says under her breath, and leads me to the sofa. Before I have the chance to sit down, she tugs off my underwear and, once again, I'm naked before her while she's still half-dressed. I give her a look and she must be a fast learner. She unbuckles her belt and quickly gets rid of her jeans. Then she tilts her head as though asking, *Is this what you wanted?* A new rush of warmth spreads inside me. It's definitely a big part of what I want.

I wrap my arms around her and hold her near-naked body against mine, inhaling her scent, reveling in the touch of her hard muscles beneath her soft skin.

"Lie down for me, please," she whispers and, by now, she doesn't have to ask me twice.

I lower myself onto the sofa and Hera crouches beside me. She kisses me and I throw my arms around her neck, while she pushes my bent leg up against the backrest. I can feel the air brush my wet lips, my swollen clit.

"God, you're so beautiful," Hera says, a crack in her voice that tells me she means it with all her being. "I want you so much. It's crazy."

But then her lips find my nipple again and while one of her hands grabs hold of my breast, the fingers of the other create patterns on my inner thigh. My exposure lifts my already growing arousal to boiling point again. This is how I am with her. Easy to combust. Ready for her when she wants me. And she wants me, there's no getting away from that.

She lifts her head away from my breast and looks me in the eye while her finger zones in. She circles my clit, once, twice, ever so slowly. My breath starts to come out ragged. I want her too. Like this, in exactly the way she has maneuvered me into this position—outmaneuvered me, even. And now, my body is only desire, throbbing with impatience and anticipation, as my clit pulses under her touch.

She looks down at me, between my legs, so I only see the top of her head, and her robust shoulders. Her gaze on me there magnifies all the sensations I've been succumbing to again. Then, with that light, soft touch she has, she slowly slides the tip of her finger inside. She leaves it there, unmoving, and looks up again. It's only when her gaze is firmly locked on mine, that she pushes her finger inside of me completely.

I moan and let my head fall back a little, while still keeping my gaze on hers. My limbs stiffen with pleasure. Hera's fucking me and all the fires that I managed to dampen since she left her house this morning come roaring back to life, until, with her thumb deftly stroking my clit, they culminate into the fire to end all fires once again.

After I've come and Hera's lying on the too small sofa with me as best as our two bodies can manage, I whisper in her ear, "Hello to you too."

"Are you still hungry?" Hera asks.

"Absolutely ravenous." I'm lying on my side and pull her close to me.

"Shall I make us some dinner?" I can feel her lips move against the skin of my neck as she speaks.

"Still not hungry for food yet." I kiss her neck. "I want you." I nibble at her earlobe. "I think I've waited long enough." My hand travels down her back and halts at the clasp of her bra. This kind of model is too sturdy for me to undo with just one hand, so I try to maneuver my other hand behind her back, but we're too closely pressed together.

"Any chance we can move this upstairs?" I ask.

"How about after dinner?" she says. "I need to eat something first."

I'm not willing to let this go. Perhaps I haven't made adequately clear how much I want her—a desire she must be able to understand, what with the way she just ravaged me as soon as I walked in the door. "Then let's stay here."

"Kat," she says, and tries to push herself up. She slides half off the sofa and it seems to change the air between us, seems to transform it from electric to awkward. "Maybe later, okay?" Hera climbs to her feet and towers over me. "I really need to eat."

"Do I detect some *hanger* in the builder?" I quip, trying to lighten the quickly darkening mood.

"I've been on my feet all day, doing some pretty heavy-duty work. I need fuel to keep going." She stands there shifting from foot to foot, claiming to need food—which is a perfectly reasonable demand—but I can't seem to shake the impression that she's actually trying to say something else entirely.

"Okay." I watch her find her jeans and T-shirt and slip them on swiftly.

She crouches down and puts her hands on my thigh. "You relax for a bit. Take a shower if you like. We can talk while we eat."

I nod. She kisses me briefly on the cheek and then, bare-foot and scrumptious, saunters to the kitchen.

Chapter Twenty-Eight

HERA

AFTER HER SHOWER, Katherine borrowed one of my T-shirts. It's a bit short and small for her, making her look extra desirable. Her make-up has been washed off and, all throughout dinner, I couldn't keep my eyes off her.

It's only after we've nearly polished off a bottle of wine that I find the courage to say what is almost unsayable. We've retreated to the sofa we fooled around on earlier, Katherine leans heavily into me, and I revel in the pleasure her weight against me brings. The coziness it creates. How it makes this house feel more like my home again.

"I'm, erm, not very good at being touched in an intimate way," I mumble.

Katherine does me the courtesy of staying in position— and not turning to look me in the eye.

"What do you mean by that exactly?" Her voice is only mildly inquisitive.

"It's not something that is of vital importance to me."

Katherine doesn't immediately say anything. The in and out of our breath is the only sound in the room. "May I ask why?" she says after a while.

"I'm not sure there's a why. That's just how it is." I wish I could say this with more aplomb, with more gravitas.

Katherine does turn toward me now. She pulls her knees onto the sofa and faces me. Before she speaks, she takes my hands in hers. "Has it always been like that?"

I chuckle. "You make it sound as though I have some sort of condition."

"That's not how I wanted it to sound. I'm just curious... because I like you."

It's hard to keep my hands in hers. "I understand if this is a deal breaker. That's why I'm telling you now."

It's Katherine's turn to chuckle nervously. "I don't think it's a deal breaker. I'm just trying to understand." She tilts her head. "Your partner. Sam. She never touched you?"

"She did, before..." This is an almost impossible conversation to have. I don't have the words for it. I can't even explain it to myself—despite trying many times. "It's just not a part of my life anymore."

Katherine sucks her bottom lip between her teeth the way I've seen her do many times by now. "I can't sit here and look you in the eye, and honestly tell you, that this isn't hard for me to understand." The clasp of her fingers around mine becomes firmer. "I—I want you in that way, Hera. So much. I mean, I happily gave myself to you. Very happily, but it was always under the assumption that I would reciprocate."

"Sex doesn't always have to be about reciprocation."

"I think I know that." She drops my hands and straightens her spine. "You don't have to educate me on all the things sex can be." She narrows her eyes. "It's not because I used to be an escort, is it?"

I shake my head vehemently. "No. I promise you that has nothing to do with it."

"Good." She huffs out a sigh, as though if I had even hinted at that, she'd be out of the door in no time. "Is it a matter of trust? Of going too fast? Admittedly, things have moved quickly between us once we—"

I shake my head again. "It's how I am. How I've become. Maybe how I've always been, although it's not that easy to find out."

"Do you…" She takes my hands in hers again and looks at them. "Do you masturbate?"

Even though I feel like I owe her answers to these questions, it doesn't make them easier to reply to. "No," I say.

She nods slowly. "I feel like I should be able to deal with this better, but I'm not quite sure what to say."

"It's a lot to take in, especially after I pounced on you like that… I should have had this conversation with you a lot sooner. But, um, I hadn't anticipated things progressing so quickly all of a sudden."

"That's what I have such trouble understanding," Katherine says. "You clearly feel sexual desire. You obviously want me with all that is in you. But you don't want to have an orgasm? You don't need release from all that tension?"

"I get my release when you come."

"Really?"

I nod.

"So, right now in this moment, when I'm sitting here in front of you in this T-shirt that barely covers me, what is it that you feel?"

I shoot her a grin. "I very much feel like ripping that T-shirt off you."

"And I very much feel like ripping yours off you," Katherine replies, melancholy in her glance, reminding me that, even though the conversation might have briefly taken a lighter tone, this is not the sort of thing that can be resolved just by having a quick chat.

Moreover, I have no reply to what she's just said. What could I possibly say? I surely can't take the liberty to have my way with her again—I probably should have restrained myself before.

"Do you want to watch *The Caitlin James Show* with me?" I ask. Because to me, watching TV with Katherine by my side can just as well be a pinnacle of intimacy.

"Sure." She cocks her head. "She's coming to the Pink Bean next Monday to pitch a new angle for that interview she so desperately wants to do with me." Katherine leans into me again.

"You're a very interesting woman, so you can hardly blame her."

"Don't you start as well." Kat puts her head on my shoulder and, in that gesture, I can sense her willingness to stay—to give this a shot regardless of what I've just confessed.

While I switch on the TV and find the right channel, I vow to take some time this weekend to articulate what I find so unspeakable. Katherine deserves more than what I've just given her.

Chapter Twenty-Nine

KAT

"I could so easily fall in love with her," I say to Liz and snap my fingers. "Just like that, actually."

"Then why don't you?" Liz grins at me.

I sigh. "It's even more complicated than I first thought."

"Isn't it always?" Liz brushes her hair out of her eyes. "Life's complicated. If anyone knows that, it's us."

"Simply knowing things are complicated doesn't really change anything about the situation."

After a long day at the Pink Bean, during which I didn't really know what to say to Rocco—except that, perhaps he was right to be worried about our working relationship if things go south between Hera and me—I remain preoccupied, unable to confide my innermost thoughts to my best friend.

This entire day my brain has been busy mulling over what Hera said last night. So much so, that I called Liz and asked her if I could stop by after work, even though what I really needed was a hot bath and a very long night's sleep.

"Do you want to tell me what makes it so complicated? Except for you being a former call girl, of course. But if that's it, let me hook her up with Jess. She can tell her all about the tricks we have up our sleeve." Liz's lips curve into a wide smile.

"That's just the thing. I'm not allowed to show Hera my tricks. Any of them."

"What do you mean?" Liz twirls her beer bottle between her fingers. "You haven't had sex yet?"

"She doesn't want me to touch her," I blurt out and, as I say it, I realize I really needed to voice that to someone else.

"I see." Liz seems stumped for words for a bit, but then says, "Like in the stone butch kind of way or because she believes you've touched too many a lady already in your life?"

I snort at the way she phrases it. I knew she was the right person to talk to about this. I couldn't possibly discuss it with any of my gay male friends—never in a million years would they understand.

"I suspect the first. Although I get a feeling it's much more than just that."

"Wow." Liz lifts the beer bottle to her mouth. "How do you feel about that?"

"I'm not really sure." I drink from the crisp white wine she has poured me. "I'm still processing."

"Perhaps it took you by surprise."

"You can say that again. The first time, I thought she was just tired, you know. Fair enough. But yesterday she told me, *after* she made love to me."

"I'm sure you've had clients like that," Liz says matter-of-factly. "I sure had my fair share of them, but I always thought it was... I don't know. Fear more than anything else stopping them from wanting to be touched."

"I don't know Hera well enough yet to work out what it is, but it is definitely a thing. And I really, really like her, and I almost feel guilty for being so dramatic about this. Like it's untoward in some way to question someone's sexual proclivities, because maybe it is just her nature, you know. But that's how I feel. Massively conflicted."

"You have every right to feel conflicted, Kat. You even have the right to turn the tables on her. What if it were the other way around? Would she continue to see you?"

"Good question." I shake my head. "I really can't imagine it. Her appetite for me is rather... voracious." A throbbing rises between my legs at the mere thought of it. "Maybe it's more a question of compatibility. Like with gays. Top or bottom."

Liz snickers. "Maybe. Compatibility is a big thing in every relationship."

"Also... in what we used to do, seduction was one of the main parts of what we did. To drive someone crazy like that. I truly got off on that, otherwise I wouldn't have been able to do it for so long, and to have to completely ignore that part of me to be with Hera. It seems unimaginable."

Liz arches up her eyebrows. "Maybe you should seduce her until she can't stand it anymore."

"I've considered it, but after our conversation, it would just be disrespectful."

"Do it stealthily." A grin appears on Liz's face. "Subtly drive her so insane she won't have another choice."

I shake my head. "That's not how I want it to be."

"I know." Liz nods. "You want to be wanted."

"It's such an essential part of who I am."

"What are you going to do?" Liz's voice has dropped into a lower, much more serious register.

"I don't know." I shake my head. "I truly don't."

"My best advice is to talk to her again. Try to get her to tell you what's going on in her mind. It's probably all you can do."

"I want to keep seeing her." My tone is as insistent as the

sentiment behind my words. "It's not as if I don't have my own shit to deal with as I enter into this relationship." I find Liz's gaze. "Was it hard for you? When you started seeing Jess?"

"Not hard, but definitely strange. I wanted it. I wanted something else than what I'd grown so accustomed to. And it took some convincing because dating a hooker simply isn't for everyone. At least you need to give Hera credit for that."

"She did give me a really hard time about that."

"Try to find someone who won't." Liz snickers and holds up her hands. "I loved being an escort, but being with Jess has made me want to quit as well."

"Do you regret quitting?" I ask.

"Sometimes I do, yes. But you're probably the only one of my friends who understands that."

"My life is just so incredibly different than before. It's much busier, for starters. But it's also… is it odd to say that, at times, I miss being an escort?"

"I think it's perfectly normal," Liz says.

I huff out a sigh. "Look at us, two old hookers reminiscing about the good old days."

Liz bursts out into a belly laugh. "No one is safe from nostalgia."

"Life is strange, don't you think?"

Liz lifts her beer bottle. "And we just have to roll with the punches."

Chapter Thirty

HERA

It's Sunday and I still don't know what to do with myself. Katherine and I have only exchanged a few non-committal text messages since she got up early yesterday morning to open the Pink Bean. I can only conclude her enthusiasm for being with me has waned since we had *that* talk.

I try to go about my usual Sunday morning business of reading the newspaper extras and drinking too much coffee, but the coffee reminds me of Katherine, and I can't focus on the long reads in the weekend section.

I wonder if I should book an emergency appointment with Jill, try to move our Wednesday evening time together to tomorrow, but, as much as I appreciate her, and I believe in what we do together, I know she can't really help me.

I haven't spoken to Jill about any of my sexual issues since Sam has died—there seemed no more reason to focus on them. This is also one of the reasons why I didn't want to start another relationship. Not only because I never want to go through the excruciating, paralyzing pain of someone being taken away from me again, but also to avoid needing to have the conversation I tried to have with Katherine.

I'm happy with how I am and I don't want to be pressured into defending myself. The only conclusion I can possibly draw from this is that Katherine deserves someone who is more suited to her. I let myself go when I was with her—I practically ravaged her—and that's on me. I let myself be intoxicated by her abundance of charm, by the warmth of her flesh. And she accepted my advances under the logical assumption that all would be reciprocated.

Maybe I should try writing her a letter. Perhaps I can articulate myself better, but I honestly don't know what more information I could divulge about my inner workings. To me, this is just how it is now. I could dredge up the whole history of the intimacy between Sam and me, how it changed over the years, but, frankly, I don't want to do that. That's Sam's and my private history and it doesn't concern anyone else—not even someone I think I'm falling for.

Or maybe, I should just call Katherine. Even though the thought of speaking with her makes me nervous, I prefer it over dealing with the inadequacy of text messages. I check the clock on my phone. It's almost eleven. I know she needed a lie-in, but surely she's awake by now.

I don't give myself more time to get worked up about it and dial her number. It rings a few times, then goes to voicemail. I don't leave a message. She'll know I've tried to reach her.

After trying to call her, I definitely can't focus on the newspaper anymore. Because now I'm wondering if she heard her phone, saw who was calling, and decided not to pick up. It's a possibility.

I decide to go for a walk before I drive myself crazy at home, which is already too filled with memories of her—I can't even look at my couch without my skin breaking out into goosebumps.

After I pull a sweater over my head and glance at myself in the reflection of the window, I say, in hushed tones, "Why can't you just do it, Hera? Why can't you just give yourself to her?"

But I can't. And it may very well be the end of us.

Just as I'm about to head out the door, my phone starts ringing. My heart skips a beat.

It's her.

I pick up as quickly as I can. "Hey." I instantly go all warm inside.

"Hey, you," Katherine says. "Sorry I missed your call."

"No worries." The warmth spreading through me is quickly turning into something else. Desire.

"Was there a particular reason for your call?" Kat's tone is different. She sounds more cautious than excited to be talking to me.

"I was wondering if you wanted to get together later today?" I ask. "I understand if you don't," I add, for some reason I don't quite get. It must be the tension building in my gut, crushing that initial flash of desire.

"I do, Hera, but…" She pauses.

The tension coils into a knot.

"I need a day of doing absolutely nothing," she says.

"Okay." I should probably ask if she wants to do nothing with me, but by now, I'm afraid to.

"Maybe tonight?" she asks. "Shall I give you a call later?"

"Sure. Yes. That's fine," I stammer. As I say it, it's as though I know in my heart of hearts, that she won't call me tonight. And that, if I want to see her again, I need to force something. I need to snap out of this. "I would like to, um, talk to you. I need to say some things. Please." I'm not sure why I'm suddenly pleading because I've no idea what these things that I so desperately need to say to her might be.

"Come by tonight?" she says. There's a subtle difference in her tone—as though she wants to give me another chance. "Around six?"

"I'll be there."

"See you then."

We hang up and I realize this is not the kind of phone conversation two people who have slept together would normally have—it's the conversation of two people who have considerable doubts about whether they should be together.

———

I arrive at Kat's empty-handed. At least that's what it feels like, even though I've brought a bottle of wine. Apart from that, I only feel an inevitable emptiness inside of me. Like my brain is still hanging on to something my body already knows I've lost.

Kat hugs me after she's let me in, and it's not a quick, dismissive hug. Her arms around me feel surprisingly inviting. Maybe, with her, it's the other way around. Perhaps her body is still willing to go through the motions to counteract the thoughts swirling in her mind.

"How was your day of doing nothing?" I ask.

Kat stares at me, as though instead of making small talk, I've just asked her to resolve all the mysteries of the universe.

"It was pretty awful, to be honest." She sits and I follow her lead.

What a contrast with the last time we greeted each other, when she allowed me to be all over her only a few seconds after laying eyes on her. She's dressed down in jeans and a wide, loose-hanging blouse. I can't detect any make-up on her face.

"I guess that had something to do with me."

"Should I get us a drink?" she says, ignoring my statement. "Do you want a beer?" She gets up again and rubs her palms over her jeans.

"Kat." I reach out my hand to her. "Let's just talk."

"Okay." She sits again. "I don't really know where to start. I wouldn't exactly call myself an expert at relationships." She chuckles nervously.

"I wouldn't call myself that either," I say.

"Yet you were in one for how many years?" Kat stares straight ahead.

I angle myself toward her so I can at least see her body language. I get the impression she'd rather sit with her back to me.

"More than twenty years," I say.

"I think that makes you the expert of the two of us," Kat says.

"I met Sam when I was in my late twenties," I say. "I'm not the same person I was then. I'm no more an expert than you are."

Kat sighs. "I'm thirty-eight and I've had one relationship worthy of calling it that, even though it didn't last very long. That's it. That's all I have to show for my brief years on this planet. Maybe I'm just not cut out for relationships."

"I dare to disagree." I try to inject some lightness in my tone but it comes out all wrong—like I don't mean what I'm saying.

"The truth is," Kat says and swivels toward me a bit more, "that I have no idea what to do with this. I'm sitting here, next to you, and a big part of me just wants to break out in the silliest of smiles, just because I'm sitting next to you." She grimaces. "Honestly, Hera, if I had my way, I'd have jumped you as soon as you walked through the door. Which, even though I'm inexperienced, feels quite normal at this stage of our relationship. If we can even call it that. But I can't because you don't want me to. And I know I need to respect that, but in doing so, I have no idea where this could possibly go."

"I—", I begin, but not quickly enough, because Kat cuts me off.

"Please, I need to say one more thing." She swallows hard. "I appreciate your honesty, and I feel I need to be honest with you as well. There's no other way." She clears her throat. "When I was an escort, I met many women who were in long-term relationships in which nothing sexual ever happened. Then they ended up with me." Her voice trembles as she speaks.

I wish I had allowed her to pour us a drink now. What is she comparing us—me—to? But just as she's trying to be respectful toward me, I owe her the same courtesy. Which results in me not having anything to say at the moment. The silence quickly grows heavy between us and, tongue-tied or not, I know I need to say something.

"I didn't—" My voice breaks already. I take a deep breath. "After Sam died, I knew that was it for me. I knew I would never venture into another relationship again. For many reasons, of which you know a few. So, I guess… I think, that we both feel the same way about this. I think we both know this isn't going to work." As I speak these words that seem so final, my brain is frantically trying to come up with a solution. Some magic thought that has never previously occurred to me.

Nothing materializes. I've had all weekend to think about this. Why would I suddenly find a solution out of this impasse now?

"You have a strange way of showing people you don't want to be in a relationship with them." Kat's tone is almost venomous now. Bitter. Hurt.

"I shouldn't have let it come this far." I shuffle in my seat.

"Don't you want what we had? Even if it was ever so fleeting?"

"Part of me does," I admit. "But another part of me knows I'll never be able to give myself to you in the way you expect—the way you would always want me to. I'm sorry. I can't open myself up that way any longer."

"Why?" Her eyes are pleading and wet. "Why is it so hard?"

I can only shake my head. Because the crux of it, it seems, I'll never be able to explain to anyone else. Sam tried to understand, from the meager explanations I cobbled together—words I strung together so she'd have at least something to hold on to—but it was never a resolved issue between us.

"I'm sorry I can't give you more. I just can't." I feel as inadequate as I sound, so I get up. As far as I'm concerned, there's nothing left to say. "It's best if we don't take this any further. Best to end it now." The last few words come out poorly articulated.

"You get to decide that for us as well." Katherine stands up. "You don't even want to try to find a solution?"

What solution? I want to throw back at her. But I've said enough. I drew the only possible conclusion. It's over. I know it and I think Katherine knows it too.

"I'm sorry." I glance at her kitchen. I guess I won't be remodeling it then. "I'll stop coming to the Pink Bean. We won't have to see each other again."

"Jesus Christ, Hera." Kat's fists are balled. "You're just going to walk away? I was trying to have a conversation and you're just shutting the whole thing down?"

"It's for the best," I whisper. My heart breaks as I look into Kat's furious, sad face. How I wish I could take her in my arms—and let her do the things she wants to me.

"It's for nobody's best," Kat hisses. "But if that's how you want it." She turns away from me and walks toward the window. Her back straightens and she wraps her arms around herself.

I'd better let myself out.

Chapter Thirty-One

KAT

I HAVEN'T SAID a word to Rocco about Hera, earning me a few meaningful looks and the inevitable sexist remark, "Must be that time of the month then."

If it were anyone else, I would have opened up to him, but I can't give him a suitable answer when he asks why. Although I do know I'll have to tell him sooner rather than later.

I'll just tell him to ask his aunt why we broke up before we even got the chance to get properly started.

When Caitlin comes into the shop, I just want to disappear. I'm not interested in whatever angle she has come up with to get me on her show. I'm in the sort of mood where I want to tell her to stick her arguments where the sun doesn't shine—and to ask her to never mention her TV show to me again.

"Hello, hello." She greets Rocco and me with a wide smile. "I'll have a flat white and whatever you lovely people are having, of course."

"Caitlin, darling," Rocco says. "My mother won't shut up

about you. Will you put me out of my misery and come to dinner some time?"

"What a wonderfully passive-aggressive invitation. How could I possibly refuse?" Caitlin's beaming like she's having the best day of her life.

"Lovely," Rocco says. "Anyway, let's not pretend you've come to see me. I'll just prep your order while you have a chat with Kat."

If I had remembered Caitlin was coming over today, I would have asked Rocco to invent some sort of excuse for me. To avoid me needing to have yet another conversation I don't want to have.

"Uh-oh," Caitlin says as I sit down opposite her. "I detect a *mood*. Or is it just the Monday blues?" She cocks her head. "Things not working out as planned with Hera?"

I wave my hand. "That's over and done with already, so." I try to be stoic about it but tears sting behind my eyes nonetheless.

"Oh, shit. I'm so sorry, Katherine. That was very insensitive of me." She reaches out her hand and puts it on my wrist. "Apologies."

I inhale deeply. "It's fine. And it's for the best." I briefly look her in the eye. "Please excuse me, but I'm really not in the mood to be pitched to. And I'll never appear on your show, Caitlin. You need to let it go."

"We don't have to talk about the show." Her thumb caresses my skin.

Rocco clears his throat before putting our coffees down. I can't look at him either.

"Am I disturbing something?" he asks.

"Just give us a minute, darling," Caitlin says.

"If it's women stuff you're discussing, I don't want to know anyway," Rocco says, but from the way he says it, I can tell he knows something's up. Something else I haven't told him. He saunters off.

"You're very clearly cut up about this," Caitlin says.

A tear escapes the corner of my eye. I quickly brush it away. "Honestly, we were barely together. I'll get over it quickly." I should get over it quick enough, even though it doesn't feel like that will happen at all. But I'm just being silly.

"Do you want to talk about it?" Caitlin offers me a warm smile. "I know I'm loud and brash, but I'm a good listener. And I've seen a thing or two in my life."

I look at Caitlin and I see all she stands for, with her open relationship and her life filled with love and brimming with sexual vitality. Yet, if there's one person I know who could even begin to understand this, it might very well be her.

"Even though Hera broke up with me, I feel I gave her no choice. I feel like I made her do it so I didn't have to say the words."

Caitlin drinks her coffee but keeps her hand on my arm. She nods slowly, which encourages me to continue.

"We're both mature women who've had quite the life, you know. We were both coming at this with loads of baggage. She with losing her long-term partner and me, well, you know my story. And I thought because of that, it could somehow work, but I failed to see that Hera's reticence was much more about herself than about me. And I should have given her more time. I should have been kinder. Because now I feel like I've squandered my chances."

"Kat," Caitlin says softly. "What happened?"

"She—I—" If it's hard for me to say, I imagine how hard it must have been for Hera. "She doesn't want me. I mean, she can't bear to be touched. In a sexual way."

Caitlin nods again. "Does she identify as asexual?"

"No, I really don't think so. If she does, she hasn't said as such."

"You need to stop beating yourself up about this. It's not helping anyone," Caitlin says.

"I just let her leave. And why? Because I wasn't allowed to get her off? Maybe it's the ex-hooker in me." I nod vehemently. "It must be that. The hooker can't get her new girlfriend off."

"Here's a suggestion." Caitlin leans over the table. "How about I take you home? You're in a right state."

I sigh. "This is my business. We've only just opened. I can't just take a day off."

"Of course you can. There's two of you, remember?" She gives my wrist a squeeze. "Leave it with me." She makes to get up.

I quickly shoot out of my chair. "No," I say sternly. "I don't need anyone to do me any favors. I can take care of myself. I always have."

Caitlin holds up her hands defensively. "Fair enough. Sorry to be so 'Caitlin James' about it." She flashes me a smile. "But I mean it, Kat. You shouldn't be working. You clearly haven't told Rocco so just tell him what he wants to hear, that you're feeling unwell, and go home. I'll go with you. Let's talk about this properly." She steps from behind the table and puts a hand on my shoulder. "Let me help you." She leans in. "I believe I can."

She seems very sure of herself and I could do with some help today.

"Okay." I make my excuses to Rocco, inwardly making a promise to myself that I will call him tonight to tell him about Hera and me, once I've regrouped a little.

———

"Do you think you can accept her the way she is?" Caitlin asks. She's sitting in the same spot Hera sat in yesterday.

"No," I say honestly. "I think I'd constantly try to *fix* her."

"But that's only because you don't understand her. All compassion starts with understanding."

"Compassion? I don't want to be with someone I pity."

"Compassion is not the same as pity. Come on, Kat." Caitlin didn't come here to easily let me get away with things. "You must know there's a spectrum. All aspects of sexuality can be fluid. This includes the desire to be touched."

"It's not just that." I huff out a sigh. "It's her complete ineptitude to have a conversation about it."

"Maybe that's how you can help her." Caitlin's face softens. "I'm not saying it's an easy thing. In fact, it's hard. But worthwhile things are sometimes very hard."

"Good god, no speeches, please. Doing what I used to do, I've seen some things too, Caitlin. Yes, it's hard, and I don't want it to be. All I wanted was to fall in love."

"I'm not judging you," Caitlin says. Unlike Hera yesterday, she has accepted a drink. She circles a finger over the rim of the glass. "I'm just trying to put things in perspective."

I shake my head. "I appreciate that, but no matter what you say, Hera looked pretty determined when she ditched me, so even if I manage to look at things from a different angle, it's not going to change her mind, nor is it going to change *her.*" Maybe I should look at the list of therapist names Hera gave me last weekend. I wonder what she'll be talking to her own therapist about this week. Will she be able to put it into words for Jill?

"You don't know that." Caitlin puts her glass on the coffee table and fixes me with a stare. "I don't know where you got the dream notion that the beginning of a relationship is always easy. Well, I can guess, of course. So much of our modern aspirations can be blamed on the ideals we see on television every day. But I can assure you that it's not always easy. It certainly wasn't for Jo and me."

I huff out a chuckle. "I can imagine no relationship is easy for you in the beginning. Non-monogamy can be a hard sell to someone who's falling in love with you."

Caitlin shakes her head. "It's not about that. I don't go introducing myself to potential love interests like that. What I'm trying to say is that everyone's complicated. Everyone has a story. The trick is to make your stories align enough so you can have a start together."

"I don't think that's possible for me and Hera. Would we even be having this conversation if we stood a chance? Would I need all this convincing, first to convince myself and then to convince her?"

"You don't know. You never know. There's no answer to that question. The only thing you can do is try. If you feel it here"—she puts a hand on her chest—"then you owe it to yourself to try. I can see you're hurting. I can see it means so much to you. That's why I think you should try."

"In your experience," I take a breath and lean back, "do you think there's a possibility that Hera will ever inch toward the other end of the spectrum?"

Caitlin smiles at me. "Not a day goes by that I didn't wish I had a crystal ball."

"You and me both."

"The only real question you need to ask yourself, Kat, is whether Hera is worth it. Worth the wait. Worth the possible sacrifice you'll have to make. Worth accepting how she is, now and in the future."

"Then there's the minor detail that she has made it abundantly clear she doesn't want a relationship," I say, not without sarcasm in my tone.

"Clearly, she's fooling herself. Why else was she going out with you?" She drums her fingers on the armrest of the sofa. "Chances are, Hera hasn't got things all figured out either. She's probably just as miserable as you are."

I can't help it. A small flare of hope lights up in my chest. I want to believe Caitlin, although it's mainly myself I need to believe in. In my capability to be the person Hera needs me to be. In my willingness to try.

"Should I call her?" My pulse picks up speed.

"I can't tell you what to do, Kat, but, erm…". Something glints in Caitlin's eyes.

"What?"

"If you and Hera get back together as a result of this chat, will you pay me back by coming on my show?" She laughs heartily.

"You are relentless." I squint at her. "The answer is no and will always be no."

"You can't blame a girl for trying." Caitlin winks at me.

Indeed, you can't, I think, as I start coming up with my plan to get Hera back. Or, at the very least, have one more conversation with her. I'll give her a few days. Make sure she's had her appointment with Jill, who looked sensible and kind. Maybe on Thursday, I can get Hera to talk to me again.

Chapter Thirty-Two

HERA

It's hard to walk into Jill's office, especially after she has seen Katherine and me together. It seems like a lifetime ago that we were at Alyssa's show at the gallery.

"Hera." Jill greets me with a different kind of smile. She may think she knows what I'm going to say, but then she hasn't taken a proper look at my face yet. "Sit and give me some good news," she says.

My face must be expressionless, because Jill just gives me a hopeful smile.

"There's no good news," I say. "We tried and failed."

"What does that mean?" The smile slides off Jill's lips.

"It means that Katherine and I didn't even make it through the weekend."

"What happened? You looked so full of promise last Thursday? You could hardly keep your eyes off her."

"I messed it up." That knot that coiled in my stomach on Sunday is still there, still hardening—like a harsh reminder of what I said to Katherine. "It was good for a minute or two, but then I—I just had to end it. I've said it time and time again. I don't want another relationship. Sam died. It was hard. I did the work; I grieved; built up my life again. That's enough for me. I don't need more."

"I call bullshit," Jill says. "But, please, do elaborate."

She's got my hackles up already. "Ever since Sam died, have I told you any differently?" I'm starting to get sick of everyone pretending to know me better than I know myself.

"Not in words, no, you haven't," Jill says.

"What else is there?"

"So much, Hera. So very much." She crosses one leg over the other. "I was glad I saw you with Katherine. I like to think I can read people and situations rather well and there was plenty of chemistry between the two of you. I didn't need to hear either of you speak to conclude that. I witnessed it. I felt it. So much promise. So, tell me, is it over already because you don't want to be in a relationship at all, or because you don't want to be in a relationship with her specifically?"

"Definitely not because of Katherine specifically," I blurt out. "She's amazing. She deserves much, much better than me." A lump swells in the back of my throat.

"Why? I've been sitting across from you on a weekly basis for many years now and I can tell you for a fact that you're no less than any other human I've ever met. So why, when you're so clearly infatuated with Katherine, would someone else be better for her?"

"Because…" I should have canceled the appointment if I didn't want to talk about this. "I don't necessarily think there's anything wrong with me, but ninety-nine percent of the population would disagree. Katherine included."

"Did you have a difference of opinion?" Jill genuinely doesn't seem to know what I'm getting at.

"You could call it that."

Silence from Jill now. It's up to me.

"We had… we had sex. Well, not really as far as she was concerned, I guess. I told you about this before. In the very beginning when I started coming here. I don't seem to feel any need for sexual satisfaction. It just doesn't interest me. It hasn't for a while."

Jill nods. "Of course I remember, Hera."

"Which makes me rather unsuitable for a relationship. Unless I find myself a 'pillow princess', as Katherine referred to it."

"A what?" Jill asks.

"A woman who, um, likes to receive but not give back."

"Right." Jill nods. "Well, I'm sure those women exist. There are plenty of men out there like that so why should it be any different for us?" She sends me a tight smile, making me wonder about her own personal situation for a split second.

"Maybe, but, honestly, I can't be bothered going out looking for them. How would I even find them?"

"Let's go back to Katherine for a minute," Jill says. "When you say you had sex, do you mean that some things happened between you?"

I nod and swallow. The lump in my throat makes it difficult.

"And you enjoyed being with her like that?"

"Yes."

"And, up to a point, she enjoyed being with you?"

I chuckle at Jill's coyness—I'm in desperate need of a chuckle. "She most certainly looked as though she was enjoying it." My chuckle turns into a wide smile at the memory. I take a few seconds to revel in it. In the memory of Katherine's gorgeously voluptuous body, all of it ready for me. A surge of heat shoots through me, only to die with a sad whimper because of how swiftly it all ended.

"And you didn't think you could take things from there? See where it went?" Jill asks.

"No, because that would be unfair. For starters, I'd be giving her false hope because I will never change."

"But can't you see you've changed so much already?" Jill says.

That gives me pause. I don't feel like I've changed at all. I examine Jill's face. Maybe it's sad that my therapist knows me better than my own sister. I could never talk about any of this with Hilda. It's just impossible. Just as impossible as me changing in certain ways. Or maybe I've become so entrenched in this idea I have of myself, that my mind can't even envision the possibility of change.

"You have, Hera. And I should know. I have notes to fall back on. You're nothing like the woman who first came to see me and, these days, you're also no longer the woman solely defined by the loss of her partner."

"That may very well be." I did go back to work. I did, in my own way, sleep with Katherine. "But some things will never change."

"Not necessarily, Hera."

"You've lost me." I look at her expectantly. I'm not that stubborn that I don't want to change in a way that might give me another shot with Kat—I just have no clue how to go about manifesting said change.

"Change is not a big bang. It's a slow, incremental process. It's you, showing up here every week for all these years, doing the work. It's you, taking a chance on life again by remodeling Rocco and Katherine's coffee shop. It's you saying yes to renovating Katherine's kitchen. It's you going through the process while barely noticing it. You wouldn't have gone out with Katherine six months ago. Maybe even two months ago, you wouldn't have gone to the gallery opening with her, knowing I'd be there. Ever so slowly, you're opening yourself up to more aspects of life again. You're allowing yourself to blossom again."

"Maybe," I say. "But—"

"No, Hera, no buts. Surely, you must have felt this as well."

"Of course," I admit. "Mainly because of Katherine, though. And now she's gone."

"Which brings us to the million-dollar question: do you really want her out of your life?"

"If you put it like that, then the answer is no. But, and I really do need this particular 'but'." I lock my gaze on Jill's for a second before continuing. "She said so herself. Sexuality is very important to her and I don't think she has it in her to accept me for who I am."

"How about a different kind of relationship, then? A platonic one, for instance?"

"You mean that we should just be friends?" I shake my head. "I think that ship has sailed and, well…"

"What?" Jill insists.

"I'm very attracted to her."

Jill quirks up her eyebrows. "Hera, let me tell you something, seeing as that is what you pay me to do." She throws in a smile. "Regardless of the reasons, you've been sexually dormant for a long time. Then you meet this woman who is literally sparkling with vitality and sexuality. I met her and I've seen it. It only took me a split second to come to that conclusion. Of course you're attracted to her. And, lo and behold, she's attracted to you as well. Allow yourself to enjoy that sensation. It's so much rarer than you might think."

"But that's just the thing. I can't enjoy it." The words come out almost automatically, but deep down I know they're a lie.

"I think you can."

I blow some air through my nostrils. "I thought this was meant to be a safe space. An hour per week where I can feel understood."

"It's not my job to understand you, Hera. Nor am I being paid to coddle you. My task is to make you see that you are worth exactly the same as anyone else and that, for that reason, you're entitled to happiness. For the record, I believe we've made excellent progress so far." She uncrosses her legs and leans her elbows on her knees. "Let's sum things up, shall we? You have the hots for Katherine. She has the hots for you. Tell me, what's the worst that could happen if you gave it another shot?"

"The worst has already happened." My tone isn't as insistent as before. I want to believe Jill with all my heart, but I can't see how I can do that. It's like I'm missing a step in between where my thought process is and where she wants it to go.

"But you have the power to undo it."

"I don't believe I have."

"You do if you want to." Jill grins at me. "I know you're as stubborn as they come, Hera, but you're never going to convince me otherwise. I can try to make you see these things, and ideally, I'd take more time to do so, to allow you to draw your own conclusion, but I think you might be running out of time when it comes to Katherine." Her grin softens. "If only you could sit in my seat and see what I see when I look at you. If I could have held up a mirror to you last Thursday to show you the grin on your face when you stood next to her. Don't deny yourself that any longer in your life, Hera. You've done that long enough. Don't let fear take that away from you."

"Fear?"

Jill nods. "The sneakiest, most damaging, most paralyzing emotion there is. Responsible for all missed opportunities in the universe." She narrows her eyes. "Can I challenge you?"

I shrug. "You're probably going to say that's part of your job as well."

"I want to give you a homework assignment, but I want you to start on it right here and now."

"Okay." I might as well go along with it.

"Get your phone out."

I fish my phone out of my back pocket.

"Start a new text message."

"To whom?"

"To whom do you think?"

"You want me to text Katherine?" The grip on my phone intensifies.

Jill nods. "And I'll tell you exactly what to write."

"No. You're going too far."

"I know I am. This is not professional. I'll admit that. But I also know that if I ask you to contact her after you leave here, you're going to find a dozen excuses not to."

"You can't force me."

"Of course I can't force you, but I can tell you, as someone who knows you very well, that you won't regret it. And if you text her now, she may text back before the hour is up. I can then help you with a possible reply." Jill sits there beaming a smile at me.

"But I need to think this through some more. We haven't resolved the whole—"

"This is not something you have to think through any more, Hera. This is something you need to *do*." She sends me another smile. "The best way to beat fear has always been action."

I glance at my phone. I wanted to delete Katherine's number last night, but I couldn't bring myself to do it.

Something inside me lights up at the prospect of contacting her. And having Jill guide me through the process makes it easier.

"What should I write?"

"Hi. I've been an ass. Can we talk?" Jill says. When I look at her she has a goofy smile plastered across her face. "Just kidding."

Even though this doesn't really feel like the right time for a joke, I appreciate the lightening of the mood.

"How about this," Jill says. "I miss you. Can we talk?"

My palms start sweating. "I miss you? That doesn't really sound like something I would ever text to anyone."

"You never texted Sam that you missed her?"

"She was always there. I never had a chance to miss her."

"Not even when you first got together? Before you lived together?"

"That was decades ago."

"What would you write? Put it in your own words," Jill says.

I glance at my phone. At Katherine's name in the 'to' field of the message. What would I say?

"I should probably apologize." I look at Jill.

She nods. "That would be a good icebreaker."

"Okay." My fingers tremble as I start typing.

I'm sorry for all the things I said on Sunday. Can we talk?

"Now press send," Jill says.

I do as I'm told. She was right. I wouldn't have done this on my own at home—I wouldn't have had the nerve.

Jill glances at her watch. "You can wait here until she replies, if you like. You're my last client of the night."

"*If* she replies," I say. I put my phone on the table between us. I scan Jill's face. I can't help but think she's getting something out of this as well. She has crossed the line between client and therapist, the line that she has insisted for years should always exist, twice this evening.

Maybe it was seeing each other outside of this office. Maybe she has gotten truly invested in my future with Katherine, which is either still possible or eternally doomed.

We'll soon find out.

Chapter Thirty-Three

KAT

WHEN MY PHONE lights up with a text, hope sparks in my chest. But it's Wednesday evening and this is Hera's time with Jill—which is surely a time when texting is not allowed.

I'm apprehensive when I pick up my phone. It might be Alana, giving it one last try. Or worse, Caitlin—although I think she has well and truly received the message now. It could also be Rocco, checking in on me. I know Hera hasn't been responding to his texts or calls and he's worried she'll start locking herself away in her house again.

I look at the screen. It's a message from Hera.

I read it again and again. After my conversation with Caitlin, I had planned to contact her. To ask her to meet one last time, if only to not have things end on such a sour note between us. I hadn't expected her to contact me. What should I do? Text back or just bite the bullet and call her?

I decide to call her. Perhaps I can deduce something more from the tone of her voice than from these words on my phone screen.

Who am I kidding? I just want to hear her voice. And she did say she was sorry—that's most baffling of all.

My heart beats in my throat as I call her. It rings three times before she picks up.

"Hi," she says, her voice much more assured than I had expected. "Thanks for calling." Ah, no, there's the tension.

"Thanks for texting," I say. "The answer is yes. We can talk. Whenever suits you."

"Erm." There's a pause and I hear some shuffling on the other end of the line. Or is that a muffled voice?

"Are you not alone?" I ask. I strain my ear. Is that Rocco I hear? Did he get through to her after all? Gave her a talking to? It's certainly his style with anyone else, but I can't imagine him giving his aunt a stern lecture.

"I'm with Jill," Hera says.

I only met Jill briefly, but I'd like to go over to her practice and give her a big hug.

"Is it too late to come over tonight?" Hera asks.

"No," I blurt out. I don't care that I have to get up early tomorrow. I need to see Hera. I probably wouldn't sleep a wink if we set a date for tomorrow, anyway. "Please, come over. Or I can come to yours."

"I'm still out and about. I can be there in twenty minutes," Hera says.

"Okay. I'll see you then."

"Okay," Hera says and hangs up.

———

Hera arrives seven minutes earlier than she estimated. I've been counting down. When I open the door I'm both nervous and almost beside myself with excitement.

Even though she's wearing a variation of the clothes she always wears, and they might as well be the same as the ones she wore when she was here last on Sunday, she comes across as completely different. She hasn't come to break up with me again, to double confirm her sentiments about our relationship, which makes me relax a little. But still, the things she said to me can't be un-said, and we have a lot to discuss.

She waves off my offer of a beer because she has to drive, so I present her with a glass of water instead.

I invite her to sit and force myself to sit next to her, even though my legs want to pace—at least until we've both said what we want to say.

"I was surprised you texted me during your time with Jill." I start things off.

"It was a homework assignment she didn't trust me to do at home." Hera runs a hand through her hair.

I chuckle. "Have I told you that I really like Jill?"

"Look, Kat, hm… I've had some time to think and I've had this chat with Jill and, I guess, the conclusion is that, if it were up to me, I'd like for us to try again. I mean, I don't suddenly have all the answers but I shouldn't have walked out on you like that on Sunday."

"I understand why you did. I could have been kinder and more understanding."

Hera shakes her head. "I disagree. This isn't about you being more understanding. And yes, when I came here on Sunday, a big part of me did arrive with the intention of breaking things off. But another part of me wanted to explain more about how I feel. About how I am. But I didn't do that at all. Mainly because I didn't know how, so I chose the easiest road and I just left." She looks at me with a steady gaze. "So, thank you so much for agreeing to see me. It means a lot to me."

"I've had time to think as well and it's really not all down to you."

"Well, at least we're talking." Hera's grin is almost shy.

"The past few days, I've been thinking that, increasingly,

life is all about what we are able to communicate. And I don't mean just in words." I say.

"I did a pretty bad job of communicating," Hera says.

"You have to take the circumstances into account. I probably shouldn't have said that thing about a certain type of client I had." I just want to take Hera in my arms, but I'm also reminded of what I said to Caitlin—about always wanting to fix her—which is not something I can repeat tonight.

"I'm not going to lie," Hera says. "Jill spurred me on to text you, and then you called, and now I'm here. But I don't really know what to say." There's her pleading gaze on me again. "Where do we go from here? Is only the intention of being with each other going to be enough?"

I inch a little closer to her. "Who knows what's enough? All I know is that it's a start."

Hera glances at my hands.

"I should have talked to you before we ended up in bed. It's not an excuse, but things did suddenly move very fast."

"Tell me about it. I was just driving you home and, out of nowhere, there was your hand on my knee." I try a smile.

Hera nods, as if she's guilty of something. "I just—I find you irresistible and simply feeling that way about someone has caused some serious clashes with the identity I've made up for myself."

"And what would that identity be?" I scoot a little closer still.

"I think you know." Her lips don't smile, but her eyes do. "Some kind of untouchable butch builder." She snickers. "Maybe I should start tearing down my own walls."

I burst into a chuckle because it's such an un-Hera-like thing to say. Maybe Jill put these words into her mouth. But it doesn't matter where they came from. It's the sentiment behind them that counts. Like Hera's already taking the first swing of the hammer to that very sturdy wall around her heart.

"Maybe I can help you with that," I offer.

"You might break a fingernail or two in the process." Hera's smile does curl up the corners of her mouth now.

"You can't make an omelet and all that," I say, mirroring her smile.

"I can't make you any promises, Kat. I am still who I am —who I've become. And if we do decide to see each other again, I will need you to be patient."

"I've waited for someone like you for a very long time. Patience shouldn't be that much of a problem." I reach for her hand.

"What do you need from *me*?" Hera asks.

"For starters, I'd really like you to redo my kitchen," I joke. I stroke my thumb over Hera's palm. "I need you to talk to me. That's all. And I know it's hard for you, but I need you to try."

"I will," Hera says. "Although I'm not sure I have much more talking in me tonight."

"For tonight," I say, "It's enough that you're here."

"I'd like to stay," Hera says. "I'd like to just sleep in your arms." She tilts her head and leans in. "And right now, I'd very much like to kiss you."

"Both things can be arranged." As her lips touch down on mine, I feel all the way into my bones, that Hera has taken the biggest hurdle already. She came back and showed a little bit more of herself to me. As our kiss deepens, the words I just spoke to her echo in my mind: for tonight, it's enough.

Chapter Thirty-Four

HERA

I GLANCE AT MY SISTER, my lifeline after Sam died. I don't need to tell her everything, but I most certainly want to share certain things with her.

"I've met someone." I find and hold her gaze.

"You don't say." Hilda winks at me.

"Don't tell me Rocco has beaten me to it." I expel a sigh.

"I don't need my son to tell me when my sister has got the hots for someone."

I shake my head. "I've barely spoken to you. How would you know?"

"How would I know?" Hilda feigns indignation. "I only grew up with you. I've only known you for all the fifty-one years of your life. You're still my little sister. I don't need much to put two and two together. Especially not when Rocco tells me you can't keep away from The Pink Bean." She slants a little in my direction. "Apparently he's worried about you as well."

I roll my eyes, even though Rocco's concern touches me. "I knew it."

"We're family. We have no secrets. Especially if the

woman you have the hots for is Rocco's best friend and business partner. But I'm glad you've finally found the time to tell your one and only sister." Hilda runs a hand through her long, wavy hair.

"It's still early days. There really isn't that much to tell."

"Hey." Hilda's gaze softens. "I'm glad you've met someone. You've come a long way since…"

"Since Sam died." I might as well complete her sentence. I might as well say the words that have been so hard to say for all those long, dark months.

Hilda nods. "I like Katherine," she says. "She's a good person, I know that much."

"You have no objections to your sister dating someone who used to, well"—I clear my throat—"you know." It still seems hard to say out loud, especially to my sister.

"I've known Katherine much longer than you have and I've no problem with her. She's Rocco's best friend and I trust my son's judgment."

"I should probably have done the same instead of making up my mind about her before I had a chance to get to know her."

"You shouldn't blame yourself for having a very human reaction," Hilda says.

"Still. It was a crappy way to behave."

Hilda shrugs. "We all have our faults and we all make mistakes. The sooner we accept that, the happier we'll all be."

"That's very philosophical of you." I drink the wine she has poured me.

She shrugs. "When enough people die on you, you're forced to look at life differently." Her gaze skitters away. "Sam's death was a blow to me as well."

I nod. "I know."

"She confided in me, you know. She… told me things. Things that, perhaps, weren't always so easy to tell you."

"About how I wasn't always the easiest person to be around?" I can say it with a hint of a smile on my lips now.

"She certainly didn't have to tell me that." Hilda chuckles.

"Neither one of us were saints."

"She loved you regardless. She accepted you, Hera. With all your idiosyncrasies and all your ambivalence about, well, certain things."

I shake my head. Hilda may think she knew what was going on between Sam and me, and all the things we never got to smooth over, but she doesn't know the half of it.

"And it was so hard seeing you have to go through that," she continues. "Not just her loss, but your guilt about all the things you thought you put her through."

"Things weren't good between us." I don't think I've ever said those words out loud to my sister—only to Jill. It's different speaking to Hilda about this, because she knew Sam well. They were friends. "They hadn't been for a while."

"I know that. As I said, Sam confided in me. More than you think."

I briefly scan Hilda's face. I'm not sure I want her to share with me the things my dead partner told her about me. I also strongly suspect—although, how can I truly be sure?—that Sam wouldn't have told her the details, the crux of it all.

"I went through the change before you did, Hera. I know all about it," Hilda says.

I huff out a nervous chuckle. "You're my sister and I love you dearly, but I'm not sure I want to have this conversation with you."

"We don't have to go into specifics." Hilda leans over the table again. "But it's about time you forgave yourself. Sam's never coming back to tell you that she forgives you for everything. You're the only one who holds that power now."

I shake my head. "I'm not sure I ever can. She died too soon, too suddenly for that. We were meant to get past that bump in our road together and her death meant we couldn't. That we never will." Tears sting behind my eyes. "When she died," my throat swells, "we hadn't spoken in days. Not had a proper conversation, anyway. I hadn't told her I loved her for a very long time. For all I knew, we might not even have made it. If she had lived."

"You were together for a very long time," Hilda says. "Every marriage, every single partnership goes through the lowest of lows. It's human nature. It's life and life will always happen. And death, unfortunately, waits for no one."

"I just wish…" I try to push the tears back where they came from. "I wish I'd had a chance to tell her that, despite everything, I still loved her."

"Hera." Hilda looks me straight in the eye. "Of course she knew."

"I certainly didn't show her."

"You don't always have to show somebody you love them." She narrows her eyes. "Trust me, Sam knew. And I know because she told me. Okay? Because I told her how bloody stubborn you could be sometimes and how you needed time to adjust to certain changes but that all of that didn't mean that you loved her any less."

I can't hold back the tears now as I look at my sister and a thought that I haven't been able to articulate shoots through my mind. A thought I could never share with my sister.

If I couldn't allow Sam, the woman I loved more than anything and anyone—my partner who died on me before I had the chance to figure any of this out for myself—to touch me, how could I ever allow anyone else to do so again?

Chapter Thirty-Five

KAT

When I arrive at Hera's, I have no idea what might happen. Even though she stayed over on Wednesday, her warm, naked body pressed against me throughout the night, nothing else happened and not much more was said.

We've spoken on the phone since, but Hera is a woman who needs to be experienced live. Half of what she wants to say, but can't express with words, I need to read off her face and translate from her body language.

She opens the door wide and kisses me on the cheek, almost politely.

Once she has closed the door, she grins at me, and says, "Please tell me tomorrow's Rocco's turn to open the Pink Bean?"

I nod. "We take turns on Saturdays and I opened last week, so." I look into Hera's eyes and something in her glance tells me this Friday evening will be very different from the last. Not because she will—miraculously—allow me to be all over her tonight, but because she appears to no longer be in the paralyzing grip of fear.

"Good." Only then, does she pull me close. She wraps

her arms around me. "I need to tell you something," she whispers in my ear.

———

It's a beautiful evening and Hera's taken me to her back patio. She has fixed us each a grapefruit mimosa—I've let it slip that it's my favorite tipple.

"I'm not very good at explaining things." She holds up her hands. "I think that's why I was so dead set on becoming a builder. At least in my choice of profession I could express myself with my hands."

You've expressed yourself plenty with your hands already, I want to say, but I know it's not appropriate. She wants to tell me something that is important and difficult. My attention can't help but be sidetracked for a moment by her big strong hands, though.

She sips from her mimosa and pulls a bit of a face. "Did I put too much grapefruit juice in?" she asks.

"No. They're perfect."

"Okay, if you say so."

"I do." I send her an encouraging smile.

"When Sam…" She clears her throat and starts again. "When Sam died we were… How to put this? We were going through somewhat of a cold war period in our relationship. Things were not good. Not in our daily life and certainly not in the bedroom." Hera stares at the liquid in her glass. I can already tell a grapefruit mimosa will never be her drink—for starters, it's way too pink for her.

"It had been going on for a while. It's one of the reasons I sought therapy. Even though, sadly, Jill couldn't fix me quickly enough for Sam and me to make up before she died. For me to take that crucial first step to repair our relationship." She snickers. "In a way, it's kind of silly. But hindsight and all that, you know." She drinks and pulls a face again. "I was going through menopause and it not only seriously fucked with my head, it fucked with my body as well. I tried all sorts of things. Every patch and hormone treatment you can think of, but nothing really seemed to help. I got more sullen, more depressed, ever more disgusted by my body. I grew so unbelievably uncomfortable in my skin, of course I didn't want Sam to touch me. I stopped touching her as well. We stopped having sex altogether. Which didn't help matters." Hera briefly looks me in the eye, then glances away again.

"To cut a long story short. We grew more and more apart. Most nights I slept in the spare room. I didn't know what to do with myself and with this whole menopause and midlife crisis business. It's as though it plunged me into this big existential crisis. Things were bad. And then she died." Hera's voice breaks. "She was just gone."

I wish we didn't have this table between us. I need to stop myself from getting up and throwing my arms around her. But I can tell Hera's not done yet. She has more to say.

"The ironic thing is that after Sam died, my doctor tried me on a new hormone replacement combo that actually worked. I started feeling better about myself." She sighs. "Of course by then she was gone and I no longer had the chance to tell her how stupid I'd been. How disrespectful of her needs and her desires. Disrespectful of our relationship as well because I'd had actual thoughts of leaving her." Hera wraps her fingers tightly around the delicate Champagne flute. "Try standing upright in front of your dead partner's coffin then." In one swift movement, she brings the flute to her lips and knocks back all of its contents. "The truly excruciating part was that it was all in my head. I got trapped in this infinite loop in my mind, because, once she was gone, all I wanted was for her to come back. But I could only see it then, when she was already dead. When it was too late." She puts her glass down and pinches the bridge of her nose.

"Hera," I whisper. "I'm so sorry you had to go through that."

"She was the woman I loved and I hadn't kissed her for weeks. How's that for loving someone?" Hera's voice breaks, but then she seems to regroup. She straightens her frame. She's still staring straight ahead. As though she's still afraid to look at me—as though what she has just told me might make me dislike her, while it only makes me grow fonder of her. Because I know this is hard for her, but she's having the courage to show herself to me. She's finding the words she believed were so unspeakable.

"Hera." I can't stop myself any longer. I get up. I need to touch her. I need to make her feel some warmth. I crouch in front of her and put my hands on her knees. "I'm sure Sam understood, if not all, then at least part of what you were going through. Isn't that what the people we love do? They know us better than we know ourselves and they understand us, through the good and the bad."

"I treated her so appallingly that, after she died, I vowed to never enter into a relationship again. I think the coping mechanism I developed when I was at my worst, the complete shutdown of any physical intimacy, has become so ingrained in my mind that I don't know how to get past it now. Even when my body is clearly telling me it wants more." Hera looks down at me. Her mouth is set in a downward grimace. I just want to kiss it off her. I want to see a smile on her face again as soon as possible. But I can't kiss her yet. I can only make my intentions known by gently squeezing her knee.

"I can understand how awful Sam dying like that must have been for you. She was still so young and you were going through that rough patch, but Hera, you're still alive. You're not dead. You need to find a way to live your life without punishing yourself."

"Turns out that's bloody hard to do." Hera looks me in the eye. Her face has softened although I can still see the struggle in it. The battle between wanting to chastise herself eternally for being what she considers a below-par partner and what meeting me has awakened in her.

"I dare to disagree." I push myself up because this crouch is getting quite uncomfortable. I hold out my hand to her. "It certainly doesn't have to be as hard as you're making it."

She takes my hand but doesn't get up.

"How about, just for tonight, we go about things a little differently?" I may not have a great relationship track record, but I do have some experience in making people let their guard down. "How about…" I give her hand a tug and she lets me pull her up.

"You're surprisingly strong." Hera grins at me as we come face to face. "How about what?"

"How about we go inside and we approach this from the opposite direction?"

"Can you be a bit less cryptic, please?" She grins at me.

"I know you're scared. And I know you have an endless stream of thoughts running through your head. But I also know, for an absolute, indisputable fact, that you want me. Why don't you let me show you just a tiny glimpse of how things can be between us and we take things from there? Who knows, maybe we can silence some of those voices in your head for good." I inch closer to her. "All due respect to Sam, for your loss, and what you went through, but I'm not Sam. I'm Katherine. My more extravagant friends sometimes call me K.Jo. And I'm here for you, because, guess what, Hera Walker?" I bring my lips to her ear. "I think I'm falling in love with you."

She lets go of my hands and curls her arms around me, holding me close.

"I think I might be falling in love with you too." Hera mumbles her words, but I hear them loud and clear. They reverberate in my ear for a long time after.

Chapter Thirty-Six

HERA

KAT LEADS me inside my own house. Maybe we should have met at her place, where there aren't so many pictures of Sam strewn across the lounge.

But I let Katherine take the lead. I need to let her. I know what will happen if I take it from her. My brain will start short-circuiting again and I will thwart all her wonderful, thoughtful intentions.

Even though I invited Katherine over to have a much-needed chat, I think I've said all I can say for one night. I've said more than I have said to anyone—apart from Jill—in a very long time.

Last night's conversation with Hilda had me tossing and turning for a while, her words rummaging through my head, keeping me awake, until I found some small comfort in the fact that Sam could, at least, talk to Hilda, while I shut myself off from her. While I was trying to explain something to Jill that I would only truly come to understand after Sam died.

I needed time and I didn't know we wouldn't have the

time. But I realize that I couldn't know this then. It was impossible for me to know that Sam's time was up when I rebuffed her advances for the umpteenth time, saying, "Later." I wasn't to know that, for the two of us, there was no more later.

Hilda was right. I'm the only one who can forgive myself for that. And just maybe, Katherine leading me up the stairs of my own house the way she's doing now, can help me with that. Because one thing's for sure: I need a little help. Frankly, I need all the help I can get. Because I'm still alive, even though, for the longest time, it felt like a crucial part of me had died with Sam.

Kat stops in front of my bedroom door.

"I'm not going to do one single thing you don't want me to do," she says solemnly. "But do know that every single thing I do, I'll want to do with all my heart."

She stands in front of me the way I've come to know her. So tall and charismatic and impossible to ignore. For a split second, it occurs to me how foolish I was to walk away from her last Sunday. A woman like this. The exact same sentiment applied to Sam when I had thoughts about leaving her, while all I ever really wanted was to be with her. Even though I didn't know how to do it, how to break through that wall. I had no clue how to demolish the thought patterns I had carefully constructed to save myself from some upcoming pain—while the most excruciating pain was already tearing me apart. Tearing us apart.

It's for Sam that I nod at Katherine. It's for Sam that, today, I decide to trust Kat and her great big heart—because Hilda was right about that as well. It's for Sam that I'm letting Katherine in. I'll never get the chance to do that with Sam anymore. But Sam is dead and I'm alive. And here I stand, gazing into Kat's dark eyes.

"You're so beautiful," I say. And maybe because of the darkness in my heart I didn't think I deserved to be touched by such beauty. But my mind is changing. Three women who have survived with me have taken care of that. My sister, my therapist, and Katherine Jones. My nephew's best friend. A woman I deemed so incompatible with me, I sabotaged my feelings for her from the very beginning.

"Right back at you," Kat says, and her smile melts me to the very core. "Shall we go in?" she asks, her voice soft and warm.

"Yes, please."

She opens the door and we walk into my bedroom.

Once inside, something about Katherine changes, a slight shift in her demeanor. As though, now that's she's gotten me over the threshold of this room, she knows she's got me.

She might be right.

She brings her hand to the top button of my shirt—I dressed up for her visit—and asks, "May I take this off?" Her head is tilted and her voice husky and low.

I couldn't even protest if I wanted to. Something in me has changed as well.

"You don't have to ask permission for everything you do," I say. "I trust you, and you need to trust me to let you know when I want you to stop."

"Deal." Katherine's smile is so wide and inviting that, before she has the chance to undo one of my buttons, I pull her in for a kiss.

This kiss is different from all the others we have exchanged since we met, because, as I kiss her, I let go of my biggest fear. Whenever a thought creeps up on me that I'm betraying Sam or myself or, even, deceiving Katherine by doing this, by allowing this, I shut it down firmly. I talk back, the way Jill has taught me to do, something I never seemed to have gotten the hang of until now—and I simply enjoy the exquisite sensation of Katherine's lips on mine.

I enjoy the anticipation, the thrill in the air, because I'm no longer afraid of what might happen. I'm no longer wasting all my energy and focus on coming up with plausible excuses for why I want her to stop. The biggest excuse dissolving when I told her the truth. When I admitted my inadequacies as a partner and a lover. Not only to her, but to myself. I've not forgiven myself for any of that just yet. But Katherine has promised to help me with that and, just as I trust her to only have my very best interests at heart when she removes my jeans later—as I know she will—I trust that she will help me with finding that forgiveness somewhere inside myself as well.

She has already done so much for me.

"You're distracting me from the task at hand," she says, when we break from our kiss. Her red lipstick is smeared all over her mouth and the sight of it makes me smile. It's a smile that emanates all the way from my core. My entire body is smiling as I look at Katherine, as I take her in, drink her in, let her presence overwhelm me. As I relinquish control in a way I haven't been able to do in years. Sometimes you need to start over, I think, as my gaze follows the motions of Kat's hands on my buttons. Sometimes you need to hit that reset button and try again. Because being with Katherine will never erase who I was with Sam, on my good days and my bad days, but it will give me a chance to try to be my best self again.

She guides my shirt off and ogles my bra. But before she touches me again, she hoists her own top over her head and gets rid of her own bra first.

The sight of her bare breasts makes my mouth water. I've

been such a fool to deny myself this because standing here with Kat, knowing, in every fiber of my being what's going to happen next, makes me feel much more alive than I ever was in the months before Sam died. It's a hard thing to admit but it's also a comforting thought, because this is how life is. It knocks you down one day, only to pick you up the next.

Sometimes I'm happy, sometimes I'm sad; mostly, I'm somewhere in between. Then a woman like Katherine comes along, a woman with her own myriad of complications, but a woman so radiant, so confident, so sure of herself when she comes for me, it would be foolish to resist any further. It would be foolish to resist that burst of happiness she brings with her when she walks through my door. When, as now, she brings her hands to my back, and unhooks my bra.

She throws it onto a chair, then looks me in the eye, before dropping her gaze. Her glance on my breasts makes my nipples rise up, as though they're reaching toward her. She glances up at me again, briefly, looking for signs of me wanting her to stop—but I don't want her to stop.

She lifts her hands to my breasts and cups them ever so gently. Her touch is so warm, so exhilarating, such a shocking reminder of things I'd never thought I'd feel again, a single tear rolls down my cheek. It falls off my chin, onto the back of her hand. She leans in and kisses it away, while her hands softly cup my breasts.

It's then I know that someone like Katherine is what I've needed all along. Someone to kiss away my tears, to break down my walls, to give me pleasure once again. As her fingers curl around my nipples, I'm beginning to believe that I might just deserve it—that I might just deserve her.

I revel in the sensation of her hands on my breasts, her fingers on my nipples. I keep my eyes wide open so I can see her face. A small part of me is afraid that, when I close them,

I'll see Sam's face. With that look she gave me toward the end. All desperation and need. So I focus on Katherine's lovely features. Her big brown eyes. The lipstick I smudged on her lips earlier. She tilts her head a little. Another question. But it's one I don't have to reply to, not anymore. She can read it in my eyes now, I'm sure of that.

Kat lifts my breast to her lips and takes my nipple in her mouth. I do close my eyes then—her face is out of view anyway. On the back of my eyelids, while Kat's tongue skates along my nipple, I don't see Sam. I don't see anything at all. And isn't that the point of closing my eyes? To no longer see and to magnify the sensation of her tongue lavishing itself on my nipple. Because that's what it feels like. She started off gently, but now she's sucking my nipple into her mouth and all I feel is her hunger for me. The difference with the last time I faced Kat's hunger is that, now, I feed off of it myself. My desire grows with hers. My thoughts are no longer in the way. Kat wants me and I want her. It really can be that simple.

Before Kat focuses on my other nipple, she pauses briefly. I open my eyes and catch her glancing up at me. God, her eyes. In them I see a blend of kindness and unbridled lust. It's not the first time I've come across that look in her eyes. It's the kind of look, I know now, that will thaw the coldest of ice queens. How did I manage to resist it before? Because I sure can't do that anymore now.

I give her a slight nod of the head so she'll know I want more. Much more.

Instead of enveloping my other nipple with her lips, she takes my hand and leads me to the bed. We lie down, I on my back and Kat half on top of me. Our breasts are pressed together and I don't know what I want more. For Kat to lick my nipples again or for her to gaze into my eyes like this for a good while longer.

"I want you," I say. My voice is not shy or timid—there's not a glimmer of doubt in it. I want it all. I want her.

"You've got me," she says, and kisses me on the lips, while her hand meanders to the button of my jeans.

My limbs don't stiffen—nothing about me is rigid anymore. My body welcomes her because my mind's letting her in.

As she lowers my zipper, it's as though, with that act, she lowers the last barrier around my heart—around my desire. It's a freeing action, one that makes me tug my jeans off my legs in an almost helpless manner. But Kat is here to calm me down. She doesn't say anything, she just puts her hand on my belly, which falls and rises quickly in time with my sharp, intoxicated intakes of breath.

Then I realize I was wrong. Taking off my jeans wasn't the final barrier. Spreading my legs for her is. There's so much release in the simple motion of letting my knees fall apart. It's an invitation. A heartfelt invitation for her to enter my most intimate space. It's where I want her. But first, there's that look again. I can still make out some kindness in her eyes, but they're so dark with desire now that her glance raking over my body is enough for me to respond. And respond I do. By lowering my underwear. By freeing the path for her. And sure, she has seen me naked before, but this is a totally different kind of nakedness. This is me opening up to her, as wide as I will ever go. This is me under the spell of desire, under the spell of Katherine Jones.

Kat takes over and, torturously slow, guides the last piece of clothing off me. I need to spread for her—again. The flow of air between my legs is thrilling. My clit stands to immediate attention, which baffles me most of all. The way my body has taken over, whereas before, it was my mind that was in full control.

I'm not sure how she's done it, but in a matter of

seconds, Kat is naked as well. She must have picked up some special skills in her former life. I amaze myself again by being able to think of her like that, like the escort that she used to be, and not shut down completely. On the contrary. I open up more, spread my legs a little wider for her.

"I want you," I repeat, nothing but urgency in my tone now. All the years without this blissful kind of intimacy catch up with me in that moment, a moment that's been building since I met Kat.

She doesn't respond with words this time but, instead, nestles herself between my legs. She kisses my lower belly while her hands reach for my breasts. Involuntarily, at least that's how it seems, my hips move toward her. I feel her nipples against my thighs but, most of all, I feel her body close to my clit. Close, but still too far.

Kat kisses a path down my belly to my inner thighs. She peppers me with hot, wet kisses—all promises of what's to come.

I bury my hands in her hair because I need to hold on to something—to her. Her lips are inches away from my clit. I can feel her breath on me there already. Years of sensual deprivation pool in my core. All my lust focused on one woman and what she's doing to me with her mouth. Her lips are just above my clit now, and already, I'm close to exploding. To reaching the ultimate surrender. Because I was wrong once again. *This* is the final stage. The moment her tongue connects with my clit.

Her mouth on me there is unspeakably warm. It sparks in me such a rush of lightness, I may as well be levitating off the bed. I feel like I've just taken the most potent happiness drug on the planet—maybe I have.

Kat licks me between my legs and I feel it everywhere, in every last fiber of my being. It changes the fabric of me forever. I already know that, after this, I won't be the same.

Every time she flicks her tongue over my clit, I'm a fraction further removed from the bitter, buttoned-up woman I allowed myself to become. And I know, deep in my heart, that this was the only way for me to break out of this shell.

At last, I'm ready.

About the Author

Harper Bliss is a best-selling lesbian romance author. Among her most-loved books are the highly dramatic French Kissing and the often thought-provoking Pink Bean series.

Harper lived in Hong Kong for 7 years, travelled the world for a bit, and has now settled in Brussels (Belgium) with her wife and photogenic cat, Dolly Purrton.

Together with her wife, she hosts a weekly podcast called Harper Bliss & Her Mrs.

Harper loves hearing from readers and you can reach her at the email address below.

www.harperbliss.com
harper@harperbliss.com